KU-444-737

DR PERFECT
ON HER DOORSTEP

BY
LUCY CLARK

AFTER ONE
FORBIDDEN NIGHT...

BY
AMBER McKENZIE

MILLS &
BOON

Lucy Clark is actually a husband-and-wife writing team. They enjoy taking holidays with their children, during which they discuss and develop new ideas for their books using the fantastic Australian scenery. They use their daily walks to talk over the characterisation and fine details of the wonderful stories they produce, and are avid movie buffs. They live on the edge of a popular wine district in South Australia with their two children, and enjoy spending family time together at weekends.

Amber McKenzie's love of romance and all the drama a good romance entails began in her teenage years. After a lengthy university career, multiple degrees and one formal English class, she found herself happily employed as a physician and happily married to her medical school sweetheart.

She rekindled her passion for romance during her residency and began thinking of the perfect story. She quickly decided that the only thing sexier than a man in scrubs was a woman in scrubs. After finishing training and starting practice she started writing her first novel. Harlequin's *So You Think You Can Write* contest came at a perfect time, and after a few good edits from her wildlife biologist childhood best friend the manuscript was submitted. The rest is history!

Amber currently lives in Canada with her husband. She does her best to juggle her full-time medical practice with her love of writing and reading and other pursuits—from long-distance running to domestic goddess activities like cooking and quilting. Multi-tasking has become an art form and a way of life.

DR PERFECT
ON HER DOORSTEP

BY
LUCY CLARK

All rights reserved including the right of reproduction in whole or in part in any form. This edition is published by arrangement with Harlequin Books S.A.

This is a work of fiction. Names, characters, places, locations and incidents are purely fictional and bear no relationship to any real life individuals, living or dead, or to any actual places, business establishments, locations, events or incidents. Any resemblance is entirely coincidental.

This book is sold subject to the condition that it shall not, by way of trade or otherwise, be lent, resold, hired out or otherwise circulated without the prior consent of the publisher in any form of binding or cover other than that in which it is published and without a similar condition including this condition being imposed on the subsequent purchaser.

® and TM are trademarks owned and used by the trademark owner and/or its licensee. Trademarks marked with ® are registered with the United Kingdom Patent Office and/or the Office for Harmonisation in the Internal Market and in other countries.

First published in Great Britain 2014
by Mills & Boon, an imprint of Harlequin (UK) Limited,
Eton House, 18-24 Paradise Road, Richmond, Surrey, TW9 1SR

© 2014 Anne Clark & Peter Clark

ISBN: 978-0-263-90791-9

Harlequin (UK) Limited's policy is to use papers that are natural, renewable and recyclable products and made from wood grown in sustainable forests. The logging and manufacturing processes conform to the legal environmental regulations of the country of origin.

Printed and bound in Spain
by Blackprint CPI, Barcelona

Dear Reader

I've always loved reading linked stories—really getting to know characters and their family and friends—and now, with Stacey Wilton stepping out and leading the way, the Wilton triplets are making their mark. Stacey, Cora and Molly are three very different women, but they're joined in the bonds of sisterly love.

For ever the down-to-earth, sensible sister, Stacey thinks she's lost her chance at love—until she meets handsome Pierce Brolin. Such a gorgeous but determined man... I loved Pierce from the start. I love the way that he, like Stacey, who is guardian to her younger siblings, has such a strong grasp on the importance of family, on not taking the people he truly cares about for granted. It's inevitable that when these two meet they'll have an instant connection which will help them embrace all the various siblings—and rabbits—that weave their way throughout the story.

If there's one thing I've learned from the very important research required to write this story, it's that you're never too old to go on a swing!

Warmest regards

Lucy

Dedication

To our gorgeous Abby. You are such a delight. Never stop!
—Ps121:7-8

Recent titles by Lucy Clark:

HER MISTLETOE WISH
THE SECRET BETWEEN THEM
RESISTING THE NEW DOC IN TOWN
ONE LIFE-CHANGING MOMENT
DARE SHE DREAM OF FOREVER?
FALLING FOR DR FEARLESS
DIAMOND RING FOR THE ICE QUEEN
TAMING THE LONE DOC'S HEART
THE BOSS SHE CAN'T RESIST
WEDDING ON THE BABY WARD
SPECIAL CARE BABY MIRACLE
DOCTOR DIAMOND IN THE ROUGH

**These books are also available in eBook format
from www.millsandboon.co.uk**

**Praise for
Lucy Clark:**

'A sweet and fun romance about second chances
and second love.'
—*HarlequinJunkie.com* on
DARE SHE DREAM OF FOREVER?

CHAPTER ONE

STACEY WILTON PULLED the car to the side of the road. She looked across at the house, nostalgia rising within her. Turning the key to cut the engine, she unbuckled her seatbelt and opened the door, her gaze never leaving the house. The late-afternoon rays from the sun combined with the blue of the September sky only enhanced the beauty of the place.

It looked so different—smaller, somehow. Which was ridiculous, because houses didn't grow or shrink. And yet it was still the same as her memory recalled. The front garden had been re-landscaped, the large tree she and her sisters had used to climb was gone, and no shade fell over the front windows, but instead the garden was alive with rows of vibrantly coloured flowers, enjoying the spring weather. Stacey smiled. Her father would have loved that.

She leaned against the car and drank her fill of the place she'd called home for the first fourteen years of her life. It was a place she'd never contemplated leaving, but she'd soon learned that life was never smooth. Her mother had walked out, abandoning them all.

Stacey and her sisters had been almost five years old, excited to start school, when their mother had declared that she'd had enough. Their father had been the local GP, working long and erratic hours. He'd employed a young nanny—Letisha—who, many years later, he'd married.

When he'd been head-hunted to run a new palliative care hospice in Perth Arn Wilton had accepted the position without consulting his teenage daughters.

'Why do we need to go?' Stacey had asked him, tears streaming down her face as he'd packed yet another box.

'Because this job is too good to pass up, Stace. I get to be a part of something new and exciting as well as incredibly important. This is the first palliative hospice just for children.'

'But what about all your patients *here*? What about your practice? I was going to become a doctor and then one day work with you here.'

'Stace.' Arn had sighed with resignation and placed a hand on her shoulder. 'It's time to move on.'

'Just because of a job? It doesn't make sense, Dad.'

'Well, then, think of Letisha. You love Letisha, and now that we're newly married it's not really fair to ask her to start her married life in a home where there have been so many unhappy memories. Tish deserves better, don't you think?'

When Stacey had opened her mouth to continue arguing her father had given her a stern look, which had meant the discussion was over.

Stacey and her sisters had packed their lives into boxes, said tearful goodbyes to their school friends, and hugged their neighbours, Edna and Mike, with tear-stained faces.

'I've never lived next door to anyone else,' Stacey had told Edna, who had been like a second mother to her.

'Adventures are good,' Edna had told her. 'And we'll keep in touch. I've given you enough letter paper and stamps to last you for a good two years at least.' Edna had smiled at her. 'We'll see each other again, Stacey.'

'Promise?' Stacey had asked.

'Promise.'

Then the Wilton family had left Newcastle, on Australia's east coast, and headed to Perth on the other side of the country. There they'd settled into their new life, and many years later Letisha had given birth to Stacey's new sister. Indeed, over the years their family had grown from three to six children.

Now, finally, after almost two decades, Stacey was returning to the job she'd always dreamed of: taking over the old family medical practice her father had once run. She hoped it would provide stability for all of them—especially after the events of the past eighteen months. Her father and beloved stepmother had passed away in a terrible car accident, leaving Stacey and her sisters as guardians of their younger siblings. Not only that, but Stacey had been jilted at the altar by the man who'd been supposed to love her for the rest of her life.

No, the past eighteen months had been soul-destroying, and her coming back to a town she'd always regarded as a place of solace was much needed.

'Can I help you?'

Stacey was pulled from her reverie by a man standing just at the edge of the driveway next to the house she was staring at. He was very tall, about six foot four, and wore an old pair of gardening shorts and a light blue T-shirt which he'd clearly used as a painting smock, if the splatters of green, yellow and pink paint were anything to go by. He had flip-flops on his feet, a peaked cap on his head, and a pair of gardening gloves on his hands. A pile of weeds was on the concrete driveway near his feet. How had she not seen him there before?

'Can I help you with something?' he repeated, taking off his gloves and tossing them carelessly onto the pile of weeds.

Stacey shifted her car keys from one hand to the other. 'No, thanks.'

'Are you sure? You seem to be quite entranced, just looking at my house.' He angled his head to the side, giving her a more concentrated look. 'Are you sure you're feeling all right?'

She waved away his concern and smiled politely. 'I'm fine… It's just that—well I used to live here.' She pointed to the house. 'When I was little.' She called her words across the street, feeling a little self-conscious as one or two cars drove between their impromptu conversation. When the man beckoned her over it seemed like the most logical thing in the world to cross the road and go and chat with a complete stranger.

'You've cut down the tree,' she said, pointing to where the tree used to be.

'Had to. It was diseased.'

'Oh. How sad. I guess it has been a while, but I do have such happy memories of climbing it—and swinging on the tyre swing.' Her sigh was nostalgic as she continued to peruse the garden. 'I really like the flowers. Very pretty.'

'Thank you. I don't mind doing a spot of gardening. I find it relaxing.'

'And painting? The house used to be a cream colour, but I think the mint-green looks much better. Good choice.'

The man nodded. 'I found painting very…therapeutic. I'd never painted a house before, but now I have. Both inside and out. One more thing crossed off my bucket list.'

Stacey gave him a puzzled look. 'Bucket what?'

'Bucket list. You know—a list of things you'd like to do before you pass away.'

She shook her head. 'I've never heard it put like that before. A bit morbid, isn't it?'

The man grinned—a full-on gorgeous smile that highlighted his twinkling blue eyes. Bedroom eyes, her sister Molly would have called them. Eyes that could mesmerise a woman from across the room…or across the road.

'Not morbid,' he continued, shaking his head a little. 'Adventurous. For example, if you had on your bucket list, *Talk to a strange man about bucket lists* then you could go home and cross that right off, feeling like you've actually accomplished something new today.'

Stacey's brow creased further. 'Why would I have that on a list of things I'd like to accomplish before I die?'

The man surprised her further by laughing. Was he laughing *at* her? Or at this bucket list thing he kept gabbing about?

'Never mind.' He held out his hand. 'I'm Pierce.'

She put her hand into his, ignoring the way the heat from this hand seemed to travel up her arm and explode into a thousand stars, setting her body alight.

'Stacey.' If she was the type of person to believe in instant attraction then she might be flattered by his smile. Thankfully she left that sort of emotion and nonsense up to Molly.

'Nice to meet you, Stacey.' Pierce gestured towards the house. 'Would you like to come inside? Take a look at some of the other changes we've made?'

We? He was most likely married, and as this house was perfect for children no doubt he had a couple of those as well. He seemed honest, personable and quite kind, but first impressions could be deceptive. Perhaps she should ask him some more questions, just to be sure.

She knew the Edelsteins still lived next door, as Edna had called her earlier that morning asking her to make a house call to review Mike.

'He's too stubborn to come to the clinic,' Edna had told her. 'But he'll listen to you, Stace.'

That was how Stacey found herself here, coming to see Mike and Edna. But now she was being invited by a stranger into the house where she'd grown up. Still, she should test the waters before going inside with him. Better to be safe than sorry.

'Do the Edelsteins still live next door?'

He nodded. 'That Edna… She's a talker, isn't she? Yesterday she stood at her fence for a good two hours and chatted to me while I did some gardening. I kept asking if she'd like to come and sit down on the veranda on the swing and have a nice cool drink—but, no, she was quite happy leaning on the fence and telling me all about her gallstone removal.'

Stacey smiled and nodded, pleased with the way Pierce's words held no impatience as he spoke of Edna. 'Same old Edna. And Mike? How's he doing?'

A frown furrowed his brow. 'Not too good, I'm sorry to say. I popped over last night just to check on him after Edna told me he's been getting increasingly dizzy when he stands up. Plus his asthma has flared, due to all the pollen.' Pierce pulled on his gardening gloves as he spoke and started tidying up the mound of weeds, placing them into the gardening recycle bin. 'His asthma meds are only just keeping things at bay.' He shook his head, concern evident in his tone.

Stacey nodded. This information was marrying up with what Edna had told her.

'Of course in typical fashion Mike's refusing to admit there's anything really wrong with him, but if things aren't brought under control soon he runs the risk of contracting pneumonia.'

'You sound very concerned.' Again she watched his expression, and when he met her eyes his gaze was quizzical.

'Of course I'm concerned. That's why I offered to give him a private check-up.'

Stacey's eyebrows hit her perfectly straight fringe. 'You're a doctor?'

Pierce nodded. 'GP. I've been doing locum work at the local hospital in the A & E department—just a few shifts a week while I finish getting things sorted out around here.'

A *doctor*? Her level of trust for Pierce increased. He was a doctor as well as passing her test regarding his neighbours. 'Well, thank you for checking up on Mike. What was your clinical assessment?'

'Clinical assessment, eh?' Pierce pondered her words as he removed his gardening gloves and then snapped his fingers. 'That's *right*. Edna said a doctor used to live in this house and that some of his kids were also doctors.'

'That would have been my dad—Arn Wilton.'

'She said he was the only one who could ever make Mike see sense about health matters.'

Stacey's smile was nostalgic. 'He and Mike were always good friends.'

'Were? Did they have a falling out?'

'No. Not those two. Mates until the last.' Stacey looked down at the ground. 'My father and stepmother passed away eighteen months ago.'

'I'm sorry to hear that, Stacey.'

Pierce's tone was filled with compassion as well as understanding. She met his gaze once more and shrugged, annoyed with the tears that instantly sprang to her eyes.

She blinked them away, wondering why she was telling this stranger so much about her life. It had to be this house—the memories it brought back.

'Losing parents is never easy. Mine both passed away almost a decade ago and still there are days when I miss them a lot.' He exhaled slowly, then shrugged one shoulder. 'I have questions. Ones only they would know how to answer.'

'Yes.' The word was heartfelt, as though somehow the loss of parents and the pain it caused had formed a bond between the two of them. 'Instead it leaves us floundering around, trying to figure things out on our own.'

He nodded, but didn't stop looking intently at her, and for some reason Stacey found it nigh impossible to look away. Pierce seemed to be a decent and caring man—a family man content to care for his home as well as his neighbours. She had no idea why he was only working as a locum at the local hospital, but presumably he had his reasons for not wanting to take on a more permanent position. Perhaps he wanted to spend some time working his way through his bucket list.

She paused as a different thought occurred to her. Perhaps he had a terminal illness, or was recovering from one. He didn't look gaunt. In fact he looked positively healthy. Stacey stopped her thoughts. This man was not her patient. He was not a puzzle for her to solve, to figure out what was wrong with him and then try to find a solution. But it was such an integrated part of her personality—especially being the oldest sibling in her family.

'By five minutes.'

She instantly heard her sister Cora's protest, which came every time Stacey stated that fact. Nevertheless, five minutes was five minutes, and Stacey took her responsibilities seriously.

'Anyway…' Pierce was first to break the silence as he put the lid down on the green recycle bin. 'I didn't mean to take our conversation in such a maudlin direction. You asked about Mike. Chest is extremely tight, asthma meds are providing basic relief, but I think the chest pains might be worse than he's letting on. Edna said he'd been dizzy, but I didn't take my otoscope with me and when I suggested he see someone about it, to make sure it wasn't the start of something a bit more sinister, he growled at me and kicked me out of his house.'

'He always did have a good bark.' Stacey's smile was instant as she followed Pierce towards the house, quietly amazed at how comfortable she was around him. 'Edna asked me to pop over once I'd finished clinic.'

'That's why you're here? To give Mike a check-up?'

'Yes, but I can see Edna's car's not in the driveway, so I'll wait until she gets home.'

'And your question about neighbours was a test, eh?' He grinned, crossing his arms over his broad chest. 'I take it I passed?'

'Yes.'

'Excellent.' He jerked his thumb towards the house. 'Does this mean you feel safe enough to come and take a look around inside?'

Stacey nodded, excitement starting to build. She told herself it was because she was getting the chance to see inside the house, rather than because she was getting to spend a bit more time with the handsome Dr Pierce.

'Where are you working?' Pierce asked conversationally as they crossed the veranda and entered the house.

'I've recently bought my father's old GP practice.'

'The one up the road? Shortfield Family Medical Practice?'

'That's the one. Phillip Morcombe took over the practice from my father sixteen years ago, and when I realised it was up for sale—' Stacey stopped as she stood on the other side of the threshold, her gaze drinking in the living room of the house which held all her earliest memories.

'Oh!' She clutched her hands to her chest. 'That's where my sisters and I used to lie on our stomachs after school and watch half an hour of television.' She pointed to the middle of the room. 'And the bay window. There used to be a curtain that separated it off from the rest of the room and that used to be our secret corner, where we'd spend hours whispering our best secrets to each other. Or we'd curl up with a book and just read.' She smiled. 'Well, Cora and I read books. Molly could never sit still. Still can't.'

'How old are your sisters? You sound so close.'

'You don't know the half of it,' Stacey said with a grin. 'We're triplets. Non-identical,' she added, as a matter of routine. She waited, expecting the usual reaction of, *Wow. Triplets? I've never met triplets before,* or *Can you sense each other's emotions?* or *How far apart are the three of you? Who's the eldest?* but all Pierce did was smile widely.

'What a lot of fun you must have had.' His tone sounded almost wistful. 'So close, so connected.'

Stacey mulled over his words as he headed around to the kitchen and dining room. 'Are you an only child?'

'I was. For quite a while. I was fifteen when my sister was born. She was born very late in my parents' life, but they loved each and every moment they had with Nell.'

He walked into the kitchen and pointed to a framed photograph up on the wall—one of him and a lovely-looking young woman who was staring at him with open delight, as though he'd just handed her the moon.

'That was taken six months ago, at Nell's twenty-first

birthday. I'd just given her the keys to this house. Independent living.' There was a thrill of pride in his tone as he looked at the picture of his sister.

Stacey processed his words. 'You've done all this work with the house for your *sister*?'

'It's been Nell's goal. She's been working towards it for so long and we're almost ready...in about another three months' time.'

'You're not married?' Why had that question sounded as though she was fishing for information? 'Er... I... You don't have to answer that. It's really none of my business.'

'Married? Me?' Pierce shook his head emphatically. 'No. *No.* No, no, no, no, no.'

'So that's a no?' she remarked drolly, wondering if his determined answer hinted at matrimonial issues. She tried not to frown, tried not to lump him into the same category as another specific male she knew who had also had deeply rooted issues with marriage and commitment.

'I'd do anything for Nell.' As he said the words he quickly checked his watch, then gasped. 'And that includes going to meet her at the bus stop. Come on, Stacey.' Pierce grabbed her hand and tugged her back through the house, across the veranda and into the garden. 'We're going to be late.'

'We?' She pulled her hand free. 'Er... I'll leave you to it.'

'But you have *got* to meet Nell. She'd love to meet someone who used to live here. She adores this house. She picked it out five years ago and told me that was the house she was going to live in when she was twenty-one. She's very stubborn and adamant, my sister.'

'Well, then, I'll go next door and see if Edna's home yet and—'

'There's no time for discussion now.'

Pierce grabbed her hand again and started tugging her along with him as he quickened his pace, pointing in the distance to a bus that was drawing closer.

'That's her bus! We've got to make it to the bus stop in time. Usually she can cope if I'm not there to greet her, but her whole routine has been a little out of whack lately—what with her promotion at work and all the new things she's had to learn. Hence me meeting her bus is the one absolute she needs in her life right now.'

Pierce spouted this information quickly as they continued towards the bus stop. When he broke into a jog as the bus drew closer Stacey had no option but to go along with him. As they jogged she had to confess she was rather intrigued at the way Pierce spoke about his sister.

They arrived at the bus stop just as the young woman from the photograph was climbing down the back steps of the bus, stepping onto the pavement. She looked around, anxiety etched on her features, but the instant she saw Pierce running towards her, the anxiety cleared and a wide, beaming smile brightened her face.

'I got scared. I could not see you, Pierce. But now you are here.' Nell, who had shoulder-length blonde hair and blue eyes that matched her brother's, spoke every word perfectly, but with little inflection.

Pierce let go of Stacey's hand before enveloping his sister in a hug. 'Sorry, Nellie. I was gardening and forgot the time.'

He took Nell's bag from her and slipped his arm around her waist as Nell started off down the street, counting her steps. She didn't seem to notice Stacey at all, and as Pierce beckoned for her to follow them, Stacey's sharp medical mind began sifting through the information she knew.

Nell had been born to a more mature mother, and

clearly needed a strict routine. She hadn't paid any attention to Stacey, even though Stacey had been holding hands with Pierce. The fact that Pierce hadn't tried to introduce Stacey, instead allowing his sister to continue counting the steps from the bus stop to the house, alerted her to the fact that while Nell might appear to be a beautiful young twenty-one-year-old on the outside, mentally her age was far younger.

It wasn't until they were standing on the front veranda of the house that Nell stopped counting and turned to smile at her brother. 'I got it right. The same number as yesterday.'

'That's great, Nellie.' He removed his arm from his sister's waist and turned to indicate Stacey. 'There's someone I want you to meet.' It was only then that Nell seemed to notice Stacey's presence. 'Nell, this is Stacey.'

Dutifully, Nell held out her hand to Stacey and shook it firmly. 'Hello, Stacey. I am very pleased to meet you.' She nodded and smiled, as though she was secretly proud of herself for getting the greeting correct.

'Good girl,' Pierce said softly. Nell let go of Stacey's hand, her smile increasing at her brother's praise. 'I know this is your house now, Nell, but when Stacey was a little girl she and her sisters used to live here.'

Nell looked from Stacey to Pierce and back again, as though slowly processing the words. 'Really?' Her eyes widened with delight. 'Did you sleep in the same room as me? The pink room?'

Stacey smiled and nodded. 'The room was definitely pink.'

'Why don't you show Stacey your room now?' Pierce encouraged as he opened the door, holding it for the women to precede him.

'Yes!' Nell entered the house and clutched her hands

to her chest with the excitement of a child at Christmas. 'I *love* my room. Did you love it, too, when it was your room?'

'Yes. I really did.' Allowing Nell's excitement to affect her, Stacey followed the young woman down the hallway.

Nell was delighted to show Stacey her doll collection, as well as a cupboard full of puzzles. Jigsaw puzzles, wooden puzzles, metal ones too.

'You must be very good at puzzles, Nell.'

'Yes. I am. My brother says that I have an amazing puzzle brain.'

She grinned, and Stacey couldn't help but instantly warm to her.

'He is so funny.'

'Afternoon snacks are ready,' Pierce called, and Nell immediately turned and set off for the kitchen.

'I like afternoon snacks. Do *you* like afternoon snacks, Stacey?'

'I do, Nell.' Stacey smiled as she watched Nell politely thank her brother before sitting down at the kitchen bench to attend to her food. They all ate, Pierce having prepared fruit with cheese and a glass of juice for himself and Stacey as well.

'How was work, Nell?'

'It was good, Pierce.' Nell swallowed her mouthful.

'Nell works as a researcher for a computer company. She solves a lot of their internal programming issues.' Pierce offered the information for Stacey's benefit, but Nell nodded as though to confirm it.

'That sounds impressive,' Stacey added.

'It is.' Nell ate another mouthful.

'Did you do anything exciting today?'

Pierce continued with his questions and Stacey had the feeling it was all part of their routine.

'Yes. I solved the number puzzle Mr Jorgensen could not do. He said I did it really fast.' Nell preened a little, feeling good about herself. 'I like puzzles.'

Once Nell had finished eating she stacked her plate and glass in the dishwasher before announcing that it was time to watch television. Off she went, leaving Stacey sitting at the table with Pierce. He watched his sister in the other room, a proud smile playing about his lips, and when he looked back at Stacey he saw she was watching him intently.

'Higher functioning autism,' he stated as he drank the last of his drink.

'She's doing very well for herself,' Stacey remarked, finishing her juice.

Pierce nodded as he collected their glasses and stacked them in the dishwasher. 'She is, and I have to say I'm very proud of her.'

'So I can see.' Stacey grinned. 'And thank you for the snack. I can't remember the last time I actually sat and had an after-work snack.'

'It's Nell's routine.'

'What happens if you're at the hospital when she gets home from work?'

'I try to be here most days, but if I'm not at the bus stop to meet her then Edna or Mike usually help out. And if that's not possible, and I know I'm going to be delayed, I'll ring Nell and let her know before she gets off the bus. But thankfully those days are few and far between.'

'If you need further support I'd be happy to add Nell to our practice nurse visitation list.'

He nodded. 'I was going to suggest something like that. I'm so glad you've bought the practice. We all thought it was going to close completely.'

'I know. My father's old partner retired last year, and since then there have been various locums running it.'

'A practice can't survive like that. It definitely needs someone at the helm.'

Stacey spread her arms wide. 'As you see.'

'You're running it by yourself?'

'Uh…with my sisters. Well, sort of. We all own the practice equally and Winifred the practice nurse, who has been there for years, is staying on—thank goodness.'

'Ah, yes. We've met Winifred several times. She's lovely.' Pierce leaned back in his chair and watched her for a moment. 'I take it both your sisters are doctors, too?'

'Yes. We went through medical school together, did all our GP training together.'

'And what do you mean by "sort of"? Your sisters are "sort of" running the practice with you? How does that work?'

Stacey frowned as she thought about Molly's new plans to study surgery. She was proud and delighted with her sister's accomplishments, but it did put her in a bit of a bind.

'Actually, my sister Molly has decided to study surgery.'

He raised his eyebrows at this. 'She's been accepted to a surgical training programme?'

'Yes.'

'Here?'

'Yes, at Newcastle General. A place came up at the last minute so she took it. Effective immediately.'

He nodded. 'Good for her.'

Pierce leaned one elbow on the table and rested his head on his hand, giving her his undivided attention. She shifted in the seat but forced herself to remain calm and collected as she placed her hands in her lap.

He continued just to sit there, watching her as though she were a complete mystery to him. When he raised a questioning eyebrow she spread her hands wide. 'What? Is there something on my nose? Do I have milk on my lip?'

Pierce smiled and shook his head. Good heavens! Did the man have *any* idea just how lethal that small, gorgeous smile of his could be? The way it caused the corners of his eyes to crinkle with delight? The way it made her feel as though he wasn't trying to judge her, just trying to understand her? For all intents and purposes this man was a stranger to her, and yet for some reason she felt so comfortable around him. It was an odd sensation, but with both Cora and Molly telling her to loosen up, to step outside her comfort zone, start living her life for *her* instead of everyone else, and with Pierce smiling at her so acceptingly, Stacey found herself telling him things she usually wouldn't tell anyone.

'Yes—yes, it *is* good for Molly. She's always wanted to do it. But it does leave me somewhat in the lurch. Cora, my other sister, is over in Tarparnii at the moment, working with Pacific Medical Aid.'

'An excellent organisation. I have…friends who do a lot of work with them.'

Stacey wondered at his hesitation. Were they his friends or weren't they? 'Are you interested in going to work there, too?'

He shrugged. 'Maybe. One day.'

'It's not on your bucket list?'

Pierce grinned. 'There are a lot of other things on my bucket list so I'll attend to them first.' He gestured to the house. 'And first on the list is to get this place completely shipshape for Nell and her soon-to-be housemates.'

'She has friends who are moving in, too?'

'Two other fine young ladies who she works with. Loris is in a wheelchair, which is why I need to finish getting all the ramps made, and Samantha has high-functioning Asperger's.'

'Sounds like it's important for me to get to know all of them.'

'Yes. Your medical practice will be the closest one for all of them. But where Nell is concerned, if she knows you on a more personal level then she's more likely to come to you when she needs help.'

'And we'll help in any way we can.' She smiled politely.

Pierce nodded with thanks, then looked at her thoughtfully. 'Hang on a minute. If Molly's studying surgery at the hospital, and Cora is overseas, then who *is* running the clinic with you?'

'Molly does a day here and there, and she's promised to find me a locum to cover for her.'

There was silence between them for a minute, with the clock on the mantel ticking loudly. Pierce continued to watch her intently, leaning his head on his hand. Stacey started to feel highly self-conscious as he just looked at her…stopped everything and *really* looked. What did he see?

'All right.' Pierce straightened up and slapped his hand onto the table, making her jump. 'I'll do it!'

'What? What will you do?' Stacey asked, startled by his abrupt behaviour.

'Call your sister. Tell her the search is over.'

'What search?' Stacey stared at him as though he'd grown an extra head.

'The locum search.' He stood and held out his hand to her. 'Dr Pierce Brolin, at your service.'

Stacey shook his hand, still a little dazed. 'I'm not sure I underst—'

'I'm coming to work for you. I'm your new locum.'

CHAPTER TWO

STACEY UNLOCKED THE front door of the family medical practice and headed to the light switch, illuminating the reception area and waiting room. It was early. Just after seven-thirty on a Monday morning. And although her first patient wasn't due to walk through the doors for another hour she'd been too nervous to sleep.

She sniffed. The air still smelled faintly of paint, and she quickly located the air filters she'd purchased last week and switched them on. If it wasn't for the rain outside she'd open the windows, but the September weather was giving them the runaround—one day sunny, the next pouring with rain.

Stacey walked through the practice, opening blinds and switching on the equipment that needed to be on. She refused to dwell on the second consulting room— the one which would be assigned to Pierce Brolin, whose first official day in the clinic would be starting in about an hour's time.

Had she done the right thing? It was true she needed a locum. It was true that Pierce was not only available but also extremely willing. His credentials were certainly impressive—especially his extensive experience in autism spectrum disorders—so she couldn't understand why he wasn't working in his chosen specialty.

'I'm more than happy to fill the gap while you wait for your sister Cora to return to Newcastle,' he'd told her when they'd met last week to sign the legal contracts.

It had been on the tip of her tongue to ask him *why* he was happy to help out here and there, but it really was none of her business. Perhaps he was content to get things settled for Nell without having the stress of a full-time workload hanging over his head. All that mattered was that Pierce was a qualified doctor who was willing to help her out.

She had to leave it at that, had to keep her emotional distance from him, because he was definitely an enigmatic man who was able to make her feel as though she were the most important person in the world. The way he smiled at her, the way he shook her hand, the way he gave her his undivided attention when he talked... All of those little things were things that Robert had never done.

She closed her eyes as an image of Robert's stern face came to mind. Her ex-fiancé, although professing to love and care about her, had never really shown it. She'd always rationalised it—Robert wasn't the demonstrative type—but now that she'd had quite a bit of time to reflect on her failed relationship she'd come to realise that he simply hadn't loved her as much as he'd said.

He'd never held her hand in public, never leaned over and whispered something intimate in her ear, never looked at her across a crowded room as though he wanted everyone to instantly disappear just so he could be alone with her.

When she'd been sitting at her consulting room desk, with Pierce on the other side, carefully reading the locum contract, Molly and Winifred both hovering around and chatting, Stacey had been far too aware of him. His broad shoulders, his thoughtful brow, his twinkling blue eyes when he'd lifted his head and looked at her, somehow making her feel as though he could see right into her soul…

And that had been the moment. That one true moment in time when nothing else seemed to matter. Her mouth had instantly gone dry, the other people in the room had disappeared from her view and it had been just the two of them, Pierce had stared into her eyes and she'd stared back into his. Neither of them had moved, and she could have sworn that the spinning of the earth had actually slowed down, capturing them both in a bubble of time. It had been an odd sensation, but for that one split second Stacey had felt…*accepted*. Without reservation, without condition.

She shook her head, clearing it of the image. 'And he'll be working here,' she murmured as she made herself walk into the consulting room he'd been assigned.

Even now she could picture him sitting behind the desk, looking up at her as she came in to speak to him about something, their eyes meeting and holding once more. Did she yearn for that sensation again because he'd made her feel accepted? Or did she fear the sensation because he'd so easily been able to penetrate the fortress she'd worked hard to put in place after Robert had broken her heart?

She glanced around the room, opening one or two of the cupboards to ensure they were properly stocked with everything he might need. She wanted today to go well, for Pierce to be happy working here.

After she'd left his home over two weeks ago Stacey hadn't been sure which way to turn. She'd known basically nothing about the man, and yet there he'd been, offering his services to help her out. Was he just being kind or was he a bit loopy?

All she could remember doing at the time was murmuring a polite reply to his declaration that he was going to work with her and then excusing herself. Her thoughts had been in such a jumble that she'd almost forgotten to check on Mike Edelstein—which had been the main reason for her being in that part of town. She'd walked out to her car to retrieve her medical bag, and been surprised to find Pierce waiting by the Edelsteins' front door by the time she reached it.

'We may as well review him together,' he'd stated, before knocking on the door.

Stacey had barely had time to collect her thoughts before Edna had opened the door and welcomed them both inside.

The other woman had hugged Stacey close. 'It's good to see you again, love,' Edna had said as she'd embraced Stacey. 'Although I wish it was in better circumstances. But at least now that you're here we might finally get Mike to see some sense, eh? He always had time for you, Stace.'

Mike had indeed been happy to see her, but when Stacey had insisted upon giving him a check-up he'd fussed about, telling her she was blowing the entire thing out of proportion.

He stabbed a finger at Pierce. 'If this young whipper-snapper hadn't been hanging around the side fence the other day he never would have heard me coughing.' Mike glared at Edna. 'At least that's what he *said*. But chances are Edna dragged him inside because she was stressing over nothing.'

'Mike—' Stacey began, but Mike was in full swing, his words peppered by coughs.

'Came right over, he did. Sticking his nose in where it doesn't belong, telling me I had problems with my lungs.

Well, of course I do. I've had asthma for most of me life, and I know when it's bad and when it's good and right now it's fine. Just fine, I tell you.'

But the instant Mike finished protesting his body was racked with a coughing spasm.

Stacey instantly rubbed Mike's back, encouraging him quietly to relax and breathe slowly. Her soothing tone must have done something, because Mike's bluster seemed to disappear.

'There's one thing I want to remind you of,' she said as she placed her medical bag beside his comfortable lounge chair.

'Yeah? What's that?' he asked, lifting his chin and meeting her gaze, pure stubbornness reflected in his eyes.

'You may be stubborn, but I'm my father's daughter—which therefore means that my stubbornness trumps yours every time.'

Edna laughed. 'She's got you there, Mikey.' And then, as though everything was now right with her world, Edna declared that she'd go and put the kettle on.

With resigned reluctance, Mike agreed to the check-up.

'Pierce was right,' Stacey said as she packed away her stethoscope and closed her medical bag once her review was complete. 'Your asthma is very bad and your ears are red. Your throat's not the best, either. You'll need some antibiotics, and I want you up at the hospital first thing tomorrow for a chest X-ray to check you're not on the way to contracting pneumonia. Spring is notorious for ailments such as chest infections, and right now it's the last thing you need—what with the rabbit jumping season quickly approaching.'

'Oh, we don't compete any more,' Edna said in a loud whisper as she carried in a tray of tea and biscuits. 'Our ol' Vashta passed away a few years ago. What a champion that rabbit was.' Edna sighed and looked wistful for a moment, before shaking her head once more.

'But you still go to watch, don't you?' Stacey asked, 'I was telling the children about it just last night and all of them were eager to go. Lydia was even asking if we could get a rabbit ourselves. She adores them.'

'Really?' Light shone in Edna's eyes as she'd placed the tray on the table and stood next to Stacey.

'I was also hoping that if I was stuck at the clinic, or if Molly was in surgery, you two might be able to take the children to the rabbit jumping show for me?' Stacey's tone held a hint of pleading, and as she watched them closely, knowing Mike had always loved to help others, especially when it concerned his favourite animals, she saw a flicker of light come back into his old eyes.

'Lydia's interested, eh? How old is she now?'

'She's seven—and just as stubborn as me.'

'Hmm…' Mike stroked his chin with thumb and forefinger. 'Seven, you say? Seven's just about the right age to start.'

Edna reached out and held Stacey's hand as they both watched Mike closely. He contemplated this information seriously for a moment or two before nodding.

'OK, then. I'll go to the hospital and take the antibiotics and do whatever else it is you want me to do—but only because it's important that I'm there to instruct little Lydia right from the beginning. There are many responsibilities that go hand in hand with wanting to raise a champion jumper. This isn't a normal pet we're talking about. She has to be one hundred per cent committed to the entire process.'

'Excellent. I'll inform Lydia when I get home tonight. She'll be ecstatic. But…' Stacey levelled Mike with her best no-nonsense look '…you must do everything I, or Pierce, or any other doctor who treats you prescribes. Deal?' She held out her hand, never once breaking eye contact with Mike.

Mike sat up a little straighter in his chair and held her gaze before he reached out and shook hands with Stacey.

'Deal.'

Edna squealed with delight and clapped her hands. 'Mike agreeing to treatment *and* the chance to pass on our love of rabbit jumping to the next generation!' She kissed Mike's cheek and then gave Stacey a big hug.

Stacey smiled before packing up her equipment into the medical bag and handing the prescription for antibiotics to Edna.

'Well played,' Pierce whispered close by.

Stacey hadn't realised he was standing so close. She looked at him over her shoulder.

'Gotta have a few tricks up your sleeve when it comes to persuading Mike to do something.'

'So I see.'

He accepted the cup of tea Edna offered him, as did Stacey. Mike started to breathe more easily, thanks to the medication Stacey had given him. He relaxed back in his chair, a smile on his face, as he regaled them with anecdotes about his beloved sport of rabbit jumping and exactly what he'd need to teach Lydia.

By the time they left Mike was settled and Edna was happy.

'It's good to see that you have an excellent bedside manner,' Pierce said as he walked her across the road to her car.

Stacey unlocked it and stowed her medical bag in the back seat. 'Thank you.'

'I'm going to enjoy working alongside you, Dr Stacey.'

And then he'd taken her hand in his, gently shaking it, and the action had been more slow and intentional than in a normal brisk business handshake.

'*Very* much.'

Stacey closed her eyes and rubbed her hands together, the memory of that hand-shake, the memory of his deep, sensual tone, still managing to make her tremble. What was it about him that seemed to tilt her world off its axis? When she thought about Pierce she had the oddest sensation of excitement, of anticipatory delight. But she'd had those sensations once before, with Robert, and look how *that* had turned out.

Opening her eyes, she turned away from Pierce's consulting room, forcing herself to stop thinking about the way it had felt to have her hand wrapped securely in his, or the way his eyes had seemed to be able see right into the depths of her soul. He was just another doctor who was helping her out. Nothing more. The slight buzz of awareness she felt whenever she was around him was simply because she was grateful.

There was no need for her to try and figure him out, to understand why he was content to work in part-time jobs, helping out here and there in a medical capacity. The fact of the matter was that his help was needed and she'd accepted it for the next three months until Cora's return. Where or what Pierce Brolin did after that was nothing to do with her.

She headed to the kitchen and turned on the coffee machine, checking there was sufficient milk in the fridge to get them through the rest of the day. 'Business,' she told herself sternly. 'It's all just business.'

'Knock, knock.'

Stacey gasped at the sound of the deep male voice,

spinning around so fast she bumped her hip against the fridge door.

'Pierce!' She rubbed at her hip.

'Are you OK? Sorry. Didn't mean to startle you. I thought you would have heard the bell as I opened the front door.' He twirled a small key chain around his finger before putting the keys into his trouser pocket.

'I was...thinking.' *About you*, she added silently, and quickly turned away, busying herself with making coffee.

'So I heard. It's all just business, right?'

Stacey closed her eyes for a second, unable to believe he'd heard her talking to herself but glad that at this moment he couldn't see her face. 'Something like that.' She needed to change the subject. 'Can I get you a drink?' She turned to face him. 'Tea? Coffee?'

'No, I'm fine.' He pulled out a chair and sat down at the small kitchen table. 'Thought I'd get in early and go over my patient notes for the day.'

'Fair enough.'

'How about you? Couldn't sleep?'

She frowned for a moment, knowing she could never tell him that she'd awoken around five-thirty that morning from a dream in which he'd been caressing her cheek, his gaze intent on hers, seeing into her soul once more and making her feel more alive than she'd ever felt before.

'Er...busy thoughts.' Well, that was sort of true.

'Aha. Anything to do with rabbit jumping?'

When she angled her head to the side in slight confusion, he elaborated.

'I was talking to Mike last night—who, I must say, is doing much better. Anyway, he mentioned that you've recently bought two potential champion rabbits.'

Stacey forced herself to relax and nodded. The rabbits. A very safe topic. 'Yes. Lydia and George insisted on having one rabbit each.'

'How old is George?'

'Nine. He said if Lydia was old enough to get a rabbit then he was doubly old enough because he was two years older.'

Pierce watched as she moved around the kitchen, making herself a cup of coffee. How was it she could perform the simplest of tasks with such grace? All her movements were fluid and seamless, and he was entranced. In fact ever since he'd met Stacey Wilton he'd been intrigued. Bit by bit he was discovering more about her, and each new piece of the puzzle was unique as well as confusing.

George? Who was George? He'd presumed that the seven-year-old Lydia she'd mentioned was her daughter. Did Stacey also have a nine-year-old son? If so, where was the father of these children? She didn't wear a wedding ring, and there had been no mention of a husband. He tried to remember whether Mike or Edna had said anything, but Mike had been far more interested in discussing the rabbits rather than the children.

'Sounds fair.' He kept his tone at a neutral level whilst his mind tried to compute any new information he might uncover. 'I know Nell's very interested, but I don't think we'll be buying a rabbit any time soon.'

'She's more than welcome to help Lydia and George if she likes. We only live two blocks away from you, so our houses are within easy walking distance.'

'Thank you, Stacey.' He seemed genuinely surprised by the offer. 'That's nice of you.'

She pulled out a chair and sat at the opposite end of the table to him. 'Having Nell come round might actually prove a worthwhile diversion for Jasmine.'

'Jasmine?'

'She's just turned fourteen, so at the moment she's nothing but hormones.' Stacey slumped forward a little and sighed.

A fourteen-year-old as well! Stacey must have been a young mother. Either that or she was older than he'd initially thought. He managed to hide his surprise. 'Ah. I remember that phase with Nell—which, believe me, wasn't easy. Trying to explain hormones and why she would feel such extremes in her emotions was difficult, especially as our parents had passed away only a few years before. But we figured it all out in the end.'

Stacey sipped her drink. 'That helps put things with Jasmine into perspective. The teenage years are the worst, in my opinion. But of course Jasmine doesn't think I understand. She's still mad at me for dragging her away from all her friends in Perth, three-quarters of the way through the school year, to the other side of the country.'

'I guess it's not easy for you—especially without your parents around.'

'No.' She sat up a little straighter and stared down into her coffee cup. 'Cora keeps telling me that Jasmine will settle down, and Molly's really good with her, but she blames me for everything at the moment, whether it's my fault or not.'

'It's just a phase, Stacey. She'll grow out of it.'

'Let's hope she does that before I lose complete and utter patience with her.'

Pierce chuckled. 'Where are the kids now?'

Stacey checked the clock on the wall. 'Probably finishing off their breakfast and getting ready for school.'

'How do they get to school?' Did she have a nanny?

'Molly's on a late shift. She and I usually coordinate if we can, but now that Jasmine's a little older she's responsible for getting George and Lydia to school each morning.'

'Jasmine won't be tempted to cut class if there's no one to check up on her?'

'Oh, gosh. I hadn't even thought of that.' She stared at him for a moment, holding his gaze, the despair slowly disappearing from her face.

Did the woman have any idea just how beautiful she was? Especially when she looked at him like that, all vulnerable and soft. Right at this moment in time he didn't really care how many children she had, or what sort of shenanigans she might be facing at home. All he was aware of was how lovely Stacey Wilton was. She was the reason why he'd been unable to sleep that morning, with his thoughts turning to what it might be like to work alongside her, to see her on a regular basis, and whether or not something else might be brewing between them.

Then she blinked, and with an abruptness that startled him she stood and finished her coffee before taking the cup to the sink and washing it.

'At any rate, I'd best go and review my own set of patients before the busy day begins,' she mumbled.

And within another moment, Pierce found himself alone in the small kitchen.

'Uh…' She poked her head around the door. 'Just let me know if you need help with anything. And er…welcome to Shortfield Family Medical Practice.' She didn't quite meet his gaze as she spoke, and as soon as she'd finished her little spiel she headed off once more.

Pierce exhaled slowly and pushed both hands through his hair. Stacey Wilton was a whirlwind of a woman—buying her own medical practice, moving her family across country, juggling a full-time job and three children. She was dynamic, thoughtful…and incredibly sexy.

He hadn't wanted to think of her in such a way, especially as they would be working together for the next few months, but he'd come to accept it as fact. The way she held herself, the way she walked with a slight swish of her hips, the way she occasionally tucked her shoulder-length brown hair behind her ear... Her eyes were the blue of the sky on a cloudless day, and her lips were... Well, whenever he thought about the shape of her mouth his gut would tighten, because the urge to actually see what those lips tasted like was a thought he hadn't been able to dismiss at all.

It wasn't as if he lusted after every new woman he met—in fact quite the opposite. After Catherine had ended their engagement six years ago he'd tried to date, but as soon as they discovered he was his autistic sister's sole guardian most women would usually choose not to see him again. Catherine, of course, had been different. She'd been instantly loving and accepting of Nell. But even that had had its flaws.

He stood up quickly, almost knocking over his chair, determined to control his thoughts. There was no point in reflecting on the past—not now, when he was at the beginning of the next junction of his life. Just three more months. By then Nell would be completely settled at the house, along with her two housemates, and he could finally accept his dream job—the job he'd been offered several times already but had been forced to decline. Until Nell was ready there was no chance he'd ever be able to leave.

As things stood, he'd been putting his plans into place for a long time, ensuring Nell understood as much as possible about what would be happening, teaching her how to talk on the internet chat channel he'd set up and other things like that. He wasn't going to leave his sister in the lurch—she was as much a part of him as his arm or his leg—but the chance to finally complete his research, to work with other staff who shared his passion for understanding as much as possible about autism spectrum disorders, would be brilliant.

He'd already completed a lot of research, written and published several scientific papers on the positive and negative effects of independent living in the autistic adult, and he knew he'd figured out how to provide the right amount of independence and support for Nell—support which could be given via computer or phone. He was so close to achieving his goal, to finally being able to accept the position he'd been coveting for years. The last thing he needed was to form some sort of romantic attachment to a woman who was clearly devoted to her own family.

Stacey was lovely. There was no denying that. But he still had no idea whether or not she was married. And so Stacey Wilton, for several reasons, was off-limits—even to his thoughts.

CHAPTER THREE

OVER THE NEXT week Stacey couldn't believe how easy she found life working alongside Pierce Brolin. It really was as though he'd been sent from heaven just when she needed him most. He was even still working two shifts per week at the hospital, determined to honour his commitments.

'Nell was asking to see you again,' Pierce mentioned on Thursday afternoon, after they'd finished a hectic clinic.

Stacey had ventured into his consulting room to see how he'd fared during the busy day, and when he offered her a chair she gratefully accepted.

'Oh, that's nice. How is she?' Stacey sat down, sighing with relief at finally being off her feet.

'More interested in meeting your rabbits than in seeing you, if I own the truth.' He grinned as he spoke and Stacey laughed, the lilting sound washing over him. He swallowed and ignored the effect. They were colleagues and friends. Nothing more. 'How about dinner this Saturday night?' Friends could have dinner.

Stacey thought for a moment. 'Are you sure you're prepared for all of us to come?'

'The whole gaggle,' he confirmed. 'I'd like to meet

the children and the rabbits, and if your sister's free ask her to come along, too. The more the merrier.'

Stacey frowned for a moment. The children *and* her sister? Didn't he realise that they were one and the same? Well, apart from poor George, who was clearly not a sister.

'Nell won't be upset with having too many people in the house? We're a pretty rowdy bunch.'

'She's usually pretty good with people if she's been properly prepared. Plus it's good for her to stretch her boundaries. It's one of the reasons why she's desperate to live independently, and the more people she knows and can rely on the better it's going to be for her.'

'True. I've read your papers on the subject. Very interesting.' She tried not to colour as she spoke, not wanting to confess that she'd actually looked him up on the internet and discovered a link to his scientific papers. In fact he appeared quite the expert on the subject of adults with autism and their integration into society.

'Thanks.' He nodded once, acknowledging her praise, but quickly continued. 'So you'll all come?'

Stacey thought over his invitation. 'Well, I'll tentatively accept on behalf of us all, but if I can let you know definite numbers tomorrow that would be great.'

'Glad to see you don't rule the roost with an iron will.'

'No. We're very much a democracy—except when it comes to bedtime.' She shook her head and chuckled. 'George always has to push the limits.'

'That's what nine-year-old boys do, I'm afraid.' Pierce joined in with her laughter, his curiosity about Stacey and these children still highly piqued.

During the week he'd discovered that Stacey wasn't married, or involved with anyone, because he'd overheard one of their more senior patients asking her when she was going to settle down and get married.

Stacey's answer had been polite. 'Not just yet, Mrs Donahue.'

Even though he'd tried to ignore his naturally inquisitive nature, he hadn't been able to stop himself from trying to figure her out. While he respected her privacy, there was something about Stacey—something about the way she seemed to be so tightly wound, taking life very seriously. He knew from talking to Mike and Edna that Stacey and her two sisters had recently turned thirty-one. That was hardly old, and yet she seemed so much older in her mannerisms and in the way her life seemed to be so closely structured.

Perhaps that was the reason he was interested in getting to know her a bit more. Perhaps he'd unconsciously decided to help her to find life a bit more vibrant, a bit more happy during his time here. For the moment, though, he realised the conversation they'd been having had come to an end, and it would look silly if he just continued to sit in the chair opposite her and stare, as he was doing right now.

'OK, then. Saturday night around six o'clock—family approval and patients willing?'

He stood from the chair and came around the desk, aware that Stacey was watching his every move. He leaned on the desk and crossed his legs at the ankle, trying to ignore the way her light visual caress made him want to preen.

'Uh…sure.' She looked down at her hands for a moment, clearing her throat. 'What would you like me to bring? Drinks? Dessert?'

'Don't bring a thing.'

'But I have to.'

Her words were serious, absolute, and it took a moment for realisation to dawn on him. She needed to bring something, to feel as though she was contributing. Those were the rules of polite society and Stacey Wilton adhered to them. Pierce was probably more slap-dash, more than willing to take care of all the preparations and give Stacey the night off, as it were, but he could see that being told to do nothing was stressing her more than being asked to contribute. It reminded him of his mother—always busy, always willing to help, always putting others before herself—and for a moment a wave of nostalgia swept over him.

'In that case, how about dessert?'

She visibly relaxed, and Pierce was pleased to see the smile return to her face.

'Excellent. Dessert it is.'

'I'm looking forward to it.'

'You may regret saying that,' she said, chuckling and held up her hands. 'George likes making desserts, and his favourite colour is blue. Needless to say we've been having a lot of blue-coloured desserts of late, so don't say I didn't warn you.'

Pierce laughed at her words and nodded. He was about to reply when the bell which was over the front door to the clinic tinkled, alerting them to the fact that someone had just walked into the waiting room.

She checked her watch. 'A bit late.'

When Stacey started to rise from her chair he immediately held up a hand to stop her. 'Don't stress. I'll deal with it. You rest.'

As he headed off before she could protest Stacey watched his purposeful, long stride. So bold, as though he knew exactly where he was going in life and how he was going to get there. If that really was the case, she envied him.

Although as far as she was concerned she *did* know exactly where her life was headed—especially as Lydia was only seven years old. Stacey's life wasn't her own, and there was nothing she could do about it. Cora had her research into island diseases and her work in the Pacific island nation of Tarparnii to contend with, Molly was following her dream of becoming a general surgeon, and Stacey—dependable, sensible Stacey—was stuck at home raising her half-siblings.

She knew she shouldn't complain, and most days she was able to handle these negative emotions, but today, being asked out to dinner by a handsome man, and for one moment pretending that he was asking her and only her, had reminded her of what life had been like before her parents' death. That was the way things had been a few years ago when she'd met Robert, when he'd taken her to the most lavish restaurant in Perth, gone down on bended knee and proposed to her in front of an entire restaurant full of guests.

'I love you', he'd professed. 'Be my wife?'

Of course she'd said yes. She'd loved him. But the instant her father and stepmother had been so cruelly taken from them Stacey's life had all but disappeared, with everyone simply expecting her to take over. Unfortunately Robert hadn't anticipated Stacey and her sisters becoming the children's legal guardians. He hadn't been able to understand why the younger children hadn't gone to live with Cora or Molly, and when Stacey had informed him that they would all be staying together—that the younger children needed all of their older sisters, that they all wanted to grieve together—he'd been unable to comprehend it.

Robert had therefore made his own decision and decided to call off their wedding. Unfortunately, he'd forgotten to tell her he'd changed his mind until she'd turned up at the church, dressed in white, sad because her father wasn't there to give her away. The groomsman had briskly apologised to her and then handed her an envelope which Robert had given him only twenty minutes earlier. In the envelope had been a short and concise note in Robert's bold handwriting, informing her that he'd changed his mind. There had been no apology, no other explanation.

Stacey shook her head, clearing her thoughts and swallowing over the lump in her throat. She blinked back the few tears that were starting to sting her eyes and forced herself to take five soothing breaths. Of course, as she'd belatedly realised, there'd been far too many things wrong with their relationship—such as the way Robert had always made her second-guess herself, or made her feel guilty for ruining their scheduled dates because her clinic had run late.

During this last year and a half she'd scooped up what had been left of her dignity, finished off her contract with Perth General Hospital as an A & E consultant and decided that a more sedate pace of life was in order. Seeing her father's old Newcastle GP practice up for sale had been the godsend she'd been waiting for. It had been her dream job when she'd been an innocent fourteen-year-old, wanting to follow in her father's footsteps. With so many things going wrong she'd been determined to make *this* dream become a reality.

It was only because Cora and Molly had supported her, as they'd always done, that the dream had even been realised. It hadn't been easy, uprooting the children and moving so late in the year, but everyone had coped well except for Jasmine. She frowned as she imagined what Jasmine's retort might be when Stacey told them all that they'd been invited over to Pierce's house for dinner. But it was their first official invitation since moving here, and it would be good for all of them.

Stacey had a hunch that Jasmine would be delighted to meet Nell—especially as the school Jaz had attended in Perth supported integration of children with disabilities. But when she finally arrived home that night, and sat down at the dinner table to enjoy the delicious meal of spaghetti bolognaise and salad which Molly had prepared, Jasmine's reaction was exactly as predicted the instant Stacey told them all about the invitation.

'I don't want to go!' Jasmine shouted.

'Well, *I* want to go,' Molly countered, giving Stacey a wide, beaming smile and waggling her eyebrows up and down as a means of indicating that she thought Pierce was cute.

Stacey ignored her antics.

'How sweet of Pierce to invite us all. Sorry, Jaz.' Molly put her arm around her half-sister's shoulders and pressed a quick kiss to her cheek—a move Jaz wouldn't tolerate from Stacey. 'Looks as though you'll just have to stick it out and come too.'

'I'm old enough to stay home by myself,' she retorted hotly, slamming her knife and fork onto her plate. 'I'm not a baby any more.' As she said the words she glared at Lydia, who was innocently enjoying her dinner and not paying one bit of attention to her sister's tantrum.

'No one's saying you are,' Stacey returned, but no sooner were the words out of her mouth than Jasmine pushed her chair back from the table and ran off to her room. Stacey closed her eyes and sighed. 'If Jasmine really wants to be treated in a more adult fashion then she's going to have to accept the responsibilities of being a part of this family—and that means attending events and accepting dinner invitations rather than having tantrums.'

Molly nodded. 'I'll speak to her when I'm finished eating.'

'Thanks, Mol.'

They both knew Molly would get much further than Stacey. It was basic psychology. Jasmine needed someone to blame for all the pain she was feeling and Stacey had been chosen as the winner. Most of the time she was fine with that. She understood Jasmine far more than the young girl realised, and knew that time really would heal the wound of losing her parents. But sometimes being on the end of her sister's cutting words was difficult to cope with.

'So we're all going, then?' It was George who asked the question, looking expectantly at his big sister.

'We are, George,' she confirmed, and the little boy grinned. 'We also need to make a dessert, so would you be able to hel—?'

'I'll help. I'll help,' he volunteered quickly, and Stacey blew him a kiss of thanks.

'What about Flopsy and Andrew?' Lydia asked.

'Yes, the rabbits can come, too.' Both Lydia and George cheered at this news, the two of them having taken to their new pets with the utmost joy. 'And, speaking of which, don't forget to feed them before you head off to brush your teeth.'

'Yes Stacey,' George and Lydia said in unison.

'Will we meet his sister?' George continued.

'Pierce's sister? Yes. Her name is Nell.'

'Nell.' George tried the name out. 'I like meeting new people.'

'Me, too,' Lydia agreed, slurping spaghetti into her mouth.

'Me three,' said Molly, following suit and slurping her own spaghetti—but not before giving Stacey a little wink. It was code for *Everything will work out fine. Stop stressing, sis.*

Stacey relaxed a bit and was pleased when, the following day, she was able to formally accept Pierce's invitation.

'Excellent,' he said. 'Nell's super-excited. She wanted to know why you all weren't coming over tonight, as she doesn't want to wait until tomorrow.'

Stacey chuckled as she made them both a cup of coffee. 'She wants to see the rabbits, doesn't she?' she stated. 'Flopsy and Andrew will be coming, too, so please reassure Nell.'

'Andrew?' Pierce raised an eyebrow.

Stacey shrugged. 'Lydia named him. She said he looked like an Andrew.' She chuckled and finished stirring their coffees.

'Lydia sounds like quite a character.'

'Oh, she is. Determined to be an actress or an astronaut. At the moment she can't decide, but her determined spirit never wavers.'

Pierce laughed as he gratefully accepted the coffee. 'I can't wait to meet her and the rest of your posse.' It was true. He had a sense that meeting the rest of the people who mattered most to Stacey would help him piece together more of the puzzle surrounding her.

'Posse?' She joined in his laughter, amazed at how light and free she felt, even though they had another hectic clinic scheduled. To have these few moments with

Pierce was like a recharge for her internal battery. 'I just hope the noise we naturally generate doesn't scare Nell.'

'Thank you for being concerned about my sister's wellbeing,' he remarked after taking a sip of his coffee. 'I do appreciate it.'

This thoughtfulness of hers was yet another facet of Stacey's personality, and one he'd been aware of from their first meeting. She gave and she gave and she kept on giving to others, and it made him wonder just who in her life gave back to her. No doubt she was close to her sisters, but it sounded as though Molly was now super-busy and Cora was still overseas, so who did Stacey rely on for support? His natural protective instincts were increasing where Stacey was concerned and he was finding it difficult to stop thinking up ways he could help her.

They both stood at the kitchen bench, sipping their coffees, the silence quite companionable, so when the bell over the front reception door tinkled Stacey jumped, startled out of her reverie.

'Let's get Friday underway,' she remarked, quickly drinking the rest of her coffee and trying not to burn her tongue in the process.

'I'm really excited about tomorrow night,' Pierce said as they headed towards their consulting rooms. 'In fact, why don't you come over around four o'clock and Nell can show the children her puzzles. She's become quite good at sharing.' He straightened his shoulders, brotherly pride evident in his stature.

'That's great. Has it been difficult to get her to the point where she is happy to share her things?'

He shrugged one shoulder. 'It's been more of an on-going thing all her life. Our mother was determined that Nell's autism would never be used as an excuse for bad manners, so Nell was taught from a young age the importance of being polite—and that included sharing. Like anyone, she has good days and bad days. But for the most part she no longer has a tantrum if people put a puzzle piece back in the wrong spot.'

'What does she do now if they do?'

'She waits until the person has finished playing with the puzzle and then she fixes it up before packing it away.'

'Good strategy.'

'It works. So—four o'clock sound good?'

She nodded. 'That gives us plenty of time to get crazy Saturday morning done and dusted and to organise the rabbits.'

'Crazy Saturday morning?'

'George goes to soccer, Lydia has ballet at eight o'clock and then gymnastics at ten, and Jasmine has a guitar lesson.'

'Guitar?'

'Electric guitar.'

'Oh, that sounds…fun—and noisy.'

Stacey grinned. 'Actually, she's pretty good.'

'She can bring her guitar if she likes. Give us an after-dinner concert, perhaps?' At Stacey's grimace he chuckled. 'Or not.' He stopped outside his consulting room door and placed a hand on her shoulder. 'Listen, if I don't get a chance to speak to you for the rest of the day, given just how hectic our clinics are, I'll see you tomorrow at four.'

Stacey was having a difficult time focusing on his words as the simple touch of his hand on her shoulder was enough not only to cause a deep warmth to flood throughout her entire body but for her mind to comprehend little of what he was actually saying. It had been so long since a man had been nice and kind and supportive, and it was…exciting.

Usually she just battled on with her day, her week, her

life, sorting things out to the best of her ability, trying to make everyone around her happy. But at the moment it felt good to actually have Pierce standing by her side, offering his support. She had the sense that he was someone she could talk to and confide in. He also had an understanding of what it was like to raise a sibling—in her case more than one. Pierce had had to raise Nell after their parents had passed away, which couldn't have been at all easy.

Long after Pierce had dropped his hand from her shoulder the memory of his warm touch and the way his blue eyes had twinkled with calm reassurance were enough to get her through the rest of the day. However, by four o'clock the following afternoon Stacey's nerves were taut with stress once more.

Thankfully Molly had driven the short distance from their house to Nell's house, with the two rabbits safe in the cage on the back seat of the mini-van, placed between George and Lydia. Jasmine sat in the far corner, listening to her music on headphones and generally sulking.

'Is this where you used to live when you were little girls?' George asked as they climbed from the car.

'Yes,' Molly answered, handing Stacey the car keys as Stacey waited politely for Jasmine to precede her. The surly girl was clearly resenting being forced to come.

'You never know what's going to happen, Jaz,' Stacey said softly as Molly and the two children made their way up the path towards the front door, carefully carrying the rabbit cage. 'You might actually enjoy yourself. They really are very nice people. Especially Nell.'

As she spoke the words she sincerely hoped that Jasmine wouldn't kick up a fuss, because despite Pierce's reassurances she didn't want to test Nell's ability to cope with chaos.

With sullen steps and her arms crossed over her chest,

Jasmine walked ahead of Stacey towards the front door. Stacey only remembered to lock the car at the last minute. She was a little disconcerted about their descending *en masse*, about her family creating too much noise, about seeing Pierce in a more social capacity. *No.* She wouldn't dwell on the latter. They lived and worked in a fairly close-knit community, and as doctors at the family medical practice it was only right that they become friends.

Nell stood at the front door with Pierce, formally welcoming everyone, even though Stacey could see that she was more interested in the rabbits.

'Please, come in to my home,' Nell invited warmly.

'Wow!' George and Lydia remarked as they stared at the ornate ceiling before doing a slow perusal of the room.

When Lydia spied the puzzles she relinquished her hold on the rabbit cage and raced over to where Nell had set them up on the floor. 'I love puzzles,' she declared, before tipping one over and starting to figure out how all the little wooden pieces went back in.

George continued his visual observation while Stacey introduced Jasmine to Pierce and Nell. The teenager managed the smallest glimpse of a smile when she shook hands with Nell.

'Right on time,' Pierce stated, grinning widely at Stacey.

She smiled back, feeling highly self-conscious and trying desperately to ignore the butterflies that had just been let loose in her stomach simply because she was in close proximity to him.

'Are you going to marry Stacey?' George asked, breaking the silence.

'*What?*' Stacey and Pierce said in unison.

CHAPTER FOUR

'GEORGE!' STACEY WAS gobsmacked. She looked at Pierce in shock, then back to her brother. 'What on earth made you say that?'

George stared at her with his big eyes—eyes that were so like their father's. 'Well…the last time we went to have dinner at a man's house was when you told us you was going to marry him.'

George's tone was a little indignant, and the puzzled frown on his face indicated that he wasn't sure what he'd done wrong.

'But then,' Lydia chimed in from the lounge room, where she was busy finishing off the puzzle, 'he decided *not* to marry you and you had to tell everyone in the church that he wasn't coming.'

'He didn't *want* you,' Jasmine added, and her words were spoken in a tone which was designed to hurt.

'Jasmine! That's cruel.' Molly's chastisement of the girl was instant. 'Apologise to Stacey.'

'What?' Jasmine spread both her hands wide. 'Why do *I* have to apologise and Lydia and George don't?'

'Because you know better,' Molly interjected.

Stacey watched the conversation going on around her—her siblings arguing, the rabbits getting agitated in their cage, Pierce looking back and forth between them all as if he was at a tennis match—and all she could focus on was her increased heart-rate hammering wildly against her ribs. She saw Jasmine's mouth move, the framing of an apology on her lips, but the sound of the words didn't register, only the thrumming of the blood reverberating in her ears.

What must Pierce think of them all! No sooner had they stepped over the threshold than a family squabble had erupted. If this was Jasmine's way of making them all wish they'd left her behind at home, then it was starting to work. Emotional punishment, especially from her siblings, was the one thing Stacey wasn't good at dealing with.

'Stacey? Stace?'

She was vaguely aware of Molly calling her name, but mortification at the situation was getting the better of her and before she knew what was happening Stacey had whirled around on her heel and exited the house. She walked quickly down the street, moving as though on automatic. For a moment she thought no one was following her, and was extremely grateful, but a second or two later she heard a deep male voice calling her name.

Stacey didn't stop, didn't look back, and even when Pierce fell into step beside her she didn't speak a word. Thankfully he didn't try and stop her, didn't ask her to slow down, didn't offer placating words. Instead he seemed content just to walk beside her, matching her fast pace with ease. When she turned down a small lane which led to the park, he simply continued on alongside her.

She made a beeline for the swings—her favourite. The equipment at the park had been upgraded since she'd been here last, but apart from that everything was exactly the same. The familiar childhood setting calmed her somewhat, and when she finally sat down on the swing, instantly pushing herself up, she started to feel the consuming tension abate.

Pierce sat beside her on the other swing, and after watching her for a moment he followed suit and started swinging back and forth, not bothering to speak or initiate conversation. After about five minutes of swinging to and fro in silence Stacey started to slow down, her breathing more natural, her head cleared of its fog. Pierce slowed down as well and soon both of them were just sitting on the swings, rocking slowly back and forth.

'Sorry,' she ventured.

'No apology necessary.'

'I hope Nell's all right and that our silly sibling squabbling didn't upset her.'

Pierce nodded. 'Nell will be fine. She was absorbed with the rabbits, eager to get them out of their cage.'

'Good.'

'Wait a second.' Pierce held up one finger. 'Did you say *siblings*? Squabbling *siblings*? George and Lydia and Jasmine are your *siblings*?'

'Yes.' She looked at him with slight confusion, then her eyes widened slightly. 'I thought you knew that.'

'Nope. I thought they were your children—or at least that some of them were.'

She shook her head. 'Nope. We were seventeen when Jasmine was born, so I *could* have been old enough to be her mother. But my father married our nanny, Letisha, when Cora, Molly and I were thirteen.' Stacey looked down at the ground. 'My mother walked out, abandoned us, when we were almost five.'

'How terrible for all of you.'

Stacey shrugged. 'Letisha's the only real mother we can remember. She looked after us for so long, and then when Dad was finally divorced he could admit he had feelings for Tish.' Stacey smiled sadly. 'They died together in a car crash. I don't think my father could have survived being left alone again.' She kicked the ground with her foot and dragged in a breath. 'Anyway, by the time the three of us had finished medical school we had three new siblings: Jasmine, George and Lydia.'

'And now, with your father and your stepmother gone, you're raising your siblings.'

'Yes. Although the three of us share legal guardianship of the younger three on paper, I seem to have become the designated parent in practice. Though in fairness Molly and Cora are very helpful.'

'But you're the disciplinarian?' He nodded, understanding what she was saying. 'It's not easy to discipline a sibling.'

'No. It's not.' She sighed and shook her head. 'I know psychologically that Jasmine is just going through a phase, that she needs to take her grief out on someone and that someone is me—especially as I've just uprooted her from her school friends and brought her to the other side of the country. I know how she feels because that's exactly what my father did to me when I was fourteen. He took us from Newcastle to Perth.'

'But coming back home was the right decision?'

'I know it is. And I know Jasmine will forgive me one day, just as I forgave my dad. But I wish—' She stopped and gritted her teeth, trying to control the tears she could feel pricking behind her eyes.

'You wish what?' His words were soft and encouraging.

'I wish she *liked* me.' She spoke softly. 'Just a little bit. Just every now and then.' Stacey sniffed, still working hard to gain some sort of control over her emotions.

'At least she gets along with Molly, and Cora is splendid with her.'

'Except Cora's not here and Molly's embarking on a new career path, leaving *you* to carry the burden of a grieving, angry young girl.' Pierce nodded, completely understanding the situation. 'It's not easy when you're thrust into the parental role when all you'd rather do is be their sibling, comfort them and cry with them and not be expected to have all the answers.'

'Exactly.' She dragged in another calming breath. 'I just hope Lydia and George don't develop over-active hormones when *they* enter their teenage years. It's not an easy time for Jasmine. I understand that.'

'But she has to realise that this isn't an easy time for you either. How long is it since your parents passed away?'

'Eighteen months.'

'Well, that's not going to be easy for any of you—regardless of how old you are. Plus, it sounds as though you've had more going on than just the loss of your parents…at least from what George said.'

'Being jilted at the altar, you mean?' There was no point in beating about the bush, especially now, thanks to her siblings and the way they'd blurted out her past hurts.

He stared at her for a second. 'Oh, Stacey. What an idiot.'

'You weren't to know.'

Pierce reached over and took her hand in his. It seemed like the most natural thing in the world so she let him. Warmth spread up her arm and somehow filled her entire being, right down to the tips of her toes, and she just let it. Right at this moment she was tired of always being in control, of bottling up her own emotions and private thoughts.

'No, not me. *Him*. What an idiot he was to let you go.'

Stacey looked at her small hand sitting inside his big one. 'How could you possibly know that?' Her tone was soft, her words tinged with confusion. 'You barely know me.'

'I met you three weeks ago, Stacey, and although I don't profess to know *everything* about you the essentials of your personality are quite clear.'

'They are?'

He gave her a lopsided smile and she had to work hard to calm the butterflies in her stomach. It was bad enough that the touch of his skin against hers was causing her heart-rate to increase. Did she have no control over her senses where Pierce was concerned?

'Stacey, from the way you stood on the opposite side of the road, gazing with fond nostalgia at the house, I knew you were someone who had a big heart. The memories the place clearly holds for you are important, and you didn't shy away from that.'

She stared at him for a moment, then glanced down at their hands, at his thumb gently rubbing over the backs of her knuckles. She wished he'd stop, but at the same time she wished he'd never stop. Was he feeding her a line? Was he being nice to her because he wanted something from her? If so...what?

It had taken her quite a while to figure out that Robert had had his own agenda when it came to their...union. He'd wanted a smart, pretty wife—someone who understood his work and who was dedicated to helping him climb the career ladder. What he *hadn't* wanted was an instant family.

'And if you want more examples of how I know your character,' Pierce continued, his tone as intent as his words, 'let's start with your concern for Edna and Mike, or of the way you talked about sitting in the bay window sharing your secrets with your sisters. But most importantly for me it was the way you interacted with Nell. As far as I'm concerned that's always the biggest indicator of a woman's true nature, because the instant a woman discovers I'm guardian to my little sister, and not only that but she has a learning difficulty, it's usually enough to make them head for the hills.'

'A *woman's* true nature?' she couldn't help quizzing.

It wasn't until Pierce looked into her blue eyes that he realised she was turning the tables, lightening the atmosphere, wanting to remove the spotlight from herself.

'There's a story there,' she said.

Picrce nodded and slowly let go of her petite hand. 'Of course there is, and it's one which has been repeated time and time again.'

'Which begs the question have *you* ever come close to matrimony?'

He nodded. 'I was engaged. Catherine was her name.'

'Was?'

'Still is, actually. She's alive and well, but—'

'But she couldn't take the responsibility of being guardian to Nell?'

Pierce shook his head. 'No. No, quite the opposite, actually.'

'Really?'

He exhaled slowly and looked down at the ground for a moment. 'Catherine was…*is*—' he glanced at her as he corrected himself '—the type of woman who loves to be of use. She loves helping others, being there for them. She's a brilliant doctor, ended up becoming an eye surgeon, but I guess the best way to describe her is that she needs to be needed.'

'So when she found out you had a sister with a disability she was happy about that?'

'Yes, and I thought, *Wow, here's a woman who likes me, who likes Nell, who loves being with both of us, who understands what we're about.*'

'What went wrong?'

Pierce paused. 'She accepted a job overseas, working with Pacific Medical Aid like your sister Cora.'

'Was this before or after your engagement?'

'It was two weeks before our wedding?'

'She just went overseas?'

'She said that we didn't need her as much as other people needed her. That being married would tie her down, would stop her from reaching her true potential which was to help as many people as she could.' Pierce met Stacey's gaze. 'Hard to argue with someone who only wants to do good in this world.'

'And is she doing good?'

'I believe she's presently in Iran, giving the gift of sight by performing cataract operations on those who otherwise could never afford it.'

'She sounds like quite a woman.'

He nodded. 'She sends me a Christmas card every year.'

'It's good that you keep in touch.'

'It is.' He nodded.

Stacey watched him for a moment, wondering if he still had feelings for Catherine. It was clear from the way he spoke of her that he admired her. Could she ask? They were being quite open with each other so why not?

'Do you…?' She hesitated for a moment, then took a breath and plunged right in. 'Do you still have feelings for Catherine?'

'Friendship feelings? Yes. Romantic feelings? No. But I wish her every success and happiness.'

'And yet you sound so forlorn.'

'I do?' He sat up straighter and chuckled. 'Sorry. I'm supposed to be the one cheering you up.'

'Then consider me cheered. You have performed your friendship duties well.'

'Friendship?' he queried.

'Isn't that why we're having dinner tonight? To build friendships not only for Nell but for each other?'

Pierce angled his head to the side. 'I guess I hadn't thought of it like that.'

'Perhaps because you're always so busy considering Nell's needs first and your own second.'

'I'm sure you know all about that, what with having so many siblings. But I think we could definitely be friends.' He spread his arms wide. 'We're off to a good start. We're swinging together.' He winked, implying a cheeky *double entendre*.

She laughed. 'Literally.'

'Yes. So, *friend*, tell me something about you that a lot of people—*sans* siblings—wouldn't know.'

Stacey sighed thoughtfully for a moment, then nodded. 'I love cheesy music videos.'

'Huh? That *is* surprising.'

'They're just so funny. The over-acting, the bad colour saturation, the strange vision of the film-maker. Sometimes the videos have absolutely nothing to do with the lyrics, and that just makes it even more ridiculous and funny. Some of the ones from the eighties are classics—especially with special effects which were considered so cutting edge at the time but nowadays are completely woeful.'

Pierce nodded, as though seriously considering her

words. 'Cheesy music videos? I'm beginning to understand the appeal.'

'OK. Now it's your turn. Tell me something not many people know about *you*.'

Pierce opened his mouth, hesitated, then closed it again.

'Come on,' Stacey urged. 'Friends share.'

He nodded, but exhaled and closed his eyes before confessing, 'I like…to sew.'

'Sew?'

'If I hadn't had a passion for medicine and helping people I would have been a fashion designer.'

'Really?' Stacey couldn't help but chuckle at this news. 'Are you being serious or are you pulling my leg?'

He kept a straight face for a whole five seconds before grinning. 'Pulling your leg. I like to garden.'

'Well, that's hardly a secret. Your whole neighbourhood can tell you like to garden simply by the way you attend to those flowerbeds.' She swung back and forth a little. 'I liked the sewing story better, but if you ever feel like bringing your gardening skills over to my house then please feel free. I do not have a green thumb whatsoever.'

'Perhaps I can give you some pointers. We could do some potting and planting and then head inside and watch cheesy music videos.'

Stacey laughed, unable to believe just how light and happy she felt. How was it that Pierce had not only been able to shift her bad mood but make her feel optimistic?

'Gardening lessons?' She nodded. 'I might actually look forward to them.'

He stood from the swing and held out his hand to her. 'I hope you do.'

Stacey accepted his hand, but as she stood from the swing she over-balanced slightly and fell towards him.

Pierce moved quickly and caught her, with one strong arm about her waist.

'Uh…sorry.' Stacey placed her other hand on his arm to steady herself, trying to ignore the instant warmth which flooded her body, her senses shifting into overdrive as she breathed in his spicy scent.

'You all right?'

His words were soft, his breath fanning her cheek, and when she lifted her head and looked at him she realised just how close her face was to his. Her gaze dipped to look at his mouth, lingering for a second before returning to meet his eyes.

'Uh…' She sent commands to her limbs, telling them to move, her legs to support her, but the sluggish signals took a few seconds to be received. 'Yeah. Yeah, I should be fine.'

As she shifted her weight, Pierce continued to hold her hand. 'Did you twist your ankle? Hurt yourself?'

'No. I just stepped wrong. The ground's a little uneven.'

He smiled at her. 'OK.'

They took a few steps away from the swings before he released her, shoving his hands into the pockets of his jeans as they headed back down the path. Stacey racked her mind for something to say, trying to get her brain back into gear rather than fixating on the way being so close to Pierce had made her feel.

They'd been doing so well, chatting and sharing as friends. She didn't want to be aware of him. She wanted their relationship to be one of easygoing colleagues and friends. She didn't want to dream of him, to wonder what it might be like to have his arms holding her securely, to have him gazing down into her eyes, to have his lips pressed against hers.

'Uh…' She stopped and quickly cleared her throat, astonished that her voice had broken with that one brief sound. 'Um…will Nell be all right with you leaving her like this? I mean, she doesn't know any of my family and—'

'Nell will be fine. Part of her preparation for living independently has involved developing a sort of *script*, I guess you'd call it, for when a visitor comes round. But with two rabbits there for her to play with I doubt she's given anyone else a second thought.'

'Well, that's good.'

'Plus, I'm sure your sister Molly will have everything under control.'

'Probably better than I ever could.' She sighed, thinking of the way Jasmine responded so positively to Molly.

'I doubt that's true. One day soon Jasmine will realise everything you've done for her, she'll see you in a different light, and she'll appreciate you much more.'

They were almost back at the house by now and Pierce started to slow his pace. He wasn't sure he was ready to go inside to the noise and bustle just yet. Chatting quietly, intimately with Stacey had been relaxing, and he couldn't remember the last time he'd allowed himself to relax.

'Oh, I hope so.'

Stacey, too, didn't seem in any great hurry to re-enter the house, and they stopped just outside Edna and Mike's place.

Stacey looked up at the fading light of the balmy September day. 'Hopefully Jasmine's been able to engage Nell in conversation.' Stacey looked across at the house. 'I hate to see her hurting.'

'Of course you do. She's your little sister and she's been through some fairly intense life changes.'

'But George and Lydia seemed to have coped.'

'Because they're younger. Child-like comprehension is sometimes a godsend, and at other times, it's an enviable reality.' He leaned up against the fence between the two properties.

Stacey watched him in the late-afternoon light. 'Did Nell understand about your parents' death?'

'It took her a while, and sometimes she was quite confused when she couldn't find them, or when she'd find me quietly crying because I missed them so much.'

Stacey pulled her lightweight cardigan around her and crossed her arms in front in an effort to stop herself from touching him. She wanted nothing more than to reach out and place a reassuring hand on his arm or, worse, to throw her arms around his waist and hug him close, desperate to let him know that she really did understand exactly where he was coming from and what he felt. Just because they were adults, it didn't stop them from wanting to see their parents again.

'It can get rather wretched sometimes,' she agreed, surprised to find her voice catching on the words. 'I often wonder where I'd be now if my parents hadn't died…if I didn't have the children to constantly consider. No doubt I'd be stuck in a loveless marriage with Robert who, as it turned out, only wanted to marry me because I fitted all his criteria. He might have professed undying love for me, but it was only another lie to secure what he wanted.'

Pierce looked at her for a moment, then shook his head. 'Yep. He was an idiot. What I mean is—and if I may be so bold, given I don't know the circumstances— your ex-fiancé sounds quite thick.'

Stacey's smile was instant. 'Thank you.'

Pierce held out an open hand towards her. 'I mean you're intelligent, caring, thoughtful and incredibly beautiful. What sane man *wouldn't* want you?'

Stacey wasn't sure what to say. His warm, sweet words washed over her, making her feel cherished…and she couldn't remember the last time she'd felt cherished—if ever. They stood there, simply looking at each other, drinking their fill. Butterflies started to churn again in her stomach as the atmosphere between them began to intensify. The need to draw closer to him, to touch him, was starting to become overwhelming, and when she edged a little closer to where he stood she found that he was doing the same.

His gaze flicked down to encompass her mouth before returning to her eyes. He opened his mouth to speak, but before he could say another word Edna's front door opened and she came running out, all in a frantic tizzy.

'Edna?' Stacey called, and the other woman yelped with fright, clearly not expecting to find two people chatting near the bottom of her driveway. 'Is something wrong?'

'It's Mike. He's got pains. I was just coming to get Pierce and call the ambulance,' she said, indicating the cell phone in her hand.

'I've got my big emergency bag in my car,' Stacey remarked, fishing her car keys from her pocket.

'Thanks,' Pierce called over his shoulder as he headed inside with Edna.

By the time Stacey joined him he'd placed Mike in the recovery position. He accepted a stethoscope from Stacey and listened to Mike's heart.

'Ambulance is on it's way,' he informed her as she wound the blood pressure cuff from the portable sphygmomanometer around Mike's arm.

'BP is elevated,' she responded a moment later. 'How do his lungs sound? Asthma?'

'Not asthma. Probably an angina attack.' Pierce met

and held her gaze for a moment, his eyes clearly saying, *Let's hope that's all it is.*

'I'm not…an…idiot,' Mike puffed, his eyes shut. 'Silence…speaks…volumes.'

'Shush, Mike,' Edna said, bossing him around. 'Let the doctors do their work.'

'You've always been very astute, Mike.' Stacey gently rubbed his arm, wanting to reassure him in any way she could. 'Try and focus on your breathing for me. Slow, calm breaths. We're going to set up an IV, just to get some fluids into you, so that by the time the ambulance arrives you'll be in a better state to receive further treatment.'

'What's…wrong?' he panted, reaching out for his wife's hand. Edna dutifully held it, but when she looked up at Stacey, there was fear in her eyes.

'We're not sure at this stage, Mike,' Pierce added as he reached into Stacey's well-stocked emergency bag, which was more like a huge backpack, pulling out the equipment they'd need for inserting an in vitro line into Mike's left arm. 'But rest assured Stacey and I will do everything we can to help.'

'Where is it painful?' Stacey asked Mike, and he told her the pain was down his right arm and across his chest. 'You're doing a good job of controlling your breathing. Well done. Is the pain constricting when you breathe in or out or both?'

'Both.'

'Is the pain stabbing or constant?' Stacey opened the tubing packet while Pierce inserted a cannula into Mike's arm.

'Constant.' He paused. 'Sometimes stabbing.'

'Any other pain? Headache? Tingling in your legs?'

'No.'

'Good.'

By the time they'd finished inserting the drip, Edna still sitting by her husband's side, holding his hand as though she was never letting go ever again, they could hear ambulance sirens in the distance.

Pierce looked across at Stacey. 'Are you OK to hold the fort for a moment? I just want to check on Nell. No doubt the sirens are going to bring the others out to see what's going on.'

'Good point.' Stacey nodded, and wasn't surprised to find Molly walking into Edna and Mike's house less than three minutes later.

'Mike? Mike?' Molly knelt down by his side. 'Ah... look at this. Stacey's got you all ready for the ambulance. Isn't she great?'

'She really is,' Pierce remarked as he re-entered the house. 'Ambulance is just pulling into the driveway. Time to get you mobile.' Pierce ran through what would happen, so Mike and Edna were completely aware of the procedure.

'I can go with him, can't I?' Edna asked as Stacey performed Mike's observations once more, pleased to announce that his BP was starting to level out, thanks to the IV drip.

'That's good news,' Pierce told him as the paramedics came into the house.

Stacey spoke with Molly, making sure her sister was all right to stay with Nell and the children.

'They've spent a lot of time playing with the rabbits and they're just sitting down to do some puzzles. Jasmine's been really good with Nell.'

Stacey sighed with relief. 'I was hoping she would be.'

'George and Lydia are having a turn with the rabbits in the back yard,' Molly continued, talking as though she was giving a patient debrief. 'And I've checked the kitchen—Pierce has pre-cooked an amazing meal, so I'll save you both some and we'll just get on with our night of getting to know Nell.'

'Sounds like a good plan,' Pierce remarked. 'Once Mike's all settled we'll head back.'

'Agreed.' With a brisk, formal nod that would serve her well in the surgical world, Molly kissed both Edna and Mike on the cheek before heading next door.

After they'd assisted the paramedics in settling Mike in the ambulance, Edna rode along with him and Stacey and Pierce followed in Stacey's car. Stacey couldn't help but be impressed with Pierce's cool, calm and collected bedside manner. Mike hated fuss at the best of times, and to work alongside a doctor who could communicate with her via looks, nods or a brief well-chosen word was excellent.

It made her think about her long-term plans for Shortfield Family Medical Practice. At the moment there was enough work for one full-time doctor and one part-time doctor, but patients who had been fed up with seeing locums were now returning to the family-oriented practice, and that meant longer waiting lists. That wasn't what Stacey wanted. Even though Cora was due to return at the end of the year, chances were they would soon be requiring more than two doctors to work at the clinic— especially as she already had plans for Winifred, their nurse-receptionist, to start conducting immunisation clinics.

Pierce seemed the obvious choice to approach with regard to a partnership. He would be close to Nell and could keep an eye on her, he was amazing with the patients and he worked exceptionally well with her. Good doctors were hard to find, so she accepted the silent challenge to persuade Pierce to stay permanently at Short-field Family Medical Practice.

Of course there was the added advantage that he was dreamy to look at, that he made her laugh and that he could ignite an instant fire deep within her. But that was completely beside the point…wasn't it?

CHAPTER FIVE

THANKFULLY, DUE TO their prompt action, Mike was only in hospital for six days, admitted for a mild myocardial infarction.

'You were lucky this time,' stated Brian, the cardiac specialist at Newcastle General. 'But it means big changes, Mike.'

Mike groaned. 'I don't have to eat those fat-free bran muffins Edna keeps wanting to force down my throat, do I?'

Stacey chuckled at her friend's resigned tone. Pierce joined in and she looked across at him. They'd both known Mike was going to be discharged that morning, so had come to listen to what the specialist had to say and also to offer moral support to both Edna and Mike. Going to hospital could be scary enough, but sometimes being discharged could be equally unsettling.

'See? Even Brian's telling you to listen to me and to stop sneaking foods which are bad for you,' Edna chastised, before staring at Mike. 'I love you, Mikey. I need you.' She took his hand in hers. 'And if eating fat-free bran whatever means that I get to be with you longer, then that's what we'll eat. *Both* of us.'

Mike raised his wife's hand to his lips and kissed it,

glistening tears in his eyes. 'That's what we'll do, love,' he finished.

Stacey couldn't believe how blessed she was to be witnessing such an intimate connection between her two friends. After over forty years together they were still deeply in love, and she immediately missed her own parents. When she glanced across at Pierce, who was on the opposite side of Mike's bed, she could almost sense that he felt the same as her, except about his own parents.

'Good to hear,' Brian continued. 'Besides, the only reason you're going home now is because Pierce lives next door to you and Stacey's going to check on you every day.'

'What about district nurses?' Edna queried. The consultant stared at Edna, then shook his head.

'Mike? Listen to a district nurse? I'd feel sorry for the nurse.' Brian chuckled. 'From all those years of playing hockey and football with Mike, I know, Edna, that it's best if someone he loves comes and bosses him around—especially with regard to anything medical.' Brian placed a hand on Mike's shoulder. 'You're a cantankerous old man now, Mike. We both are. And it's best we take steps to protect others from ourselves.'

Mike grinned at his old friend. 'Too true.'

Stacey laughed and walked across to Mike's bedside and kissed his cheek. 'I love you, Mike,' she said. Then she whispered in his ear, 'And you're the closest thing I have to a father. *Please* take care of yourself. I need you.'

When she straightened her eyes were glistening with tears. She'd only meant to encourage him, and yet here she was, standing before the head of cardiology, blubbering.

Mike looked at her firmly, then took her hand in his and gave it a squeeze. 'I'll not let you down, girl,' he promised, his voice choking with a mixture of determination, sincerity and love.

Edna hugged Stacey. 'It's perfect timing that you're back. We need you and you need us. It's right that you're back where you belong.'

And that was exactly how Stacey felt as she walked into her clinic on Friday morning, four weeks after taking it over. Coming home to Newcastle *had* been the right decision, although Jasmine would probably disagree.

As she walked through the clinic, switching on various machines to warm them up, Stacey was surprised to find Pierce in his consulting room, given it had only just gone seven o'clock. She stopped by his open door. 'Good morning. You look as though you've been here half the night.'

He looked up from his computer screen and smiled at her as she walked in, coming to stand near his desk. 'No. Just half an hour or so. I was just finishing up an article I promised I'd write for the team at Yale.'

'Yale? Yale as in the prestigious American university?'

'Yes. Presently the team there are leading the world when it comes to understanding autism and autism spectrum disorders, but there's still so much we don't know about adult autism.'

'Which is where you come in?'

'Sort of.'

'As I've mentioned, I've read your articles. They're good.'

'Thank you.' He used the computer mouse and clicked a few times before switching off his monitor. 'At any rate, the article is now done and on its way to Professor Smith for his approval.'

'I'm sure he'll do more than approve. Have you worked with the Yale team for long?'

Pierce nodded as he stood from his chair, linking his hands behind his back and pulling downwards. Stacey tried not to stare.

'For quite a while.'

'I'm surprised they haven't offered you a job.'

'Well…' He shrugged, then lifted his hands over his head.

Stacey had been about to ask him some more questions, but the words didn't make it as far as her lips as all she was conscious of was the way his trousers dipped and his white and blue striped shirt rose up. He hadn't bothered to tuck it in and she was treated to a glimpse of his firm, smooth abdominals. Good heavens! Did the man work out every day?

She curled her fingers into her palms in an attempt to stop her itching need to walk over to him and feel just how firm those abs really were. Stacey swallowed, her lips parting to allow the pent-up air to escape, only then realising that her heart-rate had increased, and her breathing was more shallow than normal.

It wasn't until he lowered his hands, the shirt sliding back into place, that she realised she hadn't heard a word he'd said—if he'd said anything at all. Quickly she raised her gaze to meet his, hoping he hadn't noticed she'd been openly ogling him. He raised an eyebrow and she noticed a soft, slow smile tugging at the corners of his mouth. It wasn't a teasing smile but one of interest.

Interest? He was *interested* that she'd been ogling him? Mortification ripped through her and she quickly looked away.

'Stacey?'

She headed towards the door, unable to look at him. 'Yeah?'

'Stacey…'

His tone was a little more urgent and she stopped in her tracks before glancing at him over her shoulder. She swallowed.

'Er...' She cleared her throat, unable to control her rapid breathing.

He walked over to her and stood quite near. She wished he hadn't, because as soon as she breathed in, hoping to gain some sort of control over her wayward senses, all she was aware of was the fresh spicy scent which surrounded him. That and the warmth emanating from him made for a heady combination. The breath she exhaled was jittery and, knowing it probably gave him every indication that she was highly aware of him, Stacey sighed with veiled embarrassment and closed her eyes.

What must he think of her? First she'd ogled him and now she was behaving like a complete ninny, all flustered by his nearness. Her mind had gone completely blank—except for the image of him standing there, stretching his arms above his head.

'Stacey?'

'Hmm?' Her eyes snapped open and she realised with a start that he'd actually moved closer than before. When he reached out a hand and tucked a lock of hair behind her ear she gasped, her body starting to tremble not only at his nearness but at the way he'd touched her with such tenderness.

His fingers trailed slowly down her cheek. His gaze firmly locked with hers. It was as though they were in their own private world, just the two of them, time standing still. With her heartbeat thrumming wildly within her ears, she idly wondered if he could hear it.

'Your hair is so soft.'

His words were barely a whisper, but they made her tremble with the realisation that perhaps she wasn't the only one experiencing emotions of awareness. Then again, maybe Pierce gave out random compliments to women as part and parcel of his personality.

'Erm…thank you.' Her words were a little stilted, due to the lack of oxygen reaching her brain simply because of his touch. She needed to move, needed to put some distance between them, and when Pierce dropped his hand back to his side, still staring at her as though he wanted nothing more than to stand there and look into her blue eyes for the rest of the day, she forced herself to edge back.

Unfortunately she hadn't realised how close she was to the door frame and bumped into it.

'Oops.'

'Are you OK?' He put out a hand to steady her.

Stacey cleared her throat and nodded, not trusting her voice not to betray the way he made her feel. She jerked her thumb over her shoulder, indicating the hallway leading to the kitchen. Pierce smiled, as though he knew exactly what was going on, as though he understood exactly why she was unable to speak, and by the delight which was still in his eyes it appeared he really didn't mind at all.

Stacey turned, sighing harshly—more at her own foolishness than anything else—and made her way to the kitchen. Coffee. If she had a coffee perhaps she'd be able to think more clearly.

She sensed rather than felt him following her, so abruptly changed her mind and took a detour into her consulting room. Now that she didn't have his hypnotic scent winding its way around her, or the warmth of his body so near to her own, or the touch of his fingers sliding through her shoulder-length brown hair, Stacey rebooted her brain and forced herself to speak as though nothing out of the ordinary had just happened.

'I'll just put my bag down,' she called.

'Right. I'll switch the coffeemaker on so it can warm up,' he returned.

She almost laughed at the absurdity of their conversation. Polite, professional, impersonal. They were colleagues and new friends, and none of that meant they should be staring deeply into each other's eyes like lovestruck teenagers!

After taking a few calming breaths, Stacey squared her shoulders and walked into the kitchen, determined to focus on one thing—coffee.

'Is the machine ready yet?' She barely spared him a passing glance as she went to the fridge for the milk, noticing he'd already placed two cups on the bench.

'Stacey—what just happened?'

She turned and glared at him, almost dropping the milk. 'What do you mean?'

Pierce waved one hand in the air. 'You ogled me. I caressed your hair. Surely you haven't forgotten already?'

She closed her eyes for one long moment, trying to suppress the tingles and nerves and flutterings of desire she could feel returning. The coffee machine dinged, signifying that it was ready to use. Glad of something to do, Stacey worked on automatic pilot to produce two coffees, adding milk to her own and letting him sugar his coffee himself.

'Like any normal person, when they experience a situation which makes them feel mildly uncomfortable and self-conscious, I *had* planned to forget it, actually.' She forced herself to meet his gaze, even though it was incredibly difficult, and was proud of herself for accomplishing the task. 'Clearly you feel otherwise. So—all right—let's discuss it.'

'Are you always so amenable to doing what everyone else wants?' Pierce stirred sugar into his drink, watching her closely.

'What do you mean?'

'Well, you don't want to talk about those amazing few moments when I invaded your personal space and lost all self-control by touching your hair, and I do.'

As he spoke Stacey felt the fire she'd only just managed to get under control ignite again. They'd known each other for almost a month now, had been working side by side. They'd cared for their patients, met each other's families, shared meals together and she'd learned a lot about him in such a short space of time—especially about the way he treated others. She had to admit that Pierce was quite a man when it came to conversing easily...just as he was doing with her now. The way he could so openly admit that he wanted to touch her hair, be so self-assured, was an admirable quality.

'What I want,' Stacey finally replied as she picked up her coffee cup and held it in front of her, as though she could hide behind it, 'is to take the shortest possible route back to rational thought, which will undoubtedly promote a comfortable working atmosphere. Hence why I was going to push the...you...invading...personal space thing...to the back of my mind and pretend it never happened.'

Pierce leaned a little closer, invading that barrier again. 'But it did.'

His rich, deep baritone caused vibrating tingles to flood through her.

'What if I want to touch your hair again? What if I want to caress your beautiful smooth skin?'

He breathed out slowly, his words unhurried, and she found it difficult to look away from his hypnotic gaze. Was that what he wanted to do? Really?

'What if I want to run my thumb over your lips...?' He stared at her mouth for a good few intoxicating seconds as he continued to speak. 'What if I want to watch them part with the anticipation of feeling my lips pressed against them?'

Her eyes widened at his words and she couldn't help flicking her gaze between his mouth and his eyes, wondering if he was being serious, wondering if he was just teasing, wondering if he actually meant every word he was saying and was about to follow through with a demonstration. The nervous knots caused by his close proximity and her secret need to have him do exactly as he said tightened in her belly.

It *was* there. The attraction she'd been trying to fight could no longer be denied—not now that he'd spoken so openly about it.

Her tongue slipped out to wet her pink lips and she watched as Pierce's gaze took in the process. A slow, deep sigh was drawn from him. He stood there for another half a minute, his jaw clenching a few times, as though he was trying desperately to control some inner urge— even though he was still invading her personal space, still holding his coffee cup in front of him as though in need of protection from his own emotions, just as she was.

'But you're probably right,' he remarked in his normal tone, before swallowing a few times, his Adam's apple working its way up and down his throat above his open-necked shirt. He took two steps back, determined and sure-footed. 'Perhaps it *is* best if we ignore this attraction...'

He gave her a lopsided grin which did absolutely nothing to settle her nerves.

'At least for now. Winifred will be in soon, as will our plethora of patients, and we both have work to accomplish before that happens.'

Then, with a nod, he turned and walked from the kitchen, whistling as though nothing untoward or life-changing had just happened. Stacey watched him go with a mixture of confusion, uncertainty and heightened sensuality.

She shook her head. 'What on earth just happened?'

As though by some unspoken mutual agreement, Stacey and Pierce kept their distance from each other for the rest of the day. Friday clinic sessions were usually hectic, and that evening when she finally arrived home after finishing off the paperwork, long after everyone else had left, Stacey collapsed onto the sofa.

'Whatcha doin', Stace?' Lydia asked as she came over and sat on her sister.

'*Ugh*. What have you been eating?' Stacey asked as she pulled the girl into her arms. 'You're so heavy.'

'Jaz bought us chicken schn—'

'Schnitzel,' Stacey supplied.

'With vegetables from the chicken shop. It was super-yum. There's a plate of food for you and Molly. George and I put it together and put some plastic wrap on it.'

'Thank you, Lyds.' Stacey hugged her sister. 'How grown-up of you.'

'George and I ate at the table, but Jaz got angry at *nothing* and took her dinner to her room.'

Stacey frowned at this news, making a mental note to check Jasmine's room later on, hoping to find an empty plate. This wasn't the first time Jasmine had taken her food to her room to eat. It had started a month or two after their parents' death. Molly had wondered whether their sister was in danger of anorexia or bulimia, but Cora had assured them both that Jasmine was eating. However, since Cora had left for Tarparnii Jasmine had become even more withdrawn. Stacey guessed that *any* change—and Jasmine had certainly had a few—was difficult for her to cope with.

'Why is she like that? Angry at nothing?' Lydia asked, her words filled with innocent confusion. 'Am I gonna be like that when I become a teenager?'

Stacey smiled and kissed Lydia's cheek. 'No. You might get a little moody every now and then, but Jaz is... confused. She can't understand why Mum and Dad died.'

'I can. It's because the angels needed help in heaven and they chose the two best people for the job.'

Stacey's eyes filled with tears at Lydia's words. She hugged her sister close again, wanting to absorb that innocence and hold onto it for as long as possible.

'That's beautiful, Lyddie,' Molly said from the doorway, instantly coming over to kneel on the floor beside the sofa.

'It is,' Stacey replied.

Lydia scrambled out of Stacey's arms and flung herself at Molly. 'There's chicken schnotzel in the kitchen. George and I made a plate of food for you and Stacey.'

Molly hooted with laughter and stood, whizzing Lydia around in her arms. 'Schnotzel, eh? Thank goodness you kept it safe. Come on, Stace. We'd best go eat our schnotzel.'

Stacey giggled as she hefted herself from the sofa, feeling less exhausted than when she'd walked through the door. Glad it was Friday night and she could stay up a bit later, Lydia went off to play with George while the two women sat eating in peace.

Molly looked closely at her sister. 'So… Interesting day?'

'Full day. Lots of patients. Lots of hay fever and sinus problems. Plus there seems to be a gastro bug making the rounds.'

'Yeah. A few bad cases came in to the hospital when I was in the emergency department just before I left— although it could have been food poisoning. I'll check later on, when I head back.'

'You're on call tonight?'

Molly shook her head. 'Just early tomorrow morning. Split shift. The work of a surgical registrar is never done—which is why, when we get the time, we high-tail it back home to enjoy some chicken schnotzel for dinner and to catch up on sleep. And we don't feel at all sorry for the poor doctors we leave behind to cope—like Pierce.'

'Pierce?' Stacey sat up a little straighter in her chair. 'He's doing a shift in the ED tonight?'

'Yeah. He said someone wanted to switch with him and he was fine with that.'

'He's doing a night shift?'

'Yes. What's the problem with that?'

'Oh. Nothing. He was just in very early this morning at the clinic.'

Molly raised an inquisitive eyebrow. 'Worried about the man's sleeping habits?'

Stacey looked down at her meal, knowing if she kept looking at Molly she'd soon be spilling the beans about what had occurred between them that morning. 'He's an employee…sort of. So of course I'd be concerned about his lack of sleep. I mean, I wouldn't want him doing house calls or treating patients when he's half asleep, now, would I?'

'No. No. Of course not.'

Molly stared at her sister and Stacey looked back across at her.

'What?'

'Is that the *only* reason why you're so concerned about him?'

'Yes.' The word was high-pitched, and sounded false even to her own ears.

'Or is it because the two of you…shared a moment?'

Stacey's eyes widened. 'How could you *possibly* know that?' she squeaked, her knife and fork clattering to her plate. She leaned forward and said in a softer tone, 'What did he tell you? What did he say?'

Molly grinned wildly at her sister and slowly forked another mouthful of chicken into her mouth. She chewed with equal slowness and swallowed before shaking her head from side to side. 'Pierce didn't say anything. You just confirmed a hunch I had—especially after watching the two of you together last weekend at dinner. You were both so cute, so friendly, but with…something more buzzing between you which neither of you wanted to acknowledge.'

'Molly!'

'And then tonight,' Molly continued, as though Stacey hadn't protested, 'he told me three times what a great doctor he thinks you are. He's too much of a gentleman to kiss and tell.'

'There was *no* kissing,' Stacey pointed out.

'But you wanted there to be, didn't you?'

It wasn't a question, it was a statement, and Stacey realised there was no way in the world she could pull the wool over her sister's eyes. Molly knew her as well as she knew herself.

She felt all the fight seep out of her. There seemed no point in denying there was an attraction existing between Pierce and herself. She sat back in her chair and momentarily covered her face with her hands, nodding in affirmation. 'I *did* want him to kiss me. Oh, Molly.' She stared at her sister. 'What am I going to do?'

CHAPTER SIX

As Pierce sat at the nurses' station in the Emergency Department, glad of a quiet night so far, he couldn't help but think of the way he'd actually touched Stacey's hair that morning. What he'd told her had been the truth—he'd thought about touching her hair from the first time he'd seen her. It had looked so soft and glossy in the sunshine that day, as it had bounced around her shoulders, her fringe framing her face perfectly.

He'd been determined to keep his distance, to ensure that his relationship with Stacey remained one of a working friendship. But the night her family had come for dinner, the way he'd felt the need to follow her to the park to ensure she was safe, then having her open up to him about her life, had only intrigued him even more.

Who *was* Stacey Wilton? The *real* Stacey Wilton? What were her dreams and hopes for *her* future? He, of all people, knew what it was like to live for others, always putting your own life on hold for everyone else—and he only had one sibling to consider. Stacey had five.

After Mike's admission to hospital last week he and Stacey had returned to his house, where Molly had been in full organisational mode. It hadn't felt awkward, walking into Nell's house and seeing it full of other people. It had felt right, somehow. It hadn't felt awkward eating the dinner he'd prepared and which Molly had reheated, sitting alongside the sisters, all of them chatting quietly but happily. It hadn't felt awkward when he and Stacey had rinsed the plates and stacked the dishwasher, tidying the kitchen together. Everything had felt...*right*.

Along with that, Nell had loved spending time with the rabbits, and she had definitely formed a bond with George, Lydia and especially Jasmine. Pierce had discovered that out of the Wilton triplets Stacey was indeed the oldest—'By five minutes,' Molly had told him. 'And she never lets us forget it.'

He'd liked watching the easy interaction between the sisters. The tight bond they shared was quite evident. Still, all he could see was Stacey, giving her time to everyone else. Accommodating Cora's desire to head off to work as a doctor in Tarparnii. Encouraging Molly's desire to study surgery. Assisting George and Lydia as they entered the world of raising a championship rabbit jumper.

'She's quite a woman, our Stace,' Mike had said one evening, when Pierce had dropped by to check on him, and had been pleased with the other man's progress. 'She's always putting others ahead of herself. For as long as I can remember—even when she was little.' Mike had thrown some poker chips onto the table. 'I call.'

'We often worry—especially after what that terrible Robert did to her.' Edna's indignation was fierce. 'She stood at the front of that church, wearing her wedding dress, calmly told everyone there wouldn't be a wedding and apologised for any inconvenience. Molly or Cora would've been happy to make the announcement, but Stacey insisted on doing it, on making sure they didn't have to bear her burden.' Edna shook her head. 'Goodness knows whether she'll ever get married now.' She looked at her cards. 'I fold.'

'It'll be tough for her,' Mike added. 'Those kids need a stable environment, and she's doing her best to provide it for them.' Then he pointed to Pierce's cards. 'You gonna call or fold, boy?'

Pierce looked absent-mindedly at his cards, more focused on the way Stacey was constantly infiltrating his thoughts rather than on playing the game. He'd already realised she was the type of woman to put others before herself, and it made him want to do something nice for her—something unexpected, something *just for her*. But what? 'Uh...fold.'

Mike shook his head. 'Easy victory. Your mind's not on the game tonight, boy.'

'I'll go put the kettle on,' Edna said as she stood from the table and headed into the kitchen. 'You go sit in your comfy chair, Mike. Time to put your feet up!' she called.

'Yes, dear,' Mike replied, and rolled his eyes. 'Help an old man up, Pierce.'

'You're not that old,' Pierce protested, but still did as he was bid.

'She's tying you in knots, isn't she?'

The question was rhetorical and Pierce looked at Mike with a frown.

'Oh, don't give me that. I've seen the two of you in the same room together—those sneaky little looks you both have. You like her. She likes you. I get it. I've been there, too, you know. Might have been a long time ago, but my Edna had me in a right tailspin and I had no idea how to pull out of it.'

'How *do* you pull out of it?' Pierce asked as he tucked a blanket around Mike's legs and made sure the television remote controls were within easy reaching distance.

Mike laughed, then coughed. 'Sometimes, boy, you've

gotta fly right through it. No pulling up, no manoeuvring around it. Gotta go through it.'

Pierce shook his head. 'I've been down that road, though. It didn't end well.'

'Your fiancée left you and broke your heart—but that was a while ago and you're over it now. Edna told me.'

'Edna has a way of getting information out of people.'

Mike grinned. 'That's my girl.' He rested his head back and closed his eyes. 'So you're not gonna do anything about the way Stacey makes you feel?'

'I don't know.' Pierce paused, then looked at his friend. 'I've been head-hunted by a hospital in America.'

Mike opened his eyes. 'Really?'

Pierce smiled. 'Edna didn't manage to wheedle *that* titbit out of me.'

'What about Nell?'

'That's why I've spent so long setting up her independent living situation. Her new housemates will move in soon, and Nell's ready for that. She wants to do it. She knows I'll be overseas. We'll talk over the internet, and she'll have a network of people around her who are available whenever she needs them.'

Mike thought this over. 'How long are you going for?'

Pierce shrugged. 'At least six months—*if* I take the position.'

'When did they offer it to you?'

'Four years ago.'

'*What?*'

'I keep turning them down. They keep offering.'

'They must want you to work with them badly?'

Pierce nodded. 'They do.'

'Do you want to go?'

'Yeah, but—' He spread his arms wide. 'And that's always been the problem. There's always been a "but".'

'So for years you've not been able to go because of Nell?'

'Correct.'

'And now that Nell is finally settled and all ready for you to leave you're not sure because…?'

'Because what if this attraction between Stacey and myself is more than just an attraction? What if this is it? The one! What if she's the woman I'm meant to spend the rest of my life with?' Pierce began pacing up and down in front of Mike, then stopped and spread his arms wide again. 'Do you see my dilemma?'

Mike shrugged. 'You've put those Americans off for four years, laddie. What's a few more months? You've promised Stacey you'll stay until Cora gets back and you're not going to leave her in the lurch. It's not your way. So why don't you see whether this thing between you and Stacey *is* real? Give it a chance.'

'And what if it is? Does that mean I *never* get to go to the States?' Pierce raked both hands through his hair. 'Everything was going along just fine. I should have known that that would be when I finally met the woman of my dreams.'

'Your dreams, eh?' Mike chuckled. 'Then you've got nothing to worry about.' His grin widened as Edna came back into the room, carrying a tea tray. 'Dreams always come true.'

'Pierce…? Hello…?'

Sister was snapping her fingers near his face and Pierce instantly looked at her. 'Sorry. I was miles away.'

'Daydreamer!' She chuckled. 'Can you review these notes, please? Plus we've just had another drunk brought in by the police. Non-abusive, passed out in the middle of the road. I've put him in Cubicle Twelve.'

'Thanks.'

Pierce took the first set of case notes from the pile Sister had handed him and tried desperately not to think about the way he'd felt when he'd caught Stacey ogling him. Her visual caress, the way she'd responded when he'd touched her hair, when he'd later leaned towards her, looking deep into her eyes and realising he'd never felt that alive for years… Just that one moment…it had been intoxicating. It was also why he'd forced himself to walk away. Too much of a good thing could cause an addiction. But perhaps Mike was right. Perhaps he *should* give this attraction with Stacey a chance, see exactly it might lead.

The thought excited him and he smiled, thinking of what he might say to her the next time they met. If they had another tension-filled moment like the one they'd shared that morning he was determined that he wouldn't be the one to walk away. He wanted to know what it was like to kiss Stacey—well, perhaps it was about time he found out.

The insistent ringing of Stacey's cell phone woke her with a start. She sat bolt upright in bed and, having had years of practice at being instantly awake, quickly connected the call, her voice sure and firm—as though it *wasn't* half past two in the morning and she *hadn't* been sound asleep.

'Dr Wilton.'

'Stacey? It's my Gary. There's something wrong. I think he's eaten something, but he has a temperature and he's vomited, and I wasn't sure whether I should ring the ambulance because he's refusing to see a doctor, saying it's just food poisoning, but this is really bad and I didn't know what to do, and—'

'It's fine. Give me your address. I'll come over now and assess him,' Stacey interrupted, and quickly wrote down the details with the pen and paper she always kept on the bedside table. Initially she'd had no idea who Gary was, because her mind had still been coming out of the fog from her dream…a dream in which a tall, dark and handsome Pierce had brushed her hair from her face, leaned forward, pressed his lips to hers, kissing her with such tender passion…

Even now, as she did her best to reassure Gary's wife Nanette—who, it turned out, had been at school with her—Stacey could feel her cheeks still flushed with heat from the memories floating around in the back of her mind. As she ended the call and dressed she tried desperately to focus her thoughts on Gary's symptoms, planning several strategies in order to cope with a variety of possible scenarios. If Gary hadn't been able to keep any fluids down then his electrolyte levels might be low and he might require hospitalisation.

Out in the family room, Stacey collected her fully stocked emergency medical backpack from the locked cupboard and left a message for Molly on the whiteboard to let her sister know she'd been called out. Then she collected her handbag and car keys before heading out, thankful that Nanette and Gary didn't live too far away.

'Sorry for calling in the middle of the night.'

Nanette rushed out to meet Stacey, her words tumbling from her mouth as Stacey collected her backpack from the car and both women headed inside the house, which was lit up like a Christmas tree. Nanette had her two-year-old daughter in her arms, the child clearly having been woken from her sleep with all the ruckus and was not happy about it.

'That's what family practices are for, Nanette. To form bonds with the community. Which way?' Stacey's tone was firm and direct, yet she was also trying to reassure Nanette. She needed her to be calm, but given what she could remember of her old school friend that might be impossible.

'I didn't know what to do,' Nanette dithered. 'And I couldn't remember the name of your partner at the GP practice, who I saw the other day when one of my kids was sick, so I called your practice number and the answering machine gave me a cell phone number, and it turned out to be yours, but then I wasn't sure whether to call the ambulance or just take Gary to hospital myself, but when I tried to move him, to get him closer to the front door, he groaned so badly that I started trembling, and—oh, Stacey, I'm so glad you're back in Newcastle. Help my Gary. *Please?*'

Stacey continued to follow Nanette through the house, heading to the bedroom at the back where she could hear Gary groaning.

'What's *wrong* with him?' Nanette kept asking, and Stacey had to use all her mental control to block the other woman out and remain calm as she introduced herself to Gary.

The man was lying quite still, sweating and clammy to the touch. Stacey pulled out her stethoscope and lifted Gary's shirt, talking him through what she was doing. She listened to the sounds of his stomach, not wanting to palpate the abdomen, given he was already in so much pain.

She asked him about the times he'd been ill, about the type of pain he was experiencing, and after she'd taken his blood pressure and temperature she pulled her cell phone from her pocket and called for an ambulance, letting them know her suspected diagnosis.

'Appendicitis!' Nanette's high-pitched shriek made their daughter start to cry and Nanette quickly jiggled the toddler up and down, whispering soothing words.

'Is there someone who can look after your children for you, Nanette?'

'Oh. Oh. Uh… Yes. OK. This *is* happening?'

'Yes, it is.' Stacey took Gary's temperature again. 'We'll have you sorted out in next to no time,' she told him, giving him something to help with the pain.

Within another twenty minutes Gary was being wheeled on an ambulance gurney towards Trauma Room One.

'What have we got?' a deep male voice asked as Stacey quickly washed her hands before pulling on a disposable gown and a pair of gloves.

She let the paramedics give the debrief as she tried desperately to ignore the way her entire body seem to fill with trembles at the sound of Pierce's tone, but it was impossible. She was so incredibly aware of him, of memories of the way he'd tenderly touched her hair, of the way he'd stared into her eyes, of the dreams she'd had of the two of them together, and as she turned to look at him a fresh round of excitement burst forth when he smiled brightly.

'Hello, Stace.' He seemed a little surprised to see her but his smile was wide and genuine. 'No sleep for you tonight, eh?' he said as he walked over to where Gary was being transferred from the paramedic's gurney to the hospital barouche.

'No. I'm Gary's GP, and his wife called me because she was concerned. I'll just see him through to diagnosis. It'll help his wife to feel more relaxed if she knows I'm helping to look after her husband.'

He nodded. 'Fine by me if it's fine by the hospital,' he stated.

'I'm registered here.'

'Excellent.' Pierce hooked his stethoscope into his ears, ready to listen to the sounds of Gary's abdomen.

Stacey looked at her patient, pleased she'd been able to convince Nanette to go and wait in the patients' lounge as Gary had turned exceedingly pale.

'I think he's going to be sick again,' Stacey warned, and the nurses were on the ball with their assistance, attending to Gary as Pierce finished his consult.

'Right. Let's get some fluids into him, boost electrolytes, and an injection of Maxalon to help stop the vomiting. Cross, type and match. We also need to lower that temperature. Get the on-call surgical registrar down here.'

Stacey and the rest of the Emergency Department staff started carrying out Pierce's orders.

'Molly said there have been quite a few cases of food poisoning presenting at the Emergency Department?'

'That's correct. But in Gary's case I think it's something a little more sinister.' Pierce had come around the barouche and was once more listening to the sounds of Gary's abdomen.

'Definitely appendix?'

'Definitely,' he confirmed as the surgical on-call registrar walked into the room.

'What do we have?' he asked.

'Forty-five-year-old male,' Pierce began, giving the registrar a breakdown of Gary's vitals. 'Initial suspected food poisoning, but all symptoms indicative of appendicitis with possible signs of peritonitis. Bloods have been ordered, but I don't think we can wait too much longer for the results.'

'Right.' The registrar performed his own set of examinations, listening to the sounds of Gary's abdomen before nodding and hooking his stethoscope about his shoulders. 'OK, Gary. We're going to get you to Theatre as soon as possible.' He turned to Pierce and Stacey. 'I'll go see if I can find a theatre that's free and get the paperwork started. Next of kin?'

'Gary's wife is in the patients' waiting room. She's quite distraught,' Stacey supplied.

'And who are you?'

'I'm their GP.'

'Excellent. Fetch the wife from the waiting room so I can explain the operation to her and her husband and get the consent forms signed.'

Stacey nodded as the registrar left the room.

'Brisk and to the point,' Pierce murmured. 'Your sister has a much better bedside manner.'

'I'm sure he's a good registrar,' she offered as they watched the nurses perform Gary's observations once more.

'Oh, he is. There's no doubting that.' Pierce stood beside her, speaking softly so only she could hear. 'I'm just saying that you Wilton women have a certain way about you that makes everyone feel more…calm, more relaxed. It's nice.'

He smiled at her—that cute, sexy little smile that she was coming to adore. Then he winked.

The intimate action, as though linking them in their own private bubble, caused Stacey's heart-rate to instantly increase. How was it possible that with such a small gesture he was able to tie her insides into knots and make her tremble all over?

Stacey licked her lips and gave him a little smile in return, before lifting the curtain which afforded Gary and the team the privacy they needed and slipping through before Pierce turned the rest of her body to jelly with another of his full-watt smiles.

When she'd licked her lips his gaze had dropped, taking in the action, before he'd looked into her eyes for a brief second longer. It was why she'd forced herself to move, to step away from his presence—because that one look had said so much. It had said that he wanted to hold her close, that he wanted to feel her touch, that he wanted to press his mouth to hers and take them both on a ride that would send them soaring to the stars.

Stacey took some deep breaths and gave her hands a little shake as she headed to the patients' waiting room. She needed to get her mind off the way Pierce made her feel and on to the job she needed to do—which was to care for her patients. Ever since yesterday morning... when he'd caressed her hair, when he'd gazed into her eyes, when he'd stared longingly at her lips...Stacey had been hard-pressed to think of anything but that.

Before entering the waiting room she mentally picked up her thoughts of Pierce and shoved them into a box, promising herself she'd take them out later and pore over every nuance and action. For now, though, Nanette and Gary needed her at her best, supporting them and helping them. She entered the waiting room and was surprised when Nanette grabbed her and hugged her close. Stacey gave her old school friend a brief rundown on what was happening to Gary and told her that he'd need surgery.

'So I was right to call you?' Nanette blubbered as Stacey offered her yet another tissue.

'You were absolutely right. Now Gary can get the treatment he needs.'

'Can I see him?' Nanette asked.

'Of course. The surgical registrar needs to talk to both of you and Gary needs to sign the consent forms.'

Nanette grasped Stacey's hands firmly in her own. 'You'll stay with me, won't you?'

'Of course.'

At this news Nanette nodded and reached for another tissue, wiping her eyes and blowing her nose. She pasted on a bright smile. 'How do I look?'

'Like a woman who loves her husband,' Stacey returned, momentarily envious of the connection Nanette and her husband had.

Why hadn't she realised sooner that Robert's words, his professions of love and his actions, hadn't exactly matched up? Perhaps it had been because she'd been desperate to make a connection, to try and find the sort of love that her father had found with Letisha. She'd believed in things that hadn't been there, she'd made excuses for Robert's behaviour, telling herself that he was stressed from working so hard in his pursuit of becoming the hospital's next CEO. One thing Nanette and Gary's easygoing love was showing her was that she was too good to settle for second best. Didn't she deserve to be with a man who loved her so wholly and completely? With a man who would cherish her for who she was?

Nanette's smile brightened naturally at Stacey's words and she nodded with eagerness. 'OK. Let me see my gorgeous husband.'

Stacey stayed with Nanette and Gary while the surgical registrar explained the operation, and after Gary had signed the consent form he was wheeled off to Theatres. Stacey took Nanette to the theatre patients' waiting room, where there was a tea and coffee machine, comfortable chairs and some up-to-date magazines to read.

She'd just settled Nanette with a cup of coffee when Pierce walked in.

'OK. Gary is heading into Theatre now. They'll perform a scan of his abdomen in there and then start the operation. They're just waiting on the report on the bloods, but for the moment everything is under control.'

Nanette sighed at this information and visibly relaxed. 'How much longer will things take? I mean, will he be able to come home later today?'

'No,' Stacey and Pierce answered in unison.

'He'll be in hospital for at least a few days,' Pierce added.

'Are you sure you want to stay and wait?' Stacey asked, putting a hand on Nanette's arm, concern in her tone. 'You could go home, get some rest, and we can call you when—'

'No.' Nanette cut off her words. 'I appreciate what you're saying but I'm staying right here. The kids are all sorted out with my neighbour, and I'm not going home to an empty house only to sit there and wait for my phone to ring.' She put her hand on Stacey's and gave it a little squeeze. 'You don't have to sit with me, Stacey. I know you need to get back to bed or see other patients or whatever else it is you doctors do during these crazy hours of the morning.'

'She *does* need to get home and get some more sleep. *I* may have the morning off, but poor Stacey here will have a plethora of housecalls to make once the sun comes up—and all without her trusty and faithful sidekick.'

Stacey's lips twitched at Pierce's words and she raised one eyebrow. 'Sidekick, eh?'

Nanette giggled, and it was good to see the other

woman finding a small bit of lightness in her otherwise dark emotions.

'Absolutely. You're the superhero. I'm just your companion.'

'Companion?' Both eyebrows shot up this time and the smile increased.

'How about...assistant? Better word?'

Stacey shook her head slowly from side to side. 'How about none of the above? I don't want to be labelled a superhero. Too much pressure.'

Pierce spread his arms wide, as though she really were passing up a once-in-a-lifetime offer. 'Suit yourself.'

Nanette giggled again, then sighed—a long, relaxing type of sigh, indicating that a small part of her tension had been eased. 'Both of you go. I'll be more than fine here. I've got magazines to read—' She pointed to the small table. 'And free tea and coffee and these chairs,' She patted the armrest of the one she was seated in. 'Not too bad for a quick kip, and I have no children to bother me, so all in all a few pluses.'

'Now, *there's* a real superhero.' Pierce held out his hand to indicate Nanette.

The woman smiled and blushed a little beneath his gaze before literally shooing them both from the room.

'She's a nice lady,' Pierce commented as they headed back to the Emergency Department. 'How do you know her?'

'School. She was the year ahead of us.'

'And yet she knows you? I didn't think teenagers stepped outside their bonds of social hierarchy all that much.'

At the nurses' station Pierce sat down and picked up a pen, knowing he should probably stop chatting to Stacey and get back to the mound of case notes Sister had asked him to review. However, if it was a choice between paperwork and chatting with Stacey the decision was a no-brainer. Getting to know Stacey a lot better was presently top of his list of things to do.

'There wasn't too much hierarchy at our school. And besides, *everyone* knows us.' Stacey sat on the edge of the chair next to him and spread her hands wide. 'We're the Wilton triplets. Twins often get remarked upon, especially if they're identical, but triplets—let's just say we're used to being something of a novelty.'

'And do you have some psychic connection that lets you read each other's thoughts? I've heard that twins can have a bond like that. Surely it's greater in triplets?'

'I wouldn't call it a psychic connection, per se.' She thought for a moment, then shrugged. 'It's difficult to explain. I guess it's more like sharing an…emotion. I think it would be the same for any people who spend a lot of time together. The three of us have been together since birth, and I guess we…*feel* that essence of the emotion in each other.' She shook her head. 'It's so difficult to describe.'

'Like intuition?'

'Sort of but…*more* so.'

Pierce scratched his head, the corners of his mouth pulling upwards. 'You're right. You're not explaining it well.'

He tried not to chuckle when she snatched the pen from his hand and shook it at him.

'Listen, buddy. I've had very little sleep, so don't pick on me.'

Pierce couldn't stifle his laughter any longer, and the sound of his mirth warmed her through and through. What was it about him that constantly knocked her off balance, regardless of the time of day?

He held up his hands in surrender. 'Sorry. You're right, of course. Time you were off back home so you can get some rest.' He stood and told the duty sister that he'd be back soon. 'I'll walk you out to your car.'

'That's not necessary. You're needed here.'

'Not at the moment.' He indicated the eerily quiet Emergency Department. 'We're past the "danger hour", and apart from Gary the night hasn't been too bad. So...' Pierce crooked his elbow in her direction. 'If you will allow me, Dr Wilton, I would be most pleased to escort you safely back to your car.'

Stacey looked around at the staff, wondering if they were all watching Pierce being a little bit silly but also incredibly charming, but most of them were too busy to notice. So as not to hurt his feelings, and feeling quite silly herself, whether due to lack of sleep, the release of tension from the past hour or so, or simply the fact that being around Pierce often made her feel delightfully free of restraint, Stacey curled her fingers around his elbow, resting her hand on his arm.

'Why, thank you, kind sir.'

He nodded politely in her direction before they headed off towards the doctors' car park, which was situated right next to the emergency parking bays where the ambulances arrived.

Neither of them spoke for a few minutes but Stacey didn't feel uncomfortable. The sky was cloudless, the stars were shining bright in the moonlight, but the breeze was quite chilly and she actually found herself snuggling a little closer to Pierce, drawn towards his natural body warmth.

'Cold?' he asked, and before she knew what was happening he'd manoeuvred their positions so that instead of offering her his arm in a gentlemanly manner he'd placed his firm, muscled arm about her, his hand resting at her waist, drawing her to him as they walked slowly along the path. 'Better,' he stated as he snuggled a little closer.

Stacey felt highly self-conscious at being embraced by him.

He breathed in and slowly exhaled. 'How can you smell so utterly delicious at such a time of the morning? Or perhaps,' he continued, 'you always smell this good.' He breathed in deeply again. 'Beautiful Stacey,' he whispered, and his sweet words caused goosebumps to flood her entire body.

When they reached her car Pierce gently turned to face her, leaning against the driver's door and bringing his other arm around her. She was now standing firmly in his embrace. Pierce was embracing her openly…here…in the doctors' car park. Granted it was almost four o'clock in the morning, and there was no one else around, but they were on display for all to see.

Stacey couldn't help glancing over her shoulder. She wasn't used to being demonstrative in public, especially because it had been one of the main things in her relationship with Robert that he'd been adamant would never happen. No public displays of emotion or affection. Pierce was so incredibly different…and she liked it a lot.

Pierce adjusted his legs, drawing her body closer to his. 'You *are* beautiful, Stacey. Do you know that?'

She lifted her hands to his chest, unsure whether she was trying to draw him close or keep him at bay. 'I… I'm…I don't know,' she replied, shaking her head as though she didn't believe a word he said.

'Well, *I* do.' Pierce looked down at her. 'Do you have any idea what you've done to me?'

'I'm sure I haven't *done* anything.'

He smiled. 'That's not what I meant, but when you say

things like that, with your tone becoming all hesitant and awkward—well, it just makes it even more difficult for me to resist you.'

Stacey shook her head and closed her eyes, wanting him to stop saying things like that. Couldn't he see that they made her feel uncomfortable, that she wasn't used to receiving compliments?

'Why not?' he asked, gently brushing his fingers across her cheek, and it was only when he asked the question that she realised she'd spoken her thoughts out loud. 'What did that jerk of an ex-fiancé do to your self-esteem?' He cupped her cheek. 'Open your eyes, Stacey,' he commanded softly, and to her surprise, she found herself obeying. 'I don't care what any man may or may not have told you in the past, please believe me when *I* say that you are a beautiful, strong, intelligent woman and I would really like to get to know you better.' He raised his eyebrows.

She shook her head again. 'Pierce. Don't say things like—'

'I'm being honest here, Stacey,' he interrupted softly. 'I'm attracted to you and I want to spend some time with you, getting to know you.'

'We spend a lot of time together already.'

'Apart from at work,' he clarified. 'I'm happy to have your siblings around, if you feel as though you need a buffer, but I would also like to take you out on a date—just the two of us.' He was silent for about fifteen seconds, and the atmosphere between them became a little strained when Stacey didn't immediately respond. 'What do you think?' he prompted.

'Um...' She swallowed, her heart beating wildly against her chest. 'You're really serious about this? About this thing—?'

'Can't you feel it?' Pierce pressed her hand to his chest. 'My heart is pounding, Stace. It always does when you're nearby. I catch a glimpse of your smile as you talk to a patient and I'm swarmed with jealousy because I want you to smile at *me*. I hear you laugh on the phone when you're chatting with your sister and the sound relaxes me.'

'Really?'

'Yes, Stacey. Really.' There was intent in his words, as though he was desperate to make her believe he wasn't just feeding her a line. 'Other men may have put you down, may not have wanted to be seen in public with you—and, yes,' he continued before she could say a word, 'I'm aware of how you're self-conscious about showing even the slightest bit of affection in public. I want you to know that I'm not embarrassed or ashamed to be seen holding your hand, or putting my arms around you or… kissing you in public.'

As he spoke his gaze dropped to encompass her mouth. Her lips parted at his words, her heart-rate now completely out of control, every fibre in her being trembling with anticipatory delight. He sounded sincere. In fact he almost sounded slightly offended that she didn't believe him. But somehow he seemed to understand that things had been very different in her past relationships—especially with Robert.

It was nice to have him say these words to her, to reassure her. And yet she still felt as though something was holding her back…but what? Everything she'd seen of Pierce—his interaction with her family, his concern for Mike and Edna, his devotion to his sister—indicated that he was a good man and, as the old adage went, a good man was hard to find. Perhaps she should stop trying to fight him and instead accept that he was really interested in *her*. That he honestly did want to spend time with her simply because he liked her.

The realisation, the sensation of believing Pierce was telling her the truth, made her heart fill with gladness.

'Do you want me to kiss you, Stacey?'

His words were barely a whisper, but they seemed so loud, echoing around her body in sync with the pounding of her heart.

'Yes.'

The single word escaped her lips before she could stop it. For a split second she thought Pierce hadn't heard her at all, but within the next moment his lips curved upwards with delight and his head began its slow descent.

'That, my gorgeous Stacey, is excellent news.'

And without further ado he captured her willing mouth with his own.

CHAPTER SEVEN

THE FEEL OF his lips on hers made her knees go weak
and she slid her arms up and around his neck, clinging
to him as he continued to bring her dormant senses to
life. Robert had always maintained that kissing wasn't
all that important in a relationship, that intellectual compatibility was far more necessary for a functioning and
enduring life together. At the time Stacey had believed
him, but now, with the way Pierce was filling her with
light from the soft, sweet pressure of his touch, she knew
she'd been oh-so wrong.

There was warmth in his touch, tenderness in the way
he held her close. He'd called her beautiful and at the
time she hadn't really believed him. But now, with the
way he was pressing his lips to hers, taking his time,
not wanting to rush a second of this unique and powerful experience, Stacey was starting to believe he might
have actually meant it.

Pierce thought she was beautiful! Accepting this
filled her with a sense of wonder and confidence and she
opened her mouth a little more, deepening the kiss, wanting to create some of the sensations she'd only dreamed
about. He was here. This was real. And she was going
to enjoy it.

Pierce's reaction was a deep, warm groan which signified his approval of the manoeuvre. She was delightful, delectable and utterly delicious. How was it possible he hadn't experienced such wonderment combined with innocence before? There was a freshness to her reaction, unstudied and raw, and with the way she was exerting control over the situation, showing him exactly what was contained beneath that quiet, calm exterior, he couldn't help but become even more enamoured with her.

The way her mouth opened to him, the way she responded to him—it was...*giving*. It was then that he truly accepted the fact that she'd always been a giver, always putting others before herself, offering to them the things they desired. As he continued to savour the sweetness of her mouth he couldn't help the thread of confusion which passed through him. Stacey was giving him what he wanted, a heartfelt response, because giving to others was what she knew how to do.

Well, this time, he wanted her to *take*, to allow him to make her feel unique and special and cherished. Naturally, as they were standing in a car park, there was no way that things could progress now, but he had the sensation that where Stacey was concerned taking things nice and slow was definitely the way to go.

He eased back slightly, breaking his lips from hers, not surprised to find both of them breathing heavily from the sensations coursing through them. Good heavens, she was precious. Her eyelids were still closed, her face still angled towards his, her perfectly pink lips parted to allow pent-up air to escape.

Pierce marvelled in her beauty, and the need to explore her smooth, sweet skin was too much for him to resist. He brushed small butterfly kisses on her eyelids, delighted when she gasped in wonderment. Then he slowly made his way down her cheeks, tasting the freshness of her skin. The subtle scent of her perfume combined with the release of endorphins to provide a heady combination, and it was one he knew he could easily become addicted to.

With an all-encompassing tenderness she'd never felt before Pierce pressed kisses from her cheek around to her ear, where he lingered for a moment, causing her body to flood with a new mass of tingles. Then he worked his way down her neck and she found herself tipping her head to the side, granting him as much access as he wanted. He brushed her hair from her neck with the backs of his fingers, not wanting anything to hinder his exploration, his fingers trailing in the silky strands as though he couldn't get enough of the feel of her hair. How was it possible that such a simple action could fill her so completely with needs she'd never even known she had?

It wasn't until he kissed lower, brushing aside the top of her shirt collar, clearly intent on exploring further, that Stacey started to feel a sense of propriety return. She opened her eyes and tried to shift in his embrace, but Pierce spoke against her skin.

'It's all right, Stace.' he breathed. 'I'm not going to ravish you right here. I just want you to *feel*.'

'I do,' she whispered back. 'But…we're…out…in the open and…oh—' Her words were broken off as Pierce pressed kisses along her collarbone, clearly thrilled with her response to his touch as he made his way around to the other side.

'You are exquisite,' he murmured, taking his time, not wanting to rush the exploration.

Stacey tipped her head further back. Her eyes were open as she stared up at the stars, but the sensations he was evoking made it impossible for her to see clearly.

It was evident that the attraction between them was incredibly powerful.

When he finally brought his mouth back to hers Stacey's hunger had intensified, and she opened her mouth wider than before, plunging her tongue into his mouth, wanting him to see exactly how he'd affected her senses, heightening them beyond belief. With a passion and urgency she'd never felt before she surrendered herself to him and to the emotions he evoked.

She threaded her fingers through his hair, making sure he didn't break away from her just yet, loving the feel of his arms firmly around her, encompassing her, making her feel secure as well as utterly sexy.

Was this how other people felt when they were kissed by someone who really desired them? Was this what she'd been missing out on? How was it possible she hadn't known that *this* was the way to kiss an attractive man? Or that this was the way a man kissed a woman he found attractive?

Feeling as though her lungs might completely burst if she didn't drag some oxygen into them, Stacey jerked her head back, needing to make a sharp clean break in order to breathe.

'Stacey…'

Her name was a caress upon his lips and she liked the way it sounded. She also liked that he was as breathless as her, as invested as her in all these new and crazy emotions.

'You really *do* like me.' Her words were an astonished whisper, filled with awe and happiness.

'Yes. Yes, I do,' he stated with a slight chuckle, and she immediately closed her eyes and buried her face in his chest.

'Sorry. Clearly I'm a little…knocked off balance by all of this. I keep blurting my thoughts out loud.'

'Is this a common occurrence?' he queried, dropping a kiss to her head, his fingers sifting through the silkiness of her hair.

'No. That's what's so confusing. Usually I'm quite in control of my faculties.' She eased back and looked up at him. 'But you…' She swallowed and smiled up at him. 'You make me feel alive.'

'That's a good thing, Stacey.'

'I know, but I'm clearly not used to it. Hence the unusual behaviour.'

'I'll let you in on a little secret,' he said, dipping his head closer to her ear. 'I like that you're a little unusual because that means you're unique.' He kissed her cheek.

She sighed and snuggled closer to him, wrapping her arms around him and resting her head against his chest, loving the words he was saying. Having been one of three all her life, it was refreshing to hear that he thought her unique.

The cool breeze, which he'd been oblivious to while he'd been memorising each and every contour of her face, whipped up around them, with a hint of saltiness from the sea not so far away.

'It's late…or rather early,' he murmured. 'And you need to get home.'

Stacey gasped. 'You're still on shift. How could we have forgotten?'

'If there'd been a problem they would have called.' He patted the cell phone in his trouser pocket. 'Besides, I haven't heard any sirens…except for you.' He chuckled and waggled his eyebrows at her.

'That's a very cheesy line,' she stated, smiling up at him and sighing once more.

'I thought you liked cheesy?'

'I do. I really do. But you're right. I'd best get home. House calls start in exactly...' She paused and squinted at her watch, unable to see the time. 'Some time soon.'

Pierce's warm laughter washed over her.

'Where are your keys?' he asked, releasing her from his embrace with obvious reluctance.

Stacey picked up her handbag, which had at some point slipped from her shoulder unnoticed to land at their feet. She dug around in the bag and eventually pulled them out.

'Amazing what you can find in a black hole,' he commented as she pressed the button to unlock her car. 'All women's handbags are black holes. I'm convinced of it. Even Nell's—although someone at work bought her an inner purse organiser which she absolutely loves. Still, it only means she can carry even *more* things around with her.'

Stacey chuckled as he opened the car door for her. He leaned forward and pressed another kiss to her lips. 'Drive safe.'

'OK. I hope the rest of your shift is uneventful.'

'You and me both. I'll give you a call when there's news of Gary.'

'Thanks. I'd appreciate that.' She smiled at him.

'And once we've discussed our mutual patient we can discuss exactly how we're going to spend the rest of our weekend—after you've finished the housecalls, of course.'

'We're going to spend our weekend together?'

'Why, yes, Stacey. That's what people do when they date. They spend time together.'

'Date?' The word squeaked from her lips and she stared at him with surprise.

Pierce chuckled once more, and was about to say something when his cell phone rang.

'Go. You're needed,' she told him.

He leaned forward and pressed a firm and secure kiss to her lips before extracting the phone from his pocket, then he winked at her and started jogging back towards the emergency department as he answered his call.

Stacey sat in the car and started the engine. 'We're *dating*?' She stated the words out loud as she buckled her seatbelt. '*I'm* dating?' She switched on the car's lights. 'Pierce and I are dating.' She tried to state the words with absolute firmness, as though it was the most natural thing in the world. 'This is good,' she remarked as she headed out of the car park and onto the road. 'Moving forward is good.'

Stacey seemed to float through the next week with a large smile plastered to her face. Her sister Molly was delighted at this turn of events.

'You're dating Pierce? *Really* dating? Really putting yourself out there and doing something just for you?' Molly was gobsmacked.

'Yes.'

'And you're not overthinking things?'

'Nope. Just going with the flow.'

'Uh-huh.' Molly didn't sound as though she fully believed her, but she grinned wildly just the same.

When Stacey spoke to Cora over the internet chat line Cora knew something was different even before Molly blurted it out.

'You look really…happy, Stace,' she said, her tone laced with curiosity. 'What's going on over th—?'

'She's dating Pierce!' Molly squealed, jumping up and down and clapping her hands with utter delight.

From there, Stacey was plied with a barrage of questions from Cora—so much so that Cora demanded that the next time they were scheduled to talk Pierce should be there so she could 'meet' him.

'So I'm being served up for Cora's approval, eh?' Pierce said at the end of the week.

They'd just finished a hectic clinic day and were relaxing in the kitchen with a soothing cup of herbal tea. Winifred had just left and the front door to the surgery was locked. It was just the two of them, and although she still felt highly self conscious about being alone with Pierce, Stacey was more than happy to have a bit of time with him.

They'd shared several meals together over the past week, with all of Stacey's siblings and Nell, too. George and Lydia had been demanding, craving adult male attention—especially when he spun them around in the back garden or gave them shoulder rides so they could pretend to be giraffes. And he was incredibly patient with them as they showed him the progress they'd made in training their rabbits in the art of professional rabbit jumping.

Nell enjoyed playing with the rabbits, and was getting good at making Andrew jump over obstacles. She still loved playing games, now openly including the other children, and liked to help in the kitchen when it was time for dinner. As setting the table was one of the things she did every night, she continued to do that job whenever she came to Stacey's house, and George and Lydia were more than happy to hand over the task.

Jasmine was perhaps the one who had surprised them all the most, by insisting on taking over Nell's afternoon routine. 'You and Pierce work late. Nell needs someone right there for her when she gets off the bus. George is nine, so he can stay at home with Lydia—or they can come with me, too.'

'But she has an afternoon snack. You'd have to prepare that too,' Stacey had cautioned.

'Hello?' Jasmine had waved her two hands in front of Stacey's face. 'What are these? They're hands. I can prepare food with them. I'm not a little kid, you know.'

Stacey had talked this over with Pierce, who'd admitted that it *would* be good for someone to take over meeting Nell from the bus as sometimes he just wasn't able to get away from the clinic on time. And so Jasmine had taken over this responsibility and so far was doing exceptionally well.

Stacey had hoped that helping out Nell would stop Jasmine from being so surly with others, but it hadn't. And she'd stopped acknowledging Pierce's presence altogether.

'She's probably jealous,' Molly had said to her one night as they'd tried to figure out how they could handle the matter. Stacey had disciplined Jasmine, and given her consequences, but Jasmine simply didn't seem to care.

'Jealous? Of what?'

'Of Pierce. She probably thinks you've got less time for her now.'

'Has she said something?'

Molly had shaken her head. 'Not to me. I'm just spitballing ideas here.'

Stacey had closed her eyes and shaken her own head. 'How do we reach her, Molly? What do we need to do to let her know we're on her side?'

Molly's phone had rung and she'd quickly pulled it from her pocket. 'Sorry, Stace. I'm second on call.'

'Sure.'

Stacey had waved Molly's words away and within

another ten minutes her sister had gone, heading towards the hospital to assist with the patients involved in multiple car crash on the M1. As this was the main road from Sydney to Newcastle, Stacey had had no idea when Molly might return to finish their conversation. Once again she'd been left holding the ball, needing to make most of the decisions and carry out the majority of discipline.

Stacey wanted to talk to Pierce about it—see if he had any ideas—but it wasn't his problem. Besides, if she did speak to Pierce about her younger sister and Jasmine found out she might stop going to see Nell, not wanting anything to do with Pierce or his sister. That risk was too great, so Stacey was left to try and figure it out on her own.

'Do you think Cora will like me?' Pierce asked, bringing her thoughts back to the present.

Stacey smiled as she placed her arms around his shoulders, delighted that she was allowed to touch him in such a familiar way. 'I have no doubt about it.'

'Excellent. Then that leaves only Jasmine.'

'Jasmine doesn't like *anyone*, Pierce, so don't take it personally. I'm trying not to.'

'She's nice to Nell, for which I am very grateful,' he remarked. He thought for a moment, then said, 'How about a picnic next weekend?'

Stacey considered it. 'The weather's supposed to be nice. King Edward Park?'

'Perfect.' He kissed her a few more times. 'Just like your mouth. Perfect for mine.'

She smiled and sighed into his embrace, more than happy for him to take his time exploring the contours of her 'perfect' mouth. Pierce was always saying such lovely things to her—telling her she had luscious hair and that he loved running his fingers through it, or that she was beautiful, precious and deserved to be loved not only for the pureness of her heart but also because of the sadness in her eyes.

'I'm not sad,' she'd replied after Pierce had whispered the compliment near her ear the other evening when he'd been kissing her goodnight.

Pierce had brushed her loose hair behind her ears and kissed both of her cheeks. 'I'm getting to know you better, Stacey and I can't believe the weight you have to carry on those slim shoulders of yours.'

He'd placed his large warm hands onto her shoulders as he'd spoken, massaging gently, releasing endorphins that had made her want to melt into his arms for ever and never leave.

'I care about you, Stacey. More and more every day. But the sadness which you've buried deep down inside is dangerous.'

'Dangerous?' She'd tried to laugh off his words, but the sound had been hollow even to her own ears.

'If we're not careful sadness can consume us.'

'You sound as though you know what you're talking about.' She'd eased back from his massaging hands and he'd instantly stopped the motion.

'I do.'

'Grief over your parents' loss?'

'Yes. The death of a loved one can leave such a wide and gaping chasm, and if we're not careful—if we don't take the time to heal the wound from the inside out but just keep changing the dressing and applying a new bandage to the wound—then infection can set in.'

He'd brushed the back of his fingers across her cheek before pulling her closer into his arms. They'd stood there for a while, with Stacey revelling in the feel of his arms wound tightly around her, before he'd finally spoken again.

'I understand the brokenness, the pain, the desolation that grief can bring, whatever the circumstances which have caused it. Along with all of these comes loneliness, and whilst I know you have a very supportive family, and you seem more than willing and able to shoulder the lion's share of that responsibility, at times you seem so lonely.'

'Lonely?' She'd eased back slightly and looked up at him. 'I've never been alone in my life. I'm one of three. I wasn't even alone in the womb! And let's not forget I have five siblings.'

'And yet sometimes…' He'd exhaled slowly, his words filled with understanding. 'You're so lonely. I just wanted you to know that I've been there, too.' He'd bent his head and brushed his lips across hers. 'The weight of your world is not yours alone to carry. Please let me help you in any way I can.'

His words had held promise, his touch had held promise, even the taste of his lips on hers had held promise…so why was she having such a difficult time letting go of the chains that bound her? Had she been carrying the responsibility for her family for far longer than she'd realised?

When her father had married Letisha, when they'd had Jasmine, hadn't it been Stacey who had helped the most, wanting to do everything she could to make things easier for her stepmother? Cora and Molly had been delighted with their new sibling, and indeed, when George and Lydia had rounded out their family, the triplets had loved having younger sisters and a brother to entertain. But whenever they'd been asked to babysit it had been Stacey who had taken charge.

Have I always done this? she asked herself later that

night. Now that he'd pointed out the wound Stacey had thought already healed, especially since returning to Newcastle to connect to her roots, she was more than aware of the way both Molly and Cora really did leave it up to her to call the shots.

She wanted to talk to Molly about it, but her poor sister had been rostered on with such long shifts that as soon as she arrived home she'd quickly eat something before collapsing into such a deep sleep Stacey hadn't the heart to wake her.

She loved her siblings—all of them—and would do anything for any of them. They'd do the same for her... wouldn't they?

She tried not to fixate on the question as she went about her daily life, happy that George and Lydia were settling into school but with increasing concern for Jasmine's declining behaviour.

Indeed, when she informed everyone they would be having a picnic in the park the following weekend they'd all been excited except for Jasmine. Even the information that Nell was looking forward to seeing her there hadn't changed Jasmine's attitude.

'I have no idea what to do,' Stacey confessed to Cora during one of their internet chats. 'She really seems to hate me.'

'That's because you're the disciplinarian.'

'How did I get *that* job?'

Cora laughed. 'I don't know. I guess as you're the oldest triplet we've always just naturally looked up to you. At school whenever there was a problem you always came up with a solution. Some people are born leaders, Stace, and you're one of them. Just look at how you've held us all together over the past eighteen months. And when you decided to buy Dad's old practice Molly and I gave our blessing because we trust your judgement. We knew you would have figured all the angles, weighed up the pros and cons.'

'And yet I've hurt Jasmine the most by uprooting her from her friends.'

'The practice would have closed down if you hadn't bought it when you did. It's necessary for that community to have a functioning, working medical practice and you've put the needs of the many ahead of the needs of a fourteen-year-old girl who will one day forgive you.'

'Will she?'

'Did you forgive Dad when he followed his dreams and took us all to Perth?'

'Yes, but—'

'You followed your dreams, Stacey. You did what you knew was right deep down in your heart. Jasmine isn't collateral damage. Far from it. Just look at how she's helping more with George and Lydia, how she's helping Pierce's sister. Those are *good* things.'

Stacey sighed. 'I guess.'

'You've held us all together for so long—plus you've had your own personal emotional dramas to contend with. And although Molly and I are always there for you—and we know you know this—you still need those moments of solitude.'

'But I don't *want* solitude.'

'Don't you?' Cora was surprised. 'I always thought that sometimes, with the three of us living in each other's pockets all our lives, you just needed some space to breathe.'

'Do you?'

Cora thought on this for a moment. 'I think I find my solitude in adventure.' She spread her arms wide, indicating the military-style truck behind her. 'Just to speak to you like this I have to borrow a truck, drive an hour through rough, dirty tracks that any ordinary four-wheel drive would get stuck in, and then head to the top of a mountain where the satellite transmission is strongest.'

'And I appreciate every time you've done this. I know it must cut into your valuable work there in Tarparnii.'

'But you see, Stace, that's my point. I *like* going four-wheel driving—just like Molly loves dancing and going on clown patrol and joining in with every social activity any hospital runs. That's *her* solitude. Yours is to contemplate the meaning of life.' Cora smiled at her sister. 'And I know Jazzy's causing you concern, but perhaps she's just trying to find her own place—her thing she likes the most.'

'Her solitude?'

'Her happy place,' Cora offered.

Stacey sighed. 'I hope she finds it soon.'

'What about you?'

'What *about* me?'

'Have you found *your* happy place?'

'What do you mean?'

'You're different, Stace.'

'I am?'

'Yes.' Cora threw her arms in the air. 'Can't you see it? Feel it?'

'Feel…what?'

'Pierce! Stacey, I'm talking about *Pierce*. Even over the internet chat I could see he was dreamy. You've picked a winner there.'

Stacey's smile widened as she tucked her hair behind her ear. 'Oh, Cora. He makes me feel so…tingly and shiny and…and…'

'Happy?'

'Yes. That's why I guess I've been feeling guilty

about Jasmine—because for the first time in a long time I'm…happy.'

'Don't feel guilty, Stace. Accept it. Draw strength from the way Pierce makes you feel. You deserve a world of happiness—especially after you-know-who.'

'It's OK,' Stacey replied. 'You can say his name now, because with the way Pierce makes me feel I've realised that whatever it was I had with Robert it certainly wasn't love.'

'Wait. wait, wait!' Cora clasped her hands together and stared at her sister. 'What are you saying? Are you saying that you're *in love* with Pierce?'

Stacey's smile was bright and wide and filled with delight. 'I…I…think so.'

Cora squealed with excitement. 'Oh, Stace, really? This is wonderful, great—and a whole heap of other awesome adjectives.'

Stacey laughed, loving her sister and wishing she was there in person so they could hug.

'Say it again,' Cora demanded, clapping her hands.

'I think I might be in love with Pierce Brolin,' Stacey stated, and even as she said the words out loud she knew that it was far more absolute than she was willing to admit even to her sister.

She didn't just *think* she was in love with Pierce. She *knew* it with all her heart… But for now, although she adored her sisters and the close bond they shared, she needed to keep that intimate piece of information to herself.

CHAPTER EIGHT

'I SEE YOU and Stacey are spending a bit more time together,' Mike said as he tossed some poker chips into the middle of the table. Edna had already lost all her chips and gone off to make them a cup of tea.

'Yes.' Pierce had been wondering when Mike might bring up the topic of Stacey. 'I see your chips and I raise you.'

Their friendly poker games had been going on throughout Mike's recovery which, Pierce had to admit, was good. Mike was adhering to the diet his cardiologist had recommended and was also looking forward to the rabbit jumping competition George and Lydia were planning to attend.

Mike considered his cards, then tossed the same amount of chips into the centre of the table. 'Call. What have you got?'

For a moment Pierce wasn't sure whether Mike was talking about the cards or about the fact that he'd been spending more time with Stacey. Mike was very protective of all the Wilton children, taking on the role of family patriarch with pride.

'I have got a full house,' Pierce remarked, placing his cards on the table.

Mike chuckled and didn't cough once, which Pierce was pleased to note.

'That you do, boy. If you're serious about Stacey there'll definitely be a full house. Are you up to taking on that level of responsibility again? Raising siblings?' Mike placed one hand over the pile of chips in the centre of the table.

Pierce had thought about it—especially as he was spending more and more time not only with Stacey but with the rest of her siblings. She was a package deal. He couldn't have one without the other. He was the same. He would always have Nell in his life. But she was now at the stage where one of her housemates, Samantha, had moved in, and the event they'd meticulously planned and structured for many years could now finally take place: Nell living independently.

But Stacey…beautiful, wonderful Stacey. She responded to his kisses as though she'd never been kissed before, as though she'd never felt this way before, and, he'd had to admit he felt a connection with Stacey that he hadn't felt with any other woman before.

'Well?' Mike brought Pierce's thoughts back to the present.

Pierce looked down at the cards neatly laid in a row. Full house. Was he ready?

'I wanted to find out whether this thing between Stacey and myself was something special—whether it was worth pursing.'

'And is it?'

Pierce reached out, lifted Mike's hand from the pile and pulled all the chips towards him. 'Yes.'

Mike gaped. 'But what about the job? The one they're constantly bugging you to come over for?'

Pierce shrugged. 'Some dreams aren't meant to come true. I learned that lesson a long time ago.'

'Hmm...' Mike looked at his friend. 'I hope you're right.'

Pierce nodded. 'Stacey's worth it.'

'Your feelings are that strong?'

He thought about Mike's question for a moment. *Were* they that strong? *Was* Stacey worth sacrificing his main chance to head over to Yale and lead a team of researchers? He'd been wanting to do that for so long now, but Nell had always come first and there had been no way he was going to choose a job over his most beloved sister. Now Nell was settled and he was free to go, to follow his dream—the one he'd been aiming towards for such a very long time.

And yet there was the way Stacey was able to see into his heart, to understand everything he'd already sacrificed for the love of a sibling, and the way she felt in his arms—as though he'd finally found *his* home, the place where *he* belonged... Were his feelings strong enough that he would never have regrets at turning down the only job he'd ever really wanted?

Pierce's answer was a firm nod in the affirmative, yet for some reason he couldn't bring himself to speak the word *yes* out loud once more. But he was certain he was falling in love with Stacey, and he was prepared to love and accept not only her but the rest of her family, just as she loved and accepted Nell.

'I hope you're right, boy,' Mike remarked as he shuffled the deck of cards. 'Ready for another hand?'

Pierce eyed his huge pile of chips, then looked at Mike and smiled. 'Sure. What have I got to lose?'

Mike's answer was a wise old chuckle. 'If you're not careful? Everything.'

* * *

The following Saturday the sun was shining brightly, making the early October day perfect for a picnic in the park. Unfortunately, by the time they all arrived at King Edward Park, it had become clear that several other people had had the same idea, and all the council-provided barbecues were already in use.

'We'll have to queue for the barbecue,' joked Samantha, Nell's new housemate, as they spread picnic blankets beneath a large shady gum tree. Nell was already getting excited and pulling a Frisbee out of the bag she'd brought with her.

'Come on, Jasmine,' she ordered, reaching for Jasmine's hand and tugging the surly teenager along. 'Come and play Frisbee with me.'

Jasmine did as she was bid, not looking at anyone but not grumbling about it either.

'Jasmine's still not happy?' Pierce asked, placing a supportive arm around Stacey's shoulders.

'Cora says she's searching for her happy place.'

'Perhaps Cora's right. I think everyone searches for their happy place.'

They stood there for a moment, watching Jasmine let Nell boss her around. Stacey wondered whether there was something more to Pierce's words. Had he found *his* happy place? Was he happy? With her?

'She's incredibly good with Nell,' he continued, and Stacey detected no unhappiness in his voice so allowed herself to relax into his embrace.

He put his other arm around her, enfolding her against him. She closed her eyes, allowing herself to breathe in his strength, to breathe in the feel of his supporting arms around her. She'd never understood before how others could draw strength just from receiving a hug from someone else—not until she'd met Pierce. But when he hugged her like this she *did* draw strength from him, and for the first time since they'd moved to Newcastle she saw a glimmer of hope that everything would turn out all right.

'Are you two going to cuddle and kiss *all* day long?' Lydia demanded, wrapping her arms around Stacey's waist.

Pierce instantly broke the contact and bent to scoop Lydia up, then placed his free arm over Stacey's shoulder, bringing Lydia into their hug.

'What's wrong with that?' Pierce asked as he kissed Lydia's cheek. The little girl wrapped her arms about his neck and snuggled into him.

'You smell nice,' she told him.

Pierce sniffed her hair. 'So do you.'

Lydia giggled. 'That's 'cause I've got Stacey's perfume on.'

'Ah…is that what it is?' Pierce sniffed Stacey, then Lydia, and nodded his head. 'Yep. Two gorgeous girls… perfectly ripe for…*tickling*!'

And with that he tickled Stacey's neck before doing the same to Lydia. The little girl let forth a peal of laughter and Stacey chuckled, her heart delighting at the way Pierce seemed to fit so perfectly with her family.

Although Molly had been called to an emergency a few hours ago she had hopes of joining them later. But with almost all of the people she loved the most nearby Stacey really did feel as though *this* was her happy place. *Her* family—complete with Nell and Pierce.

It was as though she hadn't realised there were pieces of her life missing—not until she'd met this man and his sweet sister. She was still constantly delighting in the sensations and emotions spending time with Pierce evoked, but in the back of her mind there were questions. Questions about what the future might hold and where this relationship was going. About what Pierce really wanted from his life. Was he willing to take on her ready-made family? Or did the thought put him off, as it had Robert?

Pierce had told her about the research team—the ones he wrote his articles for. And he'd told her they'd offered him a job— the same job—several times over. Now that Nell was settled and beginning to live her life of independence was Pierce going to head overseas? To lead the team of researchers? Or did he plan to stay here?

The turmoil of her thoughts kept her awake at night. Her life had been affected by indecision, questions and trauma, and it had made her the sort of person who needed to know where she was going, to map out a path of what the future might hold. If she could deal in absolutes then so much the better, but she had also had to learn how to adapt when life threw her curve balls.

'I *said*...' George remarked, tapping her on the arm. 'When are we going to cook? I'm hungry.'

Stacey snapped out of her reverie and looked at her brother. 'Your default setting is "I'm hungry".' She ruffled his hair and smiled. 'There are bananas and apples in the picnic basket. Have one of those to tide you over.'

She glanced at the rectangular brick barbecues provided by the council for everyone to use. All of them were still being used. She glanced over to where a new family was arriving at the park, looking around to stake out their piece of shady grass. The dad carried a portable barbecue and a gas bottle.

'We should have brought our own barbecue, too,' George grumbled, pointing to the family who'd thought ahead.

'Possibly,' Pierce agreed, 'but the point of coming to the park isn't just to eat a barbecued sausage, George.'

'It isn't?'

Pierce laughed. 'Come on. I think there's a football in the bag. Let's go kick it around.'

'Can I come, too?' Lydia asked.

'Yeah, Lydia's really good at football,' George agreed, his grumbling stomach momentarily forgotten as he raced over to the bag Pierce had pointed to. Pierce released a squirming Lydia from his arms and she ran off after her brother.

'They really don't stand still at that age, do they?' Pierce commented as he leaned over and pressed a contented kiss to Stacey's waiting lips.

'You're thirty-six and *you* don't stand still,' she pointed out with a chuckle.

'You're probably right,' he agreed, kissing her again before winking and jogging off to join George and Lydia on a free patch of grass.

Stacey sat down on the blanket next to Samantha, who was more than happy to sit quietly and absorb the atmosphere. Stacey watched as the family who'd brought their own barbecue hooked up the gas cylinder and began to cook their food. A few of the other barbecues were now being vacated, but at the moment she was in no hurry to rush over there and claim one. Pierce was right. Today wasn't just about barbecuing food but about spending time together, in the sunshine, enjoying each other's company.

She slipped on her sunglasses, watching as Jasmine threw the Frisbee at Nell, who didn't manage to catch it and had to run after it. Jasmine laughed and the sound washed over Stacey like manna from heaven. For this moment in time her little sister was happy. Perhaps that was enough for now.

Stacey closed her eyes, filled with a quiet contentment.

A loud scream jolted her eyes open and she pulled off her sunglasses, her heart pounding wildly.

'What?' She blinked a few times and in the next instant a loud whooshing noise seemed to surround the area, shaking every fibre of her being.

'Stacey!' She heard her name being called and scrambled to her feet. Samantha, too, was on her feet, staring, aghast, at what was happening. Panic seemed to engulf the entire park, with some people screaming, others running, and some, like her, standing and staring, trying to take everything in at a glance.

'What do I do? What do I do?' Samantha's high-functioning Asperger's was starting to show itself.

Stacey's mind clicked into doctor mode and she handed Samantha a set of car keys. 'Go to my car and get the big emergency bag from the boot. It's a big red backpack with a white cross on it.'

'OK. OK.' Glad of something to do, Samantha started to focus, and she quickly took the keys from Stacey and did as she was asked.

Stacey stood on the picnic rug and gazed out at the scene. The world seemed to pause as she took in her surroundings, her quick mind piecing together exactly what had happened.

Pierce, Lydia and George were all standing together. Pierce had grabbed their hands, ready to lead them from any danger. Jasmine was standing further away, her hands covering her open mouth, her eyes staring off into the distance in complete shock.

Stacey followed the line of Jasmine's gaze, her own eyes opening wide as she realised why her sister looked so distraught. Nell lay sprawled on the ground, the Frisbee nearby. Nell wasn't moving.

All of this registered in Stacey's mind within one glance.

The next thing to register was the cloud of black smoke filling the air, caused by a flaming ball of gas. The man and woman who had been cooking on the portable barbecue had been thrown to the ground as well, the man writhing and yelling in pain.

'Gas fire!'

Pierce's words broke through Stacey's haze, speeding her thoughts back to normal. He was walking quickly towards her, dodging people as they ran past him. Panic was beginning to grip the entire park. He was still holding onto George and Lydia's hands.

'There must have been a damaged regulator or hose and a fat fire has ignited it,' he called to her.

When they reached the rug George wrapped his arms around Stacey's waist and Lydia just stood and stared. Stacey pointed to where Nell lay on the ground.

'Pierce! Look!'

She watched as he turned, his expression changing from one of controlled concern to one of complete despair as he took in the vision of his beloved little sister lying still on the grass.

'Go!' she urged when he stood still for a split second, his world clearly falling apart. 'Check her. I'll bring the medical kit over.'

'Uh…' Pierce nodded as though his mind was unable to compute which action he should take next. 'Yeah… yeah.' With that he all but sprinted over to where his sister lay.

Stacey turned her attention to her siblings. 'George, Lydia.' She bent down to hug them both, her words fast and stern. 'I need you to stay right here. *Right here.*' She pointed to their rug, which was on the opposite side of the park from where the explosion had occurred.

People were beginning to gather their belongings and

leave, others were on their cellphones, hopefully calling
the emergency services, others were taking photographs.
There was a hive of activity, but the first thing Stacey
had to do was to make sure her brother and sister were
out of harm's way. Their safety was paramount.

'Wait for Samantha to get back from the car and then
do exactly as she says.'

'Yes, Stacey,' they both answered, their little eyes wide
with fear.

People were everywhere, and when Samantha came
rushing back with the large emergency kit, Stacey nodded her thanks.

'Can you stay with the kids, please?'

Before Samantha could answer, Stacey took the
backpack and raced over towards the man who was still
screaming, writhing around on the grass. She could
smell burning clothes and flesh. Whilst only seconds
had passed since the explosion it felt a lot longer, with
her mind trying to process too many things at once. For
now, though, Pierce was attending to Nell, and although
Stacey wanted nothing more than to check Nell herself,
she had to prioritise.

The initial fireball which had scared them all was still
burning, but thankfully the man hadn't put the portable
barbecue beneath any trees, so although it was extremely
hot the flames were now shooting upwards rather than
billowing outwards. The man had stopped rolling and she
realised he was no longer on fire, but his body might be
going into shock or worse.

She knelt down beside him, placing the emergency
kit nearby. She called to her patient but received no response. She pressed two fingers to his radial pulse, relieved when she felt it—faint, but there. She was fairly
sure he hadn't sustained any spinal damage, especially

with the way he'd been rolling on the grass before losing consciousness. She opened her kit and quickly pulled on some gloves before finding a soft neck brace to help secure the man's spine, knowing that paramedics would replace it with a more rigid one. She called to the man again, telling him what she was doing, but he remained unconscious.

'Are you a medic?' she heard a woman ask.

'Yes.' Stacey glanced up for a moment.

'Good. I'm a volunteer firefighter.'

'Excellent.' Stacey inclined her head towards the blaze. 'You OK to deal with that?'

'My friends and I are. All the emergency services have been called. My friend's just getting an extinguisher from my car.'

'Great. Thanks.'

True to her word, the firefighter and her friends concentrated on dealing with the blaze, keeping it contained. Less than five minutes had passed since the initial eruption, and even as she concentrated on her patient Stacey could also hear several other people taking charge, marshalling families together and generally controlling the situation. It was good, because it made it far easier for her to concentrate.

Nell wasn't lying too far away and she could hear Pierce speaking to her and Nell talking back. Stacey breathed an inward sigh of relief to know that Nell was OK.

'You're all right,' she heard Pierce say. 'You've just hurt your ankle, so I want you to stay as still as possible. I'm going to get some bandages from Stacey's medical kit and take care of it.'

Stacey glanced over and saw Pierce kiss his sister's forehead before looking over his shoulder at her. Their gazes held for a brief second and she could see the relief in his eyes. His sister was going to be all right.

Stacey was also aware of Jasmine in the background behind Pierce. She was still standing in the same spot, hands still across her mouth, as though she were unable to move or think, horror reflected in her eyes. Stacey wanted nothing more than to put her arms around her, to tell her that everything would be OK, to comfort her when she needed it most, but instead Stacey called again to her patient, still receiving no response.

'Trev? Trev?' A woman crawled along the grass, coming towards Stacey. 'Trev! Get away from him!' she demanded, her words slurred, her eyes narrowed and filled with all the protectiveness of a possessive lioness.

'I'm a doctor,' Stacey told her. 'His name is Trev?'

'Yes.' The woman's attitude changed to one of hope as she came closer, reaching out to touch his head. 'What's wrong with him? Why isn't he moving?'

'I want to find out, but I need you to stay back. Give him some room.' Stacey kept her tone firm and direct. She mentally ran through what needed to happen next: do Trev's obs and assess the severity of his burns.

Thankfully, due to the volunteer firefighters, the blaze was now almost under control.

As she looked down at Trev, Stacey knew she was going to need further assistance. 'Pierce. I need you,' she called, glancing over at him before checking Trev's airway was clear.

'Acknowledged. I've just finished Nell's bandage.' Pierce wrapped Nell in a big hug and whispered something in her ear before he looked over and called to Jasmine, who was still rooted to the spot, unable to move. 'Jasmine? Can you come and help Nell, please?'

Jasmine shook her head from side to side before turning and running away.

'Jasmine! *Jasmine!*' he called, but the teenager wasn't listening. Pierce looked across at Stacey, unsure what to do.

Stacey stared wide-eyed at her sister's retreating back. There was nothing she could do. She couldn't go after Jasmine, which was her initial instinct. She needed to stay with her patient. She just had to trust that Jasmine's common sense would kick in at some point and she wouldn't stray too far from where they all were.

'I'll have to deal with her later.' The words were like dust in her mouth and her heart broke that she couldn't be there for Jasmine when she needed her most. 'Get Nell over to the rug with the others. Samantha, George and Lydia can look after her,' Stacey called, knowing she needed to focus completely on Trev rather than having her attention diverted by other personal matters.

'Right.' Pierce stood and scooped Nell up into his arms, carrying her over to the rug, where George and Lydia instantly rallied around her. Poor Samantha was doing her best to try and marshal some of the other children together—especially the two boys who had been kicking the football around with Pierce and were now quite distraught about their father—the man called Trev.

'I want to see my mum!' one of them yelled.

'What's wrong with my dad?' the other one questioned.

Stacey closed her eyes for a split second, focusing her thoughts on Trev and Trev alone. When she opened her eyes Pierce was coming round to Trev's other side.

'Status?' He pulled on a pair of gloves and reached for the stethoscope.

'Airway clear. Burns to hands, arms, both legs, and

minor damage to the face. No response to calls. Trev?'
she called again as she reached into the emergency medical kit to find a bag of saline and a package of IV tubing.
'We'll replenish fluids to avoid the possible complica-
tion of shock.'

'I love that you have such a well-stocked emergency
kit,' Pierce commented as he unhooked the stethoscope.
'Heart-rate is mildly tachy. Pain meds?'

'Suggest ten milligrams of IV morphine followed by
methoxyflurane.' Stacey's hands were busy, opening the
packets of tubing and then looking for the best place to
insert the line.

'Agreed. Allergies?'

Stacey looked over to where Trev's wife was sitting,
rocking back and forth. Someone had had the presence
of mind to wrap a blanket around her. 'Is Trev allergic
to anything?' Stacey asked.

'Left arm isn't as badly damaged as the right arm,'
Pierce commented as he assisted Stacey with setting up
the drip.

She looked over to where the volunteer firefighter was
standing back. The fire situation was now under control,
the gas in the bottle having almost expired.

'Can you help?' Stacey called the woman over, indicating the saline bag, which would need to be held.

The woman nodded and made her way to Stacey,
pleased to be of further assistance.

'Is Trev allergic to anything?' Pierce asked Trev's wife
the question again, sharing a brief concerned look with
Stacey.

The woman was clearly shocked at what had happened but hopefully wouldn't go into shock completely.
The right side of her face was starting to droop, which

might indicate nerve damage. First, though, they needed to stabilise Trev as best they could.

'Uh… Um…allergies? Um…I don't know. Is he going to be all right?'

'Does he take any regular medication? Has he had any alcohol today?'

'He's had two light beers and…uh…he takes…um… fish oil tablets. The doctor said his cholesterol is high.'

'Has he had any operations? Been hospitalised?' Pierce asked.

'No. No. He…uh…no.'

Stacey nodded and pulled out a pre-drawn syringe labelled 'morphine'. 'Check ten milligrams,' she stated.

'Check,' Pierce replied, and as soon as the saline drip was working Stacey administered the medication while Pierce told the still unconscious Trev what they were doing.

'Is that going to help him?' his wife wanted to know, watching everything they did with eyes as wide as saucers.

'It's going to relieve his pain,' Stacey offered, before they set to work on carefully bandaging the worst of Trev's leg wounds. She was ecstatic when the faint sounds of sirens could be heard in the distance. Whether police, fire brigade or ambulance, she didn't care—at least help was on the way.

Pierce took Trev's pulse again. 'A definite improvement.'

'And just in time to be transferred to an ambulance. Trev, help is here,' she told him as Pierce continued to perform neurological observations.

Stacey had just finished applying the last bandage when the paramedics came racing over. Pierce gave them a debrief while Stacey pulled off one set of gloves and pulled on another, moving quickly over to where Trev's wife sat, still staring at her husband.

'What's your name?' Stacey asked as she checked the side of the woman's face.

'Rowena.'

The word was barely a whisper, and the side of her mouth was drooping down. Stacey reached for a penlight torch and checked the woman's pupils, relieved when both responded to light.

'What are they doing to Trev?' Rowena asked, trying to look around Stacey, who was blocking her view.

'They're transferring him to a stretcher so they can get him into the ambulance. Just sit still for me a moment, Rowena.' Stacey spoke calmly but with a firmness that made Rowena look at her. Stacey pressed gloved fingers gently to Rowena's face, looking carefully.

'What is it? What's wrong?' she asked.

Stacey lifted the blanket off Rowena's shoulders and checked her right arm and side, realising there were several cuts and abrasions down the left side of Rowena's body. 'Rowena? What happened when the fire started? Do you remember?'

'Uh…' She looked at Stacey with scared eyes. 'What is it? Just tell me.'

'The left side of your face is drooping. That's why you're slurring your words.'

'I'm slurring?'

Rowena immediately went to lift a hand to touch her face, but Stacey stilled her arm and Rowena winced. Stacey immediately felt her ribs, gently checking to see if any of them were broken.

'Does it hurt when you breathe in?'

Rowena tried for a deep breath and immediately winced in pain. 'What *is* it? What's *wrong* with me?' The paramedics were securing Trev to the stretcher and Rowena's gaze followed her husband's supine form. 'Oh, why did this happen? *Why?*'

'Can you remember what did happen?' Stacey prompted again.

'I heard Trev yelling and I looked over and it was as though he was on fire—but only for a moment, and then he just dropped and…and…started rolling and yelling and…and…he was moving at an odd angle and it was all blurry and then I crawled over and you told me to get back.'

'Do you remember falling down?'

Stacey also thought back to that moment when the world around her had seemed to slow down. Where had Rowena been? Stacey looked over to where two folding chairs were still on the ground, unpacked. They were the new kind of folding chair, with firm metal rods for stabilisation. Had Rowena landed on the folded-up chairs? Had she stumbled or been thrown backwards slightly, and ended up breaking a rib and possibly damaging a nerve in her face? Stacey could definitely remember seeing her lying down, so the scenario wasn't completely absurd.

Trev was now securely strapped to the stretcher, his neck in a firm neck brace, an IV pole holding the saline drip up high, releasing life-giving fluid to a patient who still hadn't regained consciousness.

'Where are they taking him? I want to go with him,' Rowena stated.

'I need to finish checking you over,' Stacey told her as she took Rowena's pulse, knowing the woman's elevated reading might well be due to the fact that she was highly concerned about her husband.

'But I can walk. I can move. I can stand.' As though to prove it, Rowena tried to get to her feet but instantly wobbled.

Stacey put out a hand to steady her. 'Perhaps just stay still for a moment and let us get organised.' Stacey beckoned to one of the paramedics, who instantly came over, his own emergency medical kit on his back. 'This is Rowena,' she told the paramedic, whose green jumpsuit declared his surname was Wantanebe. 'Suspected L3 L4 fracture, possible damaged facial nerve. Neck brace, Penthrane green whistle, then stabilise and stretcher.'

'Yes, Doctor.'

'Pass me a stethoscope, please?' She held out her hand and had the instrument immediately provided for her.

She was listening to Rowena's breathing when Pierce came over, Trev now being secure in the ambulance.

'How are things going?' he asked as he knelt down beside Stacey, the stethoscope from her own kit still slung around his neck.

'Breathing is a little raspy on the left due to possible rib fracture.'

'How's my Trev?' Rowena asked anxiously.

Pierce smiled warmly at her. 'I'm pleased to announce he regained consciousness a moment after we'd secured him in the ambulance.'

This news definitely seemed to calm Rowena down. 'That's good, right? That's good, yeah?'

'It *is* good news,' Pierce confirmed as he pulled on a fresh pair of gloves and reached for a bandage. 'Let's get you stabilised and into the other ambulance. Is there someone who can come and be with your boys?' he asked.

It was only then that Rowena even seemed to remember her children, and Stacey was thankful the paramedic had already secured a neck brace in place, otherwise Rowena might have done some damage with the way she tried to whip her head around.

'Jeremiah and Lucas? Where are they? Oh, how could I have forgotten them?'

'They're fine.' Stacey needed to calm Rowena immediately. 'Our friend Samantha is looking after them. Just over there. On the rug under the big eucalyptus.'

She pointed to where Samantha seemed to be surrounded by several children, including Rowena's boys, George and Lydia, Nell, and thankfully Jasmine, too. Stacey wasn't sure when her sister had returned to the rug but she was relieved to see her there.

'They're all right? They didn't get hurt?'

'They're both fine. Do you want them to come in the ambulance with you?'

'Yes, and I'll...I'll call my neighbour to come and get them from the hospital.'

'That sounds like a wonderful plan,' Pierce told her, his deep voice sounding like a comfortable blanket.

Rowena seemed more capable of relaxing now, and even managed a small lopsided smile in his direction. What was it about this man that seemed to cause women to relax and melt? Was it the sound of his rich baritone? Was it the comfort in his gaze? Was it the tug of his lips into a reassuring smile?

As they managed to settle Rowena onto a stretcher and get her and her boys installed in the ambulance Stacey felt the beginnings of fatigue starting to set in.

'You're not coming with us?' Rowena asked, looking at Stacey from the stretcher.

'We'll meet you at the hospital,' Stacey consoled her. 'You're in good hands.' With a warm smile, she waited while Pierce closed the rear doors of the ambulance, then stepped away from the road, able finally to turn her attention to her own situation.

Why had Jasmine been so scared? Was Nell really OK? Were George and Lydia traumatised? Had Samantha coped all right?

She turned around, expecting to find Pierce next to her, but instead he was already heading over to where Nell was sitting on the picnic rug, still looking completely dazed. He carried her emergency kit on his back and the instant he reached Nell's side he knelt down and opened the bag.

'Let's take a closer look at your ankle,' he told her, brushing some hair from his sister's eyes.

'What happened? Why was there a fire?'

'She's been asking the same questions over and over,' Samantha volunteered as Stacey knelt down next to Pierce.

'She does that when she's upset. Even if you give her the answer it's too much for her to process.' Pierce gave his sister a hug. 'It's OK, Nell. Pierce is here. Pierce will look after you.'

'Always?' Nell's voice was soft, small and very little. It was as though the child within her was all that was available, and it showed just how vulnerable Nell really was when her world was unbalanced from its axis.

Stacey watched as Pierce smiled brightly at his sister. 'Always.'

She understood the bond between brother and sister and she was incredibly proud to see it. He was an honourable man who understood the importance of family. As she watched him tenderly review Nell's ankle, re-bandaging it and then scooping her up and carrying her to his car, Stacey felt her heart fill with a quiet, unassuming love. She wanted this man in her life. No. She *needed* Pierce in her life. She loved him with all her heart and she never wanted him to leave her.

CHAPTER NINE

AT THE HOSPITAL they met up with the burns registrar, who was able to give them an update on Trev.

'They're taking him to Theatre now, to debride and clean his wounds as best as possible, but the full extent of his injuries won't really be known for a few more days.'

Pierce nodded. 'Thanks for the information. We'll let his wife know.'

'Is Nell back from Radiology?' Stacey asked as they walked out of the Emergency Surgical Suite back towards the Emergency Department.

'No. The orthopaedic registrar told me they'd page me when she was done.'

His walk was brisk, but his shoulders seemed to be drawn further back than before and there was a constant furrow to his brow. They headed to the cranio-facial unit, where Rowena had been taken after admission. Thankfully her neighbour had come and collected her boys, so at least she didn't have to worry too much about them and could concentrate on what was happening to her.

'What about *your* children?' Rowena asked Stacey and Pierce after they'd passed on the news about Trev's condition.

'Sorry?' Stacey frowned, looking at the other woman blankly.

'Well, it must be difficult for the two of you to look after your own children when both of you end up here at the hospital all the time.'

'Oh. Those children.' Stacey nodded, belatedly realising what Rowena was talking about.

Before she could say another word, Pierce indicated the physical space existing between himself and Stacey.

'We're not married and those aren't our children,' he stated matter-of-factly.

Stacey's brow was once more creased in a frown, but this time it was because she didn't understand his tone. Yes, what he'd said was accurate and true—but it had been the *way* he'd said it…as though there was no possibility of the two of them ever being anything more than they were right now… Which was what? Boyfriend and girlfriend? Forever dating but never moving forward?

She remembered the first day she'd met Pierce. When she'd asked him if he was married, his answer had been an emphatic no. Was that how he felt? Did he still think like that? That matrimony wasn't for him?

She pushed the thoughts aside, knowing she was probably overthinking things again. And besides, Pierce was no doubt still very worried about Nell. She quickly informed Rowena that the children they'd been with at the park were her siblings, and that their friend Samantha had taken them home. There was no need to add that Molly had been at home and had called Stacey to say that both George and Lydia were safe with her. Jasmine, however, had refused to leave Nell's side.

'Oh.' Rowena settled back onto the pillows and closed her eyes. 'That makes sense, I guess. Still, you two make a good couple.' And then she closed her eyes, the medication she'd been given causing her to doze off.

Pierce's pager sounded, and when he'd checked the number he stated, 'It's Radiology. Nell's X-rays are ready.'

Stacey nodded and together they spoke with the cranio-facial registrar before heading back to Radiology. As they headed down one of the hospital's long corridors she looked at him with concern.

'Pierce?'

'Hmm?'

He didn't slow his pace, and when Stacey put her hand on his arm, indicating he should slow down for a moment, he glanced over at her with a hint of impatience.

'Pierce, what's wrong?' When he simply stared at her, looking at her as though she'd just grown an extra head, she tried again. 'Are you worried about Nell?'

'When am I *not* worried about Nell?' The words were wrenched from him, and he turned and started walking again. 'Even when Mum and Dad were alive I was always there for Nell. *Always.*'

'And that's what makes you such a good brother,' she added as she caught up with him.

Pierce exhaled slowly, adjusting his pace a little so he wasn't hurtling along the corridor like an out-of-control freight train. 'At the end of the day it's all about family.'

'And Nell's OK. Yes, she's hurt her ankle, and that's going to upset her routine, but she'll adjust. You'll help her. We all will.'

'I know.' Pierce raked a hand through his hair, then stopped, looking down at Stacey. 'You're right, of course. The main point is that she's fine. No point in thinking what might have been, or how much worse the situation could have—' He stopped and shook his head. 'If a broken or—fingers crossed—badly sprained ankle is the worst thing that happens to her today, I'll take that.'

Stacey put her hands on his shoulders, wanting to

reassure him, to help him. 'And you're not alone. You have me and Molly, and Jasmine and George and Lydia to help, and no doubt Samantha's going to be there to support Nell, too.'

Pierce nodded and drew her into his arms, but before he did Stacey looked into his eyes and saw such doubt as she'd never seen in him before. Doubt? Was he still doubting that Nell's ankle was only sprained? Did he think it was indeed broken? Or was there something else going on in his head that she simply wasn't privy to?

His arms around her, however, felt as warm and as strong and as comforting as always, and she quickly dismissed her thoughts. He was her strong, dependable Pierce once more. But he was also a man who was very concerned for his sister, and that made her love him all the more.

'Thank you, Stace.'

He pulled back and brushed a kiss across her lips, right there in the middle of the hospital corridor. She still wasn't used to such public displays of affection, but she was learning not to care what everyone else might think. She knew in her heart that the way she felt about Pierce was like nothing she'd ever felt before. And if she wanted to experience the full scope of what those emotions might be she couldn't be concerned with what other people might think of her relationship with him. It was no one else's business but their own.

'That's what friends are for,' she murmured as he kissed her again. When he smiled at her, the doubt she thought she'd seen had vanished and he was back to being his usual jovial and optimistic self.

'You,' he murmured, kissing her mouth once more before pulling back and taking her hand in his, 'are a very good friend, Dr Wilton.'

'I try my best, Dr Brolin,' she returned, and they headed to Radiology for the verdict on Nell's ankle.

When they arrived it was to find Jasmine sitting on Nell's hospital bed, teaching Nell a hand-clap game.

Nell seemed enthralled, determined to figure out the movements and then laughing along with Jasmine when she made a mistake.

'It's so good to see her laughing again,' Pierce murmured as he let go of Stacey's hand.

'I made a mistake.' Nell grinned widely when she saw Pierce and Stacey walking towards her.

Stacey smiled back at Nell, her heart warming to see Jasmine interacting with others again, but as soon as Jasmine realised Stacey was in the room she clammed up tight, the laughter disappearing, the smile slipping from her face.

Stacey frowned, completely perplexed by her sister's behaviour. Thankfully Pierce didn't seem to notice as he walked over and kissed the top of Nell's head.

'How are things going here?' he asked.

'I made a mistake,' Nell said again, laughing a little, before encouraging Jasmine to do the hand-clap routine again. Jasmine acquiesced and Stacey and Pierce watched as the two girls did the routine. When Nell managed it faultlessly, she cheered and wriggled in bed with delight. 'I solved the puzzle!' It was only after she moved that she winced in pain, having temporarily forgotten that she'd hurt her ankle.

'Steady, Nellie.' Pierce put a hand on her shoulders. 'Nice and still, remember?'

'Oh. Yes.' She nodded earnestly, but still wanted to do the hand-clap routine again and again.

'Let's see how *slowly* we can do it, Nell,' Jasmine suggested, and Stacey could have kissed her sister.

She had no idea what was really going on inside Jasmine's head, but she was a good girl at heart. Of that there was no doubt.

'Pierce. There you are,' said the radiographer as she came back into the room. 'Did you want to have a look at the X-rays? I've got them up on the screen.'

'Thanks.' Pierce and Stacey headed over to the computer monitor and stared at the X-rays. 'She *has* broken it.' His tone was a little despondent.

'But it's a clean break,' Stacey pointed out.

'Six weeks in a plaster cast. Crutches. Protective medical boot after that.' Pierce raked a hand through his hair again and that look of doubt returned to his eyes. What could it mean?

'Her recovery should be uneventful, and at your house ramps have been installed for Loris's wheelchair, so that will make it easier for her to manoeuvre about with her crutches.'

'I'll have to call her work and let them know what's happened. Once she's OK to go back I'll organise taxis to take her to and from the office. Then—'

'Pierce.' Stacey interrupted, taking his hand in hers and giving it a gentle squeeze. 'Breathe. It's OK. You don't have to figure out all the logistics right this second. Just be with Nell, reassure her. She'll be fine because she has you.'

He looked down at her as though he'd completely forgotten she was there. 'She doesn't take to change easily,' he said softly, so Nell couldn't hear him. 'The slightest thing, if it isn't handled correctly, can set her off. And once she's unsettled it can take days, weeks, even months to bring her back around.'

'I understand.' She gave his hand what she hoped was another reassuring squeeze. 'But you're not alone any

more. I'm here—along with my plethora of siblings.'
Stacey pointed to Jasmine. 'Just look at the two of them
connecting. Jasmine talks more to Nell than she does to
anyone else at the moment. This is a good thing—for
both of them. Jasmine will be able to help Nell adjust.'

'Yeah. Yeah, you're right.'

He returned the squeeze on her fingers before releasing her, but Stacey could tell he was still very upset. He
thanked the radiologist and asked if he could take Nell
round to the plaster room to get the cast sorted out.

'The sooner I can take her home, the better,' he rationalised.

'Absolutely.' The radiographer was fine with that, but
as Stacey had been the one to admit Nell officially, given
that Pierce was her brother, it was up to her to sign the
necessary forms.

'Can I stay with her?' Jasmine's sullen tones were directed at Stacey.

'Sure. You'll need to get off her bed when we wheel
it, but that would be great, Jazzy. Thanks.'

'Yes. Thanks for keeping Nell company,' Pierce added,
placing one hand on Stacey's shoulder and smiling gratefully at Jasmine.

As they watched, Jasmine's gaze seemed to hone in
on Pierce's hand before she glared at them both and carefully slid from Nell's bed. She glanced towards the door,
then back to Nell, as though she really wanted to bolt, to
leave, to be anywhere except where she was right now.
But she also knew that wasn't at all fair to Nell. Instead,
she gave Stacey one more glare before pointedly refusing to look at her any more.

'I am completely perplexed by her behaviour,' Stacey
told Pierce quietly as they stood off to one side in the
plaster room, watching as Nell had her ankle plastered

into position. The young woman was delighted to have chosen a pink cast, but the decision had only come after a lot of debate and discussion with Jasmine.

'I think I know what might be causing it,' he remarked.

'Really?' Stacey turned to look at him.

'It's me.' Pierce took his time, turning his head from what was happening to his sister to look at Stacey. 'She resents my presence.'

'No. She was like this before you and I…you know…'

That small, sexy smile twitched at the corner of his mouth and she was instantly swamped with a flood of tingles, which then set off a chain reaction of sparks igniting in every part of her being.

'Before you and I…what?' he asked, his tone deep and intimate.

'Pierce.' She playfully hit his arm, feeling highly self-conscious and trying to stop her cheeks from blushing.

His warm chuckle surrounded her and she couldn't help but sigh at the sound. How was it he could make her feel so completely feminine with just one look, one sound, one touch? 'It's nice to see your smile,' she whispered.

'You didn't answer my question,' he continued, his deep drawl thrilling her so much that another wave of tingles surrounded her.

Stacey met and held his gaze, wanting to capture moments like this when he seemed less burdened, more playful, less troubled, more sexy.

'Before you and I…?' he proffered as a lead-in.

'Became…*involved*,' she finished, and smiled at him.

'Involved, eh?'

Stacey giggled, but Pierce nodded towards Jasmine.

'See? As soon as you laughed she glared across at us. She doesn't like me.'

'She doesn't *know* you,' Stacey remarked.

Still, it probably wouldn't be a bad idea if she tried once more to talk to Jasmine, to try and get her to open up. Perhaps with everything that had happened today the pressure might have built up enough for the teenager to explode.

'Jazzy's a lot like me. Cora says that's why we clash. We both store our stress in a bottle—shoving everything down, adding pressure to stop things from affecting us. But in the end those bottles become too full and the pressure gets too great, so that one tiny little innocuous event ends up having an over-dramatic and out-of-proportion response.'

'So in order to deal with this it's best to let her "explode"?'

'It's best to let her proverbial *bottle* explode, to release the pressure—because once the pressure's released only then is there any room for the clean-out to begin.'

'Your psychology professors would have been thrilled with such an explanation.'

'Shh,' she chided. 'This is how I've explained it to Jasmine over the years, so she can hopefully begin to understand what's happening to her and start to deal with the small things by herself.'

'Will she see a psychologist?'

Stacey shook her head. 'I've tried.'

'Would you mind if I had a go?' he asked as the plaster technician began tidying up, now Nell's ankle was firmly secured in the pink plaster cast. 'Why don't I take Jasmine to the pharmacy to pick up a pair of crutches? You can organise the paperwork for Nell's discharge. We'll meet you back in the ED.'

'OK. It's just as well you're here, because otherwise Nell would have needed to stay in overnight for observation.'

The words were nothing more than a throwaway comment as Stacey reluctantly left his side and headed towards Nell and Jasmine. As he'd presumed, Jasmine was a little reluctant to spend any time alone with him, but when Nell seemed eager to have her collect her crutches Jasmine agreed.

'Thanks again for staying with Nell,' Pierce started as they walked along the hospital corridor.

'Yeah.'

'She doesn't have many close friends.'

'But she goes to work. She has a job.'

'A job that has been carefully structured in order to keep Nell's world as smooth as possible. A lot of the people who work with her are nice and polite, but they're not really her friends—or not what you and I might call friends.'

'I don't have *any*.'

Instead of contradicting her, telling her she had a lot of people who cared about her, who loved her, he didn't say anything. Jasmine looked at him expectantly, a little puzzled as to why he hadn't stated the obvious.

They walked on in silence until they reached the pharmacy. Pierce handed over the request for the crutches and when they had them they set off back the way they'd come.

'Ever been on crutches?' Pierce asked, a slight lift to his eyebrow.

'No.'

He smiled. 'Want to have a turn?'

Jasmine looked at him with stunned amazement. 'But I can't. They're Nell's.'

'Not yet.'

'Stacey will get mad.'

'I don't think so.' Pierce shook his head. 'Don't be too hard on your sister. Her life isn't all that easy.'

'But she's got everything she wants. She wanted to move back to Newcastle, so we did. She wanted to open up our dad's old surgery, so she did. She wanted to find a husband, so she did.' Jasmine gestured angrily to him.

Pierce's eyes widened a bit at the last statement but he didn't say anything. Instead he stopped walking and Jasmine followed suit, crossing her arms in front of her and adopting a stance that indicated she just didn't care.

He adjusted the height of the crutches so they were right for Jasmine and held them out to her. 'Here you go. They don't sit directly under your armpits, just a little lower. There. That's it.' He gave her some basic instructions to follow and waited for her to accept the crutches.

Her wide eyes conveyed her scepticism but she did as he'd suggested, fitting the crutches into place and then starting off carefully, keeping both feet on the ground while she adjusted to the feel of these foreign objects.

'Sometimes,' he said as they started slowly along the corridor, 'we all need a little help. Even Stacey.'

'Stacey's perfect. Always has been.'

'Stacey's heart is breaking.'

'Why? What did you do?' Jasmine's snarl was instant and she nearly overbalanced on the crutches. She concentrated and righted herself.

'*I* didn't hurt her.'

'Not yet.' The angry words were out of Jasmine's mouth before she could stop them. 'You'll hurt her. Robert hurt her.' Jasmine swallowed, starting to choke up a little. 'I heard her crying once. She thought everyone was asleep but I wasn't. She was in pain.' Jasmine angrily brushed a tear from her eyes. 'I don't want to be in pain like that. *Ever*. I'm going to be stronger than Stacey.

I'm going to make sure that no one can make me cry. I'm going to make sure that I can stand on my own two feet and not need anyone else to prop me up. Like Nell, I'll be independent.'

'That sounds very lonely.'

'Nell's not lonely.'

'Because she allows other people to help her.' He indicated the crutches. 'It's all about balance.'

As he said the words to Jasmine he wondered if his own life was out of balance. Certainly today's events had jolted things a little.

Pierce waited for a moment, then started walking slowly again. Jasmine followed, still using the crutches. 'Have you ever asked Stacey why she was crying?'

'No.'

'Why not?'

'Because…because…' Jasmine started to pick up her pace on the crutches, hopping along quite confidently now. 'She wouldn't tell me anyway. I'm just a *kid*. They all stop talking when I come into the room. They hate me.'

'Maybe they're protecting you. Show them you're ready to listen.'

'How do I do that?'

Pierce grinned widely. 'You're a smart girl, Jasmine. You'll figure it out.' Then he looked up and down the corridor. 'Hey,' he said conspiratorially. 'There aren't many people in the corridor. Want to see how fast you can go on those crutches?'

Jasmine stared at him with shocked delight. 'Can I do that?'

Pierce waved her words away. 'Why not? Look around you. Assess the risks.' He ticked the points off on his fingers. 'And stop before you fall over.'

Jasmine smiled brightly, reminding him a lot of her gorgeous big sister. 'Isn't it silly?'

'Sometimes a bit of silly is good for the soul. Ready?'

The teenager nodded and checked the long corridor to make sure she wouldn't be getting in anyone's way.

'OK. Go!'

Pierce walked beside Jasmine, keeping well clear of the crutches. By the time they neared the ED Jasmine was laughing. He looked up and saw Stacey standing in the corridor, watching her sister use the crutches, watching her sister laughing. Stacey grasped her hands to her chest in delight. However, the instant Jasmine saw her sister she lost her rhythm and would have come a cropper if Pierce hadn't been there to steady her.

'Well done!' He picked up the crutch she'd dropped and accepted the other one from her as Jasmine quickly tried to school herself back into sullen teenager pose number one.

Stacey came over and placed her hands on Jasmine's shoulders. 'Are you OK?'

'Fine.'

Jasmine tried to shrug Stacey's hands away, but this time Stacey wasn't letting her. Instead she pulled Jasmine close, wrapping her arms around her sister.

'It's so good to see you laughing again. I've missed that sound so much.'

'You're not mad?'

'Mad?' Stacey pulled back. 'Why would I be mad?'

'Because I was being silly with the crutches.'

Stacey looked at Pierce and then back to her sister. 'Well, sometimes a little bit of silliness is good for the soul.'

'Here.' Pierce held the crutches out to Jasmine. 'Why

don't you take these to Nell? You can demonstrate how to use them, but don't let her have a go on them just yet.'

'OK.' Jasmine accepted the crutches, a little perplexed as to why she was being given such responsibility, but doing it nevertheless.

'The nurse is with Nell,' Stacey remarked, jerking her thumb over her shoulder. 'I've signed the papers, so as soon as Nell is ready she can go home.'

'Thank you.'

'No.' Stacey slid her arms around his waist and hugged him close, not caring who saw them or what anyone said. Pierce had helped Jasmine to laugh again, and that not only filled Stacey with hope for her sister but also filled her heart with love for this wonderful, caring and clever man. 'Thank *you*.'

Pierce wrapped his arms around her, delighted she didn't seem to care who saw them. Given the eventful day they'd had thus far, everyone he cared about was safe. Yet there was one niggling thought that continued to churn around in his mind.

'I didn't hurt her.'

'Not yet.'

Jasmine fully expected him to hurt Stacey, to break Stacey's heart…and he had the sinking feeling she might be right.

CHAPTER TEN

THANKFULLY NELL RESPONDED well to the analgesics Stacey had prescribed, so now she was asleep, her plastered leg propped up on a few pillows, Pierce was able to relax a little. Jasmine was insisting on sleeping over in the spare bed in Nell's room.

'I'm not leaving her,' Jasmine said in a stage whisper when Stacey tried to beckon her from the room. 'I want to make sure she's OK through the night.'

Jasmine raised her chin defiantly and crossed her arms over her chest, almost daring Stacey to forcibly remove her. Instead Stacey's eyes filled with tears of pride, and for the second time in as many hours she hauled her sister close in an embracing hug.

'You're such a little warrior. I love that about you.' Stacey sniffed and then released Jasmine. 'Of course you must stay. I'm so proud that you want to—so proud of the way you protect Nell. Thank you, Jaz.' Stacey cleared her throat before making sure the spare bed in Nell's room was made up. 'Just sleep in your clothes and I'll bring you over some clean ones in the morning. Call me if you need anything.' She waited while Jasmine climbed into the bed. 'Is your phone charged?'

'Yeah.' Jasmine's puzzled eyes continued to stare at Stacey. 'Why are you being so nice to me?'

Stacey laughed a little at that and bent to kiss Jasmine's forehead. 'Because I love you, silly.'

With that, Stacey left the two girls to sleep, having already said goodnight to Samantha, who'd been very eager to get to her own bed after such a hectic day.

'Cup of tea?' Pierce asked as she walked into the kitchen.

'Yes, please.'

In silence he made the tea, both of them lost in their thoughts. 'Shall we sit on the veranda?' he asked, and when she nodded he carried their cups outside. Stacey sat down on the porch swing before accepting the cup from him.

They sat there for a while, with the clear night sky spread before them. When she'd finished her tea Pierce took her cup from her and slipped his arm around her shoulders. Stacey leaned closer, more than content to snuggle close to the man who had stolen her heart. Closing her eyes, she breathed him in, wanting to memorise every detail, every sensation he evoked within her. How was it possible she'd ever thought herself in love before?

With Pierce, she felt…*complete*. And because of that she felt confident. She didn't care who saw them together, who commented on their relationship or where things might end up. Pierce had helped her to realise she was a good person, and that at times she was too hard on herself, mentally berating herself when things didn't work out the way she'd envisioned. He made her feel like a person of worth, someone *he* wanted to spend his time with, to share his life with.

As she sat there, relaxing in his arms, allowing herself to dream of a perfect future side by side with Pierce, she felt him tense. 'What is it?' she murmured softly.

'Huh?'

'You just tensed.'

'Oh. Did I?' He shifted on the porch swing, almost overbalancing them. Forcing a laugh, he stood up and walked out to the garden. The grass was soft beneath his feet. Soon summer would come, the grass would dry and turn brown, but for now, thanks to the lovely spring weather they'd enjoyed, everything was good. 'I was just thinking about Nell…about how things could have been worse.'

'But they weren't.'

'I know, I know. But worrying about her is a hard habit to break.' He exhaled harshly. 'There are just so many things that will need to change now, and any change can trigger a decline into tantrums. She becomes so single-minded, she can't understand why I can't change things back.'

He spread his arms wide.

'When our parents died she kept demanding I go and pick them up. For months, Stacey. *Months.* Every single day. And every single day when I had to tell her that I couldn't do it, that I couldn't just get in my car and go and pick them up like she wanted me to, my heart would break. Months this went on.'

'Oh, Pierce.' Stacey stood and walked over to him, wrapping her arms about his waist and hugging him close. 'What you must have gone through—and here I am complaining about Jasmine's attitude when really I have nothing to complain about at all.'

'Your challenges are different, but you still have every right to complain, Stace.' His tone was gentle as he dropped a kiss to her head, but then he unhooked her arms from about his waist and walked further into the shadows of the night. 'My mind is trying to process everything, trying to consider every angle, every contingency that needs to be put in place in order to make Nell's recovery as smooth as possible.'

'I know everything's a bit of a jumble now, but it'll work itself out.'

'What if she endures a setback? What if this event means she's unable to live independently?'

'Well, Samantha's here now, and Loris is due to move in within the next few weeks, isn't she?'

'Yes, but that is also change. And too much change…' He stopped and sighed again.

Stacey watched him for a moment, her mind trying to process what he was saying. She understood that too much variety wasn't good for Nell, but things wouldn't always go to plan in the future—wasn't it best simply to deal with things as and when they arose? In fact, now that she thought about it, with Nell's second housemate due to move in soon it would mean that the three-bedroom home was quite full.

'Where are you planning to live?' The question left her lips before she could stop it and she quickly tried to explain. 'Sorry. I'm blurting things out again. But it just occurred to me that once Nell's other housemate moves in there'll be no room for you.'

'Correct. Initially I planned to rent somewhere nearby— just a one-bedroom flat—until after Christmas, and then I was due to head overseas.'

'But you're not going now?' Even as she said the words the thought of Pierce living on the other side of the world choked at her heart.

'I haven't planned on it. And I'm glad I *did* turn down the job when they re-offered it to me.'

'When, exactly, did they approach you?'

'They emailed me a few weeks ago and asked me to start next month.'

'What did you say?'

'I said no, of course.'

She frowned as she thought things through. 'How long have they been offering you this position?'

Pierce shook his head and walked towards the flowerbeds. 'Does it matter?' He bent down and breathed in the scent of the flowers.

'Yes, it does.'

At the insistence in her voice, he turned to face her. 'Why?'

'Because it's clear to see that you leaving and working alongside such an accomplished research team, working through a lot of the questions still surrounding adult autism, is something close to your heart. If they've been holding this job for you, offering it to you on a regular basis for years, then it's important that you go.'

As she spoke the words out loud Stacey felt as though she'd just plunged a knife through her own heart.

When Pierce didn't say anything, she swallowed and forced herself to continue. 'You write articles for them. You research on your own with limited resources. Just think of all the good you could do working alongside those other brilliant minds, utilising their funding, pooling your knowledge, making a real difference in the way society at large treats adults who are trying to integrate permanently into a normal functioning world.'

Pierce's answer was simply to shake his head.

'Hang on. You said you turned the job down a few weeks ago?'

'That's right and after tonight's events, I'm glad I did.'

'Why did you turn it down? Isn't this your dream job?'

Pierce looked up at the star-lit sky for a moment, but before he could speak Stacey continued. 'Did you turn it down because of my medical practice?'

'I promised to help you until the end of the year, when Cora returns.'

'And I thank you for that. But it sounds to me as though the university wants you desperately, Pierce. And if that's the case, then go.' She tried to stop her voice from breaking on the last word and quickly cleared her throat in case he'd heard. 'I can get a locum in.'

'I *am* your locum, and I take my responsibilities seriously.'

'So do I—and I will not be the one to stand in the way of you accepting your dream job.'

Pierce stared at her as though she'd grown another head. 'Are you trying to get rid of me?'

Stacey closed her eyes, glad that it was dark and he couldn't see the tears she was desperately trying to hold back. 'If I have to.' She breathed in slowly, then let it out, unable to believe what she was about to say. 'If I have to fire you in order to get you to take that job then I will.' There was determination in her tone.

'But what about Nell?'

Stacey clenched her jaw, knowing that what she was about to do was for his own good. 'You've put everything in place as far as Nell is concerned, and while her fractured ankle might be a bit of a setback, and bring its own new level of logistics, you've still taught her how to cope with big changes. Plus it's not as though you'd be leaving tomorrow. I'll help you organise things, and we will be there for Nell, helping her every step of the way. Shortfield Family Medical Practice isn't only her closest GP surgery but my family and I are also her friends. We love Nell.'

'I know.' Pierce walked towards her and placed his hands on her shoulders. 'And I thank you, Stacey. I thank you from the bottom of my heart for the way you genuinely love my little sister.' He looked down into her face, half in shadow, half lit by the glow of the moon. 'You look so beautiful. You *are* so beautiful—not only physically but also within your heart.' He shook his head. 'You've changed my life and…and…it would be wrong of me to leave.'

'You have to.' She bit her lip to stop herself from crying. It was breaking her heart to say these words to him, especially when the last thing she really wanted was for him to leave her.

'No. Catherine left me to further her career, and I thought it was incredibly selfish of her. It's just a job, Stacey. I'm not going to sacrifice what's important to me simply because of a job.'

'You couldn't be selfish if you tried, Pierce. And where Catherine's concerned you've told me yourself she's done amazing work, helped so many people. But when you think back to your relationship, perhaps she simply used her career as an excuse because she knew deep down inside that things weren't right.' She swallowed. 'I lied to myself where Robert was concerned, telling myself he'd change after we were married, that I could live with my career always playing second fiddle to his, that I could be restrained as far as being demonstrative in my love for him went. I was willing to settle and it was wrong of me. Robert hurt me when he left me at the altar, and I wish he'd been more upfront with me, telling me his decision *before* I left for the church, but in hindsight his selfish actions saved us both from a lifetime of misery.'

She closed her eyes again, a single tear falling from her lashes to roll down her cheek.

'I couldn't bear it if you always regretted putting me before this job.'

She trembled when Pierce brushed the tear from her cheek.

'I won't.'

'You can't say that. It's been your dream, and you've already devoted so much of your time to it. I've read the articles you've written and you can do so much more with the research team behind you.' She looked up at him, not caring that a few more tears slid down her cheeks. 'Go. Do the work you're meant to do.'

'But, Stacey—'

'No. You're fired, Pierce.'

'You're not serious.' He laughed without humour as she stepped away from his touch.

'I am.'

'No. You're just doing this because you think it's the right thing to do. Well, you can't push me into this decision, Stacey. I'll be turning up to work next week, same as always.'

'No, you won't.'

'But you won't be able to cope.'

'Of course I'll cope. I'm the queen of coping.' She sniffed and brushed away a few of the tears from her cheeks. 'I know what it's like to work in your dream job. I'm doing it right now. Running my dad's old medical practice has been my dream since I was fourteen years old, and although my selfishness might have caused some of my family members—namely Jasmine—a lot of pain, the thrill of finally being where I'm meant to be, of achieving those life-long goals—'

She broke off and smiled.

'It's…amazing. For the first time in my life I know I'm exactly where I need to be and it feels great.' She shook her head. 'I won't be the one to deny *you* experiencing that same sensation, and I'm sure if Nell had a full grasp of the situation then she wouldn't want that either. Both of you have worked so hard to get her to this stage of independent living. Years and years of work, and Nell is ready for you to go. It's what she's expecting and you risk confusing her further if you *don't* go.'

Before he could say another word she turned and headed into the house, wiping at her eyes in order to clear her vision. She located her bag and car keys before turning and heading back out again.

'You're leaving?' Pierce was half on the veranda, half on the threshold as she walked past him.

'I need to.' Before she made a complete fool of herself and begged him not to listen to a word she was saying.

'Stacey—wait.'

She unlocked her car and put her bag inside before turning to face him, the driver's door between them.

'What about us? Isn't what we feel for each other worth pursuing?'

She reached out and placed a hand to his cheek, determined she wouldn't cry. 'If you love someone, set them free.' She smiled lovingly at the man who had stolen her heart, now and for ever more. 'You are going to be amazing. You are going to achieve such great things—and those great things are going to help so many people. I could never stand in the way of that.'

Her voice broke, and before she completely lost her resolve to set him free she turned from him, climbed into the car, shut the door and started the engine.

'Stacey!'

She tried not to hear the pleading in his tone as she carefully reversed out of the driveway, only belatedly remembering to switch on her headlights. Even though they lived only a few blocks from each other she still had to pull over to wipe her tear-filled eyes because she couldn't see properly.

When she reached her house she headed quietly for her bedroom and, uncaring that she hadn't changed or brushed her teeth, she lay down on her bed and allowed the tears to fall. She loved him. She loved Pierce with all her heart. But she could never live with herself if he sacrificed his own dreams for her. His dreams were his, and he deserved the chance to achieve them.

'If you love someone, set them free. If they come back to you, they're yours. If they don't, they never were.' She recited the quote into her pillow, hoping amongst hope that one day Pierce would return to her—because she would always be waiting for him.

'Good morning, sleepy-head,' Molly remarked as she came into Stacey's bedroom. 'Or should I say good afternoon?' Molly put a cup of tea on the bedside table, then walked to the window, where she opened the blind to let a bit of midday light flood into the room.

'What?' A groggy Stacey lifted her head from the pillow, trying to open her bleary eyes. 'What time is it?' She put out a hand to search for her bedside clock, but nearly upset the cup of tea in the process.

'Steady on. It's half-past twelve.'

'Oh, my goodness—Jasmine!' Stacey sat bolt upright in bed. 'I was supposed to take her clean clothes and pick her up hours ago.'

'Chillax, sis. It's fine. Jaz called and asked if she could stay until later this afternoon. She said she was having fun helping Nell adjust and teaching her, with Samantha's help, how to use the crutches properly. Still, I thought you were probably going to go and check on Nell anyway, and besides, it gives you more time to play cutesey kissey-face with Pierce.' Molly grasped her hands theatrically to her chest and then sighed dramatically. 'Oh, most beloved, take me in your arms and kiss me until I see stars.'

'Knock it off, Molly.' Stacey slumped back down onto the pillows.

'Wait. I know *that* tone. What's wrong?' Molly came over and sat on Stacey's bed. 'What's happened?'

'It's over.'

'Between you and Pierce? But how? But why? But yesterday everything was peachy.'

'I'm not sure I want to talk about it right now, Molly.' Stacey rested her hand across her eyes. 'Would you mind doing Nell's check-up when you pick up Jasmine?'

'Isn't that the coward's way out? Besides, Nell will be expecting you.'

'Ugh!' Stacey picked up a spare pillow and put it over her face, yelling her frustration into it.

She knew Molly had a point—that Nell would be confused if Stacey didn't turn up to do the check-up and right now the last thing Nell needed was to have even more instability—but the thought that Stacey would probably bump into Pierce when she went was something she simply didn't want to face right now.

Molly lifted the pillow off her. 'I *hate* always doing what's right. I hate it, Molly.'

'Are you afraid you'll see Pierce when you go?'

'Of course I am.' Stacey flicked back the bedcovers and stepped out of bed, heading to the bathroom. When she came back it was to find Molly sipping at the teacup. 'I thought that was for me.'

'You're clearly in no mood to drink a relaxing cup of peppermint tea. You need coffee, my soul sister, so why don't you have a shower and I'll make you one? Then

George, Lydia and I, along with the rabbits as a diversion for Nell, will come with you to the Brolins' house and run interference for you so that you don't have to speak to Pierce.'

Stacey relaxed a little and rushed over to hug her sister, almost making Molly spill the tea. 'Thank you. I knew I could count on you.'

'Always.'

Stacey got dressed and had something to eat, while Molly organised the children and the animals, then drove them all round to Nell's house.

'I just love walking up this path,' Molly said. 'It really does bring back so many wonderful memories. I'm glad someone we love is living in this house and making it her home. It's like the house is ready to make the next generation of memories.'

Stacey didn't reply. She was too focused on looking around the garden, half expecting Pierce to pop out from behind a bush, wearing the same gardening clothes he'd been wearing that first day she'd met him. It seemed so long ago, yet in reality she'd known Pierce for less than two months. Still, in her heart it felt as though she'd known him for a lot longer.

When she entered the house she looked around quickly, but still there was no sign of him. Jasmine and Nell were seated at the table, doing some puzzles. Samantha was in the kitchen baking.

'I like baking when I'm feeling stressed or a little out of sorts,' the woman told them as she checked the cupcakes she had in the oven. 'Besides, I know these ones are Nell's favourite, because when I bring them to work she tells me they're her favourite, so I thought, why not make some to help cheer her up?'

'Good idea,' Stacey remarked, smiling as Nell's eyes

lit up upon seeing the rabbits, as well as George and Lydia but more so the rabbits. Stacey wasn't going to ask where Pierce was, or even if he was there. She was just going to do her job and then, if Molly wanted to chat, Stacey would head next door to check on Mike and Edna. But thankfully it was Jasmine who gave her the information she sought.

'Pierce isn't home at the moment. He got called into the hospital this morning and that's why I said I'd stay with Nell.'

'Oh.' Stacey was both relieved and disappointed at the same time. She didn't want to see Pierce and yet she yearned to see him. She loved him so much. 'Right, well…Nell, let's get your check-up over and done with. When you've finished that puzzle I need to check your blood pressure and your foot—'

'And listen to my heart?' Nell asked. 'Can I listen to my heart? Pierce sometimes lets me listen to my heart. It goes ba-dum, ba-dum.'

Stacey smiled. 'Of course you can listen to your heart.'

The check-up didn't take too long, and when Samantha asked if they'd like to stay for Sunday afternoon snack-time Molly raised a questioning eyebrow in Stacey's direction.

'Sure. Why not?' she remarked, hoping against hope that Pierce didn't return from the hospital while they were still there.

Thankfully she managed to enjoy a leisurely afternoon tea and say her goodbyes to Nell and Samantha.

Jasmine was quiet on the drive home, and it wasn't until they walked in the door and waited while George and Lydia took the rabbits back to their hutch, that she turned to Stacey and demanded, 'What's going on with you and Pierce?'

Stacey blinked, a little taken aback. 'Pardon?'

'Pierce looked half sick this morning, all pale and grey, as though he'd eaten something terrible. I asked him if he was OK and he just said, "Yeah." But I could tell there was more wrong than he was saying. And then when you came you were like a mouse being chased by a cat, and *you* looked all pale and grey, too.'

Molly placed her hands on Jasmine's shoulders, then kissed her sister's cheek. 'She's not just a pretty face.'

Jasmine merely stared at Stacey, as if to say she wasn't moving until she got an explanation.

'Well…uh…Pierce and I are…well, we're going to stop seeing each other for a while.'

'You're not going to stop me from seeing Nell?' Again there was that defiant, adamant tone.

'No. Of course not. Nell needs you—well, needs all of us—now more than ever.'

'What? What do you mean?'

Stacey took a deep breath, then looked at Molly, and then back to Jasmine. 'Pierce is heading overseas.'

'What?' Molly and Jasmine spoke in unison.

'Nell will soon be living independently, just as she's always wanted.'

'And Pierce will be free to do whatever he wants?'

There was disgust in Jasmine's tone, and Stacey held up her finger in reprimand.

'Pierce is an amazing man who has done a lot of research and written many scientific papers on the subject of adult autism—especially with regard to integration.'

'I know what integration is,' Jasmine said, before either of her sisters could explain. 'Remember the school I went to in Perth? The school I loved? My friends I loved, whether they had a disability or not?'

'Yes. Of course. Well, Pierce has been offered a job

in America and…he's going to take it. When he's there,' she went on before Jasmine could say another word, 'he'll continue his work with regard to integration with an experienced team of researchers. The work he can do there will help thousands and thousands of adults with autism to be better accepted by society.'

Jasmine pondered Stacey's words for a moment, then crossed her arms over her chest and glared at them both. 'I don't see why he has to go to America to do that,' she said, then turned and stomped off to her bedroom.

'I get the feeling Jasmine really does like him,' Molly remarked as they both braced themselves for the ritual slamming of their sister's bedroom door.

Stacey slumped down into a chair and rested her head in her hands.

'Does he have to go?' Molly's question was quiet.

'Yes.'

'Do you want him to go?'

'Yes.'

'What? Why? I thought you were in love with the man.'

Stacey lifted her head and looked at her sister. 'It's *because* I'm in love with him that I'm making him go. He deserves the chance to fulfil his own dreams just like me moving here, or you doing surgery, or Cora going to Tarparnii, or Nell living independently. Pierce has dedicated all his time and effort to Nell. He's a good man, with a big heart.'

'Will the two of you still stay together? I mean nowadays long-distance relationships aren't that difficult to maintain thanks to internet chats and emails and stuff.'

'I don't know.'

With that, Stacey stood and headed towards her own bedroom, to lie on her bed and cry some more.

CHAPTER ELEVEN

BY THE END of November Stacey was worn out. She went to work early in the morning and returned late most nights. She'd started a night clinic in an effort to catch up on the overflow of patients but also to give her time to ferry her siblings around to their various after-school activities. Most nights she collapsed into bed with exhaustion.

Molly helped at the clinic as much as she was able, but after an hour or two was often called in to the hospital, leaving Stacey and Winifred to cope with whatever patients were left.

'You can't go on like this,' Winifred said late one evening, giving Stacey a big hug. 'You'll work yourself into an early grave.'

'I know. But the new locum will start soon and then, come Christmas-time, Cora will be home.'

'It's a shame Pierce took that job in America before his contract here was up.'

'I fired him,' Stacey told her.

'What? Why would you do that?'

'Because he never would have left to follow his dreams otherwise.'

Winifred sighed and patted Stacey's arm. 'You really love him, don't you?' she stated.

'Yes.'

It was as simple and as complex as that. Yes, she loved him. Yes, she missed him. Yes, she wanted him back, to have her arms around him, to have his mouth pressed to hers.

'He'll be back before you know it,' Winifred promised. 'Go on home, love. I'll lock up.'

Stacey hoped Winifred was right—that Pierce would be back sooner rather than later. Before he'd left for the States he'd tried to contact her, but she hadn't wanted to take his calls. He'd emailed her but she hadn't wanted to read them. Cutting herself off from him was the only way she knew how to make the pain in her heart decrease.

Two weeks after Nell had broken her ankle, two weeks after Stacey had fired him and told him to head overseas, Pierce had been due to leave. The night before his flight she'd gone to bed early, not wanting to dwell on the way her heart ached for him. She'd awoken to the soft sound of someone knocking on her bedroom window and cautiously she'd peeked through the curtains, her heart swelling with love when she'd seen Pierce standing there.

Pulling on a dressing gown and slippers, she'd headed outside to see what he wanted, instantly concerned that something had happened to Nell.

'Is Nell all right?'

'Nell's fine. I'm not.' He'd hauled her into his arms and pressed his lips to hers in one swift movement that robbed her of breath. 'I've missed you these past weeks, Stacey. Why didn't you return my calls? My emails?'

'Pierce.' She tried to pull away from his arms but her efforts were half-hearted at best, because with all honesty that was the place she wanted to be the most. 'I can't do this.'

'What? Let me hold you? Let me kiss you? Stacey, I'm

not going to see you for…I don't even want to think about it. I need this—these memories—to get me through.'

'I know, but I—'

He silenced her with another heart-melting kiss, and this time Stacey couldn't help but cling to him. 'Oh, Pierce.'

'I don't know how to do this,' he told her.

'Do what?'

'Be selfish.'

'I know. You're the most giving man I've ever met.'

'And yet here I am, doing what *I* want to do.'

'For a change,' she finished. 'And, for the record, you're not being selfish. You're following your dreams and you deserve the chance to do it.'

'But what if this *isn't* my real dream? What if my dream has…changed?'

'You won't know for sure until you get to America.' She shook her head and kissed his lips. 'You'll have a great time,' she encouraged him, trying desperately to instil enthusiasm into her voice.

'It would be far greater if you were to come with me,' he said, but Stacey shook her head.

'It's not my dream, but I believe in you.'

He kissed her again. 'And that, my beautiful, wonderful, most beloved Stacey, is worth everything.'

'What time does your flight leave?' she asked.

'I need to leave for the airport in an hour.'

'Come and sit with me.' And so the two of them sat on the chairs on her small veranda, content to hold each other and look at the stars, thankful the October night was not too warm for cuddling.

When finally it came time for him to leave, Pierce kissed her with such passion that she swooned.

'Please take my calls while I'm overseas.'

'No.'

'What? Why not?'

'I can't bear to hear your voice or to see you over the internet because it'll just make me miss you more.' And she wasn't sure whether she'd be able to cope with that.

'OK, then. What about emails and text messages?'

Stacey thought about this for a moment, then nodded. 'Yes.'

'Good.' He exhaled happily before kissing her once more, then walking over to the hire car parked in her driveway.

She was glad he hadn't asked her to take him to the airport, because there was no way she'd ever be able to say goodbye to him and then watch him get onto a plane and leave her. Even this, standing in her own driveway and crying as he drove away, was bad enough.

Now, six weeks since he'd left, Stacey still found it difficult to get out of bed every morning, knowing she wouldn't be seeing him at the clinic. Her dreams were always of him, and she lived for his emails, loving the excitement she read in his words about the research he was doing and the staff he was working with.

Nell's ankle had healed nicely, and all in all she'd coped with the disruption to her usual routine quite well—so much so that she'd refused to go back to catching the bus to and from work and now had a standing arrangement with the taxi company to pick her up every morning and drop her home every afternoon.

Jasmine still went round every afternoon after school, sometimes with George and Lydia and sometimes just by herself. Then, on Friday afternoons, Nell would join the rest of the Wilton family as they all headed over to Mike and Edna's for dinner, bringing the rabbits with them.

176 DR PERFECT ON HER DOORSTEP

Mike would offer instruction and coaching in the art
of encouraging rabbits to jump higher over an obstacle.

All in all, Stacey's days were jam-packed with family
and patients and longing for Pierce, but when Decem-
ber arrived the days seemed even longer. More patients.
More ferrying her siblings to and from their various after-school events. More stress, and most of all more missing Pierce.

'Cup of tea?'

Stacey opened her eyes where she sat, slumped on
the sofa after another hard day at the clinic. She was
surprised to see Jasmine standing before her, holding a
piping hot cup of tea out to her.

'Oh, Jazzy.' Stacey was overwhelmed at the thoughtful gesture, but sat up straight and sighed with relief as
she accepted the cup. 'You are a life-saver, my gorgeous
sister. Thank you.'

Jasmine looked as though she, too, was about to burst
into tears, and after Stacey had taken the cup the teenager hesitated for a moment, before sitting down next
to Stacey.

'Mmm. That is a perfect cuppa.'

Jasmine grinned with happiness at the praise.

'It's good to see you smiling. That also helps in so
many ways.' Stacey brushed her sister's hair back from
her face. 'I've been so worried about you.'

'I was…' Jasmine bit her lip, hesitating.

Stacey waited intently.

'That day in the park, when Nell got hurt…'

'Yes?' It was a day Stacey could never forget. So much
had transpired that day. So many emotions. 'What about
it?'

'I thought I'd caused Nell to get hurt.'

'What?'

'I threw the Frisbee too far and she tried to get it, and it landed near that barbecue where the man was cooking, and if I hadn't thrown it there Nell wouldn't have been near it, and Nell getting hurt is all my fault.' Jasmine broke down into tears, covering her face with her hands.

Stacey instantly put her cup on the table and gathered her sister close. 'No. No, sweetie. It wasn't your fault. Not at all. There was absolutely no way you could have known what was going to happen. It was an accident. Not your fault at all. Oh, poor Jaz. Have you been carrying this burden with you all this time? Oh, honey.' Stacey started crying as well, feeling her sister's pain keenly.

'I was so angry at you for taking me away from my friends, for bringing us here. I wanted to punish you, and then when I saw Nell lying there...I...I...all I wanted was you. I wanted you to pick me up like you used to and cuddle me close and tell me everything would be all right.' Jasmine spoke through her tears, hiccuping now and then. 'I know Nell's OK now, but...but...'

Stacey fished around in her pockets for some tissues and managed to find two clean ones. 'I'm always here for you, Jaz. No matter what the circumstances. You're allowed to be angry with me, or Cora or Molly or any of us. You're entitled to your own emotions and to be able to show them. That's OK. We're sisters. We'll always work it out in the end because we love each other.'

'Pierce said you love me. He said that things are really difficult for you. And until he said that I hadn't really thought about it like that, you know? And now he's gone, and you're working lots, and you're really tired and you're unhappy, and I don't like seeing you like that. So I couldn't talk to you about Nell, but it was getting too much. That bottle you talk about—it was building up too much. And then...I just couldn't hold it in any more.'

A fresh bout of tears accompanied her words and Stacey held her sister, dabbing at her eyes.

'It's OK. I've got you. Everything's going to be all right,' she crooned, and after a while Jasmine stopped crying and blew her nose. Stacey followed suit and they both smiled. 'I do love you, Jaz. You're my sister. We're family. We're all we've got.'

'We've got Nell and Pierce now, too.' She covered her mouth with her hand. 'Oh, I forgot. Molly told me not to say his name around you in case it upset you too much, but—'

'It's fine. Molly's just being protective.'

'Do you need protecting?' Jasmine sat up straighter. 'Because I'll protect you, too.'

Stacey felt another wave of tears coming on—tears of happiness at seeing that fierce and determined spirit of her sister's shining forth yet again. 'Thank you. But I'm doing all right at the moment.'

'Do you miss him?'

'Of course. But it's important for people to follow their dreams.' She'd tried to keep her words strong but even she had heard the wobble in her voice. This time it was Jasmine who offered the hug, holding her big sister close, and Stacey loved every moment of it.

Jasmine sniffed. 'I love you, Stacey.'

'I love you, too. Always.' They both blew their noses again and then laughed. 'Look at us. Red eyes and red noses. We must look a sight.' Stacey stood and pulled Jasmine to her feet. 'How about some ice cream?'

'But…you haven't even had dinner.' Jasmine pointed to the kitchen. 'I've made a plate of food for you.'

'Thank you. You've been such a wonderful help. But at the moment I need ice cream. Comfort food.' Stacey headed to the kitchen. 'Want some?'

'Yeah.' Jasmine watched as her sister pulled out an ice cream tub and scooped some into bowls. 'I've never seen you like this before. All "break the rules", like.'

'Then it's about time you did.'

And that was how Molly found them an hour later, when she arrived home from the hospital, exhausted. Stacey had finished her ice cream, then eaten her dinner, and Jasmine had kept her company.

'Kids asleep?' Molly asked as she kissed her sisters on the cheek.

'Yes,' Jasmine replied. 'George put himself to bed tonight—he was so tired after his karate lesson—and Lydia fell asleep with a book still in her hands.'

They all chuckled.

'Typical Lydia,' Molly remarked as she reheated her dinner. 'Oh, I had a thought earlier today. How about next weekend we all do something together? A family activity. I'm not on call, and the kids will all be finished school for the year, so we should celebrate by doing something super-fun.'

'How about ice-skating?' Jasmine suggested.

'I'm not sure Nell knows how to ice-skate, and although her ankle has now healed I wouldn't want to risk her falling over and injuring it again.'

'Good point.' Jasmine nodded, pleased that Nell was automatically included in their family plans.

'How about bowling?' Molly suggested a moment later.

'Bowling?' Jasmine's eyes lit up. 'I used to love it when Mum took us bowling. Yeah. Let's go bowling—Nell will love it.'

'Plus,' Molly added, hugging Stacey close, 'the local bowling alley has cheesy music videos.'

Stacey grinned and hugged her sister back. 'Sounds like the perfect tonic for me. The cheesier the better.'

The following weekend, with the children excited about being on school holidays for six weeks, Stacey completed her house calls in record time—especially as Jasmine had volunteered to come along and help out. They picked Nell up from her house—Samantha and Loris declined the invitation to join them—and then went home, where they met an excited George and Lydia bouncing around in the corridor.

'Where's Molly?' Stacey asked.

'She's in the bedroom on the telephone. She said she had some loose ends to tie up.'

'Oh?' Stacey hoped her sister hadn't been called in to the hospital, but thankfully when Molly appeared a moment later she assured her sister that everything was fine and that they should head off before they missed their booking.

At the bowling alley they all enjoyed the game—Nell perhaps most of all. And seeing the delight on the young woman's face Stacey wished Pierce was there to see it. She took a photo on her phone of Nell's smiling face after she'd knocked all the pins down, then sent the picture to Pierce's phone.

'You all right?' Molly asked as she came and sat down next to Stacey while Lydia had a turn at bowling.

'Sure!' Stacey offered the word with fake bright-ness, pointing to the cheesy music video on the televi-sion monitors scattered around the bowling alley and the black lighting which made the fluorescent bowling balls stand out like neon. 'Glad I didn't wear white or I'd be glowing brightly under these lights, but the music videos are definitely worth it. Oh, the eighties! Those fashions! That hair!'

'It's fun.'

'It is. It was a good idea, Molly. Thank you.' Stacey hugged her sister.

'Uh…well, you may not want to thank me too much.'

Molly whispered the words in Stacey's ear and she felt a prickle of apprehension work its way down her spine. Stacey eased back and looked at her sister.

'Why?' she asked cautiously.

'Um…well…' The music video changed on the screen and Molly pointed to it. 'Look. Let's watch this one. Hey, kids. Let's watch this music video.'

'What's going on? Why are you acting so stran—?' Stacey wasn't able to finish her sentence as her eyes widened at what she was seeing on the television monitors.

It was Pierce. Larger than life. On every single television monitor in the bowling alley.

'What? But…how?'

Then she stared in utter shock as he started lip-syncing to one of her favourite songs—a song about love, trust and dedication to each other.

'Pierce made you a cheesy video,' Molly remarked quietly.

'He…*what*?'

'Just watch.'

And she did as Pierce, dressed in an all-white suit, holding a large bunch of red roses, was seen to be looking high and low for his one true love, searching for her everywhere, singing to the camera, his handsome face radiating an earnest and honest desire to find her. Stacey's jaw dropped open in stunned disbelief as she watched him knocking on the door to her house, but receiving no reply.

'When was this filmed? And…*how*?'

'We live in an age of digital technology, Stace,' Jasmine offered.

'Yeah. It's not hard,' George added, like the wise old man he was.

Nell was clapping along in time to the music, thoroughly delighted at seeing her big brother on the television. At the end of the video Pierce was still searching, and there was a shot of him walking to the front of the bowling alley. Stacey sat up straighter in her chair—then the television monitors went blank. But the music continued playing over the loudspeakers.

Now everyone in the bowling alley had stopped bowling and they were all pointing and gasping in delight as the man from the video walked into the bowling alley, dressed in the pure white suit which became bright white beneath the black lights. He still carried the enormous bunch of red roses—Stacey's favourite—and headed slowly in her direction.

She stood, belatedly realising she was trembling. When he reached her side he smiled at her and held out the roses. A few people around them started clapping, but Stacey didn't hear them. All she was aware of was Pierce, standing before her, smiling brightly and placing the roses into her arms. What did it all mean?

She didn't have to wait long to find out.

When the music ended Pierce held out his hand for hers. Stacey shifted the roses onto one arm and gave him her hand, loving the feel of her hand securely in his. She bit her lip, her heart pounding with love for the man before her.

'Stacey. I've missed you so very much. Too much to be apart from you any longer. You encouraged me to follow my dreams and you were right when you said I'd feel a strong sense of accomplishment when I was finally in the right job in the right place at the right time…and that dream job is working alongside you in a small family-run GP clinic in Shortfield.'

'What?' She gaped at him. 'But what about Yale and your research and—?'

'All still good. All still happening. But happening on both sides of the world. I'm setting up a sister study at Newcastle General Hospital. I'll work part-time there and part-time with you at the clinic…but I'll be working *full time* in the best relationship, the happiest relationship I've ever had the pleasure to be in.' He shook his head slowly from side to side and gazed down into her eyes. 'I've missed you, Stacey. So much it started to physically hurt to be so far away from you.'

'Oh!' Stacey tried to blink back tears of happiness, not wanting to miss a second of seeing his handsome face, of hearing his perfect words.

Then, to her further astonishment, he released her hand for a moment to unbutton his white suit jacket, revealing a white T-shirt beneath. On the T-shirt was painted, in fluorescent pink writing, the words *Will you marry me?*

He went down on bended knee and took her hand in his again. 'I love you, Stacey, and I intend to spend the rest of my life showing you that. I adore you. Please, will you do me the honour of becoming my wife?'

Stacey opened her mouth to speak but found her words choked with pure emotion, so she quickly nodded and tugged him to his feet, desperate to have his lips pressed against hers. 'Yes,' she finally whispered, just before he kissed her.

'I've missed you,' he returned. 'I love you. So very much.'

'You are my everything,' she told him, smiling with

happiness when he tenderly brushed away a few escaped tears with his thumb.

Then somehow the flowers were removed from her arms and Pierce was hugging her close, kissing her passionately in front of anyone and everyone who happened to be in the bowling alley. The round of applause and whoops of joy from their siblings went unnoticed as both Stacey and Pierce only had eyes for each other.

'How did you like the music video?' he eventually asked when Nell had insisted on finishing her bowling game.

Stacey sat on her fiancé's lap, her arms around his neck as though never letting him go again.

'Cheesy enough for you?' He chuckled.

'It was the perfect blend of tacky and ridiculousness. I can't believe you went to so much trouble just for me.'

'You're worth it.' He shook his head again.

'I still can't believe you're here. You're actually *here*. When did you fly in?'

Pierce checked his watch. 'About three hours ago. I had the idea for the video and Molly helped make it happen. We knew you'd be out on house calls this morning, so it seemed the perfect opportunity to do all the photography then.'

'But I still don't know how it was edited together so fast and—' She held up her hand. 'You know what? I don't want to know.' She pressed a kiss to Pierce's lips. 'I just want to enjoy.'

It was a lot of kisses later when Stacey looked deeply into his eyes and said softly, 'You once told me you could see loneliness in my eyes, my sad eyes, and it was true. It was there because something was missing from my life—something just for me, something precious and rare. And that's you. You were what was missing from my life.'

'Marry me soon, Stacey,' he remarked as he kissed her yet again, unable to get enough of her delectable mouth.

'Of course. And that, my love, will be a definite dream come true.'

EPILOGUE

THE WEDDING WAS held outside in Nell's backyard a few weeks after New Year. Pierce had waited only the least amount of time it took to have their banns read before he married the woman of his dreams.

'Do you remember how we used to pretend that we'd get married in this very back garden?' Cora asked as she made the final touches to Stacey's hairstyle before putting a garland of flowers carefully in place. 'Oh!' She gasped. 'You look just like we always imagined. Like a princess at a small backyard wedding with our closest family and friends and we have Mike ready to walk you down the garden aisle, giving you away.'

Molly clutched her hands to her chest before tying Lydia's sash, which had come undone again. All of Stacey's sisters, including Nell, were with her, getting ready. George was with Pierce in the room down the hall. The wedding celebrant was an old family friend of her parents and the garden was filled with their closest friends.

'Nervous?' Jasmine asked, and Stacey wrinkled her nose.

'No. Not even worried. I get to marry Pierce today. My handsome prince. This time it's the real deal.'

Molly took one of her hands and Cora took the other,

all the triplets standing together, grinning at each other, sharing incredible emotions.

'This is right, Stace. He's so perfect for you.'

'And you're so perfect for him.'

'Thank you.' Stacey looked to the two women who had been with her for ever. They were sisters, and sisters were never wrong.

Jasmine rallied Lydia and Nell into position as Edna came in to check everyone was ready.

'Pierce is impatiently awaiting your arrival,' Edna told them as Mike came to offer Stacey his arm.

Both Edna and Mike looked at her.

'Oh, your father would have been right proud to see this day,' Mike told her.

'So proud,' Edna agreed, and kissed Stacey on the cheek. '*We're* so proud—aren't we, Mike?'

'Yes. We're proud of all of you.' Mike's gaze encompassed them all. 'And of little George, of course,' he added, which made Lydia giggle, and the sound of Lydia's giggle made the rest of them giggle too.

It was just the tension release they all needed, so that when the music started Stacey proudly took her place at the bottom of the garden.

Her smile only increased when she saw Pierce standing there, waiting expectantly for her. She floated towards him, not caring whether she walked in time to the music, not caring if anything went wrong. Pierce was looking at her as though she were the most stunning woman in the world, and she knew in her heart that was exactly what he thought because he'd told her so—quite often.

'You look...*wow*!' They were the first words out of his mouth as she came to stand beside him, her simple white sundress and flat white shoes enhanced by the wild flowers in her hair and bouquet. *Au naturel*. No fuss. No big puffy dress. Not this time. *This* was her dream wedding. Simple. Casual. Family.

'You look pretty wow yourself,' she told him as she took in his light grey suit.

'Ready to get married?'

'To you? Absolutely.'

She reached for his hand, linking her fingers with his, unable to believe such a pure, perfect happiness as this existed, and that it was a happiness that, for them, would last for ever.

* * * * *

AFTER ONE
FORBIDDEN NIGHT…

BY
AMBER McKENZIE

All rights reserved including the right of reproduction in whole
or in part in any form. This edition is published by arrangement with
Harlequin Books S.A.

This is a work of fiction. Names, characters, places, locations and
incidents are purely fictional and bear no relationship to any real
life individuals, living or dead, or to any actual places, business
establishments, locations, events or incidents. Any resemblance is
entirely coincidental.

This book is sold subject to the condition that it shall not, by way of
trade or otherwise, be lent, resold, hired out or otherwise circulated
without the prior consent of the publisher in any form of binding or
cover other than that in which it is published and without a similar
condition including this condition being imposed on the subsequent
purchaser.

® and TM are trademarks owned and used by the trademark owner
and/or its licensee. Trademarks marked with ® are registered with the
United Kingdom Patent Office and/or the Office for Harmonisation in
the Internal Market and in other countries.

First published in Great Britain 2014
by Mills & Boon, an imprint of Harlequin (UK) Limited,
Eton House, 18-24 Paradise Road, Richmond, Surrey, TW9 1SR

© 2014 Amber Whitford-McKenzie

ISBN: 978-0-263-90791-9

Harlequin (UK) Limited's policy is to use papers that are natural,
renewable and recyclable products and made from wood grown in
sustainable forests. The logging and manufacturing processes conform
to the legal environmental regulations of the country of origin.

Printed and bound in Spain
by Blackprint CPI, Barcelona

Dear Reader

Welcome back to the wonderful and tumultuous world of Boston General. As an author I fell in love with Chloe and Tate when I was creating and writing RESISTING HER EX'S TOUCH, and I knew their story could not be left untold. Chloe's feelings of unrequited love and Tate's wounded pride needed to be healed.

As a lifelong Harlequin Mills & Boon® reader I thought I had learned the perfect formula for romance. Attraction, romance, love, turmoil and resolution. AFTER ONE FORBIDDEN NIGHT... has all those ingredients, but put together a little differently. Sometimes in life even the smartest and most successful people don't know what's best for them and make the wrong choice—meet Tate. And as for Chloe, everything that makes her a wonderful physician—her knowledge, her drive, her constant need to put others ahead of herself—makes her a horrible patient and an even harder woman to claim.

A modern-day story of star-crossed lovers working through their emotions and fears while continuing to dedicate themselves to the medical profession is what this book offers, and I hope you enjoy reading it as much as I have writing it.

Amber

Dedication

To my Maebyn, who was a dream in my heart
when this book began and a reality in my arms
when it finished. Thank you for teaching me the joys
and discomforts of pregnancy and motherhood.
It's been an incredible adventure that is only beginning.

A recent title by Amber McKenzie:

RESISTING HER EX'S TOUCH

**This book is also available in eBook format
from www.millsandboon.co.uk**

PROLOGUE

"DR. DARCY TO Trauma One. Dr. Darcy to Trauma One."

As always her heart began to pound and her attention became focused only on the task ahead of her. Traumas were the scariest and most rewarding part of emergency medicine. By moving and thinking quickly you could become the difference between life and death, and chief emergency resident Chloe Darcy was always half terrified and half exhilarated by the challenge.

She ran to the trauma bay and arrived as the paramedics were wheeling a patient in on a gurney. She took in the unconscious pale thin girl as the paramedics gave their report.

"Twenty-two-year-old female found unconscious by her roommate with bilateral lacerations to the wrists. Estimated blood loss at the scene was minimum one and a half liters. No signs of other trauma or drugs at the scene. She left a note. Apparently heartbroken over a recent breakup. Valentine's is the worst reminder."

Foolish girl, Chloe thought to herself. *What love or man could possibly be worth killing yourself for?*

"What has she been given for resuscitation so far?" Chloe asked, focusing on the medical care of the young woman.

"Two liters of intravenous crystalloid and five hundred milliliters of colloid expander. Her pressure has improved marginally and the pressure dressings have stemmed some of the loss."

"Thanks, we'll take it from here."

The trauma team was a well-oiled machine, with a nursing team and a respiratory therapist working with Chloe to stabilize the young woman. It took thirty minutes and a lot of blood products and fluid before her blood pressure started to improve and her pulse lowered. Chloe felt her own do the same. Once she was confident the resources were in place to deal with additional bleeding, Chloe unwrapped the first wrist pressure bandage.

The deep lacerations exposed multiple cut vessels, tendons and nerves. The girl had really meant it, and if hadn't been for her roommate she would have succeeded.

"Page whoever is on call for Vascular and tell them we need them now." Chloe didn't have time to talk on the phone. The unwrapping of the wound had led to another half-liter blood loss and she had to focus on getting her as stable as possible prior to the operating room.

As Chloe stood above the girl, holding as tightly to the pressure bandage as she could, she felt a change in the room and calm passed over her. She looked up as Dr. Tate Reed entered. As always, her heart stopped momentarily as she took him in. His tall stature and muscular frame was surprisingly well defined beneath the hospital scrubs. His most striking features, his cool mineral-green eyes, were directed right at her.

She was surprised to see him. Normally she would have gotten the general surgery resident responsible for the vascular service, not the attending vascular surgeon. She swallowed and tried to focus on her responsibility and duty to her patient.

"What do you have, Chloe?" His voice was both confident and undemanding. He walked over to stand directly beside her while she continued to hold pressure on the volatile wound.

"Twenty-two-year-old female. Attempted suicide with bilateral wrist lacerations. Total blood loss estimated at two liters. Both cuts are deep and involve all the major vessels, nerves and tendons."

She began to unwrap the wrist so he could examine the patient for himself, when his hand came down on her bare forearm.

"Don't unwrap it, I trust you," he confided.

He looked at her one more time before moving his hand and speaking to the room. "I'll book her as level E0 emergency. Please have her ready for the operating room in the next ten minutes. I'll need another five units of blood typed and crossed and sent directly to the operating room."

With a final glance in her direction he left. She stood still, focused only on holding pressure for several moments before she regained her momentum. "Type and cross for the five units. She'll need a Foley catheter to monitor urinary output and we need to notify the plastic surgeon on call that he will be needed after Dr. Reed finishes the vascular repair."

As promised, the operating room was ready for her patient within ten minutes, and only as the young woman was being wheeled into the actual operating theater did Chloe let go her hold on the injured wrist.

When she returned to the emergency department she was grateful that there were only twenty minutes left of her shift and that she wasn't obligated to start with any new patients. It hurt her to think about the girl. How bad did you have to feel before you would go to that length to escape? How much pain did you have to be in to make the idea of cutting yourself open feel better? The only comfort Chloe had was that the girl was with Tate now, and he would at least be able to make her physically better.

Chloe finished her charting and paperwork and then went upstairs to the operating room waiting area to wait for news. The only part of emergency medicine she struggled with was the lack of continuity. She would often see patients, diagnose them, arrange for their care, but rarely learned about outcomes—and it bothered her. It was like starting a book but never finishing it, and she never felt able to accept the not knowing. Some of her evaluations had cited this as a criticism. The amount of extra time and effort she spent following up on patients was not insignificant, but it was always her own time, so those who did not like it just had to deal with it—it was who she was.

It was eleven in the evening before Tate emerged into the main operating corridor. "Why am I not surprised to see you?" he commented as he came to sit on the chair next to her, pulling the scrub cap from his head and running his fingers through his short-cropped dark blond hair. There was no censure in his voice, and he looked tired but not displeased at the sight of her.

"How is she?" Chloe asked, focusing on the reason she was there—for the girl, not for Tate.

"Stable. She was well-resuscitated prior to arrival, which helped. They were all clean cuts, which made the re-anastomosis easier. Plastics is with her now. They will be there for a couple of hours, then time will tell how much function she gets back in her hands."

"Damn," she said aloud, unable to comprehend how this girl was going to cope both physically and emotionally when she awoke.

"Any idea why she did it?" Tate asked, once again

demonstrating the compassion that set him apart from many of his surgical colleagues.

"Happy Valentine's Day," Chloe responded, unable to keep the sarcasm and scorn out of her voice.

"Ah," Tate replied, obviously oblivious to the holiday. "I didn't get you anything."

The comment surprised her, but when she looked back at Tate his signature sarcastic humor glinted in the smile on his face. He had a slight curl in his lip, fitting against the sharp angle of his jaw and the clean lines of his face. She couldn't help but smile back at him.

"I'd settle for a glass of wine," she responded, and smiled until the expression on his face changed.

His smile had vanished and he was staring at her, but what he was seeing or thinking she had no idea. She didn't know what to say or do to break the silence, so instead she said nothing.

"Done."

She felt her eyes widen with surprise and remained lost for words.

"But it will have to be at my place. I didn't bring street clothes to change into and I'd rather not go out in scrubs."

She took in everything about him. He was certain in his offer, and for that reason alone she agreed.

She watched as he opened the solid metal door to his penthouse loft. She had never been inside Tate's loft before, but wasn't surprised that the interior matched the man. There was a wall of floor-to-ceiling glass that overlooked the Charles River. In true loft style there were no partitions, with the living room flowing into the dining room and kitchen. She turned and felt her heart race and warmth pass through her when she spotted the bedroom area, which featured a king-size bed raised up on a two-step platform with an exposed stone wall as the background.

There was nothing cold about the industrial style—nothing cold at all as she admired the double-sided glass fireplace that centered the room.

Tate walked past her, his arm brushing against hers. She felt a tremor of heat pass through her and touched the area, expecting her arm to be warm. He made his way to the fridge and opened a bottle of white wine, pouring her a single glass and grabbing a beer for himself. He'd remembered what she liked and she felt the same warmth his touch had inspired run through her again.

"Make yourself at home. I'll be right back."

He gestured to the slate-gray couch that paralleled the fireplace and she did as she was told. He emerged from the closed bathroom moments later, dressed in jeans and a long-sleeved red shirt that clung to his skin, defining the muscles beneath. His feet were bare, and if she had ever doubted the magnitude of his sexuality she didn't now.

She looked at her reflection in the glass of the fireplace and for the first time in years felt dull in comparison. Her barely controllable red hair, long legs and unconcealed curves and rich emerald-green eyes typically made her stand out—but not next to Tate.

He joined her on the couch and she took a sip of the cool dry wine to calm herself. "So why is it that the most beautiful and sought-after woman in the hospital is alone on Valentine's Day?"

Beautiful? Did he really think she was the most beautiful woman in the hospital? Sought-after? Did that mean he believed the rumors that she'd used her beauty to get ahead of her peers? Looking into the cool green of his eyes, she saw no malice in the comment but she wasn't prepared to answer truthfully none the less. She was alone on Valentine's Day because the only man she was attracted to and had had feelings for in the past three years was sitting beside her and up until a few months ago had been taken by her best friend.

"I could ask you the same thing," she replied, trying to keep their conversation light and her feelings hidden. Tate was off-limits. He had been as Kate's boyfriend and he still was as Kate's ex.

"You think I'm beautiful?" He smiled, a teasing glint in his eye.

"I think you're sought-after," she answered, envisioning the trail of nurses who seemed to materialize around him.

"Not by everyone." His tone had changed and his eyes had darkened almost imperceptibly. She knew he was thinking of her best friend Kate, his ex-girlfriend—the one that had got away.

Regret and frustration coursed through her. She hadn't meant to bring up Kate, but truthfully she was always there between them. She had met Tate when he and Kate had started dating, and had been horrified when she'd realized her feelings for him went beyond friendship. It had been like a cruel torture. The closer he had become with Kate, the more she had gotten to know him, the more her feelings had grown, and the more unattainable he had become.

Kate and Tate's breakup had been bittersweet. She no longer had to conceal her feelings but she had also lost her connection to the man she was falling for.

Chloe felt as if she was burning up and moved to take off the black sweater wrap that she had layered over a long-bodied tank top. The long-sleeved tailed garment had been wrapped around her tightly against the winter cold and she felt flustered in her attempt to disentangle herself from it. Strong hands covered hers, stilling her actions, before he moved on to untying the knot in the tails, his hands sure and steady as he opened the garment and slipped it from her shoulders. In doing so the tips of his fingers brushed against her bare skin, the action causing shockwaves to course down her body. She shuddered in response.

"I thought you were too warm—are you cold?" Tate asked.

No trace of his self-defeat was left, and Chloe felt as if she had one hundred percent of his attention.

"No."

He rested his hands back on her bare arms, as if to check her temperature himself, and once again she trembled in response.

"You did it again." He was analyzing her, trying to make sense of her reactions.

"I know." What else could she say? She might not be able to control her body's reactions to him, but at least she could control her words.

His hands moved up her body, his fingers pressing into the muscles of her neck while his thumbs brushed against her cheeks. Cool mineral-green eyes stared at her hard before his lips parted. "Why are you here, Chloe?"

She closed her eyes and savored the feeling, waiting for their connection to break. She didn't want to answer the question, but she had no choice.

"Because you asked me." She opened her eyes to find Tate's entire attention focused on her, and she felt naked underneath his intense gaze. The only part of her body he touched was her neck and her face, but it was as though she could feel him all over, with every part of her body yearning to be touched by him.

"Why?" he asked, not pulling her toward him but not releasing her from his hold.

There were so many reasons that she couldn't describe them, and she wasn't sure he would understand.

She wet her lips that suddenly seemed as dry as the desert and dared to match his gaze. "Does it matter?"

The look in his eyes changed slightly, and there was a barely perceptible turn of his head. "Not tonight."

Her lips parted in response, but before the words came out his mouth came down on hers. His lips were hard against hers and he used them to tug and draw her lower lip to him. As she moaned he moved inside her, his tongue exploring and tasting what she offered. Never had she been kissed like this, and she felt helpless to hold back—not that she wanted to.

She turned her body towards him and wrapped her arms around him, her fingers moving through his hair and pressing into his scalp. He kissed her harder, deeper, his fingers tangling in *her* hair, while his other hand trailed the length of her back. She arched in response to his touch, pressing herself against him and increasing their contact.

As suddenly as the kiss had started Tate broke away from her and stood from the couch. The hand he extended toward her quickly pacified her sense of loss. Without words, she placed her hand in his and let him pull her from the couch. She trailed him as he led her to the bedroom platform. At the edge of the bed she watched him pull off the shirt that she'd thought left little to the imagination—until she saw him in the flesh. Every muscle was perfect and defined. She reached out and let her fingers softly move over the strong breadth of his shoulders, his chest, and then along his washboard abdomen until they ended at the top of his belt and jeans.

He started in the same place, his hands moving around her waist as his fingers grabbed enough fabric to pull the tank top from her body. She had never felt self-conscious about her body, but at that moment she felt very aware of the state of her own arousal. Tate's hand encircled her waist again, but this time over the bare skin he had exposed. She shuddered at the heat she felt coming from his touch and felt him pull her to him in response.

"Definitely not cold," she heard him whisper as his warm breath surged against her neck. His lips followed as he found her weakness, each kiss and taste stoking the fires within her. She dug her fingers into his sides and pulled him back to her and was rewarded by the hard ridge that pressed into her.

He released his hold on her as he stepped back, just far enough to remove his jeans. He held her eyes as he did the same with hers, until she was standing before him in her blue lace bra and underwear. He didn't close the distance between them and she watched his eyes trail up and down her body. It was excruciating anticipation, and she didn't know how to express what she wanted, so she echoed his earlier action and held out her hand.

He didn't take it. Instead her palm made contact with his bare chest as he reached behind her and unfastened her strapless bra. Her swollen breasts spilled out as the garment fell to the floor. She felt his fingertips brush against the sides of her breasts, then her waist, until they reached her hips and the small strings of her underwear before they too were tugged from her body. He didn't leave her naked alone, stripping himself of his last remaining article of clothing with no modesty until he stood equally naked before her.

She gasped as he lifted her up and toward him. She held on tightly, wrapping her legs around him as he held her effortlessly. She felt cool sheets touch her back as she felt the pressure and heat of Tate come down on top of her. His mouth returned to hers with the increased passion that being completely skin to skin ignited. His hand moved, sweeping the side of her breast before he finally cupped her in his hands. She moaned at the experience and her reaction was met by his lips, which closed over the opposite nipple.

She spread her legs wide beneath him—a silent plea for what she really wanted.

She watched as he reached over to the nightstand and withdrew a small foil packet. She thought she could see his hands shaking as he unrolled the condom down his impressive length. She reached out to steady his hands and in response to her gentle touch he entwined her fingers in his, moving her hand and arm over her head, pressing her into the pillow above.

He once again settled between her legs and in one precision movement filled her. The spasm of her muscles around him echoed in the grip he reinforced on her hand.

She cried out with a pleasure she had never experienced before. She wasn't a virgin, but nothing had ever felt like this before. She wrapped her legs around him, anchoring him to her as he moved within her, pushing her further and further into ecstasy with each thrust. She didn't get a break as each movement in and out of her triggered every nerve in her body to fire, until she felt she was on the verge of shattering from within. Without warning she was past the point of no return and she cried out, clutching him to her as her muscles contracted reflexively around him. One more stroke and Tate was with her, his own convulsions joining hers.

He collapsed against her and she could feel the dampness of his skin and the warmth of his breath against her neck. She couldn't resist the feel of him, satiated and re-laxed against her, and gently ran her fingertips of her free hand up and down his back. It was an act of intimacy beyond the passion they had just shared.

She lost track of time, savoring the feeling of close-ness, of Tate inside her, until he lifted himself away. He was staring down at her, levered above her, still deep inside her. He was looking at her for answers, for an ex-planation of how they'd got to where they were and what to do next. She had none.

His hand brushed her hair away from her face. "I can't talk about this right now," he said, and she heard enough regret to break her heart.

"Okay," she replied, lost for any other words. He with-drew from her body and left to go to the only closed room in the loft—the bathroom.

She sat upright and covered herself with one of the oversized pillows. She wanted to move—needed to move, needed to gather her clothes and what was left of her heart and dignity and get the hell out of there. But she couldn't move. Every muscle in her body was paralyzed by the surrealism of what had just happened. *Tate—she'd had sex with Tate*. But it hadn't just been sex. It had been the most cataclysmic physical and emotional experience of her life and in that moment she realized she loved him. And he regretted it. Did she? She had vowed never to act on her feelings, but now that she had how could she dream of taking it back?

The sound of the door opening brought her attention back to reality. Tate strode naked to the platform, with no embarrassment or attempt to hide his nudity. He was spectacular. She had never appreciated the draw of the naked male form until now. She was sure in the knowl-edge that the sight of him and the memory of how he'd felt inside her would be forever burned into her body, mind and soul.

He turned down the covers on his side of the bed and gestured for her to get in. It was an offer she shouldn't accept, but it was too hard to say no. As she crawled beneath the sheets he walked to the other side of the bed and did the same. He turned off the lights from a master panel on the nightstand, leaving only the amber glow of the fire and the reflection of the city's lights through the windows. She lay there still, not knowing what to say or do, until she felt his strong arm snake around her and pull her against him.

"Go to sleep," he whispered, his lips only inches from her ear and the length of his naked body pressed against her back and bottom.

Impossible was the last thing she thought, before she closed her eyes and her mind gave way to the complete physical and emotional exhaustion of her body.

Tate woke from a deep sleep and felt his body stir and harden. He wasn't alone—could feel himself pressing against soft skin and tight curves. He opened his eyes to the early-morning light and saw it: red. Red hair covered the pillow that lay beside him. Red hair that was unmistakable.

Chloe. As he acknowledged her identity in his head a replay of last night's events rolled through his mind. He could see her tremble with his touch, her nipples pressing against the thin fabric of her tank top, the way she'd let him undress her and then reached out for him. And there was the way she'd felt, tight and uncontrolled beneath him so that he had barely managed to hold on for her release.

It was painful to think about it as he felt himself

engorge further, pressing deeper into her tight, rounded bottom. He wanted to kiss her neck, caress her breast and slip back inside her—in part for release, and in part to prove to himself that they hadn't been as explosive together as he remembered. But the cold light of day streaming in from the floor-to-ceiling windows stopped him.

How had he let this happen—and why? He hadn't just taken any ordinary woman to bed, he had taken Chloe. Chloe—the beautiful, smart, no-nonsense, caring woman he had known for years. It wasn't as if he had just realized Chloe's beauty. He had always felt an attraction to her. But by the time they had met he had already started pursuing Kate, and he'd classified his feelings for Chloe as those of a normal red-blooded male. What had happened last night? Damned if he knew. All he knew was that the attraction he had suppressed for years had boiled over—with considerable consequences.

He ran his fingers through the tumble of red hair adorning his pillow. This was going to end badly. He wasn't naïve about the nature of the medical profession. Women still had to work harder to prove their equality, especially in fields dominated by men. Women like Chloe—though he couldn't think of *any* woman like Chloe—had it the hardest. Looking at her, no one would imagine that she could be as smart and gifted as she was beautiful. Worse, few believed that her success was due to hard work alone.

He had heard the rumors about her and resented them. Unfortunately coming to her defense would only fuel the fire. Personally, Tate could care less what people thought or said about his personal life. He made his own decisions—for himself and no one else. But as a woman and as a resident Chloe didn't have that luxury.

The rumors would be vicious. The effect on her career would be unpredictable. And for what? What did he have to offer her? He had tried to settle down for a life of commitment and had it thrown back in his face. He wasn't prepared to go down *that* road again, but he also wasn't prepared to hurt Chloe just to satisfy a need in him he hadn't known existed until last night. He had crossed a line last night that he'd had no business crossing and hated himself for it.

He needed to end this before it started—or went any further.

Chloe stirred, her eyes opening to unfamiliar surroundings as she took in the flood of natural light and the expanse of the room around her. She blinked and the scenery remained unchanged. She looked down, acknowledging her nudity before confirming to herself that last night had not been a dream. She was in Tate's loft and they had made love.

Slowly she turned towards the other side of the bed—only to find disappointment at its emptiness. The feeling did not last long as her eyes caught sight of him sitting across the room in the kitchen, staring back at her. He appeared to have showered and was already fully dressed in black pants and a crisp navy blue button-down shirt with a pewter tie at the collar. An uneasy feeling came over her.

"Good morning." She waded into conversation cautiously.

"Last night was a mistake."

His words broke through her and her perfect dream instantaneously changed into a nightmare. He remained across the room, still making no effort to close the distance between them.

"I think it would be best if we forget it ever happened and moved on with our separate lives. Take your time this morning. I have to go to work, but the door will lock behind you."

She didn't have time to argue with him. She didn't even have time to respond. She just watched dumbstruck as Tate walked out, pulling the door shut behind him and signaling the end to their conversation. How could he just walk away? Easily, she thought. He didn't have feelings for her. A physical attraction, yes, but not the same depth of emotion she felt for him or he had felt for Kate.

She remembered him after their breakup—how angry he had been, how devastated. She was a simple night's mistake compared to Kate, whose loss had almost destroyed him.

CHAPTER ONE

Six weeks later...

CHLOE STOOD FROM her chair and felt a familiar wave of nausea and dizziness encompass her. She steadied herself before considering moving again. If she had thought things couldn't get worse, she had been wrong. Her relationship with Tate remained unchanged. She had made attempts to talk to him but it was clear he was avoiding her. The hope that every day she would feel better, less rejected, was long since gone and every day she felt worse.

She needed to finish with her last patient and go home. The symptoms which she had originally attributed to heartbreak had become unremitting, and it was getting harder and harder to function. Ironically, the last patient of the evening emergency shift was feeling the same. An "LOL" in distress: a "little old lady" presenting with feelings of weakness and dizziness.

These patients were always complex, taking a lot of time and attention to detail in order to rule out conditions that could cause the patient serious harm, and most commonly nothing was found. In this case Chloe had managed to work out a cause and had reduced her blood pressure medications. If only her own case was that simple.

"Are you okay?"

A voice cut through her thoughts. She turned too quickly and immediately regretted the action, feeling her heart beat overtime to maintain her balance and remain standing on her feet.

Her attending physician, Dr. Ryan Callum, was staring at her intently and Chloe was grateful that it was him. He was seven years older than her and had completed a decorated military career as a trauma specialist before starting practice at Boston General. He was very attractive, with an athletic frame, a rare combination of brown hair and blue eyes, and a collection of scars and military tattoos that completed the package and led to him being sought after by the entire nursing staff. To Chloe, he was a trusted friend and mentor.

"I'm fine."

"You're lying." He wasn't angry, but he was making it clear he did not believe her.

"Yes, but you are a good enough friend not to push the issue."

He reluctantly nodded his agreement and Chloe relaxed. She didn't have the energy to pretend right now as she rubbed her aching shoulders.

"You would tell me if you needed something, right?"

She looked at her friend and a little bit of her misery and pity lifted. She might not have love, but she had amazing friends who would do anything for her. If only she knew how she could be fixed.

"Yes, I would."

"Okay, then, go home. You look like hell."

"Thanks, I will."

Chloe discharged her patient and made her way to the women's locker room, located within the emergency department. Her head throbbed, and pushing open the door took the last effort she had inside her. Between the rows of lockers was a bench and she'd stepped toward it, planning to rest, when a sharp pain in the right lower quadrant of her abdomen overtook her. The pain was so severe that she didn't feel the impact as her body hit the floor. She tried to call for help but didn't get the words out before curtains of black entered her vision.

Someone was screaming, but it wasn't her. Everything was muted as she struggled to see and hear what was going on around her. She felt herself being picked up and carried by a pair of strong arms.

"Tate," she whimpered as the pain gripped her again.

"No, Chloe, it's Ryan."

Disappointment filled her before she lost consciousness again.

Tate scanned the operating room slate for the night's booked cases. The locked doors to the secure unit opened and a porter entered, carrying a sealed box from the blood bank. The unit clerk who had been assisting him shifted her attention from him. "Is that the blood for Theater Seven?"

"Yes, it's the second four units of packed cells and two units of fresh frozen plasma matched for a Chloe Darcy— D-A-R-C-Y. Date of birth: March twentieth, 1983. Blood bank number: 4089213."

"Perfect. You can leave it there and I'll take it back to the room."

Tate's body had frozen at the sound of her name and his eyes landed on the box, confirming everything he had heard. The box was labeled just as the porter had read— for Chloe. He replayed the exchange. This was the second four units, which meant Chloe was in serious trouble.

"I'm already changed. I'll take it in," he told the unit

clerk as he picked up the box and made his way toward Theater Seven without waiting for her response. It was ironic that for the first time in the operating room he felt fear. Never had he felt that when working, but right now he was helpless. It was a novel and terrifying feeling all at once.

He fastened a mask across his face and paused at the window in the door. There were two anesthetists at the head of the bed and the patient was surrounded, but he couldn't tell by whom. On the operating room floor a collection of bloody sponges lay soaked through and counted off. He could see the suction canisters that were filled with over two liters of blood. Was it Chloe's blood? It looked like a scene from a trauma case, and he couldn't comprehend that Chloe lay in the center of it.

He walked into the room, his confusion growing as he identified members of the gynecology team as the operating surgeons. At the same time his eyes glimpsed the trademark red hair that flowed from the top of the operating table. It was definitely her.

He handed the box to the circulating nurse. "Do you need help?" He directed the question toward the team, needing to do *something*.

"You need to leave, Dr. Reed."

The voice came from the gowned surgeon in the hibiscus-blue cloth scrub hat. He narrowed his focus on her and through the confusion surrounding the case was able to identify Erin Madden, chief gynecology resident. Her voice and hat identified her without her needing to look away from the operative field. He had known Erin casually for years, and more so in the past two through her friendship with Kate and Chloe, but even so he wasn't in the mood to be told what to do. He normally encouraged resident autonomy, but not today—not when it involved Chloe.

"Dr. Thomas?" He addressed the staff surgeon whose back was to him.

"Dr. Madden is right. This is not a vascular case, Tate. We are going to have to ask you to leave."

He looked around the room once more, noticing the discomfort of the nursing and other teams. It felt like a betrayal from the people he worked with day in and day out, but on the other hand he knew enough to know that he had become a distraction—one that Chloe couldn't afford.

"Okay." And he left, going as far away from her as he could handle being, which was right outside the operating theater doors.

His mind raced with possibilities? What the hell had happened to Chloe? How did a healthy young woman end up in a critical condition without warning? And why the hell was gynecology in there?

A previously unimaginable explanation filled and settled into his mind. He watched, his eyes oscillating between the anesthesia monitors tracking Chloe's vitals and the actions of the surgical team.

"Tate." He heard Kate's familiar voice and felt a hand on his shoulder.

"I think she is stabilizing. They kicked me out of the room, so I can't tell for sure. But they have stopped calling for blood and I can see the anesthesia monitors. Her heart-rate has come down and her blood pressure is back up."

"What happened?" Kate asked.

"I don't know. They won't tell me anything. The usual patient confidentiality. I only got here about fifteen minutes ago. I was checking the operating room slate to see how many cases were lined up for tonight at the front desk when the porter from the blood bank came to drop off blood. I overheard him verifying her name and blood bank number with the unit clerk."

"Who is in with her?"

"Gynecology." His resentment was coming through clearly.

"Oh."

"Is it a hemorrhagic ovarian cyst?" Kate asked.

"I don't know, Kate. Like I said, they won't tell me anything."

She stopped asking questions and he wondered if she had come up with the same diagnosis he had. Either way he was grateful for the silence. He needed to keep his entire focus on Chloe.

Twenty minutes later Kate gently pushed Tate to the side and went through the operating room door. He watched the interaction, unable to hear the exchange between her and Erin Madden, but noting that she was getting further than he had. She pushed through the doors again, returning.

"She's okay. They won't tell me what happened, but they opened her up, stopped whatever was bleeding, and she's stabilized. She is going to go to the Intensive Care Unit overnight because of the large amount of blood products she received."

"Thank you, Kate," Tate replied, his eyes still trained on the window, not budging from his spot outside the door.

"Tate, they have asked us to leave and I think we should. She is stable and there is nothing we can do except get in the way and distract the team."

"I'm not leaving her."

"We're not leaving her, Tate. We're helping her by getting out of the way and letting them do their job. The same thing we ask other people to do for us." She grabbed his arm and pulled him a little, to ease him away from his spot. "Tate, we need to go. You know Chloe would never want us to see her like this."

His mind replayed all the ways he had seen Chloe and he knew she was right. Staying away from her had been the hardest thing he had ever done, but it was for her he'd done it. God knew that every time she had tried to talk to him there'd been nothing he wanted more than to take her in his arms and kiss her, to see if everything they had done together had been real and not just a memory that had reached fantastical proportions in his mind.

Who was he kidding? In truth he was terrified of the feelings she'd brought out in him and what it would cost him to have and then lose her.

He looked back at Kate, feeling nothing for her. How could he have been such a fool? He respected Kate, and intellectually she made perfect sense, but he had never been in love with her and she had never sparked the intensity of emotion that Chloe did in him. He had asked her to marry him because it had seemed like the next logical step, just like the series of steps he had taken in his training. He was tired of the single life, needed a wife, wanted a family and Kate met the criteria he was looking for. His use of logic had failed him for the first time in his life. Kate's rejection had angered him and wounded his pride at the time. Now he was grateful for the near miss.

"Are you in love with Matt McKayne?" he asked, without emotion.

She seemed surprised by the question, whether it was

at his directness or his reference to the man he knew she was in love with, he didn't care.

"Yes. I think I always have been—even when I hated him."

"Then you should be with him. Forget everything that has gone wrong between you and be together."

"It's not that simple, Tate. I can't trust him."

"Kate, *that's* not simple," he replied, pointing toward the door. Then he took one last look through the window and walked away—from both Chloe and Kate.

His steps were slow and purposeful as he returned to the front desk and the unit clerk he had spoken to earlier. He took a deep breath, steeling himself for the response he was dreading. "Am I up next after the ruptured ectopic pregnancy?" he asked as casually as he could while his heart was racing.

He held his breath as the unit clerk double-checked the confidential surgical slate that listed patient names, procedures and diagnoses. "Yes. As soon as they are done with Dr. Darcy we will be sending for your patient, Dr. Reed."

"Thank you," he mumbled and he kept walking, not thinking about his destination but more of the confirmation he had hoped not to receive. Chloe was pregnant—or had been pregnant. Was he the father? Was he responsible for the pregnancy that had almost killed her?

The door to the operating room opened again and Ryan Callum walked through.

"Is she still in?" Ryan asked, with a coldness Tate had not expected emanating from him.

He wasn't in the mood to play games. "Yes. Do you know what happened to her?"

"Yes."

Tate waited, but no more words came from the other

man and new hostility radiated from him. Ryan, who
had never been confrontational, had changed from the
direct, no-nonsense man he had been. The question was
why? In a night with so many unanswered questions it
was the last thing he needed.

"I'm asking," Tate replied, not trying to escalate the
conversation, knowing he had a thin grip on his temper.

"If Chloe wanted you to know something she would
have told you."

Told him what? That there was a reason Ryan Callum
knew about her pregnancy and he didn't? It was a thought
he couldn't stomach and he wanted it out of his mind.

"What's that supposed to mean?"

"You're the brilliant surgeon, Tate, figure it out."

He didn't want to have to think about any more than
he already was. At the moment he would much rather be
the father of her life-threatening pregnancy than think
there was a possibility that Ryan was.

"So I'm to blame? Is that what you think?"

"She said your name, not mine, as I carried her near
lifeless body to get help. That is what I think."

The image flashed before his eyes, and judging from
the scene in the operating theater Tate knew Ryan's char-
acterization was right. Before he could respond Ryan
walked past him toward the bank of theaters, which was
fortunate because he had no response. Did that mean he
was the father? Ryan hadn't ruled himself out, but what
did it say about Chloe that she would ask for *him* as she
lay dying?

CHAPTER TWO

EVERYTHING HURT. IT was her first thought as outside sounds began to intrude. She tried to move, to ease the ache, but nothing in her body responded. She took a breath and became immediately cognizant of pain and pressure in her mouth and throat. She tried to pull at it, but couldn't move her hands. When she finally moved she felt the resistance of straps on her wrists.

A monitor rang out and it calmed her as a familiar sound. She felt a hand curl around hers and tried to hold it.

"Chloe, it's Kate."

Kate. She didn't know where she was, but Kate was here. She heard her friend's voice again, but couldn't make out the words. She strained to understand, wanted to move, to breathe, but everything was so hard and met with such resistance.

She heard the alarm ring again as she struggled.

Someone with a voice she didn't recognize entered the room and she could hear Kate directing the woman before she felt a hand calmingly stroke her forehead and hair.

She only understood a few of Kate's words but it was enough. "Stay calm, okay? Intubated...Intensive Care Unit...tube out. Stay calm."

She focused all her efforts on opening the heavy lids of

her eyes to see Kate as her dark hair and her face slowly came into focus. She had to work twice as hard not to give in to the temptation to close them again.

There was another voice she didn't recognize, and once again she couldn't understand everything, so instead focused on Kate.

"Chloe, you heard that? I have to go for a few minutes while they evaluate you. No room for big dumb surgeons on these occasions. I am not going to be far, though, and will be back here as soon as they let me, okay?"

She processed the information and finally, with great effort, managed to move her head in understanding. She watched Kate's eyes fill with relief and felt her friend squeeze her hand one last time before she left.

Over the next few minutes she was aware of the room filling with more and more people. She was also aware that if she wanted the tube out she was going to have to concentrate on everything she was being asked to do, even though it was a struggle. After what seemed like a lifetime she took her first breath on her own, and even the irritation in her throat couldn't dampen her relief. She felt a nurse thread the oxygen nasal prongs around her face and into her nose as air gently began to blow, and she was grateful for anything that made breathing less hard.

As fast as the room had filled it began to empty, until only one person remained. With only one person to focus on it was easier, and she recognized the face, dark tortoiseshell glasses and pulled-back blonde hair of her friend Erin Madden pulling up a chair beside the bed. Through her emerging fog she could tell Erin wasn't here as her friend. Why was gynecology involved in her care?

"Chloe, do you know where you are?"

She nodded, her mind having put together the fact that she was in the Intensive Care Unit.

"Did you know you were pregnant?" Erin asked softly.

Pregnant. No. That couldn't be right. She couldn't be pregnant. She had only been with one man in the past two years and Tate had worn a condom. Wouldn't she have known if she was pregnant? She had been bleeding off and on for the past month, but her cycle was screwed up because of all the stress. She had been nauseated and dizzy, but that could be stress too. Wouldn't she have known if she was pregnant with Tate's baby? A warm flush passed through her as she thought about a child.

"I'm pregnant?" she managed to ask, her voice still weak.

"No, Chloe. You *were* pregnant. The pregnancy was ectopic, in your right fallopian tube. It ruptured. That is what led to your collapse. We did an emergency laparotomy and had to take out your right fallopian tube to stop the bleeding. You also were transfused with a lot of blood products, so we decided to keep you in the Intensive Care Unit. But you are okay now, Chloe. Your blood work is stable and there are no signs of anymore bleeding. You are going to be okay."

"I lost the baby." It wasn't a question for Erin, but more a confirmation to herself of everything she had just heard.

"Yes. I'm so sorry, Chloe."

Grief filled her. It was the final insult. It shouldn't hurt to lose something she had never known she had, but that didn't stop the pain. Maybe it was fitting that she felt the same way about her baby's father. She had never had him either, but that didn't make losing him any easier.

She looked around the room, surrounded by glass and curtains and monitors that would show everything about her. She didn't want to be here.

"I want to go home, Erin. I *need* to go home." She

couldn't be here—not in public, not where she worked, not where Tate worked. Not knowing he was so close and wanting him to be with her at this moment so very badly and knowing he wouldn't be coming.

"Chloe, you are barely twenty-four hours post-op. You know you are in no condition to go home. You just started breathing on your own and haven't even sat up yet."

She tried to push herself up, to prove that she could do it, but her body betrayed her. Between the physical exertion the act required and the sense of dizziness that swept over her she barely lifted herself for a few seconds before collapsing.

"Chloe, please let me handle this. I am going to have you transferred to Obstetrics, where no one knows you and you can have some privacy."

She knew she didn't have a choice. She couldn't leave even if she wanted to. The obstetrics ward... Pregnant woman and babies... Could she do that? Now? On the other hand Erin was right—it was a ward where no one would know her.

"Okay," she assented, before closing her eyes, exhausted physically and emotionally. She felt Erin pull the blankets over her. "Thank you for everything," she managed, right before sleep overtook her.

Chloe stirred, the pain in her abdomen still sharp and making her restless. She felt a hand sweep her hair from her face. Kate. She had told her best friend to go home but apparently she hadn't listened.

Pain coursed through her as she tried in vain to find a comfortable position and a soft moan escaped her.

A hand fell onto her arm and she instantly knew that it was not Kate beside her. The hand was heavy and large and she recognized Tate's touch. She didn't open her eyes.

She wasn't ready to face him. She heard her call bell go off and Tate asking for a nurse.

The exchange was brief, and within five minutes Chloe felt some of the pain dissipate from her body— but not her heart.

"I know you are not sleeping, Chloe."

Tate's voice broke through her thoughts. She opened her eyes to meet his. Each of them was trying to decipher the other. He looked tired, with new shadowing along his face and a redness in his eyes that served to heighten the light green irises. Despite her need for him she felt overwhelmed by his presence.

"How did you know?" she whispered.

"Because I've watched you sleep," he answered, as though the statement held no intimacy.

"No, I mean how did you know I was here?" she asked, not wanting to betray any of the information she had barely had time to digest.

"I'm on nights this week and saw you in the operating room."

She grimaced at the thought of him seeing her exposed—not one she enjoyed.

"Is the morphine not enough? Do you need something else?" he asked, misreading her cue.

"No, I'm fine." A complete overstatement, but she felt vulnerable and not ready for this conversation.

"You scared me."

The honesty in his face and his statement humbled her.

"I'm sorry."

"Is there a reason you didn't tell me?" His voice had quietened.

"What do you mean?" He was searching for an answer but she didn't understand the question.

Tate stared at her as though he could learn the answer

if he just looked hard enough. She looked back at him, equally searching for an answer. "Was there a reason you didn't tell me about the pregnancy?"

He knew. She didn't know how, but he did. He probably had known before she did. Just one more insult in what was already an untenable situation. He was asking her if he was the father of her baby. What must he think of her if he thought there might be more than one possibility?

She blinked hard, trying to calm herself against the ugliness she felt inside. When she opened her eyes he was still staring at her, waiting.

"Does it matter, Tate?" The hurt in her voice was apparent even to her own ears.

"Yes, it matters."

"Why?" she demanded.

"It just does, Chloe."

"Because if you were the father then, what? You would take pity on me? Feel guilty? But if you weren't then everything people say about me must be right and you can walk away and count your blessings for your near miss? I'm sorry, Tate, but neither of those options works for me. I think you should go."

"We're not done, Chloe."

She wanted to cry and tried hard to keep in her tears. She took a deep breath to steady herself. "Be honest with yourself, Tate. We never started. I need you to go."

"What if I want to stay, Chloe?"

"Then you should have stayed six weeks ago. Or at least listened to me when I tried to talk to you afterward. But you wanted nothing to do with me then, and you don't get to change your mind now. I want you to leave." She could hear the pleading in her voice but she didn't care.

She couldn't do this—not now, when she had already depleted every physical and emotional resource she had.

"But the baby...?" His voice was hushed but still she heard the small crack that betrayed him.

"There is no baby," she told them both, and the words hurt as much as anything she had felt. Tate blurred before her eyes and she couldn't read him as tears formed. She watched him get up and walk away from her and felt both relieved and wounded by his departure.

She heard the curtains close and the sliding door of her intensive care room slide shut and she closed her eyes, willing the tears to stop. She couldn't do this—not here.

She barely had time to process the sound of the guard rail going down, or the weight on her bed, before she felt herself being picked up as strongly, and yet as gently as possible, and held tightly within a strong embrace. She felt pain tear through her abdomen, but it was nothing compared to what was going on in her heart. She shouldn't do this—she shouldn't feel better in Tate's arms. But she did.

Her complete loss of control over her life overwhelmed her and she gave in to the urge she had been fighting since she woke up. For some reason she knew she didn't have to be brave right now—she didn't need to put on the funny, reassuring front she had for Kate. Right now she could just *hurt* and it didn't matter. She had nothing to lose with Tate; she had lost everything already.

She felt his grip tighten as the sobs began to rack through her body, each movement both bringing and taking away the pain. He brought his chin down to rest on her head while his hand stroked up and down her back.

"I didn't know about the baby," she confessed into his already soaked scrub top.

"It'll be okay, Chloe. *You* are okay," he murmured in reassurance.

"It's not okay. How could I not have known about my own child?"

"It wouldn't have made a difference."

No, it wouldn't have. A child between them wouldn't have changed Tate's mind or his feelings toward her. "I didn't deserve a baby."

"You didn't deserve any of *this*."

"Didn't I?" She had done the unthinkable. She had fallen in love and slept with her best friend's ex, who the morning after had found her lacking. The only reason Tate was here now was because he felt sorry for her, but to be honest not more sorry than she felt for herself.

He pulled her gently away from his shoulder, reaching up to cradle her face in his hands. "No, Chloe, you didn't."

She wished she could believe him. She had never put much stock in karma before—you couldn't when you spent your life treating people you were sure didn't deserve what was happening to them. But now she wasn't sure.

She felt fresh tears forming in her eyes at the pain of her thoughts and from staring into Tate's eyes too much. He really looked as if he cared for her. If only that was the case.

She felt his lips press against the dampness of her cheek before she was once again tucked into his arms and held tightly. She didn't know how long they stayed like that. She didn't even remember him leaving. But when she woke he was gone.

Post-operative day two was excruciating. Everything felt like a struggle. First thing in the morning a nurse had come to help her "dangle', which had basically turned into a torture exercise of being forced to sit upright with her legs dangling off the bed, maintaining her balance. She'd lasted for less than five minutes and then slept for the next three hours to recover. When she woke Kate was there, propped in a bedside chair reading a heavy hard-cover text that almost completely covered her. She was comforted by her friend's presence.

"Hey," Chloe greeted her, watching as Kate's focus shifted and she herself was assessed by the good surgeon.

"You look better," Kate said reassuringly.

"That's not saying much," she replied, still having to work to keep her eyes open.

"Do you want to tell me what happened?" Kate asked tentatively.

She hadn't thought about much in the last twenty-four hours, but what she *had* thought about, other than Tate and the loss of their baby, was what was she going to tell Kate?

Kate—her best friend, the person she had been clos-est with during the past decade. She couldn't lie, but how much of the truth was too much? Especially when the explanation for how she had gotten to this day was unexplainable even to herself.

"I had an ectopic pregnancy that ruptured." Nothing had prepared her for what she saw in Kate's face. She wasn't even sure she had been that surprised.

"I didn't realize you were in a relationship," was all Kate managed after minutes of silence.

Beyond the words she could see the hurt in her friend's eyes. The thought that Chloe had been keeping something from her was painful for Kate.

"I'm not, Kate." Truer words were never spoken.

"Oh."

She knew that Kate was not going to ask her more, but felt she owed her friend more of an explanation. "I slept with someone a few weeks ago. It was a mistake. It didn't work out."

Kate didn't respond immediately. She seemed to be processing the information until her look of surprise was replaced by one of understanding. "I'm sorry."

"So am I." And she was. A lifetime spent thinking about the man you loved who'd got away would have been better than the crash-and-burn drama that had unfolded with Tate.

"Is there anything I can do?"

"I don't suppose I can convince you to help bust me out of here?" she asked faint-heartedly, realizing that she likely couldn't even make it as far as the elevator right now.

"No, sorry. No chance of that happening. Try again."

"I would love my own clothes and stuff to take a shower."

"That I *can* do. So you'll be wanting your make-up and finest lingerie, then?"

Kate winked at her and Chloe was grateful for the lightening of their conversation.

"Definitely. Goes great with these disposable mesh underwear I am ashamed to admit are surprisingly comfortable."

"Is it hard being a patient?"

"Yes, but I haven't figured out what is worse: feeling helpless or being a patient where I work."

It was the truth. She was so used to *doing*, to being active, multi-tasking, and now she couldn't perform the simplest of tasks for herself and was dependent on people she was used to impressing with her abilities. It was hard to be this vulnerable.

"It is a big change, but the first couple of days are the worst. By tomorrow you'll be moving around a bit more and you will be home in a few days."

"Not soon enough." She waited for a while, trying to decide if she really wanted to know the answer to her next question. "Does everyone know?"

"No. The story around the emergency department and amongst some of the other services is that you had a hemorrhagic ovarian cyst. I think the residents in your program are planning on sending flowers. All your shifts have been covered for the next eight weeks so that you don't have to work before the board exam."

"Eight weeks seems like such a short and a long time all at once."

"It's not too long, Chloe. You need to focus on yourself for once. If you had a patient who had just gone through the same experience you would counsel her the exact same way."

"I agree completely."

A new voice came from behind the curtain before it was opened to reveal Ryan Callum.

"Hi," Chloe greeted him, embarrassed again at her lack of knowledge about that night, but knowing Ryan had to have been there.

Kate rose and stared at Ryan, then at her. "I'll leave you two alone. I'll be back later this afternoon with your stuff." Kate gave her one final look and then left, pulling the curtain and the door shut behind her.

"I didn't mean to interrupt," Ryan responded, taking Kate's now vacated chair.

"You're not."

"How are you feeling?"

She could see the clinician in him assessing her and did her best to reassure him.

"I'm okay, and Kate assures me that every day is going to be a little better." She was counting on that in more ways than one. "Did you take care of me the other night?"

"Yes. I don't think I've ever been more scared."

"I'm sorry."

"Don't be. I wanted to stop by and make sure you were okay. I also wanted to make sure you knew that no one in the department other than me saw the results of your beta-HCG that night."

She felt a flush of embarrassment pass through her, but also a sense of relief at what Ryan was telling her. No one else had seen the positive pregnancy test, which explained why they all believed she had had a ruptured cyst. Having managed to maintain her privacy was a small relief.

"Thank you," she said gratefully.

"Don't thank me. I don't want anything standing between you and your future staff position here at Boston General—which, by the way, will be waiting for you whenever you are ready."

"Thank you," she said again, this time struggling to keep tears from her eyes.

"You're worth it, Chloe. Please remember that."

She could tell he was holding something back, which was far from normal. "Why do I feel like there is something you are not saying?"

"Because there is. But I don't think this is the time or any of my business."

"Since when did you hold back your praise or your criticism, Ryan?" she goaded him, not wanting anything to change in her life more than it already had.

"Tate Reed."

Her heart stopped and she briefly looked around to ensure Tate, or anyone else for that matter, had not come into her room. What else did Ryan know? What else had happened that night?

"What about Tate?"

"I want you to be careful, Chloe."

"It's a little too late for that, don't you think?" she responded, understanding that somehow Ryan knew about her involvement with Tate.

"Just be careful. I don't know Tate well, but I know his type. And if the hospital administration was ever forced to choose between their prized vascular surgeon and you, you wouldn't win."

"Tate would never..." she started, and then stopped herself. She didn't know what Tate would or wouldn't do. "Thank you, Ryan—for everything."

CHAPTER THREE

POST-OPERATIVE DAY THREE was better. She could move around her room and was able, with some assistance, to take a shower, which felt better than any pain medication she had received. Her nausea was still there, but less than what it had been, and she imagined it would be a while before all the hormones of pregnancy were cleared from her system. She used similar reasoning to explain her new-found propensity toward tears. She cried when she was frustrated, she cried when she thought about what she had lost, she even cried when the nurses were kind to her.

Kate had brought her things and she struggled to keep her eyes open as she read one of her textbooks: another attempt at distraction. A new knock at the door signaled the end of her struggle. Kate peered around the privacy curtain that separated the door from her bed, the smile on her face the first thing visible. Chloe automatically smiled back.

"I have news," Kate announced before she could even cross the room.

Chloe could tell she was barely containing herself and felt her own excitement build. She pushed herself up in bed, happy to have made the effort to put on her own clothes, even it was only her favorite yoga pants and a fitted gray sweater.

Kate pulled up the visitor's chair right beside her. "Matt has asked me to marry him and I've accepted."

"Oh, my God," Chloe gasped. One look at Kate was all it took for her tears to return. Never had she seen her so joyous. She reached up and Kate met her halfway.

"He loves me—he always has," Kate explained.

Chloe simply hugged her harder. Of course Matt loved Kate. She was perfect. She squeezed her eyes shut, trying to block out a burgeoning feeling of jealousy at all Kate had. She needed to stop this. She was lucky to be alive and she had friends she loved who loved her. She just didn't have the man she was in love with.

They broke apart and she was once again rewarded with the look of pure happiness on Kate's face.

"I wanted you to be the first to know."

"I'm so happy for you. And for Matt."

"So you'll be my maid of honor?"

"Nothing would make me happier than to stand beside you on your wedding day."

"Wedding day?"

A voice intruded into their moment—a voice she knew by heart.

Tate, dressed in charcoal tailored pants and a fitted yellow dress shirt, stood in the corner of the room. She hadn't seen Tate since she had left the intensive care unit, but that hadn't surprised her. He had said what he needed to say and they had nothing left between them.

"Matt asked me to marry him and I've agreed," Kate answered elatedly.

"Congratulations, Kate."

Kate rose from her chair and Chloe watched painfully as the two embraced. Was Tate thinking of his proposal to

Kate? The one she had rejected? She couldn't read Tate's response, and any further conversation was cut short by another knock at the door.

Erin and Ryan walked in together, and soon her little room was full of people who all loved and cared for her, and she felt ashamed at the self-pity and jealousy she had been indulging in.

Erin had already been in earlier that morning, on her official morning rounds, but Chloe had gotten used to her checking in before she left for the day.

"I just came to see if you needed anything," Erin explained, her eyes fixed only on Chloe. Maybe she too felt the awkwardness of the Chloe-Tate-Kate love triangle.

"I'm good, thank you."

"When do you think Chloe will be discharged?" Tate asked Erin.

"She can be discharged tomorrow if she feels well enough to go. But she can't stay alone for the first few weeks."

"She can stay with me," Kate volunteered.

Chloe stared at her friend and knew she had been genuine with her offer, but she couldn't accept. Not with Kate's new engagement and her long overdue reunion with Matt. She wouldn't intrude on their time together.

"No, Kate, you need to be alone with Matt."

"Chloe, you are welcome to stay with me."

All eyes turned to Ryan, who didn't seem at all bothered by the surprise his offer had garnered. She was friends with Ryan, and he had saved her life, but she had never crossed that far into his personal life.

"I don't think that's a good idea."

Tate was glowering at Ryan, and Chloe felt her anxiety rise along with the escalation of tension in the room.

"Why not?" Ryan replied, his ease in contrast with Tate's decree.

"Because Chloe is still a resident and you are her attending physician."

Oh, God, had he really just said that? Didn't he remember that Kate had been a resident and he her attending physician throughout their entire relationship? She looked at Kate, who had made the same connection and seemed just as embarrassed by what they both knew was coming.

"Just because your intentions toward Kate were less than admirable does not mean mine toward Chloe are. Chloe needs a safe place to recuperate. I can provide that, no strings attached."

"I agree with Tate." Erin's voice interrupted the men's discussion.

All eyes turned to her. Chloe didn't care what came out of Erin's mouth—she was just grateful the two alpha males had been interrupted before it had got ugly...or uglier.

"I don't think *you* are the right person to comment on propriety," Ryan rebuked.

If the room hadn't been quiet already, Ryan's remark would have sealed the silence. Ryan did not suffer fools lightly, but she had never seen him as confrontational as he had been with Tate and now Erin. The attack on Erin's personal life both surprised and disappointed her.

"*Enough.* I appreciate everyone's concern, but I am an adult, capable of making my own decisions and deciding what is in my own best interests. Erin, are you sure I can't go back to my apartment as long as I don't overdo it?"

Erin took a deep breath, seemingly shaking off Ryan's comments before turning to address Chloe alone. "Yes, I'm sure. With your low hemoglobin and naturally low blood pressure I think you are at high risk for dizziness and fainting and you shouldn't be alone."

Chloe couldn't fault her reasoning or her recommendation. The idea of waiting to be found again was terrifying. She looked between Kate, Ryan, and Tate, considering the three less than desirable options before her. She wouldn't intrude on Kate's happiness. So that left Tate and Ryan. If Ryan hadn't just surprised her with his behavior she would have accepted his offer. She was used to rumors that she'd used her beauty and sexuality to advance her career—what was another log on the fire?—but she had no idea why he was so angry with Tate. And though it did not feel like romantic jealousy she didn't want to take that risk with someone who was going to be a long-term colleague once she became staff herself. That left Tate. But he hadn't offered despite his argument with Ryan.

She drew in a deep breath. "Tate, could I stay at your loft?"

No one said anything. Not Kate, not Ryan, not Erin, and definitely not Tate. She watched as her words penetrated through, with only a slight change in his eyes registering their impact. Finally he answered.

"Yes, it's the least I can do."

She almost gasped, fearing what he would say next. Was he going to declare to everyone he was the father of her pregnancy?

"Kate deserves some time alone with Matt to celebrate their engagement," he finished.

She was too crushed by his words to think about whether they had been genuine. It was still about Kate—it always had been. Would it be always?

True to his promise, Tate appeared again in her room the following morning, ready to take her home to his loft.

She had spent a near sleepless night trying to decide if she really could live with Tate, and when she had slept her dreams had been torn between the pleasure and the pain she had felt the last time she had been at his loft. She had finally given up and showered and dressed early, wanting at least to feel like herself before facing him. Her black tights fit her comfortably and provided support for her abdominal wall, and the red cable sweater dress felt soft against her skin and made her feel more feminine that she had in days.

She had gotten used to the appraisal that accompanied his visits.

"Have you been discharged?"

"Yes."

"Okay. Let me get a wheelchair and I'll get you out of here."

"I don't need a wheelchair."

"Chloe, you cannot even walk once around the unit before needing to sit for a break. So your options are a wheelchair or I carry you—pick."

The image of being held in his arms and carried through the hospital reminded her of the finale in a romantic movie and she was momentarily lost in the vision. Then his other words sank in. He likely had not just guessed at what her activity tolerance was, he had been checking up on her. It both pleased and annoyed her.

"Wheelchair, please."

"Not as much fun, but okay."

She was taken aback by his return to humor and she smiled too as he left the room to get the chair.

Her smile was brief, and it faded as Tate pushed her through the hospital halls. She watched as nurses, residents and other physicians did double-takes at the sight of them together. She had always garnered some attention, but had never been bothered by it until now. She had always been able to take comfort in knowing that she was more than what people saw and that their perceptions were usually not the truth. This time there was the high likelihood that no matter what indecent scenario they were imagining between her and Tate the truth was a lot worse.

She stopped looking and focused on her hands, folded in her lap. She still had bruising from the numerous intravenous lines and her hands were as pale as the rest of her.

"Everything okay?"

Tate's voice sounded from above her.

"I'm fine."

"You don't seem fine."

How had he noticed her discomfort without even looking at her?

She wanted him to keep moving so she needed to reassure him that she was physically okay and not about to be sick or faint from the chair. "I'm uncomfortable with people staring."

"I thought you would be used to it by now."

"Why would I be used to people staring at me?" she asked defensively.

"Because you're gorgeous, but you don't let that get in your way. It intrigues people."

She wanted to know more. To know how else he saw her. How he felt about her. But she didn't know what else to say so she raised her head and squared her shoulders as they finished their journey toward the parking garage.

Erin and Tate had been right, though she did her best to hide that particular truth. Once at his building the walk from the main entrance to his loft door was too much. She wanted to sit, or at least to lean against something, as a now familiar wave of dizziness threatened to make the choice for her. She needed help and it was a hard truth to swallow.

"Dammit, Chloe," she heard as a strong arm snaked around her, pulling her up to rest against Tate's strong frame.

She barely noticed him unlocking and opening the large steel door before she felt another arm reach under her legs as her feet left the floor and she was carried inside.

"I can walk," she protested.

"Sure."

The soft weave of his couch was soon under her, and the loss of the heat from Tate's body was replaced with the weight of a soft chenille blanket that covered her whole body and the glow from the fireplace. She wanted to close her eyes, but was instantly aware of the green eyes at face level with her own as Tate bent beside her.

"Enough with being strong, Chloe. I know I'm not your favorite person right now, but you need to learn to ask for help."

"Why do you say that?" She wasn't angry with him and hoped he didn't think she was. She was just frustrated with the situation they found themselves in.

"Because it doesn't do anyone any good to take unnecessary risks."

His words struck her. Tate was a risk, but to her he felt necessary. "Why don't you think you are my favorite person right now."

"Because I'm responsible for your pregnancy."

"You are not the only person responsible, Tate. I was there too. And if things hadn't turned out this way I would have been happy about the baby." She was out on a ledge, letting him know how she felt. Did he feel the same way? "Do you want children?"

"Yes. It was one of the reasons I wanted to get married."

"To Kate." She finished his sentence, not wanting anything left unsaid between them. She also noticed he'd used the past tense. Had the loss of Kate eliminated marriage and children from his plans?

"Yes, it was one of the reasons I proposed to Kate," he admitted. "I didn't realize you and Ryan Callum were so close."

It was a question disguised as a comment. It was also a way to change the conversation. She decided to let him. Discussing his past relationship with Kate was too painful.

"He's my mentor."

"He invited you to stay at his house." The same approach, the same hidden question.

"I think my collapse scared him," she answered honestly.

"He's not the only one."

"Why?" she asked honestly. How could he profess to have felt scared when he had not wanted anything to do with her in the weeks prior?

"Why what?"

"Why were you scared?"

"Because I care about you, Chloe. Surely you know that." His words flooded through her and she felt both warmth and annoyance. How would she know he cared about her when he'd walked away from her and never looked back?

She couldn't let it go. "You stopped speaking to me after we slept together." She tried to leave her pain out of her words and focused on the facts.

"That wasn't because I didn't care."

"Then why?"

She watched his frustration as he ran his fingers through his hair. "Because I'm not good for you, Chloe."

"Don't you think I should be the judge of that?" she asked searching his eyes for an answer.

"No, I don't." He rose up and walked away, signaling the end of their conversation.

Despite the cost and quality of his couch there was nothing that was going to make this night comfortable. He resisted the urge to shift again, taking penance in his discomfort. Even if he had been in the world's most comfortable bed it was unlikely he would be able to sleep. Not with Chloe so near.

He had had weeks to think about how they had gotten to where they were now. He had been weak—that was how. He had meant what he said to her: he wasn't good for her.

Chloe—of all the women to take to bed. Months of sleeping alone, licking his wounds and trying to restore his pride had definitely blurred his boundaries. It wasn't just that a woman had wanted him; it was that *Chloe* had wanted him. He had had his choice of woman since he was fifteen, but she was different. He respected her. She was capable and strong and an amazing physician. She was also a dedicated friend. Most importantly she was Kate's best friend.

Up until a year ago his professional life had been his only life. He had relentlessly pursued his career, moving through each step with ruthless succession from his degrees from Ivy League institutions with honors to the top residency and fellowship programs in the country. By the time he was in his mid-thirties he was one of the top ten vascular surgeons in the country, recruited with a large salary and various other incentives by one of the top tertiary centers.

He hadn't gone without women during that time. He enjoyed sex—it was like operating, a series of movements and responses that led to the culmination of something intensely satisfying. But the women he'd chosen knew the score, and while he'd respected them, and what they offered, he'd felt no other emotion toward them.

Then he'd met Kate. He hadn't intended to become romantically involved with her. He had started as her mentor within the Department of General Surgery, helping her hone her skills and making sure she had the right opportunities and surgical cases that would allow her to grow as a surgeon and show others what she was capable of. She had quickly exceeded his and everyone else's expectations and their relationship had transitioned to friendship.

Being around Kate outside of the hospital, outside of work, had opened his eyes to what he wanted in a woman. He didn't want a woman whose entire life's ambition was to gain her "Mrs." He was looking for a partner who would stand beside and challenge him, as opposed to the old adage of the "woman behind the man." Kate had seemed like the logical choice, so he had pursued her with the same intensity he had his career.

Never in his life had he failed at anything. He knew when he was going to win, and when something was a losing proposition, but not with Kate. He had asked her to marry him and she had said no. As a man who had never failed he hadn't taken it well. But all the anger he had felt at the time now felt completely misplaced. He shouldn't have been angry with Kate for refusing him. He should have been angry with himself for pursuing her at all. What had felt like all the right reasons had been anything but. He hadn't been in love with her.

How had he expected to live a life of intellectual companionship, mutual respect and admiration with no spark? No heat? A poor decision that he'd thought was behind him was now front and center. His past relationship with Kate was going to ruin any potential future with Chloe. How could he expect Chloe to see him as anything other than Kate's past?

Chloe. His mind had a reel of images of her. Chloe trembling with his touch. Chloe beneath him, losing control. And Chloe lying on an operating room table almost dead. The catastrophic result of their night together should have been enough to end any attraction to her, but it hadn't. Emotionally he had no idea how he felt about her. Physically he wanted to touch her, to comfort her, to be one with her until everything about them made sense.

CHAPTER FOUR

SHE FELT COLD. She brought her knees up and curled on her side, only to be rewarded with a pain that spread throughout her abdomen. She could hear screaming, followed by yelling, but she couldn't tell what was going on and all she could see was black. She concentrated hard on opening her eyes, and when she did everything else disappeared.

She grasped the sheet to her, feeling more vulnerable than in the cold of her dream. She struggled to slow her breathing and calm herself as she took in her surroundings. The sheets were not hers. The room was not familiar. In an instant she remembered she was at Tate's.

"Are you okay? Can I get you something or help in any way?"

His voice projected across the loft and with a moderate effort she was able to push herself up and see him. He was seated at the breakfast bar, drinking from a coffee cup, his laptop in front of him. His attire was casual, no suit or tie. He wore a sweater in warm cream and designer jeans.

She glanced at the bedside clock. It read ten in the morning. How had she slept for that long? Wasn't it also a week day?

"You are not at work?" She stated the obvious.

"No, I'm working from home."

"Tate, you are a vascular surgeon. How do you work from home?"

"I canceled my elective cases for the next two weeks and have arranged for my on call to be covered."

"You didn't need to do that."

"Yes, I did. I know you, Chloe, and I can't trust you to take things easy. If you are still at high risk for dizziness and fainting than you shouldn't be alone. That means whether you are at your place or mine."

She wanted to argue with him, embarrassed by what she knew to be the colossal sacrifice he was making, but she couldn't. Her near collapse yesterday and her fears of something bad happening to her with no one around to help circumvented any argument.

"Thank you."

She moved toward the edge of the bed and before her feet hit the floor he was at her side.

"I'm okay."

"Prove it."

She looked at his face, freshly shaven, at his green eyes, clear with one eyebrow raised, and knew that there was no way he would be backing down. She was surprised that she found herself feeling more honored and protected than annoyed.

She managed to move to a standing position—the physical task she had found the hardest and the most painful since her surgery. Once on her feet she moved toward the bathroom, Tate inches behind her. As she passed through the bathroom doorway she stopped and turned around toward him.

"Happy?"

"I wouldn't go that far, but you did great."

A look at his face confirmed his words. Of course he

wasn't happy—what was there to be happy about? She had invaded his life and he was now being forced to care for her. She should be grateful, and she forced herself to reserve her feelings of sadness until she was truly alone.

"Thank you. Now, if you'll excuse me…?"

"Leave the door open."

"What?" she questioned, shocked by the request. The bathroom was her only possibility for privacy. She hadn't yet had a chance to see what she really looked like post-op, and wanted some time alone to finally see the scar that would forever remind her of what she had lost.

"The bathroom has a separate toilet and door for privacy, but if you are going to be in the shower with hot water and prolonged standing I'd like you to leave the door open so I can hear if you need me."

"Is that the only reason?" she teased, needing to lighten the conversation and her thoughts.

"I have a photographic memory Chloe. I can see you naked any time I want. Go shower. I'm here if you need me."

For the next four days they didn't leave the loft. She slept and studied, and spent more time talking to Tate than she had in the years prior. She knew a lot from the time they had spent together while he was dating Kate, but now they had the opportunity to talk just the two of them and she loved their conversations. They talked about everything—their families, their past, their education and career plans—and Chloe really began to feel as if she truly knew him.

She was reading a textbook chapter on abdominal pain when the front door buzzer rang. Tate didn't appear surprised and buzzed the person up without speaking. There wasn't time to ask questions as he made his way to the front door.

Her mouth fell open as he met and greeted an older woman. With her classic silver-gray bob and the same height and eyes as Tate Chloe knew it was his mother. She immediately tried to make herself presentable, adjusting the cream cowl neck sweater she was wearing and trying desperately to rein in her hair, which she had left to tumble freely past her shoulders.

The pair made their way to her and she tried to stand, but the pain and tightness she still felt in her abdomen slowed her.

"Oh, dear, please stay sitting," Tate's mother admonished thoughtfully.

Tate smiled, and she couldn't help but share his sentiment.

"Mom, this is Chloe Darcy. Chloe, this is my mother—Lauren Reed."

She reached out to shake her hand but instead was enveloped in a warm embrace.

"Lovely to meet you, Chloe. I'm so glad to hear that you are doing well."

An overwhelming feeling of being cared for overrode her thoughts about what Lauren Reed knew. Had Tate told her about the pregnancy? If he had she seemed unconcerned with their circumstances.

"Thank you, Mrs. Reed."

"Oh, please call me Lauren."

"Thank you, Lauren."

"I asked my mom to stay with you while I run some errands this afternoon."

Chloe blushed, both at his thought and at his mom being asked to be her "babysitter." "That's not necessary."

"I knew you would say that—that is why we both

agreed not to mention it to you. I'll be back in a few hours. Have fun."

Had he really just winked at her? Chloe made a conscious effort to keep her jaw from dropping as she watched Tate grab his jacket and keys and leave.

"Can I get you a cup of tea, Chloe?" Lauren offered.

"Yes, please." Truthfully, she would have preferred something stronger as she had no idea how to handle this new setting.

She watched as Lauren moved through Tate's kitchen with obvious familiarity. She knew Tate was close with his family, but it was still lovely to see how close as his mom effortlessly put together a tea service and returned to sit beside Chloe.

"Thank you for the tea, and for taking the time to spend with me today."

"It's my pleasure, Chloe. It is not often my son needs me these days, and I appreciate the opportunity to meet the reason why."

She was still smiling, and Chloe got the feeling there was a lot she was not saying.

"I appreciate everything Tate has done for me."

"Well, don't appreciate my son too much. We both know he has his faults, and he needs to be reminded of them every once and a while."

"Excuse me?"

"Tate's stubborn and independent. It's been great for his career but not for his personal life."

If Chloe hadn't already been surprised by the day's events, she would have been shocked now.

"Don't get me wrong, dear. Your friend Kate is a lovely girl, but she wasn't right for Tate. She didn't inspire him. My son needs to be challenged. Tate needs to be uncomfortable."

It seemed as though Tate's mother knew more about their dynamic than she had thought. Chloe's mind replayed all the ways she had made Tate uncomfortable. From the aftermath of their first and only night together to his nightly attempts to sleep on the couch. If her goal was to make him uncomfortable then she had succeeded.

"Mrs. Reed—" she started, before noticing the reproachful elevation of one of her companion's eyebrows. "Lauren," she corrected herself. "Tate and I are not in a romantic relationship."

"It saddens me to hear that, my dear, but I have faith that it won't stay like that for long."

"I'm not sure..."

Lauren placed her hand on Chloe's and she paused mid-sentence.

"Chloe, I know my son well and I trust him. You should too. Now, enough with this seriousness—tell me more about you."

Two hours later Chloe was laughing so hard she thought she might need to restart some of her pain medication to deal with the soreness in her stomach. It was nice to have the lingering uncertainty of her relationship with Tate lifted for a short time. It was also nice to get to know Tate even more through the stories his mother told of his childhood with three younger sisters.

The front door of the loft slid open and Tate came through, with a bouquet of flowers in one hand and the other a collection of shopping bags.

He smiled at them both as he moved to join them, putting down his collection. "I see you two have done just fine without me."

"I was just telling Chloe about the time you were so desperate for a little brother you cut Emily's hair and insisted we all start calling her Eli."

"Not my finest moment," Tate acknowledged, with an obvious pride in his former self's ingenuity.

"Well, Chloe. It was wonderful to finally meet you and get to spend the afternoon together. I look forward to doing it again sometime soon."

"You are welcome to stay for a while, Mom."

"I know, Tate, but truthfully I came to visit Chloe—not you. Now, if you'll excuse me, I'll leave you two as I found you. Take care of her, Tate. She's worth it."

Chloe felt herself turn the shade of her hair as Lauren once again embraced first Tate and then her, prior to leaving the loft.

"I would ask what you talked about while I was gone but I'm too afraid of the answer." Tate grinned.

"She's wonderful, Tate. You are lucky to have her—and so close by."

"I know. Even if she *does* have the habit of involving herself in my personal life."

Chloe felt herself blush, thinking back to Lauren's words about her son. She hoped she was right about Kate, and that Tate had come to recognize that too. She looked back at him and the collection of goods around him.

"Do I need to put those in water?" she asked, looking at the bouquet of brightly colored flowers.

"I can do it. I want you to open the rest first."

She stared at the large pile of packages and realized Tate had gone out shopping for *her*. "I don't know what to say…"

"Don't say anything—just open."

The first bag contained her favorite line of bath products. Bubble bath, shower gel and lotion, all in her favorite citrus and sandalwood scent. She looked up at him questioningly.

"I thought you deserved to smell like *you*."

She didn't know what to say, so said nothing and moved on to the next package. She pulled out the largest bag of wine gums she had ever seen. She looked up at him again, with the same surprise in her eyes.

"What you like to eat while you study."

Without response she moved to the third bag. It contained a collection of designer yoga pants, long-sleeve tops and hoodies. He answered this time before she could ask the question.

"I thought you deserved to be comfortable and knew these were your favorite."

She got to the last bag, only to discover high-waisted cotton underwear—granny panties. She was horrified and tried to stuff them back in the bag. She couldn't even look at him this time.

"Those won't rub on your incision," he explained, almost as embarrassed as she was.

Truthfully, her low-cut briefs had been rubbing painfully, but how he knew that she had no idea. She was touched by his thoughtfulness. Few men would be caught dead making this kind of purchase.

"Thank you."

They both stood and reached for the flowers. His hand closed over hers and for a moment stayed there as they met each other's eyes. He was so close she could smell the masculine scent of his soap—the one she had shared for the past few days. She wanted him to kiss her, but he didn't.

"I'll get you a vase if you want to arrange the flowers."

"Okay," she managed.

They both made their way to the kitchen and she unbundled the bouquet and set about trimming the stems. She started opening drawers in search of kitchen scissors when she saw it—a square light blue ring box. She wanted to put it back, to shove it to the back of the drawer and never look at it again. But she couldn't. Instead she slowly opened the lid to discover a diamond ring. She didn't have to think for long about what it was and who it was meant for. It was the ring Tate had bought for Kate—the one he had proposed with. But why had he kept it?

"Careful with that."

Tate's voice cut through her thoughts.

She felt like a kid caught with her fingers in the candy drawer. Without thinking she reached out and handed it to him. She watched as he closed the box and replaced it in the drawer.

"You kept the ring?" she finally managed.

"Yes."

"Why?"

"I have my reasons."

She could tell by the look on his face and his tone of voice that he didn't want to discuss it further. She did. His answer told her nothing. Did he think Kate was going to change her mind? Or did he want a reminder of their past together. How did he feel about Kate?

But all the questions that Chloe had in her mind were going to remain that way. Their conversation was definitely over, and Chloe was not going to get any of the answers she was looking for.

CHAPTER FIVE

AFTER TWO WEEKS Tate returned to work and Chloe welcomed the privacy. She needed to regain her independence, and that wasn't going to happen if she was constantly attended to by Tate.

A knock on the loft's industrial door snapped her from her train of thought. She put down the resuscitation algorithms she had been reviewing and braced her abdomen, using her other hand to steady herself as she made her way to the door. Kate, dressed casually in jeans and a light purple fitted shirt, was on the other side, with a new glow about her. She was beautiful, and for the first time in her life Chloe felt self-conscious next to her. She looked down at her black yoga pants and loose-fitting blue sweatshirt and knew she paled in comparison. Jealousy hinted at the edge of her consciousness and she did her best to push it away.

"Hi, stranger."

And Kate's familiar smile washed away any negative thoughts she had been feeling. Kate embraced her gently before they both moved back into the living room.

"How are you feeling?" Kate asked.

"Tired, sore," she replied. *Confused*, she added to herself. "On a happier note, how are things with you?" she added, needing to change the topic. She had had enough time to think about her own life recently.

"Wonderful. It's funny that for so many years I thought this would be the worst time of my life, with exam stress and getting ready to leave, but instead it is the best. Matt found a new apartment for us in New York to start our new beginning together, and we've decided to get married in the Hamptons on the August long weekend."

Kate's smile was infectious, and despite her problems Chloe felt a similar wave of happiness pass through her. A sparkle caught her attention and she immediately wondered how she had missed it. On Kate's left hand was a large emerald cut diamond flanked with two smaller similar side stones on a polished platinum band. It was stunning.

"Oh, Kate, it's so beautiful—and absolutely perfect for you," she gushed with emotion.

"I know. Everything feels right for the first time in a really long time."

Chloe's envy returned full force.

"Are things weird, living with Tate?"

Chloe was unprepared for the complete change of focus. She looked into her friend's soft gray eyes and knew there was nothing behind the question—and certainly no knowledge of what had happened between them.

She tried her best to put on the same smile she had for the past two years when talking about Tate. "Tate's been very generous, letting me stay at his loft and taking time off to stay with me. I'm very grateful."

She watched a flicker of doubt cross Kate's face she knew she hadn't sold Kate on her feelings. She was happy when Kate let the matter drop.

"And Ryan?" Kate asked.

Chloe was surprised again by the question, and the

change in Kate's tone and facial expression as she asked about the other man. She looked even more serious than when she had been discussing her and her ex's living arrangements. On the other hand things *had* been weird that day in her hospital room, and Chloe herself wasn't as confident as she once had been in her perception of the other man.

"Ryan's been great. He's called a couple of times, and next week he is going to come over and help me practice some oral examination questions for the Boards."

"Is it awkward, seeing him?" Kate asked.

"Because of the pregnancy?" Chloe asked, her confusion still present.

"Yes."

"It was at the beginning, but Ryan has been really discreet and understanding about everything that happened and we are moving past it."

"Do you think you will be able to work together still?"

"Yes, definitely. We are both professional adults, and both very good at our jobs, so it shouldn't be hard. Probably easier than *your* plans to come back here to work in the same department as Tate, the man you were almost engaged to, once you are done with your fellowship."

She didn't mean to sound defensive but she knew that she did. It was just hard to imagine that on top of everything her relationship with Ryan had also changed.

"I guess... My relationship with Tate seems like a lifetime ago."

"It was nine months ago," Chloe corrected.

"Yes, but things are so different now, and we have both moved on."

"Kate, he professed his love for you and asked you to be his wife."

"He didn't mean it."

"How can you be sure?" Chloe asked. Her heart was still convinced that Tate was hung up on his Katherine.

"Sure of what?"

"How do you know Tate is over you?" Because *she* certainly wasn't over them, and she wasn't convinced Tate was either.

The slide of the heavy loft door ended their conversation as they both directed their attention to the man walking through it. It was one of his rare daytime appearances at home and Chloe had to wonder how much it had to do with Kate's visit. He did, however, seem surprised at his ex's presence.

Kate stood from the couch. "Hey, I just came over to visit Chloe."

"I can see that. You are welcome anytime, Kate."

"Thanks."

The exchange held no tension but it was still painful to watch. Tate tossed his keys into a bowl at the front entry and removed his suit jacket, draping it over one of the chairs in the living room before coming to sit with them. Chloe felt herself running her fingers through her hair before she was aware of the action. She sighed audibly; nothing was going to make her close to Kate's beauty— not at this moment, and maybe never in Tate's eyes.

"Are you tired? Do you want us to leave so you can rest?" Tate asked, his attention focused on her.

"No, I'm fine."

Two pairs of eyes looked at her skeptically.

"Really, I'm fine. I'm not used to doing nothing, and it's hard not to be able to do the things I used to do."

"Like...?" Tate asked, and she hoped she didn't seem ungrateful for everything he had done for her.

"Go outside," she said. She felt as if she was going crazy, being alone all day with nothing but her own thoughts, but she had promised Tate she wouldn't go out alone.

"Let's go out, then. If you want we can go out for dinner tonight. Somewhere close by and familiar, but still *out*."

"That would be great," she agreed, her outlook already improving.

"Kate, would you like to join us?" Tate asked.

She looked at her friend expectantly, willing her to say no.

Kate repeated Chloe's words. "That would be great."

"Then it's settled." He pulled off the tie that had been knotted at his neck and undid the collar of his shirt before proceeding into the kitchen to make arrangements.

Chloe stood again and made her way toward the bedroom platform, opening her designated drawer and searching for something that would both fit and be flattering. She managed to settle on a previously loose-fitting royal-blue jersey dress that now clung to her still swollen breasts and the curve of her hips. It would have to do. Her brief pregnancy and the post-operative changes to her body had ruled out the majority of her wardrobe.

She gathered the uncontrolled waves of her hair into a ponytail and used what little make-up Kate had packed to add some color back to her face. When she was done she knew it was an improvement, but nothing compared to Kate.

When she exited the bathroom she found Kate and Tate both on the couch. The quiet conversation that they'd been having was immediately stopped by her presence. Maybe she was wrong—maybe things *could* become more uncomfortable between her and the two people she loved most in this world.

She put on the same smile she had for the past two years. "So, where are we going?"

"Kate suggested Italian."

"Sounds great— let's go."

The small restaurant was familiar, and a comfort to Chloe. She hadn't realized how isolated she had felt until she was out. The *maître d'* hugged and kissed both women affectionately before shaking Tate's hand, recognizing him on sight. "Dr. Reed we have an excellent table for you and your companions this evening."

"Companions" was a safe descriptor, Chloe thought as they were led to a curved booth that had already been set for the correct number. Tate grasped her arm as she gently lowered herself down onto the leather. He didn't follow, and Kate entered the other side, moving to the center as Tate sat opposite her.

The first few minutes were filled with silence as they all examined their menus and selected their meals.

When the waiter returned Tate ordered a bottle of red wine and appetizers for the table and they each ordered.

"I was hoping you were going to pick the steak," Tate commented after the waiter had left.

"Why would I pick the steak?"

"To help replace your iron."

"Is that why your housekeeper keeps preparing meals and stocking the fridge with red meat, leafy greens and fortified cereals?"

"Maybe," he answered, with a small satisfied smile on his face.

Kate's laugh broke through and Chloe couldn't help but join in.

The *maître d'* arrived with their bottle of wine, uncorked it, and offered a small amount to Tate for his approval. Once approved, he began filling glasses. Chloe declined, not sure how the wine would affect her ongoing nausea and mild dizziness. The *maître d'* filled Kate's glass and paused mid-pour, his eyes fixated on Kate's ring.

"Congratulations, my dear. I didn't realize there was cause for celebration. Dr. Reed has magnificent taste in both women *and* rings."

Chloe felt her mouth fall open and her eyes widen in horror at the man's assumption. He obviously knew Tate, and had known them both as a couple. She looked at Kate, who looked equally as uncomfortable and speechless.

"Thank you, Antonio." Tate graciously accepted the intended compliment with no obvious embarrassment.

Chloe watched as Antonio left, still speechless. Had that really just happened?

"Well, he is right on at least one account." Tate remarked as he took a large sip from his glass of wine. "Beautiful ring, Kate."

She wondered if he was comparing it to the one *he* had bought for Kate.

"Thank you. We've set a date for the August long weekend in the Hamptons. I hope you can come."

Chloe looked over at Kate, who was fidgeting nervously, turning her ring round and round on her finger.

"I wouldn't miss it."

How was it possible that *she* was the most uncomfortable with this conversation? But, looking between the two of them, she realized she obviously was. Thankfully the conversation changed to work, and Chloe breathed a sigh of relief. Then their appetizers arrived, followed by their main courses.

They talked about the hospital and the upcoming Board exams. Tate and Kate even briefly asked about each other's families, and Chloe couldn't get over the level of comfort and how at ease they were with each other after everything. Times had changed, it seemed— not just for Chloe, but for Kate and Tate as well. She wasn't sure which scenario she was more comfortable with: Tate and Kate not speaking to each other immediately post-breakup, or this back-to-normal resolution.

She looked down at her plate of seafood linguine and realized that she had barely touched her pasta. It tasted amazing, but her appetite was still not back and the ever-present feeling of nausea she had struggled with over the past few weeks still had not subsided.

"Are you okay?" Tate asked, his eyes directed at her full plate.

"Yes," she answered. "I just haven't gotten back to my regular appetite yet."

"Has this been too much?" Kate asked.

Yes, she thought to herself. Not the outing and not the meal, but the combination of the three of them together felt like too much.

"I'll get the check and take you home."

Before she could answer Tate had signaled for their waiter, who presented himself promptly.

"That's not necessary. You two should stay and enjoy your meal. I can get a taxi."

"No, I'll take you home." Tate was resolute, and she knew not to argue the matter further.

"I'm sorry," she apologized to Kate.

"Don't be. It's normal to still be exhausted by the little things. It will get better, I promise." Kate reached out and squeezed her hand reassuringly.

They drove back to Tate's loft together, dropping Kate off at her car before entering the underground car park. Once back inside, Chloe felt spent.

"Are you going back to the hospital tonight?" she asked, not knowing what his new routine would be but hoping for some privacy to digest the evening.

"No. I thought we could relax and watch a movie together. If you fall asleep that's okay too."

She was taken aback by the normalcy of his suggestion. They really didn't *do* normal. They did passion and distant and awkward to a tee.

"That would be great. Give me a few minutes to change out of this dress and wash my face."

"Sure."

She walked back toward the bathroom and changed into loose-fitting shorts and a T-shirt. It wasn't exactly the finest lingerie, but it was what she had with her and it covered her body and eased her self-consciousness. When she emerged from the bathroom most of the lights were off in the loft and the television that was stowed within one of the tall bedroom cabinets had arisen from its hidden resting spot. She was surprised to see Tate on what she thought of as "his" side of the bed, still fully dressed and on top of the covers. He had not moved from the couch or even approached the bed in the past weeks.

"I thought you would be more comfortable lying down than with both of us on the couch."

"Thank you." She moved slowly up the two stairs onto the bedroom platform, watching as Tate pulled back the covers as he had done once before for her, waiting for her to join him. He had placed some extra pillows on the bed to support their upper backs and heads.

"Do you have any preferences?" he asked as he used the remote to turn on the large flat screen.

"Something funny; nothing serious or violent. I don't need any more nightmares." She yawned.

The television went to "mute" and Tate turned to face her. "You're having nightmares?"

She regretted her words almost immediately. She'd been having nightmares even before her collapse and hospitalization. Her dreams had become much more vivid and she had become much more sensitive to the stimuli around her. Now, after her collapse, it was worse and she would frequently have dreams of patients she couldn't save. Sometimes that patient was herself and sometimes it was her lost baby.

"Yes."

"Do you want to talk about them?" he asked gently.

"Is it okay to say no? I already feel tortured enough during them; it's hard to think about them a second time."

"Of course."

The volume returned to the television and within a few moments he had selected a famous animated children's film, featuring a fiery redheaded princess heroine.

"I thought you would appreciate something familiar."

She turned toward him. No sound escaped him, but she could see from the subtle movements coming from him that he was laughing silently at his own reference. She smiled at this return to his trademark sarcasm.

He smiled back. "Truly, Chloe, my sisters and my nieces all swear it's a great movie for both children and adults."

"We'll see..." she said, in the same teasing banter.

She wasn't sure when she nodded off, but it was a deeper sleep than she had achieved in the past two weeks. And Tate didn't leave her for the couch.

The first time she stirred she felt a strong arm cross over her and his soft words echoed through the darkness. "You're okay." This happened several times through the night, until she was welded against him the way she had once been. Somehow she remained conscious of where she was and her dreams of helplessness remained at bay.

After that evening she was never alone. She didn't dare question how he had managed to avoid nights on call for a total of four weeks now, but instead relaxed into the solace he provided. Every night he would sleep next to her—fully dressed and on top of the covers she was tucked beneath, but next to her just the same.

She feared she was growing dependent on him. She needed to remember that this was not permanent and that once she was recovered they would go their separate ways.

She pushed away the textbook she had been reading and stood. She was feeling better and better every day, with her incision pulling only slightly at the corners and her nausea subsiding.

She walked to the bathroom, which had soon become her favorite room in the loft, both for its privacy and its luxury. She stripped from her clothing and entered the shower. She would miss this shower. The large glass enclosure was imposing, but also comforting. The showerhead had multiple settings, perfecting the pressure of the hot water that sprayed all over her body.

The sound of the shower water was one of the few that could drown out her thoughts. She stood until the heat began to overwhelm her senses and threatened to interfere with her still precarious balance. Dense steam covered the mirror and filled the room, which preserved her solitude as she made her way to the large double sink and mirror. She wiped the excess water from her body and wrapped a towel around her before she started on her hair. She worked through the long red waves as best she could, soon tiring and taking breaks between sections, letting her body weight rest against the counter.

She felt a hand cover her own before she saw him. The shock led to a small gasp and the final loss of her balance. She reached out to the hard granite for support. Unfortunately in the process of doing so her loosely slung towel fell to the floor.

"*Oh, God*," she thought, and was surprised to hear her voice expressing the sentiment.

"No, just me—Tate." Tate, quiet and sarcastic.

She smiled and just for a moment forgot that she was standing in front of him completely naked. She started to bend for the towel, but was beaten to it by Tate, who had already bent to retrieve the lost covering.

He stopped midway in rising. Chloe didn't dare to look down and instead closed her eyes. He was at eye level with her lower abdomen and she felt his hand trace the incision that now ran along the top of her bikini line. Despite the fact that he had already seen her naked, had already been deep inside her, this felt more intimate than anything prior. His face was very close to her most private of areas and she was completely naked under his fully clothed assessment. He placed his hand flat against her abdomen and she could feel him through the numbness she had acquired. His hand slid upwards but stopped short of her breasts, which she felt his eyes appraising even though she still couldn't bring herself to look.

She finally opened her eyes as she felt the towel being fastened securely around her. Apparently he found her lacking, and the sting of rejection burned throughout her body. She had barely glimpsed his face before he grasped her shoulders and turned her toward the mirror.

She remained silent, transfixed at the slow appearance of her reflection as the steam cleared from the mirror.

Tate took the brush from her hand and worked it through her long hair, gently teasing away the tangles with his fingers and being careful not to pull at her scalp. It was hard not to melt into the moment. His actions were intimate, but his earlier evaluation and rejection kept her tense. He didn't look up from the task at hand until he was finished, and then his face rose to meet her gaze through the mirror's reflection.

"When is your follow-up appointment?"

The words surprised her and a chill coursed through her body.

He walked away from her briefly, returning with his robe. The black terrycloth was warm and heavy on her shoulders as he helped her thread her arms through the too-long sleeves. She appreciated the physical barrier.

"When is your follow-up appointment with Dr. Thomas?" Tate asked again, and she was just as surprised by the question on its second asking.

"Next week. Why?"

"I'll have to rearrange my schedule."

"That isn't necessary. I can take a cab."

"I want to be there."

"Why?"

"I have some questions."

"What's happened has happened and nothing can change that."

"I know."

His acceptance surprised her. "So what is the point, Tate?" Her frustration was breaking though.

"I need to know that you are going to be all right."

"I am." She needed to believe that even more than she needed *him* to.

"I'm still going."

"Be reasonable, Tate. My appointment is at the hospital. How is it going to look if people see us together?"

"I could care less."

He meant it. Maybe it was ego, maybe it was confidence, or maybe it was just that Tate Reed's love life had been the center of the hospital rumor mill for so long that he really didn't care. But she did. She had learned not to let the rumors about her supposed love life faze her, but the thought of the hospital being abuzz about her picking up where her best friend had left off was too much.

"I care."

"You shouldn't."

"There are a lot of things I shouldn't care about, but that doesn't change the way I feel, Tate."

"I'm sorry."

She turned from the mirror to look at him directly and she could see the truth behind his words. He *was* sorry. Sorry for *her*. She could only fear why. Did he know about her feelings?

"It's not your fault." It wasn't. Hadn't she always known where his heart lay?

"Isn't it?"

She couldn't continue this. "No, it's not. I think I should move back to my apartment."

"I'd like you to stay until after your follow-up appointment with Dr. Thomas."

"I don't think that is a good idea."

"When has *anything* between us been a good idea?"

It was him again—same old Tate—and even if his words were true they still hurt.

"Never," she conceded.

"Then why break our pattern now?"

"Because this isn't normal, Tate. We're not a couple and we cannot keep acting as though we are."

"Is that what you think I've been doing? Acting?"

His eyes had narrowed and she immediately felt as if she had said something more hurtful than she had intended.

"No, Tate. You've been great the past few weeks. But this isn't who we are, and I can't keep relying on a combination of your generosity and guilt to make you take care of me. I need to stand on my own feet again."

Surprise and discomfort were apparent as he tensed the features of his face and withdrew slightly from her. "It's not like that."

"It's exactly like that. Up until my hospitalization you wanted nothing to do with me. I understand why, and appreciate the change of heart, but this—us—isn't what you had planned."

He looked as if he wanted to argue the matter further but no words left him as he stared at her.

"I'll drive you home when you're ready."

"Thank you." A sense of relief she hadn't known she was holding in left her as Tate finally turned and left the bathroom. She watched him, waiting for the door to close behind him, but he stopped and turned back toward her.

"Chloe, I still intend to be with you at your appointment next week." The door clicked shut behind him.

So maybe they were not completely done.

CHAPTER SIX

SHE LASTED THREE days at home before she truly thought she was losing her mind—or would if she didn't go back to work. It wasn't just the isolation at Tate's apartment that had been getting to her, it was the complete departure from her previous life that she couldn't stand. She loved and needed her work. It was the part of her normal life which she had been searching for most desperately.

She was more nervous about her first day back at work than she had been for her first day of residency. But she walked into the emergency department and her nerves eased. The familiar hum of the department felt like home.

She went to change into her scrubs. The women's change room was not any different, despite the fact that she had almost died on the floor. She shuddered and walked quickly to her locker, pulling on the dark blue top and pants, annoyed that she still had some post-operative swelling in her abdomen, making the pants more snug than normal.

She entered Section B—minor treatment—and smiled. Standing at the triage desk was Ryan Callum, and she appreciated the familiar face.

"I didn't know you were on today," she remarked casually, wanting things between them to remain as they always had been.

"Apparently some of us don't know when to stay home. Welcome back, Chloe."

He was smiling at her but she could still feel his concern and assessment.

"Thank you—for everything." She knew that was all that needed to be said between them.

She went to grab for a chart when the sound of a child's wailing pierced through the department. The sound wasn't new, or even out of place in the Emergency Department, but there was something about this particular cry.

She found her answer in the red face of a toddler who was being held down by one of the other residents in an attempt to establish an intravenous line. It wasn't a cry of pain, but a cry of terror. There was a nurse, but no other people in the room—no parents. The child looked terrified.

"Dr. Russell?" Chloe called, and both the resident, Andrew Russell, and the child paused in their battle to focus on her. "Can I speak to you for a moment?"

She could tell he was angry but she didn't care. She didn't say a word until they were outside the cubicle with the sliding door shut.

"Yes, Dr. Darcy?" Dr. Russell's tone was unmistakably bitter.

"What is that child presenting with?" she asked, not rising to his confrontation.

"How is that any of your business?"

"Andrew, what's wrong with that child."

"I didn't realize you were back. Must be nice to get five weeks off. I wonder what entitled you to special treatment? Come to think about it, I don't need to think about that one very long." He looked leeringly down toward her chest.

"Dr. Russell, I suggest you regain your professionalism before you say something you will regret. Now, what is wrong with that child?"

"You won't be Chief forever, Chloe."

"No, you are correct on that. As of July first I will be attending staff at Boston General—so, as I said, Andrew, don't say anything that you are going to regret."

She watched as disbelief and then resignation passed over him. She knew that she was the only resident to be hired direct from training in the past ten years and if Andrew had any hope of ever returning to Boston General he had to keep himself in line.

"She's a three-year-old who fell from two and a half meters in height at daycare. After the accident she was somnolent and unresponsive and now is combative and irritable. I'm trying to establish an intravenous so she can be sedated for a CT scan of her head." His arrogance had returned.

"Why are you doing a scan?"

"For the reasons I just explained."

"But look at her now. She is very oriented, responsive, and quite frankly terrified."

"That doesn't mean she doesn't have a brain injury."

"I agree. But what I disagree on is exposing a three-year-old to potentially scary treatment, not to mention unnecessary radiation."

"So what do you suggest I do?"

"Call Pediatrics, ask that the child be admitted for observation, and find her parents. That is what she needs."

"Will there be anything else?"

He knew she was right, but that didn't change the animosity between them.

"Dr. Russell, I guarantee that when you present your new plan to Dr. Callum and the pediatric attending you will be commended for your conservative management. Why don't you go do that?"

She watched as he walked away before she went back into the cubicle. The little girl focused on her and she watched as her little chin began to wobble and tears filled her eyes. Chloe moved slowly, choosing to sit next to the little girl and doing her best not to intimidate the already frightened child.

"Hi, sweetie, it's okay to be scared. No one is going to hurt you."

The little girl was still eyeing her suspiciously. She looked between Chloe and the nurse, her fear still very apparent. The nurse was still holding the intravenous supplies and looming above them both.

"Cassie, we're good here."

The nurse took her direction and left. The little girl instantly relaxed and Chloe left silence for a few minutes. She watched, rewarded, when the little girl slowly scooted down the bed toward her.

"Do you want to go and play with some toys?"

She nodded and held out her arms, waiting to be lifted. Chloe reached for her and hoisted her into her arms, swaying slightly at the weight of her and the unexpected difficulty of the task. She steadied herself and then made her way out of the cubicle toward the pediatric play area.

"Jaclyn!"

Chloe swayed for a second time as the little girl jerked in her arms. Chloe turned in the same direction, to see a woman running frantically toward her. When the woman reached them the little girl jumped from her arms and into her mother's.

"Oh, thank God," the woman cried. "How is she? Is she all right?"

"She's much better now. We've asked a pediatrician

to come and see her, and possibly admit her overnight for observation, but I think she is going to be just fine. You can wait with her over in the pediatric play area, if you like."

"Thank you so much for taking care of her."

"She's easy to take care of."

Chloe watched as the woman walked away, with the little girl, Jaclyn, still holding her tightly. A mother and her child. *She* wanted that. She had assured Tate that she was going to be all right, but that didn't mean she hadn't spent the last five weeks worrying. Would she ever be a mother? Would she be able to have a successful pregnancy after everything that had happened? Would she find another man she would love and whose child she would want to have?

She shook away her thoughts and went to grab another chart.

Four hours later she was exhausted. She had spent the day suturing, casting and following up tests, but she felt spent despite the simple treatment needed by her patients.

Chloe rested her head on her hand as she scrolled through the computerized images that had sliced her patient's abdomen into sections for review. The radiologist had reviewed the same images and attached a report, but she always looked first. Finally she saw it: the inflammation in the patient's right lower quadrant and the swollen prominence of the appendix. It wasn't a surprise. Her exam had already made the diagnosis, but confirmatory imaging made it an easier sell on consultation.

Ryan joined her at the monitors. "If you already knew it was appendicitis why did you get the CT scan?"

"Because a CT scan clearly demonstrating appendicitis will get the patient to the operating room faster than asking General Surgery Service to take my word for it.

This way they can take one look at the images and book the patient instead of a medical student, then the resident, re-examining the patient and maybe still ordering a CT scan because they don't trust their own exam skills and are too scared to be wrong."

"So it was easier to expose the patient to unnecessary radiation and expensive testing than to argue your findings?"

He was challenging her, as he always did. She should be grateful that he wasn't going easy on her.

"Today it was," she admitted, her usual sense of fight replaced by the exhaustion her first shift back had created.

"I think your plan has backfired," Ryan replied, looking up with a new coolness in his voice.

She raised her head to look in the same direction and met Tate's eyes staring across the department at her. He was wearing scrubs and was accompanied by one of the general surgery residents and a medical student.

"The entire team appears to be here to discuss and evaluate your patient."

Tate strode toward them, his focus clearly on Ryan. "Ryan."

"Tate."

She immediately knew things were still hostile between them. Both men were behaving out of character and a spirit of antagonism radiated between them.

"I was surprised to hear that Dr. Darcy had a consultation for our services. I would have thought the Emergency Department would have been a little more accommodating," Tate commented, his criticism lacking any veil.

"The Emergency Department has always been supportive of Dr. Darcy in all the professional choices she makes—including her decision to return to work."

His emphasis on the word *professional* was making it clear to both of them that he didn't support the recent personal choices she had made.

She looked at both men and knew she needed to end this before something was said aloud that she didn't want said. The general surgery resident was clearly uncomfortable with this deviation from the norm. Having his staff come downstairs to supervise a basic appendicitis consult was demoralizing. And the medical student didn't seem to know any better.

"The patient is a twenty-four-year-old woman coming to the Emergency Department with a one-day history of increasing abdominal pain that has now localized in the right lower quadrant. It hurts her to move and she is lying very still. She has nausea and vomiting associated with the pain and no other symptoms. On exam she is febrile, with a pulse of one hundred and thirty, and blood pressure is normal. She has rebound pain, guarding and tenderness over McBurney's point on exam. Investigations show an elevated white blood cell count of eighteen thousand and normal hemoglobin, electrolytes and kidney function."

She relayed the history, providing all the relevant information for the benefit of the medical student, trying to transition the discussion back to medicine and teaching.

"Ask Chloe why she ordered a CT scan on such a clear-cut case," Ryan said.

Tate's eyebrows were raised at her. He was not willing to play directly into the conversation Ryan was orchestrating. The gesture was as good as the question, though.

"I ordered the CT to definitively prove appendicitis." She waited, knowing that Ryan was not going to be satisfied with her response.

"Chloe was just arguing that General Surgery will

no longer take a patient to the operating room based on history and exam alone, no matter how classic the presentation."

It was said as a challenge, from one department to another, about how they provided patient care. It was also an escalation of a testosterone-fueled dispute she would have never predicted from either man.

"I don't think it best practice to make assumptions about what *any* service would or wouldn't do. Dr. Munnoch, please go and consent the patient for surgery and discuss aspects of informed consent with our student."

The resident and the medical student left.

"Chloe, can I speak to you for a minute?" said Tate. It was less of a question for her and more a direction for Ryan to leave.

"Okay," she affirmed to both men, and waited for Ryan to go before choosing her next words. "What are you doing here?" she asked, as patiently as she could manage.

"I was going to ask you the same thing," he replied, his annoyance even more clear in the absence of observers.

"I'm working, Tate. This is where I work."

"I don't have a problem with that, Chloe. Where and with whom you work is none of my business."

"What is that supposed to mean?"

"Ryan Callum is very protective of you."

"Ryan Callum has always been there for me and he helped save my life. Surely if anyone can understand the relationship between a mentor and a protégée it's you?"

Her temper had gotten away from her and she regretted her words even as they met her own ears. Drawing a comparison between her and Ryan and Tate and Kate wasn't fair, or accurate. There was nothing romantic between her and Ryan.

"This isn't about Kate," he replied defensively, not missing the undercurrent of her remark, but his voice only carrying as far as her.

"*Everything* is about Kate," she stated, knowing it was the truth between them.

"That's far from the truth."

They were getting nowhere. "Tate, what are you doing *here*?" she asked again, as a means to end their conversation's previous trajectory.

"I agreed to take some General Surgery on call to make up for my recent absence. I was surprised to hear from my resident that *you* were the consulting physician. I wanted to make sure you were okay to be back at work."

"You don't need to worry about me. I can take care of myself." For the second time that day she felt a clinical appraisal as Tate's eyes ran up and down her body.

"We'll see about that. What time are you done?"

"I'm just finishing up. The appy was my last patient."

"Page me when you are done and I'll drive you home."

"That isn't necessary," she replied with frustration.

She understood where Ryan and Tate were coming from with their protective overtures, but enough was enough. Despite everything that had happened she didn't doubt her own capabilities, and they shouldn't either.

"That wasn't an option, Chloe. I'm either driving you home to your apartment or my loft. Those are your options."

It wasn't worth the fight. When had she ever been able to change Tate's mind about anything? "Fine. I just need to sign off the chart and change."

She walked away and back toward the change room, discarding her scrubs into the hospital linen basket and getting back into her own clothing. Her jeans were even more snug than they had been that morning, and they dug uncomfortably into her lower abdomen.

After thirty seconds of discomfort she gave up and undid the button and the zipper. She retrieved a hair tie from her pocket and threaded it through the buttonhole, using the loop end to secure the button a few more inches away from where it had previously been fastened. She untucked her white button-down dress shirt and slipped on tall brown leather boots over the skinny legs of her jeans before leaving.

"Everything okay?"

Tate's voice greeted her before she'd even realized he was standing outside the women's change room door.

"Didn't anyone ever tell you it's creepy to stand outside women's change room doors?" she replied, with both humor and aggravation.

"No, but—as I told you a few days ago—I really don't care what other people think."

Chloe Darcy was going to be the death of him—if she didn't bring herself to permanent harm first. He'd hated dropping her off at her apartment, and equally hated the sight of his empty loft. His love of the masculine open concept design had vanished and now the space felt large and empty. Unfortunately he was more than aware that what was bothering him most about the space was that she wasn't there.

When had what seemed so wrong—Chloe Darcy in his bed and his life—started to feel so right? It wasn't what he had planned...it wasn't even something he had pursued. Two words that had defined every achievement in his life: planning and pursuit. But Chloe had just *happened*, and he felt more insecure with her than he remembered ever feeling before. He had no idea where he stood with her, or if there was the possibility for anything more.

Had he ruined their chances by being with Kate? There were so many questions that needed to be answered. He couldn't read her. Except that since her hospitalization there was a new sadness about her that she tried to keep to herself. Was it the loss of the pregnancy? Or was there something more?

Ryan Callum was an unwanted facet to this situation. It didn't help, seeing them together. Even an outside observer could see that Chloe was clearly more comfortable with Ryan than she was with him. He had never in his life felt jealous of anything or anyone, and it was a new emotion he didn't enjoy. The sight of Ryan and Chloe together made him want to throw away everything he had worked for and earned in favor of a macho display of aggression he had never considered before.

Then there was Chloe herself. She was different, and something was telling himself to pay attention to those changes. He didn't know how but he had a definite feeling that there was something still linking them together.

CHAPTER SEVEN

SHE STILL HADN'T gotten used to being a patient. Sitting in the waiting room of Dr. Thomas's outpatient clinic, she thumbed through a magazine meant to help her pass the time until it was her turn. She had arrived ten minutes earlier, after getting blood work done, and now was both anxious for the appointment and about Tate's arrival.

She had managed to dissuade him from picking her up, but not from attending the appointment. It was funny that despite all they had shared and the personal nature of their acquaintance she was still uneasy about having him hear future predictions of her fertility. Being declared permanently damaged would be hard enough for her without knowing it was another way she wasn't good enough for Tate Reed.

"Chloe Darcy," a nurse called from the front of the clinic.

Chloe rose and followed the nurse to one of the examination rooms, turning with one last glance toward to the clinic's front door and breathing a slight sigh of relief at Tate's absence. She didn't know what had changed his mind, but she was grateful none the less.

She waited another ten minutes before Dr. Thomas entered the exam room. "You look better," the middle-aged man greeted her as he came to sit at the desk beside her.

"Thank you."

"How are you feeling?"

"Okay. I'm occasionally sore, but the incision has healed well. Still tired, and occasionally nauseated, but I am not sure how much of that is recovery versus my Board exam in two weeks."

Dr. Thomas's eyebrows rose as he wrote down some notes. "I remember those days well—you'll be fine. Did you get the blood work done?"

"Yes, about an hour ago."

"Okay, why don't you get changed while I go and see if the results are ready? I've paged Dr. Madden to come and see you as well. She'll be in to discuss the blood work and do the exam. There is a drape on the bed—everything off from the waist down."

She watched as he left and closed the door and then complied with his instructions. She slipped off her jeans, followed by the low-rise bikini briefs that fell below her incision, tucking them neatly into the folded jeans, then smiling at the idea of hiding your underwear from a person who was about to see you naked. She covered herself with the drape and waited.

The wait seemed like forever. Then a knock at the door sounded and she held her breath, still waiting for Tate's promised appearance. It was Erin Madden. The petite blond had achieved average height in heels and had her hair down, which was a rare occasion.

"Hey, Chloe. Dr. Thomas paged me to let me know you were in for your follow-up and asked me to come see you. It's hard to believe it has already been six weeks. How are you feeling?"

"Okay. Good days and bad days, I guess. I went back to work this week and that has helped. But I haven't been studying nearly as much as I planned and will be more than happy then this exam is done. I'm surprised to see you still at work. I would have thought you would have been off studying too."

Erin's face held the same hopeful and yet exhausted expression Chloe had come to recognize as the same look *she* had worn for some time.

"You know what they say about best intentions."

"Well, I'm here, aren't I?" Her usual humor was to cover the pain she still felt about the events leading up to her pregnancy.

"How are you feeling *really*?" Erin asked, pulling the stool from the end of the bed so she could sit and talk to her friend.

"Disappointed, frustrated—take your pick. It's hard to admit that I made such a mistake, both in getting pregnant and then not even having the medical sense to realize it. I want to be able to move past it, but I can't seem to get back to normal. I still feel tired, nauseated, and I have no control over my emotions, which just leads to more frustration."

"You may be being slightly hard on yourself."

"I know."

"Chloe, would it be okay if I examined your abdomen and we did a quick bedside ultrasound?" Erin asked, and for the first time in their conversation Chloe felt uneasy.

Something was not right.

"Of course. What are you not saying, Erin?" she asked while at the same time turning to lie on the examination table as Erin washed her hands and then moved the drape to sit low on her hips.

Erin didn't respond immediately, but her face was doing a poor job of concealing her thoughts. Chloe both felt and watched her friend's hands move over her abdomen, her fingers pressing flat two centimeters above her pelvic bone.

"Your blood work from this morning shows a persistently elevated beta-HCG."

"What does that mean?"

"It shouldn't still be elevated. If we had performed a salpingostomy and removed only the ectopic pregnancy than some residual placenta might be present in the fallopian tube, leading to the elevated hormone level, but..."

"But?"

"But your tube had ruptured and we were unable to control the bleeding from the rupture site, so we performed an open right salpingectomy, removing the entire fallopian tube. The pathology report confirmed the presence of the pregnancy. So your beta-HCG shouldn't still be elevated, unless..."

"Unless what?"

"Chloe, you may not be able to move on. I think you are still pregnant."

Time stood still as Chloe replayed the words in her head and waited for something in Erin's expression to clarify her statement.

"I don't understand."

"I think your pregnancy was a heterotopic pregnancy. One inside the fallopian tube and one in the uterus. It's a rare condition, occurring in only one in every five to thirty thousand pregnancies."

"How do we find out for sure?" Chloe managed through the pounding of her heart.

"We look."

And without further discussion Erin squeezed warmed jelly onto her abdomen and placed the ultrasound probe against her. She turned toward the screen that was visible to both women and watched as the clear outline of a baby appeared. She could see a head, body, a heart flickering, and legs and arms that stretched out and explored their environment.

"A baby..." she stated with wonder.

"Your baby," Erin confirmed. "I'm just going to do some measurements to date the pregnancy."

"There is only one date possible."

"Which makes you about fourteen weeks along."

"Does everything look okay?" she asked, her surprise over the baby being quickly replaced by fear that her surgery and the medication she'd received had caused her baby harm.

"As much as I can see right now, everything looks okay. but we're going to need to do some investigations. You received a lot of blood products that they initially didn't have time to match against your own blood screen. You also received some medication we don't recommend in pregnancy, but right now you have a baby."

"A baby..."

"How do you feel about that, Chloe?"

She watched the screen in awe. Both she and Erin were silent as the small figure moved around and she tried to reconcile in her mind the fact that everything she was seeing was actually happening inside her. She watched as Erin moved the cursor over the tiny flickering heart and was mesmerized by the sound of the heart beating that filled the room.

"Wonderful."

"Okay, so we will just go from here. I am going to give you a requisition for prenatal blood work and another ultrasound in four weeks' time so we can look at the rest of the baby's anatomy."

"Erin, is it weird that I am excited and terrified at the same time?"

"No, I remember that feeling well. You're going to be a wonderful mother, Chloe. Congratulations."

A mother…a baby…*her* baby.

Chloe felt the first genuine smile she had experienced in months turn the corners of her mouth as she got dressed, no longer frustrated at the swelling in her abdomen as she took a moment to rest a hand against it before finishing dressing.

"Hello, little one, I'm your mom and I love you so much already," she whispered aloud.

She grabbed the requisitions and left the examination room and the clinic before her first thought of Tate came to mind as she saw him striding toward her, still in scrubs and a scrub cap, with a look of irritation apparent on his face.

"I'm sorry," he greeted her before she had a chance to worry about her words to him. "Another team got into some massive bleeding and I got called in to cross-clamp the aorta."

"Don't be." Her joy was too much even to let the heartache of Tate bring her down.

"Can we go somewhere to talk?"

She wanted to tell him that they had nothing to talk about, but she now knew that was not true.

"Yes."

They walked together to one of the many coffee counters in the hospital. After getting a large black coffee for him and a peppermint tea for her they took the table for two furthest from the others.

"How was your appointment?" he asked.

She thought about the baby. She needed time to get used to the idea before she added the complexity of Tate into the equation. "It was good."

"So all your tests came back normal?"

Tate was looking at her expectantly. For a brief second she had the feeling that he knew her secret, but there was no way he could and she wasn't going to be pushed into telling him before she was ready.

"Yes," she answered simply.

She tried to tell herself that pregnancy was a normal state and she wasn't lying to him, but even she did not believe that.

"Tate, can I ask you something?" she started hesitantly.

"Since when did you need permission, Chloe?"

He was smiling at her and she couldn't resist smiling back. He was right. She was known for being direct and to the point. It was one of the things that made her a great emergency physician.

"Good point. What would we have done if the pregnancy hadn't been ectopic?"

He didn't answer her. Apparently it wasn't the question he'd been expecting.

"But it was," he said eventually.

"Yes. Pathology was returned confirming the pregnancy was in my right fallopian tube." The truth—which again felt like a lie.

"So why are we discussing this?"

She could hear the frustration in his voice but she wasn't going to back down.

"Because I'd like to know." Because she needed to know now that there was a baby growing inside her.

Tate sighed and for a moment she thought he wasn't going to answer. "We would have figured it out."

"What does that mean to you?"

"It means we would have done what was best for the child. Chloe, why are we talking about this?"

"Because it's something I think about. And I wondered if it was something you think about too. The 'what if?'"

"No, Chloe. I haven't been thinking about something that was never a possibility in my mind."

She felt her face fall but in her mind knew she had no right to be hurt. Why would Tate think about the "what if?" He probably thought of her failed pregnancy as his narrow escape from a path in life that had not been of his choosing. *She* was the one who dreamed of their life together.

She couldn't tell him. Not today. She wasn't prepared to see the disappointment on his face when he realized that his lucky escape was no longer. Not when her heart was so full of love for the life they had created together.

He watched Chloe walking away, studying her every angle and movement. There were very few occasions when he resented his job but today was one of them. It had been a life or death situation that had kept him from attending Chloe's appointment, and now he had to live with the consequences.

He had wanted to be there with her. He knew she was afraid of the possibility of permanent damage and he'd wanted to support her. He'd also wanted to assure himself that she was okay and going to be okay long-term. Her nightmares had scarred not only her but him too. He already had the image of her on the operating room table burned into his mind, but her nightmares had added the sounds of her whimpering and fear to the mix too.

What *would* he have done if the pregnancy had not been an ectopic? He honestly didn't know. So many of his feelings toward Chloe had grown from the threat of losing her. If he hadn't faced that threat would he feel the same?

* * *

She floated through the next two weeks. Everything that had been challenging her dissolved into the background as she embraced her pregnancy and the prospect of motherhood. Every pregnancy symptom became a welcome burden, reminding her of the life growing deep inside her.

After spending five years preparing and living in fear of her Board exam she walked into the examination hall with full confidence in her knowledge and abilities. Eight hours later her confidence was still with her as she arrived at Kate's apartment with their long-standing plan to celebrate together still in place.

She climbed the stairs, smiling at the new effort it took. Kate opened the door with a smile too, and she knew that her friend had done as well as she had expected her to. She really was both brilliant and a gifted surgeon. They hugged tightly before Chloe walked through the door.

"Where's Matt?"

"He had a hearing in New York that couldn't be rescheduled, so we are going to get together this weekend to celebrate. But he *did* leave this in the fridge!" Kate revealed a bottle of very expensive champagne tied with a large bow and a note.

"Are you sure that is not meant for your weekend together?" Chloe asked, smiling at the gesture.

"The note reads: 'Congratulations, Kate and Chloe, I never had any doubts. Love Matt.' So, yes, I am sure." Kate worked her way through the kitchen, opening the bottle with a flourish designed for champagne and pouring two fluted glasses. She raised her glass and Chloe mirrored the action. "To achieving everything we want and to the happiness we deserve."

She clinked her glass with Kate's and brought the glass

to her lips. It wasn't until she had the briefest hint of the crisp liquid on her lips that she remembered she shouldn't drink alcohol.

"What's wrong? Is it horrible?" Kate asked, her concern evident.

"No, it's not that. I'm sure it's wonderful. Kate," she started, realizing there was no turning back. "Kate, I'm still pregnant."

Her friend's eyes reached their widest dilation before they fell from her face to her abdomen. "I don't understand. I thought it was an ectopic pregnancy?"

"It was—but it is also an intrauterine pregnancy. Twins, in a sense."

"Oh, my God. How pregnant *are* you?"

"Sixteen weeks."

"Wow!"

She watched as Kate processed her disclosure and a large smile came to her face.

"Is it okay to be happy and excited for you?"

"It's perfectly right. I'm happy for me too. And excited—and scared."

"Did you tell the father?" Kate asked, her voice tentative.

She looked at Kate, waiting to see if there was any judgment in her face. She was sure that Kate did not know about her night with Tate. There was no way Kate would have held that information inside. But just now Kate had said "the father" as though she knew who that title referred to. Maybe she had been more transparent in her feelings than she had thought.

"No. I only found out two weeks ago, and I needed some time to get used to the idea myself. And I wanted to get past the exam."

"But you *are* going to tell him, right? I mean there

is no way you can avoid the issue and work at Boston General."

"I know—but not today and not tonight. Tonight is about us, Kate. And congratulations—you are going to have to drink for two!"

Her cheer was genuine, and also meant to take them back to their original purpose and away from the thought that had not left her head in two weeks.

"As my first official duty as Auntie Kate, I couldn't be more honored. Now, let's get ready—we have a party to attend."

"Congratulations, Chloe, you look amazing." That was the comment that followed her throughout the night.

She wasn't sure if she had truly done *that* great a job, selecting the emerald-green cocktail dress with a deep V front and back and aside gathering that hid the changes to her figure, but she was gracious none the less. She knew people were genuinely happy for her—especially in light of her well known brush with death.

She was happy too. She was spending the night celebrating with most of the residents she had worked with for years in her program and in other specialties. This was the end of an era and the beginning of her real life.

The party was being held at a local pub located near the hospital and frequented by the staff. Once a year it closed to the public for this celebration, and the familiarity of both the location and the people made it the perfect choice. In the background music filled the space, and the lights were turned down, adding to the atmosphere of the evening. She visited, she danced, and she discreetly avoided the celebratory drinks that were being passed around.

"I'm probably not the first, but can I tell you exactly

how amazing you are and how proud of you I am, Dr. Darcy?"

She turned and smiled back at Ryan, who was standing behind her, holding two fluted glasses in his hands. "I couldn't have done it without you."

"You could have done it anywhere, with no help at all. I'm just happy you trained here and are staying here."

"Thank you," she said, and reached up to hug him carefully.

He handed her a fluted glass. "A toast to Dr. Chloe Darcy—a friend, an inspiration, and now my colleague."

She smiled and clinked her glass against his. As she pulled her arm away she both saw and felt a hand close over her own on the stem of her glass. She recognized the hand, and didn't need to turn to see the man attached.

"Let's dance."

Not a request—more like a caption for Tate's intentions as she felt herself being relieved of the glass and pulled toward the dance floor.

"What do you think you are doing?" she asked, trying to make herself heard over the music but not by the surrounding dancers.

"I could ask you the same question," he replied, his tone matching his actions.

"I am celebrating, and I don't appreciate being barged in on and hauled away when the mood strikes you."

Her last words had been louder than she'd wanted as the loud music faded away and a slow song filled the room. She moved away, wanting the conversation over. But once again she was pulled back, this time finding herself pressed against Tate, with his hand pressing into her low back, pressing her to him, while his other hand still held hers tightly. Her bare skin pressed against dark denim jeans and the linen of his button-down shirt.

"And here I thought you would be appreciative," he drawled, but there was no ease in his words.

"Why would I be appreciative?" she questioned, her position such that she was staring just over his shoulder, her eyes unable to meet his.

"I didn't think you would want to drink alcohol," he whispered, his words soft against her ear.

His implication caused the complete opposite effect in her. She felt her back straighten and arch as she turned to face him.

"It's not good for the baby," he said.

She wanted to run—to do everything she could to avoid a conversation she was not ready to have—but any thought of that was lost as she felt Tate's hand and arm securing her to him once more.

"How did you know?" Her voice cracked as the words passed her lips.

"You just told me."

"Tate…" she beseeched him.

"You're different. I noticed a couple of weeks ago that the changes were not all post-operative."

"What do you mean?"

"A few weeks ago, in my bathroom, I noticed a new curve to your hips and your breasts appeared fuller. Pregnancy has definitely added to your perfection."

Heat coursed through her as she remembered his appraisal in the bathroom that day. Maybe he hadn't found her as lacking as she had thought. "We shouldn't be having this conversation."

"Shouldn't we? When were you going to mention the pregnancy? Or is it none of my business?"

"Not here," she implored, her eyes once again not able to meet his.

"Then let's go."

He didn't wait for an answer and with the same force hauled her off the dance floor. He didn't stop as they made their way through the pub, out through the front door and to his Range Rover, where he held open the passenger door.

She couldn't think about speaking until they were driving. She hadn't even said goodbye to Kate.

"Where are we going?"

"We are going to finish this conversation," Tate answered.

In no hurry to start talking, she said nothing.

She wasn't surprised when they arrived back at Tate's loft. If she'd been going on the offence she would rather do it in her own territory as well. He held the door open and she walked through the entrance, stopping in the middle of the living room and turning to meet Tate head-on.

"Now what?" she asked, exasperated with the going-nowhere track they were on.

"This."

He walked toward her and for the second time that evening gathered her against him. This time their entire bodies met as he reached into her hair and held in her in place as his mouth came down on hers.

She couldn't have broken away even if she'd wanted to and she was not sure she did. Since their first and only night together this felt like the only way they communicated with each other—the only time they were in sync, the only time she was able to forget about everything that complicated their relationship and kept her from getting what she wanted.

She parted her lips, taking in the taste of him, and he took the opportunity she presented. She met his kiss, allowing him to explore her and taking no less from him. Her intensity increased with every touch of his tongue and she felt herself channel all her emotions, good and bad, into their exchange.

She heard the tearing of her dress at the same time as cool air met her back. The hands that had previously held her to him were now freely roaming her body, and areas that had been cool were now given heat from Tate's body, hands, and mouth. She felt a second tug at her dress as the straps were displaced from her shoulders and the bodice was pulled towards her waist.

She wasn't alone. The sound of buttons being released was followed almost instantly by the pressure of Tate's bare chest against hers. The slight friction created as he ground into her, with his hands still moving over her back while his lips and tongue caressed her neck, was torture for her newly sensitive breasts. Finally the two met as his large palm cupped her swollen breast and he brought the sensitive peak to his mouth. She gasped at the intensity of the sensation and Tate paused for a second, his eyes venturing away from his target to meet hers. The look they shared was almost as primal as the sensation she had felt moments before.

She whimpered as his hands left her breasts and roamed down the sides of her body. She felt her dress being hiked up to meet the gathering of fabric surrounding her waist. She felt his hands come beneath her, his grasp on her bottom firm, as he once again returned to her mouth with punishing drive. She was being lifted from the floor, her legs wrapping around Tate for support and for desire. She could feel him pressing into her, and the knowledge of everything he had to offer made her most intimate of places pulse with anticipation.

She clung to him as he carried her through the loft and

laid her before him on the bed. She finally opened her eyes enough to watch him rid himself of the now torn linen shirt and the belt he wore. Like a predator he came down on the bed over her, his body brushing her but not pressing down on her.

Braced on his forearms, he tangled one hand in the layers of red hair that had fanned out over the white duvet. His face came down to meet hers, the green of his eyes even brighter than normal, before his mouth reclaimed hers. The depth and passion within his kiss made her wonder where she began and he ended. Only as she struggled for breath, her heart racing from the heat, did he leave her lips and once again begin caressing the breasts he had teased earlier.

He alternated his ministrations with hand and mouth, each movement more exquisitely torturous than the one prior. When he finally released her breasts she felt bereft—until she realized his intentions. She felt his lips trail over her abdomen, his tongue encircling her belly button, and then he moved lower as his hands worked the material of her dress higher, exposing her from the waist down.

She hadn't worn any underwear with the dress and nothing stood as a barrier between them. His hands once again reached for her bottom and he began his path of seduction again, starting at her knee and gradually working along her inner thigh, each movement and each touch causing her to naturally open wider to him. He opened her with his tongue and she barely held herself away from completion.

She glanced down to see Tate caressing her so intimately, with a look of enjoyment on his face that made her let go completely. He wasted no time, and the same torturous seduction that her breasts had endured came again as he tasted, suckled and stroked her core, each movement bringing her closer and closer to a cliff edge, higher than she had ever climbed.

Then with one final stroke she broke, her back arching as she cried out into the silence between them. But he didn't stop as she contracted beneath him. He kissed and stroked and kept her wanting him.

He returned to lie over her, his lips softly caressing her own. It took her a few moments to realize his intention.

"We're not done," she declared softly, her hand now roaming him as his had done to her, making its way toward the ultimate fulfillment.

"I don't want to hurt you," he gritted, not stopping her but keeping himself rigid above her.

"Then give me what I want," she replied huskily as her hand delved beneath the fabric of his jeans and boxer briefs to grasp him.

She saw the struggle within him before he moved away from her, stripping himself of his remaining garments, and finally ridding her of the remnants of her dress. His eyes stopped on the swell of her abdomen and her scar before he moved over her again. In a sudden smooth motion he rolled them both, allowing himself to be flat on his back and she above him. She understood his intentions and moved herself astride him, giving herself her first intimate view of his length. He was perfection, and she couldn't resist touching him to see if the feel matched the visual. He was both soft and wet at the tip, but everything beyond felt like thick iron.

"Be careful, Chloe," he warned, his face clenched in a combination of pleasure and agony.

She leant forward, her breasts once again brushing his chest, her face centimeters from his. "Why?" she purred, reveling at the new equality she had gained in their union.

"Because I've never wanted to be inside a woman so badly."

She opened her mouth to his as she rose above him and in one movement encased him within her. They both cried out, each sound muffled by the other's mouth. She felt so full it was impossible to imagine more pleasure. Then she began to move slowly, wanting to prolong what she knew would be the ultimate release. Tate's hands fell to her hips but rested there only as she controlled their pace and his depth. She watched him as his expression transitioned from rapture to intense concentration.

"Chloe, I can't hold on much longer."

"Then don't."

And she increased depth and pace, bringing herself closer and closer. She could feel him hardening further within her, hear small sounds and noises, and then finally the hands that had rested on her dug in as she lifted herself and then came down hard and deep onto him. Tate's cry and the feel of the warmth spilling into her propelled her to her own ending.

She collapsed forward, her body spreading over Tate's as he once again tangled his hands into her hair.

"Marry me."

His words cut through her afterglow.

There was no way she had heard him correctly. She pushed herself up onto her hands, not caring as both her breasts and her hair fell forward. He didn't look as if he was joking.

"I'm sorry?" she asked, stunned by all the events of the night, but none more than this moment.

"I think you heard me."

He lay beneath her with all the confidence of a man sure of an outcome. Given everything that had just occurred between them, she could understand how he had gained this impression.

"No." She shook her head, the only movement possible as shock still paralyzed her.

"You didn't hear me?" His eyebrows rose and obvious doubt shadowed across his face.

"No, I will not marry you."

Her words surprised them both, but it was Tate's look of anger that spurred her into movement. She pulled herself from his body and practically stumbled in her attempt to distance herself from him. Love Tate? Yes, maybe she always would. But the idea of marrying a man who didn't love her—that was a purgatory that even she couldn't endure.

She turned her back on him and scanned the room for what was left of her dress. The torn heap of fabric quickly reminded her that it was no longer an option.

She walked to his dresser and opened the top drawer, knowing it was where his extra scrubs were kept. Despite the changes in her figure she still swam within both the top and bottoms, but she didn't care. She moved to the couch and sat to fasten the straps of her shoes. She raised her head to meet long legs clad in denim before her.

"You're not getting away that quickly, Chloe. You have some explaining to do."

He was still shirtless, his jeans tugged on but unbuttoned. He was gorgeous—and very, very angry with her, despite the attempt he made to conceal it. She didn't care. In what world was she obligated to explain *anything* after his nonsensical proposal?

"*I* have some explaining to do? *You* are the one who proposed. *You* have some explaining to do!"

"You're pregnant, Chloe."

"I'm very much aware of that fact." She didn't rise

from the couch, not sure she could stand on her suddenly weak legs.

"Do you have a better offer?" he retorted, his attitude as harsh as his intention.

"Say what you mean, Tate." She stood, the extra three inches of stiletto heel compensating for their difference in height and allowing her to look him in the eye.

"I don't think I need to," he replied, his lip curling with disdain at his implication.

"Oh, no, I think this time you really do."

He opened and closed his mouth. No words came through. She stood inches from him, refusing to back away.

"What do you want from me, Chloe?"

"I don't know—but not this."

"You're pregnant, Chloe. It's no longer about what we want."

"It's not 1960, Tate. A shotgun wedding is no longer the necessary next step."

"So you don't think a child needs a father?" he replied with equal derision.

"I didn't say that…" For the first time she felt defensive and less sure of herself.

"Think about it, Chloe. How are you going to cope as a single mother? You don't exactly have a nine-to-five job, or any of the maternity benefits that type of job would provide. What was your plan? To deliver and go back to work the next day? Between your student loans and childcare even your physician's salary would be tight. Unless, of course, you were planning to completely neglect your child and take extra shifts."

"I…" She was lost for words as she realized the truth behind his commentary.

"Chloe, we're not perfect. But deep down we respect

each other—and there is at least one area where we are more than compatible." His eyes instantly darkened and confirmed his words.

He was right about pretty much everything. Would she do it? *Could* she do it? Sacrifice herself and her wants for her child?

She was lost in thoughts of the possibilities and didn't notice Tate walk away from her. When he returned he reached for her hand, and she felt before she saw what he'd pressed into it.

She was mesmerized at the site of the blue square box within her hand. It couldn't be—he wouldn't... Again, like a moth to a flame, she opened the lid slowly, praying for a different result. It hadn't changed. It was the ring he had bought for Kate.

She didn't need to see more. She closed the lid—but not before her rage bested the hurt she felt inside.

She heard the sound before she comprehended what she had done. Her hand throbbed after its impact with Tate's cheek, and both of them were stunned by her actions. But the ring box still pressed into her opposite hand was enough to keep her from backing down from her outburst.

"No," she answered. "I'm not settling for second choice. Goodbye, Tate."

CHAPTER EIGHT

TWO WEEKS LATER she hadn't spoken to Tate—but she had confirmed everything he had said to her. She had checked with the Human Resources Department at Boston General and once she was on staff she would no longer be covered for any type of maternity leave. Physicians were considered self-employed, not hospital employees, and therefore not entitled to any employment benefits. She had also checked with her bank. Her student loans and her line of credit were average amongst her peers, but substantial compared to the average student. The debt would not wait for her return from maternity leave, and would require payments starting in three weeks' time.

She didn't have a lot of options. She could take a week or two off at the most and then would have to work a full-time schedule of sixty hours a week to cover her loans, living expenses and child care. The idea of leaving her newborn in the hands of stranger made her want to stay pregnant forever. At least then they could be together. She didn't have family money, or nearby support to rely on. She was an only child and her parents were both academics—college professors who had been in their forties when she was born, making them now in their seventies. They lived in Montana and visited at most once a year, their schedules still very much dependent on the academic calendar.

She was stuck, and she was going to have to ask for help. The question was from whom? Did she ask Tate for help, knowing that his help would not come without questions and conditions she would have to answer and give in to?

Or did she ask Kate, or more accurately Matt, for financial help, knowing it would be years before she would ever be able to pay him back? She had only known him for a short space of time and, while she was completely confident in his and Kate's relationship, she had already done enough with her involvement with Tate to jeopardize her friendship with Kate. Asking her fiancé for an inordinate amount of money to help her support the child she was having with her ex seemed more bold than even *she* was ready for. They hadn't discussed her child's paternity again, or the events leading to Tate's proposal, but it was likely only a matter of time before everything came out.

It was hard to be over thirty, a physician, and still feeling as stuck and confused as a teenager.

She looked around the waiting room full of pregnant women and didn't miss the fact that she was one of the few women alone. She hadn't told Kate or Tate about this prenatal appointment and ultrasound so she couldn't feel sorry for herself—she had made a conscious choice to come alone.

"Ms. Darcy," a nurse called from the doorway, and she followed the woman down toward the exam rooms.

She waited patiently, and was happy and relieved when Erin knocked and entered the room.

"Hey, I didn't know you were still around. I thought

you would be taking the last of your holidays before your move."

A small smile crossed Erin's face and Chloe couldn't tell if it was genuine or if there was something else going on.

"Well, you know what they say about best-laid plans. I've declined the fellowship in California and will be staying on here at Boston General."

Chloe did her best to mask her surprise and instead focused on the positive. "So does that mean you are available to be my doctor for the entire pregnancy?"

"If you'll have me—then, yes."

This time the smile was genuine and Chloe decided to leave things alone. She knew only too well the value of privacy.

"You have a deal."

Erin sat down and started leafing through the papers that had accumulated in Chloe's chart. "So your official due date, based on conception and last menstrual period, is November ninth. Your infectious disease blood work all came back negative and you are rubella and varicella immune. Your most recent hemoglobin is low to normal range, so we should make sure you are staying on your prenatal vitamins and adding some supplemental iron."

"Okay."

"Chloe, the test that *did* come back abnormal was your blood type and screen. You are B negative, and the antibody screen came back positive for anti-C and anti-Kell antibodies."

"Which means…?" she asked, the easygoing nature of their interaction disappearing as fear set in.

"It means the baby is at risk for anemia."

"What do you mean, at risk?"

"The baby's total risk for anemia depends on its blood.

To determine how much risk is present we need to do genetic testing of your blood type and the same genetic profile of the baby's father, to determine the odds of the baby having the affected blood type."

Chloe felt the bottom of her stomach hollow at the thought of asking Tate for anything in light of their last conversation. "Are there any other options?"

"The other option is to do an invasive procedure called a cordocentesis, which directly samples the baby's blood from its umbilical cord while it's still in utero. It has some significant risks, but it would provide us with definitive information about the baby."

"No!" she refused adamantly, her hand reflexively covering her abdomen...her baby.

"It wouldn't be my first choice either. So instead we need to test you and the father and then follow the baby with serial bloodwork and ultrasounds for signs of anemia and heart failure."

"Tate."

"Excuse me?"

"The baby's father is Tate Reed."

"I know," Erin acknowledged simply, with no judgment in her eyes or her voice. "Chloe, this isn't a paternity test. It's a genetic profile of your blood groups. We have to grow the cells over two to three weeks and then we use specific markers to look for the subgroup antigens."

"How did you know?" Chloe asked, surprised.

"Tate was in the operating room the night of your ectopic and I realized very quickly that his concern for you stemmed from something beyond friendship."

"From guilt," Chloe commented, still regretting the new nature of their relationship, which felt as if it was based solely on guilt and obligation.

"I didn't think so—but I don't have a great track

record when it comes to men." Erin shook her head and then stood. "Come with me. We need to get you to your ultrasound."

She knocked at the industrial metal door and held her breath waiting for an answer. She hadn't called ahead and the doorman, recognizing her from her previous stay, had let her up—no questions asked or notifications made. She had no idea how Tate would react to her, but knew that she needed him.

The door slid open to reveal Tate, casually dressed in washed denim and a fitted ivory T-shirt printed with a graphic. He looked neither happy nor surprised to see her.

"We need to talk," she opened, as peacefully as she could muster.

"I don't think that is in dispute," he replied, his eyebrows raised, signaling the same skepticism his response portrayed.

He slid the door wider for her to enter. He didn't move, though, and she brushed against him as she made her way into the living room. His body was as cold as his expression, but *her* reaction was the opposite. Every part of her that had touched him felt like fire. She swept the hair off her neck and pulled down the hem of her tank top, trying to limit the heat.

Without words Tate walked to the kitchen and returned with a glass of ice water. They both sat down on the center couch.

"Just like old times," he remarked sarcastically.

"Tate—" she began.

"I'm sorry," he interrupted her. "I was out of line the other night with the ring. Apparently I don't handle rejection well and my temper got the better of me. I'm sorry, Chloe."

"I shouldn't have hit you. I'm sorry," she said, echoing his apology.

"I'm not sure about that."

His sincerity was clear in his eyes and she felt her defenses soften.

"I need your help," she opened simply, before she could change her mind. She watched him, waiting for a response. He was looking at her and she had no idea what he was thinking.

"I'm glad." He had misinterpreted her, and she felt guilty for the misunderstanding.

"No, Tate. I tested positive for two blood antibodies which may attack the baby's blood cells, depending on its blood type. We need to determine the baby's risk of anemia."

She had his attention and she watched as his eyes drew to her stomach. "What do you need?"

"Blood work. They need to do some genetic testing to determine the baby's level of risk."

His jaw flexed and she watched as his Adam's apple rose and fell with his swallow. "Okay—on one condition."

"Excuse me?" she asked, unprepared for the request.

"I'll get the blood work done *after* you move back in with me."

"Tate, you can't be serious."

"I'm very serious right now, Chloe. You want something from me and I want something from you. As you have clearly demonstrated your unwillingness to consider marriage, I'll settle for having you under my roof."

"Why?" she asked, not understanding his reasoning.

"You need me, Chloe. Not just for the blood work, but everything involving this pregnancy and the baby. You're just too stubborn to see it."

"But what about what *you* want and need?"

"Chloe, do you really need to ask that?"

She didn't as she watched his eyes trail down her body.

"And what if I say no?" she challenged, though her words held no power.

"You won't. I know you. You want what is best for this baby."

"What about Kate?" The thought slipped out before she could take it back. She wanted so badly to take it back.

"What *about* Kate?" he replied, not giving an inch.

"You proposed to Kate. You wanted to spend your life with Kate—have a child with Kate," she explained painfully.

"Yes. And I also proposed to you. So far I am zero for two."

"It's not the same..." she mumbled, lost for words.

"Yes, I think we can definitely agree on that point. Kate didn't slap me."

"How am I going to explain?" she wondered aloud.

"What is to explain, Chloe? You're pregnant and you need me."

"You really are serious," she finally acknowledged.

"Yes. Let me prove it to you."

She watched as he reached for his cell phone, which had been sitting on the upholstered leather coffee table that was before them. He dialled a number but she had no idea what he was doing or who he was calling.

"Hi, it's Tate. I wanted you to be the first to know. Chloe and I are together and she is going to be moving in with me permanently."

Together? Permanently? When had that become part of the situation? She watched as he listened to the response, still having no idea who he had called. His mother? One of his sisters? Her bewilderment increased as he passed the phone to her.

"She wants to talk to you."

"Hello...?" she ventured carefully.

"I don't know what to say."

Kate's voice rang clear through the telephone line. Guilt for her actions and her lack of disclosure to Kate pierced through Chloe as she turned to Tate for a brief instant to transmit her hurt. She couldn't look at him for long, though. She was too hurt and too angry. The phone still pressed up to her ear, she walked through the loft and into the bathroom, where she shut the door.

"I'm so sorry, Kate," she apologized, and waited.

"You have nothing to apologize for, Chloe."

"Don't I?" she asked.

"No. Tate and I finished a long time ago. Chloe, is Tate the father of your baby?"

"Yes," she confessed.

"Wow, I didn't see *that* coming." A pause lingered, but Kate was still there.

"I'm sorry."

"Stop apologizing."

She could hear Kate's frustration, but she didn't know how to respond other than with her remorse. Instead she said nothing.

"Chloe, are you happy?"

"I'm overwhelmed, Kate—with everything."

"That's not surprising. Is there anything I can do?"

"Be my friend."

"Done."

They were going to be okay, and she was grateful for the one part of her life that was both stable and solid. "Thank you."

"You know it does make sense—you and Tate."

Chloe would have laughed if she hadn't felt like crying. "I think your new-found love and happiness has impaired your judgment."

"We will see. Are you at Tate's now?"

"Yes."

"Are you hiding in the bathroom?"

"I wouldn't use the term *hiding*, but, yes."

"Good luck, Chloe. I have the feeling you are going to need it."

"Thanks."

As she heard Kate hang up she wished she hadn't. She was torn between relief over the conversation she just had and anger at being forced into it before she was ready. She took a few minutes to gather herself, using a cold cloth on her face and neck to cool the combined heat of pregnancy and anger.

When she left the bathroom she found Tate in the kitchen, leaning against the granite countertop.

"Are you satisfied?" she asked, but her voice lacked the energy she needed to continue this conversation. She hadn't realized how emotionally exhausting it had been, worrying about Kate's response to her paternity time bomb.

"Yes. You look tired."

He hadn't risen to her accusation, and she did acknowledge that he lacked any hint of smugness or victory.

"Thanks. I *am* tired. In case you haven't noticed I've had a lot on my plate lately." She reached back and rubbed at her aching neck and shoulders.

He strode through the living room toward the couch, but didn't sit. "Come here."

She was too tired to fight, and in truth she was exhausted, so she did as she was told. When she reached him he gently nudged her onto the couch, but didn't join her. Instead he walked behind her, and before she'd realized his intentions he had swept her hair to the side and begun to knead gently at the muscles she had been tensing in anticipation of this meeting.

She didn't want to relax, but she didn't have a choice. The conflict between them melted as he pressed and stroked down her neck and shoulders, his fingers finding their way into her hair and pressing at the trigger points at the back of her scalp, causing momentary discomfort and then complete resolution of the tension.

"Better?" he asked, his voice lower and more comforting.

"Hmmm…" she murmured, still deep within a new state of relaxation and peace that she hadn't found in weeks.

His hands left her back and were placed on her arms before she felt herself being lifted and guided across the loft. She was too tired to ask any more questions. Without comment she took direction and lay down on his bed. She felt Tate prop an extra pillow under her side, taking the pressure off her lower back. Then a light blanket covered her as he leaned down and kissed her lips softly.

"Sleep," he commanded quietly. "We'll figure everything else out when you are feeling a bit better."

Tate perched on one of the metal and leather bar stools that lined his kitchen counter, sipping a black coffee. In the distance he could hear the sound of Chloe's breathing. Every once in a while she stirred and he waited for the pattern to resume. He had chosen this spot at the counter because it was the only way to keep himself from watching her.

He had no regrets about his method of persuasion. She needed something from him and he had come to accept that he needed *her*. Chloe made sense. She was beautiful, smart, and he respected her intelligence. But what was driving him to resort to manipulation was the way they were together. In truth, she was the first woman in his life ever to drive him crazy. How else could he explain his behavior?

But he had been completely out of line with the ring and didn't deserve her acceptance of his apology. He had kept the ring for the simple reason that it was too humiliating to return an engagement ring and admit to anyone other than himself his stupidity and resultant rejection.

He had never in his life been anything less than honorable in his treatment of women, but everything about Chloe made him willing to compromise his principles. He craved her, he wanted her, and no matter what she was going to be his and no one else's.

His initial fears about her reputation suffering from an affair between them were gone. He and Chloe were not destined for a short-term affair. All the fears he'd had of falling for her and losing her had vanished with the confirmation of her ongoing pregnancy. Their child would forever link them to each other and he would never let her get away. He knew he could make her happy and that they could have a wonderful life together, if only she would let them.

He heard a muffled song and tracked the intrusion to her purse, moving quickly to silence the call. The display flashed back at him: Missed Call. Ryan Callum.

It was interesting how falling for a woman could change a man. His initial feelings of jealousy toward Ryan were now more than familiar. He knew there was nothing romantic between them, but he hated it that that night Ryan had saved her when she had been calling for *him*. Hated that she trusted Ryan and turned to him when she needed to talk. He didn't like thinking of anyone having a closer relationship with her than he did—romantic or not.

He looked over and saw Chloe had moved only slightly and then resumed her rhythmic breathing. He placed her phone back in her purse and then noticed the envelope that had been nestled beside it. The logo was Boston General's Fetal Assessment Unit's. The baby. *His* baby. He opened the envelope and looked through the stack of pictures inside. He wasn't ready for the black and white images that flashed back at him. Feet, hands, heart and a profile of the baby's face were featured on the ultrasound images.

He sat on the couch, overcome by the feelings the images evoked in him. This was their baby. This was the person that he and Chloe had made together. He searched the pictures for details. The baby had his nose. He wanted to see more. He wanted to know more. He looked back at Chloe, but he couldn't wake her.

His conversation with Chloe replayed in his mind. It was a high-risk pregnancy—not only because of the initial ectopic but also because of the anemia. He already felt he couldn't lose Chloe, but now he felt that way about their child. He needed to do everything he could to support her and decrease any stress in her life. Despite his method, that was one of the many reasons he wanted her back under his roof.

She had asked him to get the blood work done and he would—for her. Chloe had called it "genetic testing"—in a kind euphemism for a paternity test—but he knew what she really meant. He understood her need to get the test done. She needed to prove to him that he was the father. It was unnecessary, but he was willing none the less if that was what she needed. He would do anything for her.

She had always loved her work, but now it had truly become a refuge. Tate had given her two weeks to finish her residency, organize her life, and then he expected her to be with him. She would have thought she wouldn't be nervous about living with him—she had already done so for four weeks—but this time things would be different. He had been clear about his expectations. They would be a couple in almost every sense of the word, with the exception that she still had no idea how he felt, other than that their attraction was still present and burning hotly between them. She couldn't help but think that his desire to be with her was just related to their baby, and that if there was no baby there would be no them.

It seemed that her life, which had felt out of control for the past four months, was going to continue to be so. But she had no regrets. She had their baby's best interests at heart. It had begun to move in the past week, and every flutter or stir overwhelmed her with love. She would do anything for the little person growing inside her, and if there was a possibility that her being together with Tate would provide a more stable home for their child, she would do it.

Now she was working her last shift as a resident and she wished it would never end—a stark contrast to most of her training, when she had often *worried* that it would never end.

She glanced through the charts, looking for something to take her mind off her impending fate. Chest pain— perfect. Her heart hurt too.

She walked to Critical Track Room Three and began her assessment. "Ms. O'Brien? I'm Dr. Darcy."

The patient, a forty-one-year-old woman, stared back at her, her eyes wide, her face displaying the panic she was feeling.

"Everything is going to be okay," she reassured the woman, taking a seat on the stool beside the bed and placing a warm hand on the woman's clammy arm. "When did this start?"

"About two hours ago," the woman replied, her voice breathless. Clearly she was not able to answer in a single breath.

Chloe glanced to the monitors and noted oxygen saturation of eighty-five percent and an elevated pulse of one hundred and twenty. "What are you feeling now?"

"I can't catch my breath, and there is a gnawing pain in the middle of my chest that hurts more when I take a deep breath."

"Have you ever had anything like this before?"

"No."

"Do you have any medical problems?"

"No."

"Surgeries?"

"I broke my leg a few weeks ago and they had to fix it in the operating room."

Chloe focused her attention on the woman's lower body, which had been covered by hospital blankets. She made sure the room's curtain was fully drawn before uncovering her legs. The left leg was in a cast, and above the cast the skin was swollen and reddened. She pressed behind the knee and the patient pulled her leg away in response to the pain.

"When did your leg starting hurting more?"

"A few days ago. I just thought I had overdone it."

"Are you on any medication?"

"Just some over-the-counter pain medication and my birth control pill."

"Any allergies?"

"No."

"Okay, Ms. O'Brien. We are going to start some IV medication to thin your blood and then get some tests done to confirm my diagnosis. I think you have a blood clot that has traveled from your leg to your lungs, which is why it is hard to breathe. It's called a pulmonary embolism."

She pushed the call bell on the woman's bed and waited for a nurse to join them. "Julie, can you please start a therapeutic intravenous heparin infusion? I am going to order an electrocardiogram and a CT scan of the pulmonary arteries, *stat*."

She touched the woman reassuringly once more and then left to write the necessary orders and contact the on-call radiologist to expedite the tests.

She was staring at the electrocardiogram tracing when a familiar sensation passed over her. She wasn't surprised to see Tate standing beside her. He had changed out of his surgical scrubs and was casually dressed and still devastatingly handsome, with a look of self-possession about him.

"I'm on my way home but I wanted you to have this tonight to celebrate." He passed over a box that was fortunately *not* the same ring box she was all too familiar with. Still she approached it with hesitation, never able to predict Tate's words or actions.

"Open the box, Chloe." He was irritated.

She looked around the department and then did as she was told. Sitting atop the plush velvet was a diamond-encrusted primrose key pendant on a thin platinum chain. It was breathtaking.

"I wanted to give you something to signify our new beginning. Since there is no way I'm going to convince you to put a ring on your finger anytime soon, I thought a key to unlock our future together was a good second choice. The key to the loft is in the box under the velvet."

It was the most romantic thing he had ever said to her and he looked as if he had meant every word. She wanted to kiss him, to reach up and press her lips against his...

"Dr. Darcy to Radiology *stat*. Dr. Darcy to Radiology—*stat*." Their moment was broken and she sent him a desperate look of apology before she took off, running towards Radiology.

"What's going on," she asked on arrival, her eyes drawn to Ms. O'Brien, who appeared non-responsive to the chaos surrounding her.

"She lost consciousness during the scan. We can't get a blood pressure. Her last measured was sixty over twenty-five when we pulled her out of the machine. Pulse is there, but weak and slow," replied the respiratory technician who had been called for help.

"What do we have in here?" she asked looking around the room for basic resuscitation equipment.

"Nothing."

"Then let's move her and run." Chloe grabbed the transfer roller and threw it on the stretcher beside the scan machine. She went around it and rolled Ms. O'Brien toward her, allowing the team to place the board under her and pull her over. Then they were off. "Take her to Trauma One—it's open."

She was winded from her run, her new-found pregnancy limitations still surprising to her.

She looked at the radiology technician, who seemed stunned by the turn in events. "Did you see a clot?"

"The radiologist hasn't reviewed the films yet."

"I understand that, but did you see a clot? It's important," she stressed.

"Yes, I think there is a large saddle embolus between the right and left pulmonary arteries."

"Thank you."

She raced back to Trauma One and saw the team was in action. Ms. O'Brien was wearing a non-rebreather mask and the nurses had established additional intravenous access and hooked her up to the main monitor bank. Her blood pressure was fifty over twenty.

"Give her two liters of intravenous normal saline and establish a norepinephrine infusion on a line separate from her heparin."

"Need help?"

Ryan's voice broke through the crowd and she saw him standing unobtrusively outside the trauma room.

"I'm going to start thrombolytic therapy in addition to her intravenous anticoagulation," she replied knowing she might be out on a ledge.

"Is it worth the risk of a bleed into her head?" he asked, not moving from his spot.

"Yes, she is hypotensive, with a saddle embolus on imaging and significant right heart strain on electrocardiogram."

"I'll call Pharmacy and have them send up the medication right away."

"Thank you."

She stayed with Ms. O'Brien for hours, well past the end of her shift, until she was stable for transportation to the Intensive Care Unit. Her blood pressure had stabilized and slowly her breathing had improved. She'd

regained consciousness and showed no signs of neurological damage from the risky clot-busting medication.

After she'd signed off the chart she changed back
into her regular clothes and checked her phone. She had
missed calls from Tate, her parents, and Kate. She also
noticed the time. It was a minute past twelve. She was
officially no longer a resident.

"Congratulations."

The voice cut through her thoughts.

Ryan stood beside her. "I would offer to take you for a
drink to celebrate your last shift as a resident, but given
your delicate condition and your rather protective baby
daddy I think we should take a rain check."

"As long as it's not a permanent rain check. My life is
complicated enough these days without having to worry
about my friends ditching me."

"Chloe, you know that I haven't been particularly fond
of Tate Reed recently, but I think you are doing the right
thing. A child does need two parents, and I think you and
Tate are both mature enough to work through any dif-
ferences you have and do what is best to provide that."

"I don't know what to say," she responded, stunned
by the change in Ryan's attitude.

"You don't need to say anything. You're doing the right
thing and I respect you even more for it."

CHAPTER NINE

TATE ARRIVED JUST as he'd said he would at three o'clock sharp. She finished taping the last of the boxes shut and left it with the others for the movers to put into storage. Tate's fully furnished loft and her changing body meant she had little she needed to bring with her.

"Ready?" he asked as he lingered in the doorway of her apartment.

"Does it matter if I'm not?" she answered. *This was it.*

"No, it doesn't. I'll take you as is."

They both smirked at his confidence and she watched as he took her suitcase from her and they left the apartment. Tate opened the passenger door and helped her into the vehicle before stowing her suitcase in the back. They drove through the winding Boston streets and she took in the beauty of the hot summer day. She barely noticed where they were until the vehicle stopped and her door was being opened for her.

It wasn't Tate's loft. Instead it was one of Boston's finest five-star hotels that overlooked the harbor. She took the cue and left the vehicle, having no idea why she was there but knowing the bellman didn't have the answer. She watched as Tate opened the hatch and pointed out the bags to the bellman before coming around to take her arm.

"Why are we here?" she finally asked as the coolness of the air-conditioned lobby greeted her.

"To celebrate our new beginning." He took her hand, kissing the back of it before leaving her to check in with the hotel's exclusive concierge. Within minutes he was back at her side, leading her to the elevator and then down the hall toward a corner suite.

Before she could move forward he'd reached under her legs and swept her up and into his arms. He carried her in. He didn't put her down as she took in the luxury of the suite, the sitting room and its adjoining balcony, the marble finishes and plush velvet coverings. Then they were in the bedroom, with a king-size bed and a bottle of champagne sitting on ice, followed by the bathroom, where she was finally lowered slowly to her feet. The bathtub was deep and filled with water, bubbles and rose petals.

He gently turned her away from him, his fingers finding the zip of her summer dress and lowering it slowly until the dress was released and fell to the floor. Mesmerized by the moment, she stepped out of it, unabashed in the simple bikini briefs she wore.

"I thought you might like to relax. I know you didn't sleep much last night and it's been a hectic day," Tate explained.

She turned toward him, feeling empowered by his attentions. "Are you joining me?"

He smiled ruefully. "There is nothing I would like more, but if I do it may not be as relaxing and peaceful as intended."

She was disappointed, but appreciative of his intentions.

"Call when you are ready to get out. I don't want you to slip." And after a long, appraising look at her he left.

She felt her body melt into the water. The tub was so deep that the water sat at her shoulders. She closed her eyes—and awoke to Tate's voice and soft touch.

"Chloe…" He nudged her shoulder gently.

As she adjusted to her surroundings she registered that the water had cooled considerably. "I fell asleep," she confirmed to both of them.

"Yes. Let's get you out before you become a mermaid." She stood with Tate as support, helping her balance. As she stepped out he held a warm towel from the heated towel rack and gently patted the excess water from her before replacing it with an equally warmed robe.

"Thank you," she murmured.

"Do you want to sleep a little longer?" Tate asked.

"I'm good." She looked down at her robe and realized that other than her dress she had nothing to wear. "I don't have any of my things."

Tate smiled. "I packed you an overnight bag and your clothes are in the bedroom. The box on the counter is a present from me." He smiled and left the bathroom.

She walked toward the box, gently pulling at the satin bow and lifting the lid and layers of tissue until she revealed an ivory silk nightgown with thin straps and a deep V front. A rose pattern had been embroidered at the waist, and there was a slit almost to the thigh that allowed for movement and also showed a great amount of leg. She doubted its fit, as her pregnancy now sat midway up her abdomen, but she tried. The material felt cool against her, and it covered her whole body, accentuating the fullness of her breasts and abdomen. She felt sexy, and more confident that she had in a long time.

She emerged from the bathroom in just the nightgown, leaving the robe behind. Tate had stripped from his jacket, and his dress shirt was half buttoned, sleeves rolled up. He was sitting on the large king-sized bed, where the linen had been turned down.

"You look amazing, Chloe."

She smiled at the compliment. "Thank you. So do you—always, really."

"Can I get you a drink?" He gestured toward the champagne bucket.

She smiled and placed her hand on her abdomen. "I don't think that is the best idea, do you?"

"It's sparkling grape juice—for both of us." He opened the bottle and poured two tall flutes of the bubbly liquid. "To new beginnings."

He handed her a glass as she sat down to join him and they clinked them together as he finished his toast. The liquid was cool on her throat. As she lowered the glass she found it taken from her, and the taste of the liquid was quickly replaced by the taste of Tate.

"I've missed this," he murmured against her mouth.

The warmth radiating from him and the lingering scent of his cologne was enough to intoxicate her without any alcohol. "Mmmm..." she murmured in response.

He stopped kissing her and pulled back, his hands cradling her face. "Chloe, do you want me?"

"Yes," she replied unabashedly. "Do you want *me*?" She held her breath, waiting for his response.

His eyebrow rose, and the side of his mouth rose too. He reached for her hand and placed it on his groin, his rigidity pressing through the gray fabric. "Every minute since I last had you."

She could feel his sincerity and took solace in their mutual want. This was where they were equal, and it was not a bad place to be starting from. She met his smile as she reached for his belt. He looked back with desire but didn't stop her. She undid first his belt, then the button, then the fly of his pants, and felt a great sense of pride as the weight and strength of his erection spilled into her hand. She gently brushed her hand against the last layer of fabric between them before turning her attention toward his shirt. She slowly undid every button, allowing her fingertips to brush against the hard musculature. When she reached the final button she pushed the material from his shoulders.

She stood from the bed, holding her hands up to lace her fingers within his, and then pulled him to his feet. She used the change in position to finish her earlier act of removing his trousers, followed by all his remaining undergarments.

"I'm feeling a bit underdressed, Chloe. Are you planning on joining me?" he asked in a sultry voice, showing no embarrassment. Why would he? He was magnificent, and just the sight of his masculine virility was enough to make her throb with desire.

"Yes. Would you like the honor?"

"I would." He pulled her toward him, gathering the soft material into his large hands before raising the entire garment over her head. "Better."

"Make love to me, Tate?" she asked softly, feeling more exposed by her request than her nudity.

He didn't reply with words. Instead he swept her off her feet, laid her on the bed, and complied.

Tate strode into the hospital laboratory ready to fulfill his promise to Chloe. They had spent the past week enjoying and getting to know each other and every day he was happier and more confident in his decision-making. Aside from the luxury of their bedroom compatibility he enjoyed how easy and relaxing she was to be with on the one hand, and how she could challenge and maintain his interest on the other. It was almost everything he had ever wanted.

He still felt Chloe was holding something back from him, and he would bet it had everything to do with the paternity test he was about to have done. She still felt she had something to prove.

He recognized the voice before he saw his face. Ryan Callum was at the desk, speaking with the unit clerk.

"How long does it take for paternity results to come back?" he was asking.

"Two to three weeks, Dr. Callum. We can page you as soon as they arrive."

"Thank you."

Tate was fixed on the conversation and still standing in the doorway when Ryan turned to leave. They met each other's eyes but said nothing as Tate moved aside and let the other man pass.

Why was Ryan Callum getting a paternity test? A glimmer of doubt formed in his mind and started to smolder. He knew better than anyone that sometimes a working relationship could lead to a personal one, and Chloe certainly was a draw that few men could resist. Ryan also had the benefit of knowing her beyond her beauty, which only strengthened her appeal. Had they been more than the friends they were now?

No, it wasn't possible. Chloe would have told him. There was also no way Tate was prepared to consider the possibility that he could lose everything he almost had. But why was Ryan taking a paternity test at the same time as he was?

He walked toward the unit clerk, trying to focus on the task he'd come to perform. "I'm Tate Reed. I believe some requisitions were faxed over from Dr. Erin Madden's office that I need to complete?"

"Yes, Dr. Reed. If you can take a seat for a few minutes we will get the tubes labeled and call for you when we are ready."

He nodded his agreement.

Within fifteen minutes the task was complete, but Tate had no resolution. He had broken one of the cardinal rules of medicine. He had participated in a test when he had no idea what to do with the results. If there was a possibility he was *not* the father of Chloe's baby did he even want to know? It wouldn't change things. He was committed to Chloe and they were going to raise this child together. But Ryan would know.

The world he had lived in for the past week felt different. It was no longer he and Chloe and the wonder of their new life together and parenthood. It was he, Chloe and Ryan Callum—and he wasn't happy at the new addition to what had briefly been the perfect family.

Chloe rested on the sofa, her feet up and her computer on her lap, as she scanned through the listings Tate's real estate agent had sent over. Tate's loft was perfect for one, sometimes perfect for two, but it was not meant for a family of three.

She felt before she saw the small movement on her abdominal wall as the baby stretched or kicked—or made whatever motion it was fond of doing. She smiled, always happy for a reminder of the wellbeing of her child.

When she looked back at the listings she tried to consider them objectively. Each house was more impressive than the next. At first she had been reluctant. The grandeur and the cost of the homes the realtor had forwarded were beyond her wildest dreams and beyond her budget.

She was already aware that she would be far from an equal financial contributor in their relationship. Tate had arranged for a generous amount of money to be deposited into her personal account to help with her student loans. She had objected, but she hadn't won the fight with Tate, who had argued that he would rather she take care of herself and their baby than work herself past her limits when he easily could afford to take care of all three of them.

The same went for the house. There was no way she could afford even twenty percent of the value of the homes selected, but Tate had once again convinced her that in the long term it would be better to raise their child in a real home, with a real yard, in a good neighborhood, than to move house halfway through their child's childhood, when Chloe finally felt financially equal—which might be never.

General surgeons typically made more money than emergency physicians. And as Tate was one of the top ten vascular surgeons in the country, and had been recruited to Boston General with a heavy incentive package, she had no hope of ever being equal. It was a situation she made herself accept, acknowledging the irony that in all her prior failed relationships the main breaking point had been her boyfriends' inability to accept her advanced education and increased earning potential.

At least the listings were taking her mind off her upcoming ultrasound appointment. After a week of happiness with Tate she had the uncanny feeling that at any moment it was all going to go away. She had spent years pining for Tate and trying to come to terms with the fact that she would never be with him. Now they were together, and with or without love she was happy, and slowly coming to be at peace with their life together. He was considerate, respectful, and definitely attracted to her. Their nightly lovemaking was the only time when her mind managed to shut off and when she truly felt they connected. He was also very interested and attentive to her pregnancy, making sure she was feeling well and taking the time and patience to wait to feel for their baby's movement.

Their baby. She had thought the further she got into the pregnancy the more relaxed she would become, but every day she felt as if she had more and more to lose. Erin had been very good at explaining the plan for her pregnancy and she felt well cared for, but that didn't mean she didn't worry. Her next ultrasound was one of many, and despite the joy she got from seeing her baby she also remembered the purpose of the scan—which was to look for problems. At least Tate would be there. As independent as she had always been, each day she was more grateful that she wasn't doing this alone.

She heard the key turn and the sound of the loft door opening. Tate walked through and immediately she felt the small flame that always burned for him flare to life. She craved, loved and needed his attention and attraction toward her.

"Hey," she greeted him, smiling at the breathy quality her voice seemed to have adopted around him.

"I went and did the blood work today."

It was a face she recognized but hadn't seen in a while, and she wasn't happy to see it return. Maybe he just didn't like being reminded of the original terms of their union. She already felt past that, and was looking forward to moving on together as a team.

"Thank you. Did they say how long it would take to come back?" She really didn't want to be discussing this further, but she needed to know when or if she would be able to put her mind at ease.

"Two to three weeks," Tate answered, and then he

walked through to the kitchen and away from her and the conversation.

He didn't turn back to look at her when he started to talk again, but she could almost see the expression on his face.

"Archer called me a few hours ago. He's had a family emergency and needs me to cover his week of nights."

"Oh." She didn't believe him. Not in light of the distance he was expressing. But she didn't have the strength to confront the truth that he was likely lying to her. She would rather pretend everything was as it should be than risk losing what they had slowly managed to build together.

"I already have an elective day of surgical cases booked for Monday, and a combination of clinics and administrative meetings for the rest of the week, so I won't be around much."

He was giving her notice. Their "honeymoon" was over. What had changed? Was this all about the blood work? Or had he grown tired of her already?

"Is there anyone else that can do it?" She heard the desperation come through in her voice, but desperate was how she felt. She wanted to hold on to what they had.

Tate turned and looked at her, but what he was thinking or feeling she couldn't tell.

"No, Chloe. I owe Archer this favor. He covered for me during your recuperation."

She couldn't argue with that. "What about the ultrasound?" she asked.

"I'll be there."

"Do you want me to reschedule our meeting with the realtor?"

"No, you go. I'm okay with whatever you pick."

"It's our home, Tate, you should be there," she argued.

"I will be, Chloe. But I still have a job to do. My schedule was arranged months ago—before you and the baby."

She could hear his frustration and it was another warning to leave things alone.

"You're starting back again this week too. Between your shift work schedule and my schedule we are going to be lucky to see each other at all. This last week has been great together, but it's not reality—which I think we both need to face."

There was a lot she needed to face, and everything that had made her think it was going to be smooth sailing from here on evaporated in her mind.

That night was their last together in bed. Tate had been quiet throughout the rest of the evening and she hadn't confronted him again. She had lived in fear that the change in his attitude toward her was going to span all areas, but that night he still reached for her. There was a new intensity and drive toward complete possession that they had never experienced. She cried out his name as he entered her, and with each thrust he begged her to repeat it, until they both tumbled over the edge.

Afterward he said nothing, pulling her against him but facing away.

In the morning he was gone.

CHAPTER TEN

SHE WALKED BACK in to the Emergency Department, aware that everything had changed but feeling no different. She was with Tate, pregnant with his child, and now she was on the attending staff.

"Good afternoon, Dr. Darcy." The unit clerk, whom she had known for the past five years, greeted her.

"Hello, Lexi," she responded, a smile on her face.

She walked to the main triage board and assessed the department. There was a list of who was on shift, both staff and residents, and to which section they were assigned. Next to it was a list of current patients on an electronic mounted flat screen. Names were not listed but demographics were. Location, age, gender, presenting complaint and assigned physician were all listed and updated regularly in order to keep and maintain the flow within the department. People who needed to stay had to be consulted to the appropriate service. Everyone else had to be treated and discharged to make room for the next patient.

She was listed on the board simply as Darcy, and was assigned to Section B: Fast Track. Not the sickest of patients but also not the chronic patients. It was a good place to start on her first day back.

Her first instinct was to grab a chart and begin seeing

patients, but she held herself back. For the first time she was no longer a resident. Her new role was going to be different. She was now responsible for both patient care and the education of the other residents. So instead she waited.

Within five minutes Kristen Inglewood, a third-year in the program, had made her way toward Chloe and she smiled at her good luck. Kristen was excellent, and they had worked well together when they were both residents.

"Hi, Dr. Darcy."

"Hi, Kristen, but as always you can call me Chloe. What have you seen so far?"

"A four-year-old boy presenting with a four-day history of fever, flu-like symptoms and headache."

"Why did they bring him in today?" Chloe asked, knowing there was usually something that had instigated a decision to present to the emergency department.

"New rash that started developing on the cheek yesterday and is slowly spreading toward the torso and limbs," Kristen answered confidently, obviously aware that this was a key part of the history.

"Is he otherwise a healthy child?"

"Yes. In preschool, has been vaccinated according to schedule, and has met all developmental milestones."

"Physical exam?"

"He still appears overall well. He is playing in the room, showing no signs of lethargy. All vitals are within normal limits for his age and temperature is one hundred and one degrees Fahrenheit. Eyes, ears and throat are all normal, with no signs of infection. His chest is clear, with equal respirations bilaterally, and no signs of pneumonia or decreased air entry. The rash is in a lace-like pattern, starting on his left cheek and extending in patches on his torso and left arm."

"Do you have a differential diagnosis?"

"Fifth disease or parvovirus. The other most common condition is adenovirus, but the rash is more typical of Fifth."

"So what do you want to do?"

"Nothing. The child is otherwise well, breathing normally and active. Physical examination is completely within normal limits. I think he's safe to go home with counseling on when to return if he worsens and plans to keep him out of school for the next week."

"Sounds great—let's go see him together."

"Um, Chloe..." For the first time Kristen seemed uncomfortable in their exchange, her eyes focused specifically on Chloe's abdomen.

"Yes, I'm pregnant." She hadn't made any sort of public announcement, but she hadn't had to. In the past two months her pregnancy had become increasingly more visible and now it was undeniable. Coupled with her now public relationship with Tate, she had no doubt there was not a soul in the building who was not aware of the change in her circumstances.

"I know, and congratulations on everything. Dr. Reed is amazing. I was referring to the effects parvovirus has on pregnant women and their babies. If there is the possibility that you are non-immune you should try to avoid direct patient contact."

Chloe knew that—she just had trouble remembering that she was now among that vulnerable group. Pregnant women were at risk for both maternal and fetal complications from many infectious diseases, but she hadn't ever faced any restrictions in what she could and couldn't treat. She also had never had to consider anyone other than herself in the risks she took in her profession.

"Thank you, Kristen. If you're happy and the parents are happy go ahead. I'll sign off on the chart later."

The next few hours were filled with multiple fractures, minor wounds requiring suturing, sore throats, bladder infections and rashes. Between the two of them they kept their section turning over. Chloe, who had already been a conscientious physician, was extra cautious, ensuring she used appropriate contact precautions with any patient who might have an infectious condition.

Now she sat at one of the many physician work stations on the phone, on hold, awaiting a connection with the poison control line. A university student had taken a handful of her roommate's hyperactivity medication in order to help her stay awake to study. Now the young woman was experiencing hallucinations and other psychotic symptoms and Chloe was looking for guidance on other medical side effects they might encounter.

"I brought you something to eat."

Tate's voice entered through the generic music playing on the end of the line. He was standing next to her, also in hospital scrubs, carrying a brown paper bag from the hospital café.

"Thank you." She smiled, still not sure where they were at. "I have a few more things to do, then I will try to take a dinner break."

"You need to eat something, Chloe. You are six hours into your shift and I bet you haven't sat down or eaten anything since you started. I can also bet that you will not do so until at least one to two hours after your shift is done. You need to be conscientious about more than just your job. It is not just you anymore."

"The baby and I are fine, Tate. My work is very important to me, as is the baby, and I am more than capable of taking care of both." She didn't appreciate being told what to do, or any implication that she was making bad choices on their behalf—not even from Tate, who she knew was just being overprotective in light of everything. She worried his new-found protectiveness was more about the baby than her.

"I need help in here!" someone yelled, and broke into their conversation.

Chloe got up and ran to discover her patient's psychotic behavior had escalated and she was physically tearing apart the exam room and attacking one of the nurses.

She went to enter the room, but was held back by a strong grip.

"Not a chance, Chloe."

She watched as Tate entered the room and moved behind the patient, pulling her back and restraining her away from the nurse she had barricaded in a corner.

Chloe yelled down the hall at the other staff who had also come to help. "I need Haldol—five milligrams, IM."

The syringe was in her hands within minutes and she made her way slowly into the room. Tate still held the patient, her back to him, her arms restrained, but she seemed to have calmed.

"Give me the syringe. I don't want her to kick out at you," he said.

It was an order that she followed. Tate's physical strength was enough to hold the patient with one arm as the other injected the medication into the woman's thigh. They both waited and within a few minutes the sedative effect took place.

Now she was sedated, several nurses helped transfer her onto a hospital gurney, where monitors were attached and restraints put in place.

"Thank you," Chloe said as Tate left the room.

"You need to promise me you are going to take better care of yourself. I can't always be here, and I don't like having to spend every moment you are out of my sight worrying about you."

"You mean the baby?" she inferred.

"No, Chloe, I mean *you*." He moved toward her, pressing his lips hard against her forehead before he walked away.

She stood there speechless for a few moments before she returned to her desk.

She opened the brown bag and did as she was told, eating the granola bar, the fruit cup, and making her way halfway through the bottle of water before she began to chart the incident and call in the consultation to Internal Medicine.

Every time she thought she had Tate figured out he confused her more. It was more than frustrating to someone who had spent her entire career diagnosing and figuring people out.

By the time she had done all her paperwork and handed off her continuing patients her shift had been technically over for two hours. Her stomach growled and the baby kicked out at the disruption. Things had definitely changed. She wouldn't be able to push herself the way she'd used to anymore.

She changed back into her street clothes, lingering to chat, and then slowly made her way home. As she slid open the door she was greeted by her expectation: all the lights were off and Tate wasn't home. She'd known this was likely to be the case, but it still didn't help with her loneliness. For the last five years she had lived alone and never once been bothered by coming home to an empty apartment. But somehow in the last week everything had changed, and now the empty loft was significant for what was missing in her life.

It was three days before she saw Tate again. She was lying on the sonographer's table, her abdomen exposed, when Tate entered the room and took the seat next to her. She looked at him, and he looked tired, with more stubble on his face than normal. She had deliberately avoided confirming his explanation of on call coverage for his absence, and for the first time she had hope that she was wrong. He certainly looked tired enough to have been working double shifts.

"Sorry I'm late," he whispered to her through the darkness of the room.

"It's okay," she reassured him.

As the sonographer began to scan her abdomen images of their baby were transmitted to the screen on the wall in front of them. The first picture was of the baby in profile, the forehead, nose, lips and chin in perfect outline. She felt Tate's hand closing over hers and let go some of the anxiety that had been building within her.

Though they were both medical, it was still hard to interpret all the images they were seeing, but the sonographer explained every structure she was looking at.

"Do you want to know the gender?" the sonographer asked.

Chloe turned to Tate, wanting his input.

"Whatever you want, Chloe."

"It would be nice to wait for a surprise," she said, hoping he felt the same.

"I agree. This baby hasn't been enough of a surprise yet." His beautiful smile and the glint in his eyes were vibrant enough to be seen through the darkness. "No, we don't want to know," he answered for them both.

"Okay, we are just going to start doing a study of the baby's middle cerebral artery. By analyzing how quickly the blood is flowing through the vessel we can predict with some accuracy what the baby's red cell count is."

The sonographer did not say anything else as she worked to capture the baby in the perfect position and then aligned the marker perpendicular to the vessel. She performed the same action over and over again to calculate an average. The first few times Chloe thought nothing of it, but as the sonographer got more quiet and didn't comment on what she was seeing Chloe began to feel her panic start to build.

She turned to Tate, who was alternating between watching the screen and watching her. She felt him squeeze her hand again for reassurance.

"Is there something wrong," he asked directly, after a few more minutes had passed.

"The speed in the blood vessel is high normal. It's not yet abnormal, but it's higher than we would typically see at this stage. I'm going to go and review the images with the perinatologist on call today and she may want to come and re-scan you herself. I'll be right back."

The sonographer used the paper drape that had been tucked into Chloe's lowered pants to wipe the jelly from her abdomen before she left the room.

"The baby looked okay to you, right?" she asked Tate, looking for reassurance, knowing that he didn't know any more than she did.

He used his other hand to stroke through her hair, his hand never leaving hers. "The baby looked beautiful. I would expect nothing less from our child."

The door opened and the sonographer returned, accompanied by a middle-aged woman in a white lab coat. "Dr. Reed, Dr. Darcy, I'm Dr. Young, the perinatologist covering the unit today. Do you mind if I have a quick look at your baby?"

"Go ahead."

Once again warm jelly was applied to her abdomen and the baby reappeared on the screen. Silence filled the room for several more minutes as Dr. Young took a look at the baby and repeated the artery study.

"The studies of the baby's middle cerebral artery are in the high normal range, but not abnormal. The rest of the images look normal, with a normal-sized baby and no evidence of excess fluid around the heart, lungs or amniotic cavity."

"So what's the plan?" Tate asked, before Chloe could voice the same question.

"We are going to arrange weekly ultrasounds to keep a close eye on things. I assume you've both had the appropriate blood work to determine the possible blood types the baby could have?"

"Yes," they answered together.

"Is there anything else we can do? Is Chloe okay to keep working? Should she be at home resting?"

"No, Dr. Reed. This isn't a condition that would benefit from that. Unfortunately there is nothing we can do but keep a close eye on the baby and arrange delivery if the baby starts to decompensate. The antibodies in Dr. Reed's blood have the potential to attack the baby's existing red blood cells if the baby has the associated blood type. The Kell-antibody can also suppress the cells in the bone marrow that produce the baby's red blood cells. If the baby's levels become critically low than we should see an abnormal reading on the test we just performed, or signs of heart failure. At which point it would be safer to delivery prematurely than to leave the baby in its current environment."

"What about Chloe? What are her risks?" Tate asked.

Chloe was still processing the information she had just heard—not that it was new to her, but it was still hard to hear.

"Dr. Darcy is not at any significant risk. In the future it may be harder to find blood products for her, in the event she needs a transfusion, and there is an increased risk of needing a Caesarean birth if we have to urgently deliver the baby prematurely, but overall she is quite safe."

Tate squeezed Chloe's hand again. "Thank you, Dr. Young."

The image on the screen vanished and Chloe felt her abdomen being wiped off once again.

"Dr. Darcy, the receptionist at the front desk has been instructed to rebook you for weekly ultrasounds and blood work so we can follow your antibody levels. She can work with you and Dr. Reed for a regularly scheduled appointment so that you can arrange your schedules around it. Dr. Madden will have your ultrasound report by the end of the day, as well as my recommendations. Have a good day."

They both left the room while Chloe continued to lie on the examination bed. Eventually she felt Tate rearranging her clothing and easing her upright.

"I really need everything to be okay," she confided.

"It will be," Tate answered, more confident than he had any right to be. Still, that was what she needed right now.

They walked from the exam room back to the reception desk and arranged a standing appointment that didn't conflict with Tate's regular operating schedule.

"I need to call my secretary and rearrange a few things—do you mind waiting a few minutes?" he asked.

"No," she answered honestly. She was already adding

the weekly appointments to the calendar on her phone, which had been updated to follow her pregnancy. She was twenty-three weeks. A full-grown baby was forty weeks, and she needed to make it until at least twenty-six weeks to have a chance at a healthy newborn.

The pictures hadn't prepared him for seeing the baby today. Watching the sonographer move the probe around Chloe's stomach and watching the matching image on the screen had brought everything home. This was his family.

He had never seen Chloe look more beautiful as she did with her rounded stomach and that expectant glow. But today she had made him catch his breath. He had meant his words to her. The baby *was* beautiful—because he or she already looked like their mother. He had studied the images intently and his mind had filled in the rest. Hope, anticipation, expectancy—no words could describe how much he was looking forward to meeting their child. This baby—*their* baby—felt like the final key to his and Chloe's relationship. The baby was the piece of his life he hadn't known was missing, and it would help him keep the best thing that had ever happened to him—Chloe—forever.

She was still staring at her phone, considering the possibilities when Tate returned.

"Ready to go?" he asked.

"Yes." It wasn't until she was sitting inside his Range Rover that common sense returned. "Tate, don't you have to go back to work?"

"I shuffled the rest of my day and found someone to cover my shift tonight."

"Thank you." She was more than grateful not to be alone with her own thoughts.

"I also called the realtor. She is going to meet us back at the loft and is working now to arrange viewings of the houses you liked. If this baby is going to come earlier than we expected I want us to be settled in to our new home before you deliver. We'll see them today and make a decision together, so you have one less thing to worry about."

"Thank you."

Tate reached over and placed his hand over the one she had resting on her thigh. It was funny, the effect he had on her. His touch brought both a feeling of heat and excitement and also a sense of calm and peace. Everything was going to be okay. She just had to have faith.

When they arrived back at the loft the realtor was in the lobby, waiting for them. The remainder of their day was spent looking at homes, each spectacular in its own right, and a distraction from the news about her pregnancy.

The first was a Victorian-style home that was beautiful, with marble finishes and tall white columns, but it lacked the kind of warmth Chloe could see raising a family in.

The second was more modern, and very similar to Tate's loft. It was a completely open concept, with finishes that were a study of contrasts, alternating boldly between dark and light. It had a large open staircase that transitioned the two floors. It lacked both a railing and a backdrop between steps. It was beautiful for a couple, but she had worked in the emergency department for long enough to know that you would only have to look away for a moment for a child to have a serious accident.

The third house was her favorite from the minute she saw it. It hadn't been included in the listings she had seen previously and must be new on the market. It had a wide porch, with the wide stairs to the entrance flanked by a combination of wood and stone pillars.

Recent renovations were obvious inside, but had been done in keeping with the craftsman-style design. The main floor had been changed to an open concept, with the living room transitioning to a family room divided by a half-wall featuring a two-sided fireplace. The family room was sunk by two steps to define the space. Adjacent to the family room and occupying the entire back wall of the home was a large kitchen that had been renovated to include a double oven, fridge and freezer, and an island that was large enough for a cooktop and preparation sink and still allowed six bar stools to sit opposite as a breakfast counter. The remainder of the floor featured a dining room, an office, a powder room, a guest bedroom with en suite bathroom, and a mud room.

She climbed the stairs, feeling safe and secure with the solid wood railing, wide steps and proper incline. The second-floor landing contained another open concept space, which was being used as a children's play area. She walked to the furthest door and discovered the master bedroom. The room was large enough to easily accommodate a king-sized bed and a sitting area, and also had a two-sided fireplace. She discovered a luxury master bathroom with a soaker tub that had the fireplace as a backdrop, a glass-enclosed shower with multiple shower heads and a ladies' bench, and a double sink. A separate toilet was present within the en suite room, as was an adjoining door to a large master closet that contained "his and hers" everything. She could never imagine having enough clothes to fill half of the space.

She walked slowly through the remaining rooms on the upper floor. Two smaller but by no means small bedrooms were adjoined by a Jack and Jill bathroom. The fourth bedroom was immediately next to the master and had been staged as a nursery. She felt her heart accelerate as she took in the lamb-themed room, complete with soft moss-green walls, a white crib and bedroom set, lamb motifs throughout. An upholstered rocker sat in the corner, and she couldn't resist sitting in it and gliding back and forth. She just needed a few more weeks—just a few—before this could become her reality.

The floor was completed by a third additional full bathroom that was accessible off the main landing.

"Would you like to see outside?" the realtor was asking, and for the first time since she had entered the house she remembered that she was not alone. She looked at Tate, who was smiling at her softly.

"Yes, we do," he answered for them both.

The backyard was a perfect backdrop for the home. The deck extended from the family eat-in kitchen area, making it an ideal extension for outdoor dining and entertaining. Large leafy trees provided shade and privacy. The grass around the area was thick and lush, and a children's play set was already there.

"You love it," Tate whispered, his breath warm and comforting against her ear and neck.

"I really do. Do you?"

"If it means this much to you, then, yes—I do."

He ran the tips of his fingers down her back as he made his way back toward the realtor, who had given them some privacy. He returned a few minutes later, leaving the realtor to wait outside.

"She is going to submit an offer and I have given her bargaining terms for the remainder of the negotiations. With any luck we should know by the end of tomorrow whether it is ours or not."

"Do you really think we are that lucky?" She laughed,

thinking about her hospitalization and the high-risk nature of her pregnancy.

He rested a hand on her abdomen over the baby while his lips kissed hers softly, gently parting them with his tongue for the briefest of tastes and sensations.

"Yes, Chloe, I do."

Tate was at home that night, and despite the earlier news of the day she felt more relaxed. They ordered in dinner and relaxed on the patio, with the July heat of the day still present but now bearable. There was no simmering tension or cold undercurrents between them. And at nine that evening the realtor called to confirm that their offer had been accepted and they could take possession in two weeks' time.

"That's the August long weekend," Chloe confirmed aloud, just realizing the significance of the date.

"Yes—is that a problem? Are you working that weekend?"

He was oblivious to the conflict Chloe had detected.

"No, I'm not working. It's the same weekend as Kate and Matt's wedding," she explained carefully, unsure of what reaction she would see.

His face didn't change, but he didn't say anything immediately either. She waited as he seemed to be considering his options. The invitation had arrived a week ago, addressed to both of them, but neither had raised the issue since.

"I'll ask my parents to do the walk-through the day of possession. I don't want you traveling or spending the weekend alone in the Hamptons."

"Are you sure?"

"Yes, I'm sure. Is it okay if we go to bed early tonight?

This week of nights has been exhausting, and I still have patients I need to see over the weekend."

"Sure—it's been an exhausting day for me as well."

Tate retreated to the bathroom and she heard the sound of the shower. He hadn't asked her to join him, but this time it didn't surprise her. He needed time alone so she let him be. She moved around the loft, bringing in their glasses from the patio and electronically drawing the blackout blinds. She changed into a light satin chemise and slipped into bed. It wasn't long before Tate joined her, the fresh scent of his soap filling the air. He drew a thin Egyptian cotton sheet over both of them before pulling her to him, aligning her against him in the position they always went to sleep in after they'd been intimate. She could feel his nakedness, but tonight he made no advance, and within minutes his breathing signaled that he was fast asleep.

Tate woke in the night, his heart racing, and with images from his dreams still replaying in his mind. It had been Chloe as she had been on the operating table, bleeding to death, but this time he had been holding a small infant. He'd looked up and seen Ryan Callum in the doorway, waiting for him to hand over the baby, the last part of Chloe he had.

When had he fallen in love with her? He had no idea. It was beyond any logic or explanation that he could think of. He had known a few months after the breakup with Kate that he had never truly been in love with her. But when had he fallen in love with Chloe?

Everything that he ever wanted she had, and he was tortured by the thought of losing her. The *what ifs* made no logical sense to him. He could convince himself that there was no way Ryan and Chloe had been involved.

There was no way there was even the slightest possibility that Ryan was the father of his child. But logic had nothing to do with how he felt about Chloe and his fear of loving and losing her played at the back of his mind. He just needed to make it through the next two weeks, when the test results would confirm what he and Chloe already knew. They were a family.

He couldn't lose her—not now, not ever.

He pressed himself against her, needing contact with her to erase the nightmare. She murmured contentedly, her neck arching as her bottom pushed into him. The small satin nightgown she had worn to bed had already risen up to her waist and she was bare against him. He should let her sleep, she'd said she was tired, but he couldn't resist her—he could never resist her.

He pressed his lips to the back of her neck, gently kissed the exposed skin of her shoulder. He captured her swollen breast in his hand, gently kneading the firm globe before turning his attention toward her nipple. The satin slid effortlessly, increasing the sensation. He didn't stop kissing her neck as he trailed his hand down her body, his fingers gentle but insistent as he sampled her core. She was wet and ready for him. Still he tried to remain patient, kissing her as he caressed her back and forth.

She moaned, her breathing escalating into pants and gasps. "Please, Tate," she begged.

That was all he needed to hear. She wanted him.

He elevated her upper leg and slid easily into her from behind. She was tight and contracted against him immediately. His hand returned to its ministrations as he moved in and out of her, rocking them both to the same rhythm as his fingers caressed her. He held himself back, trying to be gentle and waiting for her. It didn't take long before she cried out and arched her back again, the spasms he felt from inside her confirming her climax. He embedded himself deep within her and joined her release.

He stayed where he was, as close to her as possible. She didn't turn or move away from him. Instead he was greeted by the sound of rhythmic breathing that signaled sleep.

"I love you, Chloe," he whispered into her hair before he joined her.

CHAPTER ELEVEN

ALMOST TWO WEEKS and two more ultrasounds later Chloe was starting to feel as if things were actually going to be okay. The readings from the baby's artery hadn't changed and there were no signs of heart failure. She was transitioning into her new role as attending staff and Tate was back to being the man she'd fallen in love with—except now his attention was on her and their baby. She wasn't sure how he was making it happen, but Tate never missed a single appointment or ultrasound.

She was even optimistic about this weekend and Kate's wedding. Maybe it would be the final step Tate needed for closure. Maybe after this he would be able to fall in love again. She could hear it so clearly in her mind—*"I love you Chloe."* She just wanted it to be true.

Tate had arranged to take the day off, so they could get an early start on the four-hour journey that was going to be congested with all the other travelers planning a long weekend at the beach. She looked over at him, wondering if the attraction she felt would ever dissipate. He was stunning, in a tight fitted black T-shirt, blue jeans and aviator sunglasses. His grip on the steering wheel revealed a tan muscled forearm—a tan she knew continued throughout his body.

"How many children do you want?"

His question came from nowhere and she was happy not to be the one driving. There was a high probability that she would have driven off the road in surprise.

"Where did *that* question come from?"

"You're an only child and I'm from a family with four children. I was wondering what you were thinking?"

"I haven't thought about it."

"Did you like being an only child? Would you want just this child?"

"No, I didn't like being an only child. It was lonely—still is. I guess if given the choice I would want this baby to have at least one brother or sister to grow up with and share the family history. Would *you* want to have another baby together?"

"I would have as many children with you as you wanted."

"Don't you think we should wait to see how this one turns out first?" she joked, imagining herself running after a high-spirited toddler.

"I can't think of a better mother for my children."

He reached over and rested a hand on her knee as he kept his eyes focused on the road. She was grateful for the slight distraction. She had no doubt his words were genuine. But she couldn't help remembering a conversation they had had. He had proposed to Kate because he wanted children. Did that mean he had once pictured *Kate* as the perfect mother for his children? If he'd changed his mind about Kate, would he also change his mind about her?

She closed her eyes and tried to block the idea from her mind. She needed to put her trust in Tate. They needed at least a mutual trust between them if there was to be no mutual love.

With ease he pulled in to the inn's main entrance and put the vehicle into "park." The valet opened the door and she barely had time to slip her jeweled sandals back onto her feet. As she stood she smoothed down the fabric of her pink maxi-dress, hoping that it was not as wrinkled as she feared.

"Don't forget this." Tate handed her a straw fedora hat with matching pink ribbon. "I don't want you to burn." He pulled her toward him and kissed her before making his way into the inn's lobby.

"Chloe!" Kate's voice rang out.

They both turned as Kate ran toward them. The two women embraced.

"You look so *beautiful*," Kate gushed.

"Thank you." Chloe gracefully accepted the compliment. She rested her hands on her baby bump, proud at the progress and the changes that had happened since Kate had moved back to New York a month ago.

"It's nice to see you too," Tate teased Kate, standing slightly back from the best friends' reunion.

"Hi, Tate." Kate reached up for a brief hug. "Thank you for being the man who brought my best friend to my wedding." She teased him right back.

Chloe laughed and looked up to share her smile with Tate. So far everything felt easy, with no tension between them, and she was grateful.

"Tate."

"Matt."

Both women paused in their conversation as the men in their lives shook hands.

"Chloe, you do look wonderful," Matt greeted her, and she hugged him. She liked Matt. He made Kate happier than she had ever known her to be.

"Thank you—and congratulations to you both."

"I'm going to get us checked in." Tate left the group and made his way to the inn's front desk.

"So what's the plan?" Chloe asked. She would do anything she needed to make sure her best friend had the perfect wedding day.

"I thought you would want to rest when you got here. Tate said you still get quite tired and would likely need an afternoon nap."

"When did you talk to Tate?" Chloe asked, surprised by the knowledge that the two were still speaking often.

"When I called to check on you I wanted the whole truth, and not the stoical version you like to report," Kate replied honestly.

Her friend didn't look angry, and Chloe knew she didn't have a leg to stand on. Hadn't she spent the last six months trying to pretend she was okay to Kate when she wasn't?

"Later on this afternoon you and I have appointments at the inn's spa for manicures and pedicures, and then we have a small rehearsal dinner with you two, Matt's best man and his wife and our families." Kate's excitement was apparent.

"I think the nap was a good thought," Chloe remarked happily, sharing Kate's enthusiasm.

"Yes, well, I need you to take very good care of the little person inside you. His or her mommy is my best friend."

"Thank you, Kate."

"We are all set," Tate informed her as he re-joined them. "Kate, you'll have more than enough time with Chloe later this afternoon."

"Yes, Dr. Reed," Kate quipped, her smile never fading.

Tate led Chloe to the elevator bank and up to their room. It was a corner suite, with a wraparound balcony that opened itself up to an ocean view. Facing the window, a king-sized bed adorned in white linen was centered on the opposite wall. Nautical accents were throughout, and the adjoining bathroom was equally grand, with a two-person whirlpool bathtub and a large shower. The valet had already deposited their luggage prior to their arrival, and sounds from the ocean filled the room.

"It's beautiful," Chloe remarked, venturing out onto the balcony to take in the fresh scent of the ocean.

"It's not the only thing that is," Tate murmured. His arms were braced on either side of the railing and his lips were against the back of her neck.

"I thought I needed my afternoon nap?" she teased, knowing there was no way she would ever be able to refuse him.

"Maybe I need to have an afternoon nap with you."

The rest of the day was filled with equal pleasure and pampering. At the spa, she and Kate gossiped like the old times—about work, their families, and now for the first time about the men in their lives. Chloe didn't speak much about her relationship with Tate, not wanting Kate to draw comparisons with what they had shared, but the bride-to-be was exuberant enough in her love of Matt that Chloe wasn't sure she could have gotten a word in anyway.

Manicures were a rare treat for Kate, who couldn't wear nail polish in the operating room, and they both enjoyed being able to take the time out for indulgence.

Chloe was worried about re-introductions at the rehearsal dinner. The last time Kate's father and stepmother had seen Tate he had been their daughter's boyfriend. Now he was with her visibly pregnant best friend, and she wasn't sure how they would react.

As is turned out, they didn't. They welcomed Tate like an old friend and fussed over Chloe, whom they had both known for the past nine years, smiling the same smile that everyone else did at Kate and Matt's happiness. The entire evening relaxed into one of celebration, ending around eleven so the bride could get her beauty sleep— not that she needed it.

"Are you ready?" Kate asked, her eyes still bright and showing no sign of fatigue.

"Yes, I will be the best maid of honor anyone has ever seen."

"Then let's go." Kate smiled, pulling Chloe to her feet.

"Where are we going?" Chloe looked between Tate and Kate. Both were smiling back at her.

"Well, it's the night before my wedding and I am not going to spend it alone. Your lovely Tate has been kind enough to loan you out for the evening."

She looked back at Tate, who looked more than pleased at his surprise.

"He's a very generous man," Chloe agreed. She was pleased with Kate's openly referral to Tate as Chloe's.

She and Kate left the private dining room, giggling like the schoolgirls that they truthfully had never been. After their first meeting in medical school this felt like the only time they had ever had together when there was no stress over the next exam, or the next milestone in their careers they had to achieve before them. It was a feeling of elation that Chloe couldn't explain.

Kate's room was the honeymoon suite—the top floor of the inn, with panoramic views and the same luxuries Chloe had seen in her own room. Kate had bought them matching pyjamas and they both changed, took off their make-up and crawled into the king-sized bed. *This is what it would have been like to have a sister,* Chloe thought.

The lights from the outside boardwalk filled the room.

With the windows open a fresh breeze lifted the summer heat.

"Can you believe we are here?" Kate asked, her voice piercing the darkness.

"Honestly? No."

"I don't think I would have believed anyone if this time last year they'd told me all this was possible."

"All of this?" Chloe asked.

"Reuniting with Matt. Finally hearing and knowing that he loves me back after all the heartbreak and time that had passed between us."

"Was it worth it?" Chloe asked, feeling as if all her future happiness was riding on Kate's answer.

"Was what worth it?"

"The waiting? The pain of loving someone who doesn't love you back?"

"Yes. I would have never said that at the time, but definitely yes. Once I fell in love with Matt I knew that I would never love any other man the same way and as much as I did him. I hated him for years, thinking that he'd ruined any chance of happiness for me, but now I'm actually grateful. My love for Matt was what kept me from settling for anything less and making bad decisions that would have affected more than just *my* life."

"You mean Tate?" Chloe acknowledged painfully.

The bed shifted as Kate turned on her side to look at her and meet her eyes.

"Chloe, I love Tate. But I was never *in* love with Tate. The thing that has brought me the most happiness this year—other than being in love and reunited with Matt— is you and Tate. I meant what I said when I found out you were together. It makes sense."

"He wanted to marry *you* first."

"Yes, he proposed to me, but there was a lot more

wrong with our relationship than just my feelings for Matt. We both can see that now. I made logical sense to Tate; you drive him crazy. Sometimes fate can be our best friend."

"Is this Dr. Kate Spence, General Surgeon, talking?" Chloe joked, attempting to lighten the seriousness of their conversation and lessen the risk that she might pour her heart out to Kate and ruin the night before her wedding with her own insecurities and problems.

"No, this is soon-to-be Mrs. Matthew McKayne and her best friend, I suspect the soon-to-be Mrs. Tate Reed, talking."

"You are not really changing your name, are you?" Chloe joked with a playful nudge.

"Never—we've both worked too hard to become Drs. Spence and Darcy!"

Everything went as planned, and Chloe glowed as she walked down the aisle ahead of Kate. A spaghetti-strapped royal-blue silk dress hung from her shoulders. Two triangles of fabric covered her chest and transitioned to an empire waist, which accentuated her new figure and flowed to the floor softly. Kate was stunning in a white silk gown that had been sculpted in waves and tucks that hugged her figure and was mermaid-like in its design.

The ceremony was beautiful, timed perfectly for sunset, and Chloe cried with happiness through it all. Kate was the most beautiful and the most happy Chloe had ever seen her, and she felt no sense of jealousy, only happiness for her friend. There was so much that was positive about the day that there was no room for any negative thoughts or feelings.

Later she watched as Kate and Matt danced together

on the lantern-lit patio and she swayed along to the music from the band.

"How are my two favorite people?" Tate asked, holding a glass of wine for himself and a sparkling water for her. He was stunning in his black suit, complete with a navy tie that accented her dress.

"We're wonderful. Do you realize that our baby is now exactly twenty-six weeks? Every day we get from here on is a blessing."

"And here I thought every day you were with *me* was a blessing."

"You know what I mean."

"Can we interrupt and ask for a dance?"

Kate's voice broke through their exchange. Chloe looked up to see the happy couple before them.

"I think we can manage that." Tate stood from his chair and took Kate's hand, leading her on to the dance floor.

It took Chloe a moment before she realized the invitation also included her, and she too rose, a little wobbly on her silver heels, her focus not entirely on her long silk dress that barely cleared the floor. Before she could right her own balance Tate was behind her, his hands along her back and on her elbow.

"I'm okay," she reassured him, embarrassed by the commotion.

Kate, the bride, was standing abandoned in the center of the dance floor, and Chloe had no idea how Tate had even seen her, never mind managed to get back to her after her small lack of balance.

He didn't seem to believe her as he knelt in front of her, tightening the ankle straps on her silver heels.

"Tate, I'm okay—really."

"Be careful with her, Matt. There is no one else like her."

Matt responded with a small affirming nod and Tate walked away reluctantly back toward Kate.

Matt took her arm and walked her to the dance floor, away from Kate and Tate, before placing his hand on her side and holding her. They started moving to the slow waltz. She couldn't take her eyes off Tate dancing with Kate in her wedding dress, and even though there appeared to be nothing romantic between them it still unnerved her.

"You need to let it go, Chloe."

She turned her head to face Matt.

"Excuse me?" she asked, not sure she had heard him correctly.

"The past. There is nothing we can do to change the past, and thinking about it only punishes them and tortures us. It's not fair to anyone."

She was stunned, and worried that her emotions had always been this transparent. "How can you forget it?" she asked, thinking that Matt was probably the one person who most closely understood her situation.

"I haven't. But I also know that in my situation the only one I have to blame is myself. I made the wrong choice and it cost me nine years with the woman I love."

"I'm not who he wanted. Tate chose Kate over me, Matt."

"Did he really? I wasn't around then, but I'm not sure it was a fair competition. And even if he did, people make mistakes, Chloe. Are you really going to punish him for the rest of your lives together?"

"I'm not punishing him. We're together and having a child," she tried to argue, but as his words sank in she knew he was right. She was punishing both of them and it wasn't making her happy.

"Chloe, a few months ago you did me the biggest favor of my life by telling me that Kate had followed me to New York. Let me do the same for you. Tate loves you. Fortunately for me—and him—he doesn't look at my wife the same way he looks at you."

With perfect timing she looked up and saw Tate looking over Kate's shoulder directly at her. Saw the small upturn at the corner of his mouth and the same piercing green eyes she missed when he was not around.

The music stopped and Matt led her off the dance floor back to her chair. "Get over the past, Chloe, and you'll see that I'm right about the present."

They arrived back in Boston late Monday evening. The rest of the weekend had been relaxing and restful. Chloe missed Kate, and knew the next twenty-three months would be torture. How had she ever thought they needed time apart? The only person uncomfortable with their current situation appeared to be *her*. She thought of Matt's words, appreciating his advice and willing him to be right.

Once back in Boston they went directly to see their new home. Tate turned on the entry light and a warm glow reflected off the polished wood surfaces. The house was empty of all of its furnishings, but full of possibilities in her mind.

"I've arranged for the movers to come to the loft tomorrow while we are at work and move the basics so that we can start living here. The rest of the furnishings you can take your time and choose yourself. Or hire a designer to do it—whatever you would prefer and will cause you the least amount of stress."

"Thank you." She still couldn't believe the home was theirs, awaiting the completion of their family. She rubbed her hand over her stomach and was rewarded by the small flip-flop from inside.

"I thought you would appreciate this one design choice, though," he said, and took her hand and led her upstairs.

She thought he was going to bring her to the bedroom for a romantic surprise; instead they went through the door beside it.

It was the nursery, with all the furnishings she had seen in it before and more. In addition to the furniture and gentle lamb theme the nursery was now stocked and complete. A change table held the smallest diapers she had ever seen, and baby wipes, blankets, lotions and creams. On the dresser was a framed ultrasound photo of the baby's profile, with the caption "Love at First Sight." She opened the top drawer of the dresser to find neatly folded rows of green and yellow baby clothes. The bookshelf was piled with books for children aged from zero to five years.

"How did you do all this?" she asked incredulously. She didn't even know what half the stuff in the nursery was for.

"It was easier than I thought it would be. My sisters made me a list of must-haves for a new baby and after one trip to the baby store I think I bought double. I want everything to be ready and perfect for our baby."

"Thank you. I love it. And please thank your sisters."

"You can thank them yourself next time we see them."

"I like your family." She smiled, enjoying again the feeling of being a part of something she'd never had.

"That's good, because my family includes the both of you."

She smiled again. Matt's words echoed in her head. Was there a possibility that Tate loved her back? Did she have the courage to ask and risk the answer breaking her heart?

CHAPTER TWELVE

TATE WALKED THROUGH the Emergency Department, his eyes searching for Chloe. He had nothing he needed to tell her, but after spending four straight days together at Kate's wedding it was hard to be apart. They had arranged for him to pick her up later that evening, so they could go to the house together for their first night in their new home, but he didn't want to wait that long to see her. Tonight was the night he was going to lay it all on the line and tell her he loved her.

He walked into Section B and up to the attending physician desk. She wasn't there, but Ryan Callum was, with his back turned to him, a phone pressed to his ear. Tate had turned to leave, having no desire to talk to the other man, when Ryan's words caught his attention.

"So the child is mine."

A knife cut through Tate's chest and he had to think how to breathe again.

"Has Dr. Madden been made aware of the results? Thank you for letting me know right away. I appreciate your discretion in this matter."

Tate felt his world come crashing down. It reminded him of seeing Chloe in critical condition on the operating room table. Ryan was the baby's father. He was going to lose the woman he loved and the family he'd always wanted.

Ryan turned, and there was no avoiding a confrontation with the other man.

"What are your plans?" Tate asked, already needing to know how much time he had left. Could he still win her heart?

"Excuse me?" Ryan seemed taken aback by the question, which irritated Tate even more.

"What are you planning to do about the baby?" *My baby*. It still so very much felt like his baby.

"I don't think that is any of your business."

"Answer the question, Ryan." His need to know was paramount.

"I'm going to be the father my child deserves."

"What about her?" He couldn't even say Chloe's name. Not to Ryan.

"That's between us, Tate. Now, if you'll excuse me, I'm done talking about this."

Ryan walked away from Tate and with defeat coursing through him he let him.

Chloe walked toward Tate's office her nerves already on edge after Erin's phone call. The blood work had come back. Both she and Tate carried one copy of the dominant Kell blood-type gene, meaning the baby had a seventy-five percent chance of being affected by the antibody. The only good news was that Tate carried one copy of the C blood-type gene, so there was only a twenty-five percent chance of effect. It would have been much better the other way around, with the Kell gene being more harmful, but it was something they were going to have to live with. Erin had moved up her next ultrasound to tomorrow, and she had already been to the lab to have more blood drawn for an evaluation of her current antibody levels.

Tate's door was shut, so she knocked, thinking that something serious must have happened to keep him from picking her up and going to their new home together as planned.

"Come in," his voice directed.

She walked in, surprised to find him in the office despite the vocal confirmation she had just heard. She'd anticipated that he would be dealing with a surgical emergency, not sitting at his desk sipping from a glass of Scotch.

She shut the door behind her and took a seat in one of the tall leather-backed chairs across from his desk.

"You didn't meet me as planned," she commented, still trying to take in the picture of the man in front of her. His eyes were bloodshot, his short hair somehow askew, and he hadn't changed from the surgical scrubs he had operated in that day. The only time she had ever seen Tate look like this had been after his breakup with Kate.

"The blood work came back." His voice was a monotone.

This was not the Tate she was used to. Throughout everything he had been the positive one, the reassuring one, and she had expected, had *needed* that trend to continue.

"It's not that bad, Tate." She flipped from her need to be reassured to being reassuring. One of them needed to hold things together. She could do that.

"Isn't it?" A single eyebrow was raised as he looked at her questioningly.

"It's nothing we can't get through." She reached her hand across the table, waiting for him to take it; he didn't.

"The results don't change how you think of me, Chloe? How you feel about our family?"

She could see and feel the hurt coming from him. She'd had no idea he would feel so responsible for something they had no control over.

"No, Tate, they don't. We can get through this together."

He looked as if he didn't believe her. He certainly made no attempt to provide her with the same comfort.

"What about Ryan?" The words were apparently ripped from him out of the amount of pain he appeared to be in.

"What *about* Ryan?" she echoed back, completely lost as to what the question actually meant.

"What's going to happen?" Tate clarified, as though he was making perfect sense—which he was not.

"How would I know? How would *Ryan* even know? High-risk obstetrics and antibody complications in pregnancy are not really something the average emergency room physician knows anything about."

"He hasn't contacted you since finding out?" Tate sneered, his disdain for Ryan more apparent than ever.

The uneasy feeling that had filled her since Tate had failed to meet her as planned grew to tsunami-sized proportions within her.

"Found out *what*, Tate? Spell it out." Her compassion was leaving her and she braced herself for what was coming next.

"That Ryan is the baby's father."

For the first time since her hospitalization she felt her full temper and sense of fight return to her. She stood from her chair, her body hanging over his desk, her face as close to his as her pregnant abdomen and the depth of his desk would allow, so she could look him in the eye as near as possible.

"The only person I know to be the father of my child is *you*, Tate."

"I went to the department earlier this evening to see you. I heard Ryan on the phone. The paternity test confirmed him as the father."

He wasn't angry, despite her escalation, but that still didn't derail her temper. She collapsed back into her chair, anger seething from every pore.

"*What* paternity test, Tate?"

"The one you asked me to complete."

"Do you mean the blood work I asked you to complete?"

"Yes."

"You thought that was a *paternity* test?"

"Wasn't it?"

She saw the glimmer of doubt begin to cross his mind, but she didn't care.

"You thought I didn't know who the father of my baby was? You thought that I was sleeping with my attending staff? *Ryan?* And you actually thought I would be with you with all those things in mind? Wow, Tate. You really do think highly of me."

Tears of anger and hurt spilled from her eyes, but she didn't care. Nothing could be more humiliating than being faced with the truth about the way Tate really saw her. She had been wrong, thinking he saw past her beauty and saw her for who she truly was. She stood and headed toward the door, away from the man she loved.

She felt him reach for her arm but she pulled it away, not wanting anything physical between them.

"I heard Ryan on the phone today, Chloe. He said the child was his."

"Let me say this once and I am never, *ever* going to say it again. I have never had any type of romantic or sexual relationship with Ryan Callum or any other physician, or any other person that works at this hospital, other than you. The fact that I have to even *say* this to you now is degrading, and I do not deserve it. In the past two years I have slept with exactly one man—you. So, whether you chose to believe it or not, this is *your* baby."

"The blood work—"

"The blood work was *not* a paternity test. It was a genetic work-up for both you and I to determine all the possible combinations of blood types our baby could have beyond the routine A, B and O statuses that come up on basic screening. *That* is what came back today. The baby has a seventy-five percent chance of being affected by severe anemia, which I really thought would be the worst thing I'd hear today. I was wrong."

"Chloe—" He reached for her again.

"No, Tate, I can't. Not anymore—not knowing how you really feel."

She left the office and he didn't follow her. She didn't want him to. It hurt too badly right now, and she didn't need any more revelations from Tate to add to the grief within her.

She had changed and retrieved her purse from the women's locker room before going looking for Tate, so now she had no idea where to go.

The loft had no furniture left in it and she couldn't go to their new house—not alone, and not like this. That house represented everything she had almost had. She dug her phone from her purse and dialed before thinking.

"Hello?" Kate's voice answered.

"Hey, I'm sorry to interrupt your honeymoon, but I need you."

"Chloe?" Kate's voice was questioning, and she knew

that she didn't sound like her normal smile-through-the-pain self.

"Yes, it's me."

"Chloe, what's wrong? What's happened?"

"Tate thought the baby was Ryan's."

"Chloe…"

Kate's voice did not contain the surprise and outrage she had expected.

"Kate, he actually thought there was the possibility I was sleeping with my staff and didn't know who the father of my baby was," she explained, waiting for the response she needed from her friend.

"Chloe, I need to be honest with you. Before I learned about you and Tate I thought Ryan was the father too."

"What? How?"

This wasn't helping. It was supposed to be helping.

"Chloe, I didn't know you had anyone in your life, never mind Tate. Ryan Callum is amazing, and quite frankly the idea of pursuing a romantic relationship with your staff is not that foreign to me. After the ectopic he seemed very protective of you, and you were secretive about the paternity. I put two and two together and got the wrong answer."

"I can't believe that the two people I love most in the world both thought the worst of me."

"No, Chloe. I did not assume that you were sleeping with Ryan to get ahead with your career. I know you are more sensitive about those rumors than you pretend to be, and that wasn't what I was thinking. I thought you were in private relationship with a man who happened to be in your department and at the time was your superior. Just like Tate and I had been."

"No, Kate. *Nothing* is like you and Tate had been. And apparently it never will be. I need to go. I'm sorry for dumping all this on you. I'll be okay. I just need some time."

"Chloe…"

"Really, it's okay, Kate. Everything's forgiven. I mean, how was I to expect you to know that I was in love and sleeping with your ex-boyfriend?"

"Chloe…"

"I really have to go. I'll be okay. I'll have to be."

"Take care of yourself, Chloe—please."

"I will. Love you."

CHAPTER THIRTEEN

SHE SPENT THE night in a hotel and arrived at the hospital with enough time to change into the spare clothing she kept in her locker. Her ultrasound had been arranged for eight in the morning, as an emergency spot. She needed the reassurance of seeing her baby. She hadn't had time to tell Tate about the scan—not amidst his confession that he believed Ryan Callum had fathered her pregnancy.

Used to the routine, Chloe shifted down her pants and moved toward the right-hand side of the table within the sonographer's reach. The images were transmitted to the screen and she watched her baby. The sonographer said little as she began taking measurements. First she started to measure the fluid around the baby, and even to Chloe's eyes it seemed to have grown substantially, with the black of the fluid now overwhelming the screen. Then she started scanning the baby, her silence making Chloe look again at what she was seeing on the screen.

She had had enough ultrasounds in her pregnancy to know what things should look like, and they didn't look the same. She had also done several ultrasound courses as a part of her emergency training, so she easily recognized the fluid collections that had started in the baby's lungs, heart and abdomen.

"I'm going to call Dr. Madden and the perinatologist," the sonographer declared, before leaving the room.

There were no false reassurances provided. The baby was in heart failure; Chloe didn't need anyone to tell her that.

Erin walked through the door, her face full of concern, obviously breathless. "Chloe, when did you last have anything to eat or drink?"

She knew the intention behind the question and swallowed hard. "Last evening," she answered. "The baby's in heart failure." She stated her worst fear.

"Yes," Erin confirmed. "I'm sorry, Chloe, but we need to get you delivered."

"I'm not ready," she said, panicked. "The baby's not ready. I'm only twenty-six and a half weeks," she explained, knowing she didn't need to remind Erin of this fact, but not having the strength to ask what she really meant.

"There is no other option, Chloe. The heart failure and the reverse blood flow in the umbilical cord shows that the baby is at high risk for stillbirth at any moment. Dr. Young is reviewing the images and she is on phone to the Neonatal Intensive Care Unit now, letting them know what to expect with the baby."

"Erin, what's going to happen?" she asked, preparing herself for the worst, her mind racing with a thousand horrible thoughts a minute.

For the first time since entering the room Erin slowed herself and took the seat next to Chloe that Tate normally sat in.

"Right now the baby weighs about two and a half pounds, but some of that is swelling from the extra fluid that has built up in the baby's tissues. Following birth the baby will be intubated for respiratory support, and also given some medication down a tube and into its lungs to help the lungs mature and make breathing easier. We can use the umbilical cord to establish intravenous and arterial access so that we can both monitor the baby and provide medication and nutrition in a more direct fashion. There is at least an eighty percent chance of survival and a fifty percent chance of no major complications."

"I haven't exactly been doing great in the luck department this year, Erin."

"Chloe, we need to focus on the positive. We diagnosed the baby before anything really horrible happened and we are going to get you delivered right away."

"A Caesarean section?" she questioned.

"Yes. It's the fastest way, and the baby is still breech right now, making a vaginal delivery a poor option."

"Okay." She nodded, processing the information and agreeing to the plan simultaneously. She needed to be strong for both of them.

"They are preparing the obstetrics operating room across from the nursery. We need to walk to the unit now and get you admitted so we can deliver this baby as soon as possible."

"Okay," she said again, taking everything step by step.

Erin reached over and grabbed the paper drape that was still tucked in, wiping the jelly from her body. She offered Chloe an arm and eased her from the bed. She grabbed her bag and walked with her quickly, but as calmly as possible.

"Chloe, when you get on the unit it is going to be chaotic. Everyone is going to be coming at you, asking you questions, getting you changed, poking and prodding you to get you ready. I have to make a call and get changed into my scrubs. Just remember that you and this baby are going to be okay. Do you have any questions about the plan or the Caesarean?"

"No."

"Chloe, do you want me to call Tate?"

"Yes." She was keeping it together on the outside, but on the inside she was absolutely terrified. Tate needed to be here. It was his baby and he needed to make sure it was okay. She rubbed her stomach again, trying to transmit a sense of reassurance to the person inside her that they were both going to be okay.

True to Erin's word, the scene inside the unit was one of organized chaos. It reminded her of the Emergency Department, except this time she was at the center of the chaos and not directing the team.

She wasn't sure how much time passed before she was sitting upright on the operating table, her legs dangling in front of her, crouched over a pillow, while the anesthetist cleaned her back. She worked hard to focus on staying calm, repeating to herself and her unborn child, *It's going to be okay*, silently in her head. She barely noticed the cold antiseptic on her back, or the sting of the freezing needle. Within minutes her legs and bottom felt warm, and nurses were lifting her legs and lying her on the table.

She watched as things continued to move quickly around her. With the spinal anesthetic she once again felt like an outside observer, able to see but not to feel the cleaning solution on her belly or the drapes being applied.

She looked around at the room, which had no fewer than ten people in it. In the corner was a neonatal resuscitation bed, surrounded by the staff neonatologist, two nurses and a respiratory technician. Around her there were three nurses that she could count, Erin, and an obstetrics resident she didn't know well, but who was there to assist. The anesthetist at the head of the bed shifted the bed for a left tilt and threaded oxygen prongs into her nose.

"Is Tate coming?" she asked, realizing they were moments away from the birth of her baby. She couldn't do this alone.

The operating room door was pushed open and familiar green eyes locked with hers. The rest of him was covered in a surgical mask, hat and scrubs.

"Dr. Reed, you can take this stool beside your wife," the anesthetist instructed.

He did as he was told, not bothering to correct the anesthetist's terminology. "I'm so sorry, Chloe," he whispered, his hands gently stroking her forehead.

"I'm scared," she confessed in a whisper, only to him.

"Chloe, can you feel anything?" Erin asked, her head and scrub hat visible at the top of the extended drape.

"No." Were they touching her?

"Patient is Chloe Darcy. She is having an emergency Caesarean section. She has no allergies. There are two units of blood in the room, and she received a gram of Ancef at nine-thirty-two. Does anyone have any concerns?" the circulating nurse asked as she completed the pre-surgical safety pause.

"No," Erin answered.

"You can proceed," the anesthetist confirmed.

The room, which had been loud and busy in the build-up to this moment, was silenced. Chloe heard Erin call for instruments and the sound of the cautery and suction machines intermittently turning on and off. She glanced over to the resuscitation bed, knowing that in a few minutes her baby would be there. The entire neonatal team was fixated on her abdomen.

"Are you okay?" Tate whispered, his eyes watching her for a response to the surgery.

"I can't feel much—just some tugging and pressure," she replied, trying to focus on the physical and not on the avalanche of chaos her emotions were.

"Uterine incision," she heard a nurse call out to the team.

"Chloe, you are going to feel some pressure on your abdomen as we help push the baby out. Tate, if you want to stand up you can watch your baby being born. The baby is breech, so you are going to see legs and bum first," Erin described.

Tate looked at her.

"Go ahead," she encouraged.

She watched Tate as he watched. She heard the sound of amniotic fluid splashing the drapes and the floor and felt increased pressure as they pushed at the baby from above. Tate's face stayed set in a look of disbelief and didn't change until a small whimper broke through the silence.

She watched as the resident assistant walked the baby over to the neonatal team, but before she could catch a glimpse the baby was surrounded.

Tate sat down next to her, his hand clutching hers, which was strapped to an arm board.

"He's small, but he's okay."

She wasn't sure which one of them he was trying to reassure.

"It's a boy?" she asked.

"Yes, Chloe. We have a son."

Never had she seen any man look so proud.

"Tate, I think I'm going to be sick."

His smile quickly vanished as he turned his attention toward the anesthetist and they worked together to roll her head to the side.

She was aware of the blood pressure cuff squeezing

her arm and of the noise in the room, which appeared to be increasing.

Erin was calling for the blood to be opened and for medication and equipment she had never heard of. She didn't feel well...everything was blurry. She looked again for the baby. One of the nurses had moved and she could see the outline of his little body. His face was covered by a mask as the respiratory technician provided respiratory support.

Tate stood again from his stool and looked over the drape. This time all the blood drained from his face.

A neonatal nurse came around the bed to speak with Tate. "Dr. Reed, we are going to be transporting your son across the hall to the Neonatal Intensive Care Unit. Would you like to come with us?"

"Go," Chloe urged through the oxygen mask that moments ago had replaced the nasal prongs.

"No," Tate refused.

"Please, Tate. I don't want him to be scared and alone."

"He's in excellent hands, right?" Tate questioned the nurse.

"Yes, Dr. Darcy. We will take very good care of your son."

Tate clutched her hand strongly. He felt so warm compared to her. "You should go and be with your son," she tried to argue, but all she wanted to do was sleep.

He bent his head toward her and pushed back her hair and the surgical hat that was attempting to cover it. "Chloe, the most important person in the world to me is right here, and nothing could make me leave you right now. I didn't care if the baby wasn't mine—I was just terrified you would leave me if he wasn't. All I want is you. I love you, and I am going to spend the rest of our lives together reminding you of that every day until you believe me."

"We need another four units of packed cells and two of fresh frozen plasma crossed and in the room. Open the postpartum hemorrhage tray and have a hysterectomy tray standing by, please," Erin commanded.

"It's going to take at least an hour to cross her for more blood," the anesthetist responded.

"Then let's get on it," Erin responded, and even Chloe could hear her friend's fear.

Darkness was descending on her. It reminded her of being on the locker room floor and she was terrified. "Tate!" she cried out.

"Chloe, I'm here, and you are going to be okay. I promise you."

"I love you," she whispered, before she lost the battle and slipped into the darkness.

She opened her eyes to familiar surroundings. She was on the postpartum unit. She tried to move but felt a familiar pain in her abdomen. A hand brushed her forehead and she took comfort and settled with the touch.

"You're okay, Chloe. Rest."

She closed her eyes again and was unsure how much time passed before she reopened them. Tate was sitting at her bedside, still in hospital scrubs, his attention entirely fixated on her. Her hand moved to her abdomen, which was flat. A new wave of panic passed through her.

"He's okay. He has been stabilized and is settling into the nursery, Chloe. Erin was able to stop your bleeding with a special suturing technique and she didn't need to resort to a hysterectomy. We have a beautiful son, Chloe."

"A little boy…" she affirmed, remembering the brief glimpse she had seen.

Tate took her hand and she felt his warmth transmitted through her.

"I love you, Chloe Darcy."

Her eyes swelled and she felt the tears start to roll down her face. She felt completely not in control of anything—including her emotions.

"Because of our son?" she asked. Her fear that he was with her because of the baby was still ever present.

"No, Chloe. But I will forever be grateful to him for helping me keep you."

"Because you can't have Kate?"

She watched his reaction as closely as she could through the haze of pain and the medication she had been given. She needed to be clear. She needed complete honesty and openness. She had been through too much to expect any less.

"I'm your second choice, Tate." She confessed the painful thought that had tortured her for months.

"No, Chloe, you are my first choice. You saved me from myself. I made a horrible mistake in my relationship with Kate. I thought because she met the criteria of what I wanted in a woman that was enough. It wasn't until I met you that I realized what I really needed. I *need* you, Chloe. I need my confident, caring, beautiful partner—even if you drive me absolutely crazy sometimes."

"You avoided me. You never told me how you felt." She loved every word he was saying, but still it didn't make sense to her.

"I was scared of you and of the way you made me feel. At first I didn't trust myself to make a commitment ever again, and I thought an affair would hurt you so I tried to stay away. When I couldn't I became even more terrified that if I admitted to myself I loved you it would break me to lose you—and it would, Chloe. I don't want my life without you."

"I don't want to be without you either, Tate."

For the second time in their relationship Tate lifted her from her hospital bed and held her. His lips kissed hers before she was tucked carefully into his warm embrace and she once again let her tears flow—but this time tears of happiness.

"Chloe?"

"Yes," she whispered quietly against his neck.

"I need to hear you say the words."

"I love you, Tate. I have for a long time. I just was too afraid to tell you and hear that you didn't love me back."

"Well, you never need to worry about that, because I'm going to tell you I love you every day for the rest of our lives."

"Tate?" she said, not moving from their embrace and her spot on his shoulder. "When can I see our son?"

"Not until you agree to marry me. We need to set a good example."

She felt his smile as his cheek moved upward against hers. She pulled away to look at him, to take in this moment. He was smiling, and she didn't miss the faint dampness in his eyes.

"Yes! I never want to be without you again."

She saw his smile grow as his lips came down to meet hers. The tenderness of the moment was overwhelming. Their lips lingered and his hands held her face close to his before finally they broke apart.

She was lost in the moment as he reached into his pocket and took her hand, placing on her left hand's third finger a platinum band. On its surface was a large circular emerald surrounded by two concentric rings of diamonds.

The jewel matched her eyes perfectly, and she could tell it had been chosen just for her,

"I've been carrying around that ring for a long time, hoping that one day I would be able to convince you to be my wife."

"I'd love to be your wife, Tate." She reached for him again, unable to resist the intoxicating feeling of kissing him knowing that he loved her as she loved him.

"Then it's settled—let's go see our son."

Tate did as he'd promised, lifting her into a wheelchair and pushing her past the objecting nurses, who felt it was too soon for her to be moving. He moved her to an isolate that contained the smallest, most precious little person she had ever seen. He was perfection—two pounds, with a little diaper that was sliding from his bottom, ten fingers and toes. Take away all the intravenous lines and monitors and he looked content.

Every emotion passed through her. Pride, happiness, fear, guilt, wonder—all directed at the perfect little person before her.

"Can I touch him?" she asked the nurse assigned to their son's care.

"Of course, Dr. Darcy. I think he would very much like that from his mom."

She washed her hands before the nurse opened the isolate door and she was able to stroke his back, his little body. He was lying on his tummy, the small mask over his face helping him breathe. He seemed to calm with her touch.

"Hello, my little man. Your mommy loves you so much. He's perfect," she whispered, instinctively lowering her voice so as not to wake him.

"Of course he's perfect, Chloe—he's yours."

"He's *ours*, Tate." She saw the smile of pride return to Tate's face and could only imagine the pain he had felt, thinking he wasn't their baby's father.

"It's done now, Tate. Everything that came before today—Kate, Ryan, every misunderstanding—is done. Today we became a family, and it is the best day of my life."

"You really are perfect, Chloe—just like our son."

* * * * *

MILLS & BOON®

Want to get more from Mills & Boon?

Here's what's available to you if you join the
exclusive **Mills & Boon eBook Club** today:

✦ *Convenience – choose your books each month*
✦ *Exclusive – receive your books a month before
anywhere else*
✦ *Flexibility – change your subscription at any time*
✦ *Variety – gain access to eBook-only series*
✦ *Value – subscriptions from just £1.99 a month*

So visit **www.millsandboon.co.uk/esubs** today
to be a part of this exclusive eBook Club!

EBOOK_SUBS_2014

MILLS & BOON®

Maybe This Christmas

Author of *Sleigh Bells in the Snow*

Sarah
Morgan

Maybe this
Christmas

COMING SOON
OCTOBER 2014

* cover in development

Let Sarah Morgan sweep you away to a perfect
winter wonderland with this wonderful Christmas
tale filled with unforgettable characters, wit,
charm and heart-melting romance!
Pick up your copy today!

www.millsandboon.co.uk/xmas

MILLS & BOON®

The Little Shop of Hopes & Dreams

* cover in development

Much loved author Fiona Harper brings you the
story of Nicole, a born organiser and true romantic,
whose life is spent making the dream proposals of
others come true. All is well until she is enlisted
to plan the proposal of gorgeous photographer
Alex Black—the same Alex Black with whom
Nicole shared a New Year's kiss that she is
unable to forget…

Get your copy today at
www.millsandboon.co.uk/dreams

MILLS & BOON®

Why shop at millsandboon.co.uk?

Each year, thousands of romance readers find their perfect read at millsandboon.co.uk. That's because we're passionate about bringing you the very best romantic fiction. Here are some of the advantages of shopping at www.millsandboon.co.uk:

* **Get new books first**—you'll be able to buy your favourite books one month before they hit the shops

* **Get exclusive discounts**—you'll also be able to buy our specially created monthly collections, with up to 50% off the RRP

* **Find your favourite authors**—latest news, interviews and new releases for all your favourite authors and series on our website, plus ideas for what to try next

* **Join in**—once you've bought your favourite books, don't forget to register with us to rate, review and join in the discussions

Visit **www.millsandboon.co.uk**
for all this and more today!